W9-BRY-787

have
a
nice
day

have
a
nice
day

julie halpern

FEIWEL AND FRIENDS

New York

A FEIWEL AND FRIENDS BOOK
An Imprint of Macmillan

HAVE A NICE DAY. Copyright © 2012 by Julie Halpern. All rights reserved. Printed in the United States of America by R. R. Donnelley & Sons Company, Harrisonburg, Virginia. For information, address Feiwel and Friends, 175 Fifth Avenue, New York, N.Y. 10010.

Library of Congress Cataloging-in-Publication Data Available

ISBN: 978-0-312-60660-2

Book design by Kristina Albertson

Feiwel and Friends logo designed by Filomena Tuosto

First Edition: 2012

1 3 5 7 9 10 8 6 4 2

macteenbooks.com

To Liz Szabla,
for making every book better

have
a
nice
day

WHAT THE HELL AM I GOING TO WEAR? I should be thrilled that everything I own is at least one size too big, which, let's be honest, is three sizes bigger than I'd like to be. Still pretty much a major accomplishment, seeing as I wasn't even trying to lose weight. Major accomplishment or no, that doesn't answer the question of what the fug I'm going to wear. I could ask my mom to go shopping, but I've been home all of thirty-six hours and the two of us have said maybe twelve words to each other. And about half of those words were me asking if she bought Cap'n Crunch. Which is all I've had to eat since I've been home. If I keep eating only Cap'n Crunch, maybe the weight will just continue coming off. Screw the Special K Diet; the Cap'n Diet is the way to go. Whose bizarre idea was it to call it "Cap'n" vs. "Captain" Crunch? Does anyone else realize it's Cap'n? Avoiding avoiding avoiding . . .

Maybe I could wear my favorite jeans but with a belt. If I owned a belt. Why don't I own a belt? Perhaps it's because my pants never fall down. And I wouldn't choose to wear a belt for aesthetic purposes, because aesthetically I would look like a potato pretending to have a waist.

Stop, Anna, stop. You are better than this. You look really good. Well, really better. So much better that you actually, sort of, probably have a boyfriend. A beautiful, tall, sweet, romantic boyfriend who is also an excellent kisser. Not that you had that much (i.e., nothing at all) to compare it to, but— No. No buts. Definitely a good kisser. And he likes the way you look. He called it juicy, remember? Maybe I should get myself some Juicy brand clothes, just to go with the whole theme? Nah, that's ridiculously not me. I don't need "Juicy" splayed across my ass. Besides, I always thought it made people look like they had juicy asses, which sort of sounds like they have diarrhea. Don't need to shout that across the Midwest.

1

What to wear, what to wear?

A skirt? When do I ever wear skirts except for special occasions? But this is an occasion, right? Not really one to celebrate, although it is a debut of sorts. Maybe I should get a ball gown. That would not make me look crazy or anything. Do I need to worry about that? Looking crazy? Are people going to look at me and whisper about how pale I am and notice the bruises on the insides of my arms from all the testing and realize I haven't been in school for three weeks? Will anybody even notice?

What the fuck *are* you supposed to wear to school when you just got out of a mental hospital?

SUNDAY, ASSY SUNDAY

*Brand! *New! *Journal! For my *Brand! *New! *Life! I suppose I could have written more yesterday, my first full day home, but I was too busy pouting and kicking walls, a light bit of aggression I picked up from Lakeland, excuse me, Lake Shit. My parents, the same two people who brought me to a mental hospital in the first place, decided to surprise me with a bedroom makeover when I came home. Thing is, and this is a message for ALL PARENTS: My room *was* me. So you making it over? Was pretty much like saying you didn't like the way I looked or acted or dressed or sounded or expressed myself in any way shape or form. Come to think of it, putting me in a mental hospital kind of sent the same message. You guys were laying it on thick in the Anna Bloom Sucks department. Not only did my mother and father take down all of my posters, some of which were vintage and purchased with my hard-earned bat mitzvah money through intense online auction battles, but they tore down my beloved—albeit ridorkulous—kiddie circus wallpaper border and slapped on some Pepto Bismol–colored paint. The posters, which my parents claimed they took down ever so carefully, were stacked on top of one another in the bottom of my closet, the tape from each sticking to the next poster. I spent several hours peeling them apart, and I still managed to rip a couple. Careful my ass. It took so long to separate them that by the time I finished I was too tired to bother putting them back up.

At least I had the freedom to listen to music all day. It was stifling being in a hospital where the only times of day anyone could listen to music were a) Free Time, on a patient-controlled radio that managed to solely tune in to classic rock or hip-hop, or b) Physical Therapy, where we had the same radio stations available, but had to work out while we listened. There were no MP3 players, no computers, and pretty much no singing allowed. In my new and unimproved, pukey, pink room, I flicked around on my iPod until I found my religion: *The Ramones* by The Ramones. Hard and fast and short and brilliant. Loud enough to almost make me forget that my family was somewhere nearby outside the confines of my stomach coating of a bedroom.

The weird thing was, the music didn't sound the same.

I loved it, of course, but I was listening through different ears. Because Lake Shit changed me. I wasn't sure how yet, besides the weight loss and guy-friend, but the music felt different inside me than it used to. Almost like it was the old me that loved it so much, and the new me wasn't sure if liking the same music made me still the old me. I tried to shake the identity crisis and focused on hating my parents some more. Yesterday they set some ground rules, which sounded like *blah blah blah* to me. Until they got to the part about not getting my driver's license until things "calmed down a bit." Calm? I was calm. The apple I grabbed from the table and chucked at the couch showed them how calm I was. Which, of course, freaked them out because I never did stuff like that before I went to Lake Shit. Whose fault is that? I didn't sign myself up for crazy camp.

ASS UP

Tracy won't stop calling me. My best friend in the whole world calls me, and I should want to talk to her and tell her everything, right? But when I first saw her name on my cell, I didn't pick up. Nor the second time. After six calls in less than an hour, I started to feel guilty and answered. She was thrilled to talk to me. Like, screaming into the phone, talking ultra-fast thrilled. Which is really not Tracy. The only time T usually gets all bunged up like that is when she's watching some WWE event on her jumbo TV. But there she was, almost screaming like a little girl. It weirded me out. I guess it was sweet that Tracy wanted to hang out so badly. Why wouldn't she? She hadn't seen her best friend in three weeks due to an unseemly incarceration of the mental hospital variety, so why wouldn't she want to see me?

But why wasn't I quite ready to see her?

Tracy's life hadn't changed in three weeks. She hadn't lost fifteen pounds, seen only three hours of daylight, and had her first major kiss from her melty, gorgeous, kind-of boyfriend. Or maybe she had. Things do happen in three weeks. Unlikely, of course. Tracy is probably just the same hilarious, tough-as-nails girl who works in an overtly sexist lingerie chain store and has an unhealthy obsession with professional wrestling. Which are all of the things I loved about her. But in just three little weeks, I am not the same person I was when I used to be her best friend. I lived by freakish, nonsensical rules, like *Don't drop your pillow during Relaxation*. If you were not in a mental hospital, you would have no idea what that means. Does it even matter that all it is is some stupid type of therapy where you just lie on a floor and listen to crappy music to numb your brain into sleepy oblivion, but only if you place your pillow ever so gently on the floor? Saying it now, why did it even matter at Lake Shit? Why did I care whether I got points for doing good (*placing* the pillow), which allowed me to gain levels within a ludicrous system made to keep us in our places? Looking back, who cares if I made it to Level III? All that did for me was give me the power to choose a TV station during Free Time. Being Level II meant I could eat in the cafeteria instead of my room. It felt like such a big deal. Now that I'm home, explaining all this sounds ridiculous. None of it makes any sense in real life. And that's where I am now. Shoved back into reality after being sucked out and dropped into Loony Central. How did anybody in the mental health field come up with this as a way to make life better? All I feel is skewed.

Maybe the Cap'n will put things into perspective. I never ate Cap'n Crunch before I went to Lake Shit, but the singular request I made of my mom when I got home was that she buy me some Cap'n Crunch. It's pretty much the one thing I ate while I was at the hospital. My stomach didn't quite adjust to the wacky schedules and constant surveillance; therefore I never really took advantage of the vast menu of cafeteria options offered up. Hence, the weight loss. My mom didn't quite see the Cap'n in the same light.

"All that sugar." She shook her head.

Yeah, Ma, see, I was, like, fifteen pounds heavier when I was eating Ass-o-Bran Cereal, so maybe there is something to be said for giving in to temptation. Or at least sugary kids' cereals with a dopey seaman on the box. Ha. I said "seaman."

Was that even funny? I feel like my sense of humor has gone totally out of whack since I got back (though my gift for rhyme is working overtime). Things that are funny when you're in a mental hospital don't seem to make nearly as much sense as when you're out. Example: I keep thinking about Matt O., one of my closest friends at Lake Shit, who had been there for six months by the time I arrived. Whenever he was stuck in the Quiet Room (ironically titled, being the only room in the whole hospital where one could be as loud as they wanted. Hence, how I ended up singing Ramones songs in there as if I were at a concert and I had to yell over the giant speakers to hear myself. As punishment for throwing a plastic baby down the hall. Long story), Matt O. would cry out his mantra, which was, "When I die, I want them to bury me face-down and ass up, so the whole world can kiss my ass!" Every time I think about it, I crack up. So during one of my seventy-six conversations with Tracy yesterday, I told her that story. She did one of those pathetic forced laughs that best friends should not have to do. Because she didn't get it. Really, if I take a moment to analyze it, I know it doesn't make any sense. It's not like Matt's bare ass would be popping out of the top of the coffin (although, god, that's funny. Can you picture the burial plot: a mound of grass with a butt peaking out of the center? Hey! That is funny!). Tracy's comment was, "Wait. Why is he called Matt O. again?"

I explained, "He's been in there for six months, which is, like, years in mental hospital time. In those months, lots of people have come and gone, a bunch of them named Matt. To make things less confusing, because, of course, we were all too messed up in the head to deal with a catastrophic complication such as more than one person with the same name, they gave all of the Matts the addition of the first letter of their last name. Matt O. was technically the only Matt who was at the hospital while I was, but the O stuck around just in case."

Thus the burial ass joke was lost in a quagmire of Lake Shit red tape. And there ended my desire to tell anyone on the outside anything.

PARENTS JUST DON'T UNDERSTAND

I've started to wonder if my parents were somehow traumatized almost as much as I was by putting me into a mental hospital. I mean, my dad has barely said two words to me since I've been home. Oh, wait. That's *normal*. Truthfully, I'd prefer less than two words from him, since his words are usually critical ("Do you really need seconds?"), confused ("I have no idea what you're talking about"), or— my favorite— dismissive (which often involves zero words plus kind, fatherly hand gestures, such as a finger in the air commanding I wait while he finishes his crossword puzzle). My mom was in some otherworldly trance, where she's trying to be as nice to me as possible while a glassy sheen to her eyes meant tears from either the past or yet to come. When they sat down together to give me "the talk" (and I'm probably the only teenager in the world to say I'd rather this have been the sex talk than the laying-down-the-rules-post-mental-hospital talk), there was a nasty cloud of blame hanging in the air. I blamed my parents. My dad blamed my mom. My mom blamed herself. Dad made me promise that any time I felt "bummed" (obnoxiously inappropriate air quotes included), I should tell my mom right away. Which is wrong on so many levels, just a few being he thought my problem was that I was "bummed," that should I need to tell someone it should be my mom, and that I'd actually consider telling him in the first place. My mom, who of course wasn't objecting to the suggestion, peeped up (and, no, I don't mean "piped," because a pipe up would imply you could hear her in more than a five-foot radius), "Allen . . ."

"Don't start, Beth," as though her saying his name was starting.

"I'm not starting, Allen. I just think that it's important for Anna to know that we are both here for her, no matter what happens." I was impressed that Mom actually said something, but not enough to want to listen. I tuned them out, a little trick that Bobby, the youngest kid at Lakeland, taught me: Hum in the tiniest voice you can, so tiny that hopefully no one else hears you, whenever you want to escape a situation mentally. That way either you block out the sounds of the voices completely or you bug the shit out of them with the shrill sound. I succeeded two-fold, since I missed the glory of my mom and dad's "discussion" (it's never an argument) and managed to annoy my dad, who took a pause from belittling my mom to ask me, "What are you doing?"

"Excuse me?" I asked.

"You were humming," he explained to me, as though, in my fragile mental state, I was unaware.

"I know." I smiled at him.

Big sigh from Dad.

Big surprise.

T TIME

As nervous as I was about my reunion with Tracy, anything was better than staying home with my parents, who were never in the same room at the same time, ensuring a possible run-in with either whenever I left my room. The plan was to meet T at the mall, dropped off by my mom in a predetermined location and picked up at a predetermined time at the same location. If I strayed from the plan, even if my mom called my cell phone and found out exactly where I was, I wasn't going to be allowed out of the house again except for school until I graduated. That's what my mom said. I wasn't sure she'd let me out at all, so I milked the pity angle and told her I had nothing that fit me. That's when she laid down the rules, a pretty strong threat from a woman who couldn't even ground me when I shoved all her tampons into the toilet to watch them expand in fifth grade. If I could only see the look on that plumber's face one more time.

Tracy was waiting in between the double set of mall doors when I arrived. She enthusiastically hugged me, a foreign gesture from a girl who refused to cry in public when she found out her beloved dog of twelve years, Shasta, died. At four foot eleven, Tracy reminds me of the tiny bully in that old movie *A Christmas Story*. She may be small and cute, but she could kill you with a well-placed finger to the neck. At least that's what she told a guy when he pinched her butt at a WWE SmackDown she dragged me to.

Tracy backed away from the hug and squinted at me as though trying to figure out what was different. "You look—" she started.

"Thinner, I know. I lost at least fifteen pounds." I wondered how many times I'd be sharing my weight loss factoids.

"Well, there's that, but I was going to say pale."

"Yeah. Three weeks with practically no sunlight will do that to you."

"It's good. Vampiric, really."

"Hope I don't need to worry about being attacked by any Twi-hards," I said as we walked into the cavernous mall.

"Are you hungry?" Tracy asked.

"For blood?"

"Is that what you ate where you were?" Her eyebrows questioned whether or not I was kidding.

"Because you said I looked vampiric. It was a joke."

"Got it." She nodded awkwardly. "So . . . are you hungry?" She asked in a way that said *Do you eat anymore?* not *Do you want something to eat?* Or maybe I was just being paranoid.

"I think so," I answered. My appetite was still wonky, which was good for losing weight but annoying when people expect you to eat the way you used to.

We decided on a hamburger and hot dog place that also served excellent milk shakes. Not that I was hungry enough to eat both. Or either. It was as though I was so uncomfortable in the middle ground where I stood between Lake Shit and Real Life that my stomach couldn't quite adjust. Like on an airplane. You don't want to eat too much in case you get a stomachache and have to take a poo in the tiny bathroom, which may or may not have a working lock and which may happen right in the middle of the captain turning on the fasten-seat-belt sign. That's how my stomach felt.

I ordered a hamburger, my hospital standby when the Cap'n Crunch hibernated after breakfast, but had to settle for fries instead of Tater Tots. More places should serve Tater Tots. Tracy ordered a chicken sandwich and a chocolate cake shake, which is literally chunks of chocolate cake thrown into a shake. I considered ordering one for myself but then remembered the airplane. That I wasn't actually on.

When we sat down, there was a lot of wrapper crinkling and ketchup squirting, then some chewing and glancing around at all of the kitschy, old-timey hamburger-place photos covering the walls. Finally, Tracy produced the requisite "So . . ." To which I responded, "So . . ." I wasn't ready to tell her about Lakeland. While there, I wrote her a never-ending letter about everything and everyone that filled my three weeks, but when it came time to mail it, I couldn't. That story was mine, and I didn't want to send it away. It's like having the most intense sleepover-camp experience of your life and then having to come home and tell your best friend everything that happened to you that *didn't* include her. Except that, instead of summer camp, I was in a mental hospital with a group of depressed kids sharing everything that the rest of the world didn't know. How could I explain that?

Thank God for Tracy. She managed to break the "so" pattern by suggesting, "After lunch let's go into Boobs R Us and take one bra from every display into the dressing rooms just so someone else has to put them away." She looked at me with that mischievous Tracy smirk.

"Wouldn't you freak if someone did that to you while you were working?" I asked with a smile.

"They do. Every day. And I spend every second of my hideous job at The Slut Station putting back the crumpled-up bras with their boob juice all over them!" she yelled way too loudly for including the term "boob juice."

I busted up laughing. "Boob juice? That's nasty." I paused. "Is there really boob juice?"

"I don't mean in the literal boob-juice sense," she dismissed.

"Oh, you were referring to the traditionally figurative use of the term boob juice."

"But of course."

"Gotcha."

If every conversation could go that way for me, then great. I don't mean the boob-juice way, I just mean in the completely un-analytical, non-depressive, so-you-were-just-in-a-mental-hospital-what-do-you-feel-like-doing-now way. Maybe if conversations ever become too stressful for me, I can yell out "Boob juice!" to bring it back to happyland.

As we took our wrappers to the trash, I considered, "Do you think if you say boob juice three times, some boob juice will appear?"

"I don't know if we should chance it. Could be someone else's boob juice. And where would it appear?"

"Something to think about, for sure."

We walked into a trendy-looking store that sold jeans, and Tracy helped me pick out a new pair that fit me better now that I'm in a slightly more svelte range (or would that be less svelte?). Two sale-rack v-neck tees and one tight and revealing tank that will never see the light of day after I stuff it in the bottom of my t-shirt drawer later, and we're done spending the money that my mom rationed out to me. Tracy used her hard-earned boob cash on a most excellent puffy black jacket with faux furry trim around the hood. The jacket happened to be on a display about ten feet off the floor, but instead of asking an employee for help, Tracy grabbed one of those long, silver stick-hooks they use and fished a size small off the rack. As she maneuvered it down to a grabable position, I said, "You do realize it's only September, T?"

"The early bird gets the jacket. And you know I won't step foot in a mall once the post-Thanksgiving Christmas freaks hit."

"Unless you're reporting for boob juice duty," I noted.

"Don't remind me. They make employees park in the nosebleed section of the lots."

"Doesn't nosebleed section mean high up?"

"You know what I mean," she said, peeved, as she tried on the jacket.

"Very cute," I told her.

"Is it *too* cute?" she asked as she looked herself up and down in a mirror. Tracy was constantly fighting her diminutive stature's gift of making her look adorable in practically anything. For Halloween one year she wore head-to-toe camouflage, and every parent who answered a candy-doling door awwwed at how cute she looked. I was always a little jealous, being that most people ignored the chubby girl, especially next to the tiny girl. I suppose it could have been an issue, if Tracy weren't so hilariously anti-cuteness of any sort.

"Maybe if the fur were real, it would be too cute. You know how cute dead animals are wrapped around a hood," I joked. "I think it looks really good. You should get it."

While we waited in line to pay, I talked Tracy out of scaring the shit out of a group of tweens who sprayed every bottle of disgustingly musky perfume by reminding her that we were young and dumb once, too. "At least we didn't smell dumb," she retorted.

I managed to avoid Lakeland talk until we reached the mall doors on our way out.

"So, did you get any driving time?" Tracy asked. "At the hospital?"

Tracy has had her license for three months, practically a lifetime in driving time. Age-wise, I've been legal for a few months, if only my parents would let go of the depression leash they have wrapped around my neck.

Was this Tracy's attempt at getting me to share what all went on at Lake Shit, or was it just really only about my driving abilities?

"Nope," I answered. "No driving time. Barely any walking time, really."

"Oh," she replied, a disappointing "oh" that implied she wanted something more. Whether it was more information about the hospital or that she was hoping I would be closer to getting my license, I wasn't sure.

I suppose I could have told Tracy all about my romantic cab ride to the Shedd Aquarium with Justin, sitting so close to him that our legs became codependent to hold each other's up. How Justin, Matt O., and I were the only inmates allowed to go on that field trip because of good behavior. How Justin and I kissed in the shark reef while Matt kept our chaperone occupied. Instead, I chose to tell Tracy about the getaway cars parked outside the hospital building, one of the only outside views I had for three weeks. Since we were on the subject of cars, and all. It had nothing to do with the fact that I wasn't ready to spill the truly personal moments that were still all mine.

"Sandy—that was my roommate—and I used to pretend these two cars, which for whatever reason never moved from their parking spots, were our getaway cars. They were so funkster decked out. Pink and blue with white trim. Retro. And they just sat there, so we figured if the time was ever right to bust out of Lake Shit—that's what we all call it—we'd each get a car and go." I smiled at the memory of hours wasted looking out our locked, screened window, wishing and wondering when and how we'd get out.

Another short, grunty answer from Tracy followed: "Huh."

Not like "huh?" the question, but "huh" the filler for not having anything constructive to say but needing to acknowledge in three tiny letters that you may, in fact, have been listening. Was she not interested? Did she think I was weird for making up stories about pink and blue getaway cars? Did she think it was some antidepressant-induced hallucination, and she had to humor me or incur my crazy wrath?

My mom, ever the punctual one, pulled up at that moment, leaving me to ponder the not-so-great note where Tracy and I ended. At least it wasn't an I-want-to-end-my-life-things-can't-get-any-worse feeling. Because I've had those. That's something, right?

THE DINNER DISH

Dinner could have been cruddier for the Sunday night before my first day back at school, post-crazy. Would you believe my dad actually made it less cruddy? I'll take attendance and show you how:

> Mom: present
> My sister, Mara: present

Anna: present
Dad:
Dad: ?
Dad: ☺

Dad wasn't there! Not unusual by any means and most welcome at any time. Tonight's excuse was something to do with . . . Well, I wasn't listening. Just know that you'd rather not have him there either.

We ate a dish I'm embarrassed to call one of my favorites: tuna noodle casserole, direct from a recipe book that came with our microwave. The cream of mushroom soup really melts on your tongue. God, that sounds gross.

Most of the talking came from Mara, which is the norm. Mara talks when she's nervous, excited, or awake.

"I'm thinking of trying out for Poms."

"Is that some pomegranate juice appreciation society?" I asked to annoy her.

"Ha and ha. Pom-poms? We cheer at all the basketball games. 'We' if I get in, of course."

"You'll get in. You are chocked full of perk. And you wear a mean ponytail." I nudged her. She gave me that adorable Mara smile that melts me like a Choco Taco on a hot summer's day. The same smile she's made since she first called me "Nanna," which made me sound like a grandma. But it always made me proud to be a big sister.

Could Mara possibly ever look up to her Nanna again, now that I've had a Grade A Crazy stamp tattooed on my ass?

RODNEY

Before I went to bed, I decided I needed to do something to proactively relax. I refuse to admit that the folks at Lake Shit were on to something with their Relaxation. My mom has a large collection of yoga and pilates DVDs, so I perused the choices until I found a box that looked like what I'd expect from a yoga teacher: an Asian man with a long ponytail wearing a loin cloth, saluting the sun. Or something like that.

I popped the DVD into my craptop (which is what I call my laptop, since the only thing it's good for is watching DVDs. The Internet never fails to fail, and even when it does work it's so slow that I grow an ulcer just waiting for a page to open) and followed as the man on the box, Rodney Yee, serenely led me in yoga poses and breathing. His voice, soothing to the point of hypnosis, really did help me calm my brain for a bit about the impending, unpredictable day. If only his tiny, black yoga undies weren't so distracting.

GOOD MORNING, TOILET

Bastardly Irritable Bowel Syndrome. My stomach was so bad this morning, I felt like I had just been forced to run a mile. I went to the bathroom no fewer than eight times. A record before 7:30 a.m.? I feel so proud of my irritable bowels. The irony begins. Sixty-five hours out of a mental hospital, where I miraculously managed to stop having panic attacks and irritable bowels (Do I really have to keep saying that? The world's most humiliating diagnosis), and here I am, the real world, my own home, ready to head back to regular school, and my bowels are as irritable as my grandma after a Yom Kippur fast. What I wouldn't give to be back at Lake Shit right now, waiting to be called into the elevator, to stand illegally but tantalizingly close to Justin, the hair on our arms attracting like desperate magnets . . . Instead, here I am wearing stiff new jeans and my favorite Ramones t-shirt—a security blanket, really—preparing to return to a high school that only brought me anxiety attacks, frequent trips to the nurse's office, and a wealth of ditching and hiding in the secret second-floor bathroom in the math wing.

What are people going to say to me? Welcome back, crazy? From where? Will they know where I was? Will they even have noticed I was gone? Do I care if they know? Still have to figure that out.

Am I a total loser psycho because I would rather be back in a mental hospital? Not just any mental hospital, of course, but my beloved Lake Shit. Oh god, did I just say that? Lake Shit was by no means beloved. It was a hellhole run by adults who only wanted to get paid out of my insurance money by doing as little work as possible, and the only "therapy" I had there was group work, where the group "worked" on our problems with one another, not on our real-life problems that we would have to face again once we got out. Unless you count my one-on-one visits with Dr. Asshole (now that I think about it, that's not a very clever nickname, as fitting as it was), where all he did was berate me and all I did was count the pastel wall–numbing seconds until our meetings were over.

But none of that was what Lake Shit was about.

Lake Shit was really all about Justin. And the other kids, too. But Justin . . . God, I have Justin on the brain. And the fingers and the toes and pretty much everywhere else. How can I not when he's the most—the first—delicious boyfriend I've had, and I don't even know if I'll ever see him or talk to him again? I wonder what he's doing right now. Wait. I don't need to wonder, since I know his exact schedule, seeing as it's how I spent twenty-one days. That's so weird. And he has absolutely no idea what I'm doing. I could be sleeping with every member of the football team (not bloody likely), and he'd have no clue. Is he worried? Jealous? On to the next girl at the mental hospital with any semblance of common likes who is somewhat cute but not nearly as insecure as I am? Maybe he's really some mental-hospital player who gets himself locked up just to hook up with a pathetically depressed chick, to lodge himself into her brain so that she's so obsessed that even when she's out and free to breathe real air and other guys, all she can think about is Justin and his lanky, yet muscular body, his adorably growing-out brown hair that pokes him in his luscious brown eyes, his messed-up fingers because of a horrid accident with a power tool that instead of making him freakish only made him more delectably sensitive and layered, his . . .

What was I talking about?

Oh yeah.

My bowels.

Thanks to my bowels (if I say that word enough will it stop sounding gross and old person-ish?), I was running completely late for my first day back. I thought about walking, which was something I never even considered in the past. Chalk it up to laziness. Today, I'd have to settle for a ride on the Mom Express. The bus, thankfully, was not an option, since I technically lived too close to the school to warrant a bus ride. I'd complain, but who wants to ride the bus? Such problems, I know. Bowels, buses, embarrassing Mom car rides. It could be a lot worse. For so many of my fellow inmates at Lakeland, it was. Molestation, attempted suicide, satanic possession . . . I wondered if that would really be so bad, satanic possession. Because if you're possessed, are you even aware of it? Maybe it'd make life easier. If you have no control over your actions, but not because you're some depressed, chemically imbalanced basketcase, but merely because evil has implanted itself in your body, then what's the problem? I should look into that. Note to self: Get possessed by someone. Preferably before first period.

———

KID IN THE HALL

As Mom dropped me off, she forced a happy face through worried eyes and tensed lips. "Your dad and I need to talk with you tonight when we're all home. But I hope you have a wonderful day."

"That was encouraging," I told her and closed the car door without looking back. I had other things to fret about besides parents pretending to care.

Tracy met me at my locker, along with the comforting presence of the perpetually attached-at-the-lips couple of Julie Ganty and Chris Panlin. After Tracy shoved the two of them aside to make room for her tiny self, she asked, "Have you seen Herpetta today?" Herpetta is what Tracy calls Mrs. March, a hall monitor, who never sports fewer than three large cold sores on her mouth.

"No, thankfully. Why?"

"She must have had one hot weekend. Her lips seem to have morphed into one giant, gleaming beacon of herpes simplex one."

I laughed. Hooray! A real laugh at something Tracy said. That's one step closer to normalcy.

"So how are you feeling this morning?" Tracy casually slipped into our banter.

Fizzle. "Are you going to ask me that every time I see you from now on until—I don't know. When does one become non–The Girl Who Just Got Out of a Mental Hospital?"

"Maybe I'm not asking you because you just got out of a mental hospital. Maybe I'm just asking. Maybe you should ask me the same question. Like, T, how are you feeling today? And I'd answer, like a ball of anus droppings because I didn't sleep for shit last night."

"Uh . . ." I didn't have an answer for that one. Sometimes it's best to let Tracy's words percolate. Or fester. Either way, it felt pretty good to have Tracy just being Tracy and not tiptoeing all around me (Mom) or overcompensating with assiness (Dad) or watching me with confusion and terror (Mara). In fact, Tracy and my family were pretty much the only people I'd talked to—unless you count Sir Spits-A-Lot, the repulsive cashier at the mall—since Lakeland. As much as I was freaked out by the unknown that was school (the unknown of how my brain and stomach would react), maybe it's better than being home with the fam. Hell, if being in a mental hospital was better than being home with my family, what wouldn't be? (To which I answer: an adult prison where you have to sleep in a bunk bed with the lights on. And pee in front of everyone. Oooh—and poo. Everything comes back to the toilet.)

T and I talked about meeting up for lunch, then said our goodbyes. Walking through the halls, I was shocked by how many times I touched a person or a person touched me. By accident, of course, but even a shoulder brush or knuckle knock was forbidden at Lake Shit. At first, I completely tensed, not wanting to make contact, but soon I relaxed and let the drove of backpacks, shoulders, and elbows carry me along to English. It was almost comforting.

When I arrived at my English classroom, my heart started beating quadruple time. I was so worried about what I was going to wear and what people would think when they saw my ghostly pallor, that I completely forgot that I had only been in my classes one week before I was whisked away to Loontown. The other students would have three weeks on me with schoolwork and teacher vibeage. This particular teacher, Mr. Groban, was one that I had for a semester my freshman year for mandatory English. When I faded nicely into a desk. Now, it's pretty impossible to miss me, seeing as I was gone for three weeks, and he most certainly received some sort of notice telling him I'm all kinds of crazy and not to make sudden movements or allow me to use sharp writing implements.

What if he makes me take tests in crayon? Would that even show up on a Scantron?

I was also pretty nervous because, try as I might, I was not able to finish (get past the first ten pages) of *The Crucible*, assigned while I was at Lake Shit, so I'm for sure bordering on F territory. I've never bordered on F territory. I've never even visited D Town, and only occasionally been a sexy stranger in C County. Is this going to be part of the new Anna Bloom? Fs? Not the smartest move for the big, intense, college-prep junior year. Maybe if I sit in the back row and don't move or breathe, he won't notice that I had been gone.

HE NOTICED

After sitting through the class's final discussion of *The Crucible* (symbolism, blah blah blah), with no one seeming to notice I was ever gone (two cheerleader types looked confused, whispered to each other, shrugged and moved on, plus stoner-for-life Louis Teaf rasped, "S'up. You got any papers?"), I thought I was free and breezy, until the bell rang and Mr. Groban called, "Anna, can I see you for a moment?"

My stomach lurched at the thought of the F, of being forced to read *The Crucible* with toothpicks holding my eyes open and girls in Puritan costumes cackling at me in the background.

Wait.

My stomach lurched at the thought of Puritans, but not at sitting in class. For the first time during school since before my panic attacks surfaced last spring, I didn't think about my stomach and nerves and going to the bathroom and what if I farted in class or needed to get up or . . . What did I think about then? Certainly not *The Crucible*. My English notebook answered our question: How many times can one write "Justin" in a fifty-minute period? So as long as I focus all of my brain power on Justin (who, as previously noted, I may never see or talk to again and who probably doesn't even remember my name at this point), my tummy's golden. Screw my grades.

Mr. Groban is slightly balding with hipsteresque brown-framed glasses, and may or may not have been a little cute when he wasn't parent-old, missing hair, and an English teacher. He also has a penchant for wearing suit vests and skinny ties. It's a look. Surprisingly, he didn't want to talk about my F. I began our chat with a defensive "It was really hard to read *The Crucible* at the hospital. I just—"

But Mr. Groban interrupted, "No worries, Anna, no worries. We're done with that book anyway. On to bigger and better. I'll just leave that unit out of your grades and start fresh from here on out."

"Wow. Um, thanks." Was he actually being understanding? Is it possible for a teacher to care about me as a person more than he cares about my GPA? Or was this some piece of my post-therapy program, that all teachers were told to treat me in a kind and benign manner? So I wouldn't crack?

"I wanted to let you know that if you ever need a moment or just someone to talk to or a place to go if it's a bad day, my office is always available. No expectations from me. You don't have to talk to me, but if you need to, I'm here." Mr. Groban placed his hand woodenly on my shoulder and gave me a solid nod. "Okay then. Better prep for my next class. Tomorrow then?" he asked, like we had plans I may or may not be able to make. Which I guess was true. Who knows where my stomach would be tomorrow?

"Yep," was all I could muster. And then I grew a mustache like General Custer. And the wind began to bluster. Aside from my pathetic attempt at rhyme (although any paragraph containing both

22

the words "muster" and "mustache" should be instant comedy gold in my book), that wasn't so bad. I wonder if my pre-calc teacher got the be-kind-to-Anna note, too.

CALC-U-LATER

See what I did there? Like a *calculator,* but, oh, never mind.

Pre-calc was sort of the opposite of English. There were numbers instead of letters! I'm really on a roll! Thank you, ladies and germs! I'll be here all night!

In all seriousness (was that even funny?), Ms. Jared didn't single me out at all. Instead of acting like I had been gone for three weeks and was a total weirdo, Ms. Jared went about class like she always does, all perk and petite blondness (I pictured her as a peppy cheerleader in a huge skirt and pom-poms back in the 1800s when she was in high school), teaching us a new concept and giving us five minutes at the end of class to ask questions or start the homework. I thought I'd be lost, seeing as in math one thing builds upon another, but since so much of the beginning of the year was reminding us of the math that had drained with the chlorine into the swimming pools of summer, I hadn't missed much. The newness of the lesson kept my brain occupied enough that I didn't have to get up six times to visit my favorite, secret math-wing bathroom (don't tell me you don't have a favorite bathroom). There were only two moments during pre-calc that reminded me I had been on a loony holiday. The first was when Amber Rose Duncan, my next-door-seat neighbor, leaned over with a delicate hand on my desk and whispered, "We're glad you're back." I guess that was sweet. But did she know where I was? How? And who was she representing with "we"? The math class? The school? Or maybe Amber Rose Duncan is possessed, and she somehow knew with all her intuitive possessed brain that I befriended several folks at Lake Shit dealing with demonic possession, so she and her tenant were happy to see me. Until they devour me in my sleep tonight.

The second blip of a reminder came as I left the classroom. I decided not to approach Ms. Jared about my missing math work, hoping she, too, received the magical crazy excuse note (that I created in my mind) to not stress me. She didn't mention any note or missing homework as I left her room, but I swear I saw the tiniest wink. Perhaps she just had some whiteboard dust in her eye. Or maybe she winked at Carl Benison, who recently placed fourth in our nation's Science Olympiad. I hope it was at me. I do love a good wink.

¿QUÉ?

Physics was a jumble of science and numbers, which the teacher, Mr. Fripp, tried to make entertaining by applying them to such things as roller coasters and Sit 'n' Spins. I don't see what it has to do with real life. Fripp handed me a packet on the way out and said, "Glad to have you back. Take your time on these assignments. I don't need them back for at least a week." He smiled at me through his bushy beard, which made him look like he had been lost in the woods for six weeks. Didn't he get the No Anna Homework memo? Am I going to have to say something to him? Or worse, am I going to actually have to do the work? It hardly seemed fair that something that's not even my fault (Hi, crappy genetics and jacked-up parents!) should cause me to have tons of homework or screw up my grades.

I almost left the class without saying anything, but I decided to call forth the strength of my fellow Lake Shit patients: Matt O., who defied all hospital rules because he knew, after being there for six months, that the punishments were inconsequential; Sandy, my roommate, who faked a pregnancy, and they made her carry around a plastic baby doll until she admitted to it; and Justin, who still managed to be cool and funny and charming even though his home life sucked enough for him to attempt suicide after his hand was mangled. These people were tough, and they taught me while I was there that I could be tough, too. That getting in trouble most of the time wasn't anything, as long as you knew what you were getting into. The more I thought about it, the more pissed I got. How dare this bearded dweeb of a man think he could throw three weeks of homework at me, work I never even learned in his class because I was dealing with depression somewhere where they didn't have physics teachers, and then expect it back in one week? Did he think I wouldn't have other work to catch up on? Did he not think about the consequences of all that extra stress he just piled on?

Almost out the door, I turned around and marched over to Fripp's desk. I slammed the packet down in front of him, harder than I had planned, to get his attention. He looked up from the papers he obliviously shuffled and exhaled, "Can I help you?" His confused expression said he had no idea who I was without my designated seat assignment to tell him.

"Mr. Fripp, I don't think I should have to do the work I missed. This is three weeks of work on stuff I never even learned, so that would mean I would have to learn it, do all of the work, do all of my current work, and deal with all of the crap I'm still dealing with having been, you know, where I was." The dull look on Fripp's face made me question whether or not he did know where I was. Or who I was.

"Annnnnna." He stretched out my name, as if discovering he recognized me. "I see your point. The grades are unimportant to me, so I can wipe them if need be. However, you will struggle through the rest of the year if you don't master these concepts first. How about we set up some after-school tutoring sessions to catch you up?"

That was easy.

I told Mr. Fripp that I wasn't sure when my mom wanted me to be home this week, but I would get back to him.

Just like that, I convinced a teacher to forgive three weeks of homework out of the goodness of his own beard. Score one for the crazy girl.

I envisioned Español offering up a welcome-back fiesta, complete with burro-shaped piñata dropping brightly wrapped Mexican candies. Señora Schwartz, with her thick East Coast accent tromping all over her fluent Spanish, was a sucker for candies (sweet pun intended) and any excuse for a fiesta (and occasionally a siesta), but I received nary a glance from her oversized bosom (which glanced just as proficiently as her eyes). *¿Qué pasa?* I didn't need a piñata, but an *hola* or *¿cómo estás?* would have been *bueno.* Or at least *asi,asi. ¡Qué mal!*

After I sat down at my desk, I started to feel antsy. Not as extreme as the shitty old days, but enough that I needed to bounce my leg up and down to try and dissipate the approaching stomachache. Without the acknowledgment of the Señora, I got nervous that maybe she didn't know where I was and I'd have to explain things. And just like that, was it all coming back? Were my three weeks at Lake Shit for naught? What would I do if it all happened again? If I couldn't sit through my classes and my stomach started hurting and I needed to go to the bathroom and I wouldn't leave the house and—

The bell rang. Class was over, and I made it. I guess. My right thigh burned from all of the physical activity. Next time I have a freak-out, I'll be sure to shake my left leg. Got to keep them even.

God, I hope there's no next time.

———

THE LUNCH BUNCH

I met Tracy at the vending machine in the hall outside of the cafeteria. Our school's caf is surprisingly pleasant and relaxed compared to the fluorescent-bulbed, cliquified cafeterias of your standard TV shows and films. It surrounds a woodsy courtyard, complete with floor-to-ceiling windows that brighten the room enough so artificial lighting is minimal. Some tables are square, some the classic, long rectangle, and there are even some small, round tables scattered about. It makes the alienation thing less noticeable, like, if you sit at a small, round table by yourself with a bunch of books, that doesn't necessarily mean that no one wants to sit with you but that you want to study. Or that you want to study and no one wants to sit with you, but at least you're not all by your lonesome at a gigantic table where other kids with mass quantities of friends talk smack about you at the other end. I'm referencing that one lonely semester my sophomore year when I didn't manage to have a single friend in my lunch period. It's of the past, since Tracy and some Art class friends are in my current lunch period. But it never hurts to remind oneself of how life can be more pathetic than it is now. Or does it *always* hurt?

The vending machine is where I liked to supplement my mom-made lunches. And, no, I don't think it's weird that my mom makes my lunches. I mean, when you buy your lunch at school, someone else is making it for you, so why is it weird if it's my mom? But I didn't bring my mom's lunch today. It was a slight bit of rebelliousness on my part, a *Screw you, Mom, you put me in a mental hospital, and now that I'm out you think I'm going to do everything your way and go to school and eat your food as if nothing ever happened.*

And, totally weird, but I still wasn't all that hungry. I don't know if it was the nervous stomach creeping back (which always used to be comforted by an excess amount of food to suffocate the butterflies) or that I was used to not eating much at the mental hospital (where it was the pleasant combination of gross food, inner awkwardness, utter terror, and sexual tension that prevented me from gorging), but lunch wasn't my lunch-period priority. I was more nervous about a) what my Art class lunch friends would have to say about my absence and b) what my stomach was going to have to say the rest of the school day. And the day after that.

Tracy marched up to me with her My Little Pony lunch box and asked, "How you holding up? Need me to practice my dragon-sleeper hold on anyone?"

"Which one's the dragon?" I asked. Tracy demonstrated in the air one of her many beloved wrestling maneuvers. I don't think I'll ever fully understand her love for professional wrestling. She claims it's the combination of costumes, violence, and tiny man nipples. "I'm good for now, thanks, but I'll keep you posted. Do you have a dollar I can borrow?" In my haste to burn my mother with my forgotten lunch, I also forgot to bring money, just in case I actually wanted something to eat.

Tracy fished her chain wallet out of her back pocket. In her effort to buck any sort of preconceived female stereotypes, which is her constant battle (skanky lingerie store job vs. professional wrestling, My Little Pony lunch box vs. chain wallet, Dora the Explorer pillowcases vs. Handy Manny sheets. You know, the usual), Tracy preferred a less traditional form of money carrying. Plus, it made her feel badass that she could pull out her wallet and whip it at someone like a deadly set of nunchucks.

"Here you go. What delightful Little Debbie holiday items are available for us today? Do they still have the Labor Day flag cakes?"

"Wasn't Labor Day like three weeks ago? Surely they're on to their Christopher Columbus head cakes by now," I joked. "I think

I'm going to skip the Little Debbies today. Not really in the mood for sprinkles." I scanned the window of snacks and decided on a pack of Oats 'n Honey granola bars.

"So healthy now, aren't you?" Tracy pressed, while the granola bars dangled and dropped into the protective snack-catching bin.

I shoved my hand into the metal door and rescued my granola bars from their waiting area. "Not really. Granola bars are deceptively unhealthy. Sugar and fat and stuff. See?" I held the wrapper up to her face. "Six whole grams of fat."

"If you start only eating celery and mustard, I'm allowed to worry, right?" We walked to a bench in the front foyer of the school and sat down. I wasn't sure if Tracy purposely wasn't bringing me into the cafeteria for protective reasons or if she just needed a minute to have The Weight Conversation.

"Dude, I lost weight. That's a good thing, right?"

"Yeah, I guess. I mean, I know you wanted to."

"Everyone wants to, right? We're just, as females in the Western world, supposed to want to lose weight. Even if we look like that." I pointed my granola bars at a prepubescent-looking freshman in crotch-tastic short-shorts, her legs nowhere near rubbing where they should.

"This doesn't need to turn into some feminist diatribe, Anna. Or antifeminist, as it's sort of sounding. I just haven't eaten much with you in three weeks, and I have no idea how you lost this weight and where you might be going with it. I mean, are you on a diet? Do you have a goal weight? Are you going to hire a personal trainer named Gunther?"

"Why? Do you know a personal trainer named Gunther?" Tracy sneered, then smiled. "No personal trainer, T. No diet, really. I just don't feel like eating as much. And sorry that looking in the mirror after losing fifteen pounds makes me feel less shitty than being plus fifteen pounds did. I'm still not even average, so I don't think you have to worry." Our conversation simultaneously made me want to buy out the vending machine's Little Debbie collection and throw my granola bars in the trash.

I must have looked tragic because Tracy kicked my Converse and said, "Hey, no worries, Anna. Forget I said anything, okay? You look great. You looked great. You will look great. If I were a lesbian, I'd do you. The end."

"You'd *do* me?" I laughed.

"Would you rather I said 'make love'?" We both shivered at the grossness of that phrase, and I remembered a moment back at Lakeland when Justin and I sat in chairs next to each other during Free Time, listening to a classic rock station, and that song, "I Feel Like Makin' Love" came on. I could only wonder if anyone like Justin would ever have thoughts like that about me. One week later, he kissed me. And I knew he did.

"You want to go to the lunch table?" Tracy's question broke into my melty memory, and I hated that I wasn't locked up in a mental hospital, just rooms away from Justin, the potential for a snuck elevator arm touch or cafeteria leg bump gone when my insurance ran out. Here I was, twenty minutes left until gym class torture, then more classes, more torture, no Justin. Would there ever be a Justin again?

"Sure," I shrugged. Reluctantly I followed behind Tracy to our round, corner lunch table where Meredith Hyon, Eleanor Mang, and Tucker Cahill, all Art class friend-quaintances waited in their poised, waify manner. More often than I'd care to admit, I'd coveted their perfectly slouching skinny jeans, the way their ratty Vans protruded from their sticklike legs, how they could wear baggy t-shirts and still look twiggy. I know there's more to them than their lack of fat, as there hopefully is more to me than my plethora of it, but somehow the way they look, the ease of it, has always made them seem more legitimate in the art world than me. Even with my musical prowess, my bass playing, my utter and undying devotion to The Ramones, I'd never look as right as they do at a concert. Just because they're skinny. And I'm not.

There's more to them, Anna, I had to remind myself as I made my walk of . . . what?—Doom? Shame? Lunacy?—to the table halfway across the cafeteria. Meredith happens to be hilariously addicted to Blink 182, no matter how old they get (our favorite argument is how much older The Ramones are, to which my defense is a) some of them aren't even alive anymore, so that doesn't count and b) The Ramones are ageless and timeless and perfect, and then I stick my tongue out and give her the finger and let her know I won). Tucker is an online conspiracy theorist who is constantly trying to hack our school's network to mess with grades. Not his grades, mind you, because it's hard to go anywhere higher when you have a GPA consisting entirely of AP class As. He'd much rather lower the grades of, as he put it, "pre-corporate scum" so they can't get into the colleges of their choice, and therefore will fall into a potpit of despair where they will inevitably get Grateful Dead tattoos and follow Phish or Widespread Panic or whatever band requires outside substances to make their music tolerable until they end up on the side of the road selling hemp bracelets and attempting to create dreadlocks out of what is left of their once lush hair. Then there's Eleanor, who will not admit to anyone but our lunch table that she is addicted to World of Warcraft and has a level 75 warrior named Cha Cha.

So, yeah, they look cool, but I guess they are pretty cool, too. In their own bizarre ways.

I picked up my step and sidled up to ye olde lunch table. "Hey, guys, how've you been?" I smiled and tried to be casual.

"Anna!" they yelled in celebration. After a round of hugs, we were all seated. Eleanor produced a gift from the seat next to her. Cupped in her hands was a delicately folded paper box, decorated in Meredith's familiar drawing style. Between the large, round eyes and boxy shoes, I noticed some grease circles seeping through.

"Open it. Quick," Eleanor prodded.

Inside the box was a packet of cafeteria Tater Tots, the kind I used to buy every day pre—Lake Shit. The grease should have been a dead giveaway.

"Gee, thanks. You shouldn't have."

"We didn't know what to get you," Tucker apologized. "It was this or . . ."

"Some homemade get-well-soon cards. But that just seemed off somehow, you know?" Meredith asked.

"Yeah, I do know." I laughed a little, picturing the envelope filled with get-well-soon cards from my family and friends that I was handed upon leaving Lakeland. They didn't know what to say either. Tater Tots were at least kind of funny. "This was very thoughtful," I decided. "Thanks."

My smile seemed to melt any apprehension that may have been left over from my approach, and we relaxed into discussion about Art class. I told them about the colored pencils our Art teacher, Mrs. Downy, sent over to the hospital and how I had to stick my fingers out my hospital room door in order to get someone to come and sharpen them. The intense looks I got from the lunch crew freaked me out a bit, like I was telling them ghost stories and I was about to get to the part where the sculpture is really a clown. Maybe I wasn't quite ready for that. I shifted the talk over to them.

"So what have you guys been up to?"

Tucker started to speak, but Eleanor broke in, "Hold up. Can I just say, Anna, that you look really good. Pale, which is awesome, but did you lose weight?"

And back to me.

JUST SAY YES

Finally something good came out of my antidepressants. I mean, besides the obvious presumption that they are making me anti-depressed. Because the verdict's still out on that. Who can prove what did the trick when I started the antidepressants just a few days before entering a mental hospital? And if they were so great and all-fixing, then why did I need the hospital in the first place? Or if they are just some sort of placebo pill, what's the point of taking them if I went into a mental hospital anyway? The bullshit of science. I asked the psychiatrist who prescribed them how they worked. Like, did they find the unhappiness floating through my bloodstream and just zap it like zit cream? But he couldn't even explain it. It was one of those bogus "We're not quite sure how it works; we just know that it does." Or *do* you? Maybe it's all in people's heads. Not the depression, but the ability to get over it. Maybe it's just another piece of the billion-dollar pharmaceutical industry, and the people who make the drugs only want us to think we need them.

Like, I have wondered about that warning that certain antide-pressants shouldn't be taken until after adolescence ever since Matt O. schooled me on it at Lake Shit. Studies have shown that these drugs may actually *cause* teenagers to commit suicide. How is that possible? Is it like dropping acid and thinking you can fly? Some-how these chemicals react with the pubescent brain to make us beyond crazy, so much that we kill ourselves? Or is it just another excuse adults use because they messed up in the first place, gave us their fucked-up genes and crappy parenting, and then need someone

33

else to blame besides themselves? Or, if these drugs really do somehow cause teens to kill themselves, how messed up is that? That someone could invent a drug that can make some people feel happier and some people want to die? How do you know which it will do for you?

None of that really matters at this point because my antidepressants just got me out of gym class. When my gym teacher, Mr. Schocker, approached me (you know the guy—impossibly high-waisted shorts, uncomfortably snug around the crotch, undeniably tight around the stomach) to ask if I'd be joining the class today, I told him my doctor suggested I take it easy because the medicine I'm on may make me dizzy. Which is completely untrue. I don't even know why I said it because, as gym teachers go, this one isn't so bad. He never yelled at me for shuffling instead of running, for hanging on the sidelines during basketball, or for visiting the cramp excuse more than four times in a month. Maybe I like the idea of having an excuse. That I was actually somewhere totally screwed up for three weeks, and instead of pretending that I'm all better, new and improved, the old me but with extra shine, I deserve to milk it a little and say that I'm not. How much better am I? Just a little less fat, a little more cynical, a great deal more experienced, and completely and utterly more disillusioned with my parents and pretty much every adult in the world.

The upside of it all? Mr. Schocker caved so much and so quickly that I didn't even have to change for Gym if I didn't want to. I could sit it out, do my homework, read, or even, Schocker suggested, help him keep track of everyone's fitness goals. I told him I might not be ready for something so intense, but I'd think about it. Instead I decided to use the time to write my first letter to Justin.

———

34

HARDER THAN I THOUGHT

You'd think after spending three weeks lusting after a guy, one extraordinary day at the Shedd Aquarium ending with a most magnificent kissing session, and one last-hurrah goodbye kiss, totally initiated by yours truly even if it could get Justin punished after I left Lake Shit, I'd have a lot to say to what is quite possibly the most amazing guy I'd ever meet in my life.

You'd be wrong.

There is so much that I want to say to him—so much sappy, syrupy, Harlequin Romance, borderline soft-core crap that could fill a novella. But what would be the point? He's at Lakeland, and I'm here. He's in the city, I'm in the burbs. He's locked up with who knows what new, adorable, skinnier, less depressed girl who he can make out with during mental hospital school when no one is looking, and I'm free as a bird, surrounded by possibly eligible, pretty much disinterested males that haven't noticed me for the last sixteen years. It's a fact that I had practically no competition at Lake Shit: There was my fakely pregnant, taken roommate; a shit-talking rude girl who was already making out with someone during school time; and a girl possibly possessed by the devil who had seizures and spoke in tongues. Of course, that one girl who was semi-normal came along at the end, but she found someone else to screw around with at Lake Shit (God, is that all we did in the mental hospital? Why would anyone want to leave?). And that was it. The entire adolescent-floor female population. If that were the selection, hell, I'd make out with me. At least I listen to good music and wear cool shoes.

What am I supposed to write about now that I'm out? Do I send Justin a letter only reminiscing about the good (and groping) times we had? Do I ask him a million questions about how everyone at

Lakeland is doing? Do I try to make plans with him when he gets out? What would we even do? I can't think about that yet. It could be weeks, months even, if his insurance is good. Do I tell him what's been going on with me, post–Lake Shit, and ask him what's been going on with him, post–me at Lake Shit? Do I want to know? How much would it kill me if he did hook up with someone else? We didn't leave with any sort of expectation, no dramatic "I'll wait for you" proclamation. What if he's not even thinking about me at all? What if I can never stop thinking about him?

WORLD CULTURES

No letter written. I wasted my entire gym class making one gigantic doodle monstrosity in my binder. If I am forever lost for words, I suppose I could send the doodle to Justin. Maybe it would land in the hands of one of the Lakeland workers, they'd psychoanalyze it, determine I'm insane, and wheel me back in. That would solve the letter-writing problem. If I'm at the hospital with Justin then I won't have to write him any letters. And maybe we would make with the smoochies again. But what if I got readmitted on the same day he's discharged? Then I'd have to write him letters. What would I say?

World Cultures class was a cultural wasteland. All we did was take notes on a "classic" film, *Lawrence of Arabia*. All of that desert made me thirsty. I could even have gone for one of those Lake Shit juice cups with the metal peel-off lids that never really quenched my thirst.

Will every thought for the rest of my life return to Lake Shit?

ALL I NEED IS ART

I had envisioned the moment when I explained the state of my unfinished collage assignment to Mrs. Downy. Maybe she would excuse it, hug me, and tell me to use those newly explored feelings to create great art. Or maybe she would look at it, peer at me over her colorful, speckled glasses, and tell me to "carry on," her nod to Tim Gunn on *Project Runway*. It didn't go down either way, though. The Art room buzzed as it always did the final period of the day. Some seniors, who killed off all their class requirements in their first three years, took the last period as AP Art, which to me looked like just hanging out in the Art room with their friends for college credit. There were two actual scheduled classes in the Art room during last period: Art I, a freshmen-level class that anyone can take, and Art III, the class I'm in, where we experiment with more advanced projects and also have a lot of freedom in how those projects are executed. Because I couldn't focus and choose just a painting or drawing or photo class, this seemed like the best choice. The constant noise and commotion in the Art room made it the one place in the school I never had stomach or anxiety problems, except maybe during a critique. Usually, it was so loud and the others were so into their own thing, that it never mattered even if I did have to leave to use the bathroom, which meant that I rarely did. If only all classes could be this crazy-person accommodating.

If you were wondering, Tracy doesn't take Art. Instead she chose to be the only girl in Auto Shop class because she doesn't like the stereotype of only greasy guys under car hoods taking it. Or maybe it's *because* she likes that.

The Art class trio from lunch sat at the farthest wooden table from the door. I could have bypassed Mrs. Downy, and just pretended the collage never existed, but I would have had no idea what she expected from me. As of now, I have no idea what anyone can expect from me. Cruddy feeling.

A freshman was arguing with Mrs. Downy about a weak drawing of a hand. "But my hand looks that way. See?" He held up his oversized hand from his lanky body.

"Get that out of my face," Mrs. Downy clipped. "I can grade it now, or you can do it over. Your choice. Next?" As if the Art room were a deli.

I approached Mrs. Downy with the collage gripped in both hands. To a person on the street, Mrs. Downy would look normal: short, poised, and with a thick streak of white in the center of her long, brown hair. As a teacher, she's a little scary. When you're presenting someone with something as personal as a piece of artwork you've created, you'd expect that person to be gentle with her criticism. Not Mrs. Downy. She tells it like it is. When the nose on your drawing looked like a triangle with two holes, she'd cackle and ask, "Really?" When you handed in what you thought was a delightful, fruity still-life painting, all she'd see was how you missed the orange's shadow. And when you just got out of a mental hospital and you had to admit to a still unfinished assignment, she just looked at you for a good twenty seconds, up and down. Then a tiny smirk crept onto her face, and she said, "Anna Bloom. Good to have you back. What is this?"

"My collage?" I asked, presenting it to her like an offering to a queen who can, and will, chop your head off. "I never got a chance to finish it. They didn't give me a whole lot of time for drawing at, you know, the hospital." I was totally milking it. If I could produce tears on cue, I would. I even thought about a subtle lip quiver.

"Not to worry. You can either finish it, or move on. Of course I'd prefer you finish it. We've started photography. See me after school for a review."

"I don't know if I can come in today. My mom's kind of keeping a close eye on me and—"

"Then tomorrow. I'm here until five. Next?"

Not exactly the warmest greeting, but at least it's another non-F. Note to all of you out there who want to get out of schoolwork: Go to a mental hospital. You'll be surrounded by Satan worshippers, abuse victims, and kids dealing drugs to pay for their mother's cancer treatment, but at least you won't have to do homework.

I was still confused about what to do with the collage when I saw Meredith, Eleanor, and Tucker waving me over to their table. Tucker and Meredith stood looking over Eleanor's shoulder, so I took a spot next to Tucker to see what was what.

"Check it. It's a flip book of Cha Cha. She's totally wailing on an orc." Eleanor flipped the small pages with her thumb, and we watched an elf in sparse, green medieval clothes dice up a green globular creature wearing a shredded brown tunic. In the grand finale, Cha Cha pulls out a dagger and stabs the orc repeatedly in the head until he's a bloody pile of mush on the ground, which she then climbs, pulling a flag from behind her and planting it firmly into the orc leftovers. The flag unfurls to read "Cha Cha wuz here."

"Is that part of the new Art Three curriculum?" I asked.

"I'm not turning this in to anyone," she scoffed. "I made it in calc."

"We had a test in Calc," Tucker reminded her.

"After," Eleanor snipped.

"Overachiever," Tucker mumbled.

"Maybe some of us don't feel the need to check our answers and then write unsolicited essays to the teacher about why extra credit is necessary to bring our GPAs over their, and I quote, 'stifling capacity,'" Eleanor said with extreme bite, complete with harsh air quotes.

"How did you even see that?" Tucker yelled, frustrated and a little too loudly.

"You sit next to me, you didn't cover your paper, and I was

intrigued by the scratching of your pencil. Math tests usually involve fewer words than you provided. Really, you were just asking for it to be read. I merely succumbed to the invitation." Meredith looked at me with a hidden smile. Eleanor and Tucker have been a will-they-won't-they couple since I've known them. They even went to Homecoming together last year, although fully platonically. In fact, that's what Eleanor asked the photographer to put on their tragically captioned photo. While most people had gag-worthy sentiments inscribed on their pictures, such as "Liz + Joe 4 EVA," Eleanor and Tucker's photo, of the two of them standing a measured twelve inches apart, read "Eleanor and Tucker: Fully Platonic." How am I so familiar with said photo? Eleanor took the photo and turned it into a life-sized painting for Art II class. It's so crazy good, you can actually see the sweat beads of discomfort on Tucker's upper lip. A really brilliant piece of work. Meredith and I have a theory that Eleanor had to make such a big production out of the platonicity because she is actually deeply in love with Tucker. We figure she'll admit this right before graduation in dramatic Eleanor fashion, possibly in skywriting. Or maybe someone else's blood.

The lightness of Art class made me step back a bit from myself. If I didn't have the loon cloud hanging over my head, was I just a normal teenager at a normal high school? These three people were pretty much just in-school friends, but that kind of counts, doesn't it? And they have asked me to do stuff in the past out of school, like meet them at Denny's once or twice. But that was always when Tracy was working, and I felt like a goob going alone. Plus, it was mixed into my period of isolation due to irritable bowel syndrome tomfoolery (I imagine my bowels must enjoy being irritable to some degree, or why would they always be that way?), and I wondered if they would ever ask me to hang out again. Did I miss my chance? And would my mom even let me if they did ask again? Because being there with three people joking about something as unremarkable as math tests kind of reminded me of my friends back at Lakeland. Which oddly made me feel just a little bit more normal.

HALL TIME

Tracy waited by my locker after class, bubbling with excitement (well, this was Tracy, so maybe more like crackling with anticipation, or busting with enthusiasm. She's not much of a bubbler) over an Auto Shop story.

"You know Bernard Stevens?" she jumped right in as I approached, without a hello or sappy greeting. Much appreciated to keep the momentum of my normalcy going.

"No, not really. I think I've heard his name mentioned in conjunction with words such as 'suspension' and 'battery.'"

"Yeah, that's him," Tracy continued. "The whole time I've been in class he's been bitching about how girls shouldn't be in Auto Shop. Mr. Grubb made us partner up for oil changes, and Bernard was all trying to be the man, showing a lady how to do an oil change. We're both under the car, and he was getting really close with his creeper."

"Whoa. What's a creeper? You don't mean his . . ."

"Ween? God, no. It's the thing you lie on to roll in and out under the car. Anyway, I didn't like the approach, so I played dumb girl and twisted off the drain plug, then rolled out of the way, commando style. All of the oil went right in his face. Up his nose, in his mouth, everywhere. Some of the other guys had to hold him back, as if he could even take me. And I was all, 'Oh, I didn't know what that was for. I'm sooooo sorry. I'm just a girl, you see,' batting my eyelashes and shit. Good times."

She said it. Good times. This day was so much better than predicted. I sat through my classes semi-normally. I talked to my friendish people. I laughed. I didn't get any Fs. Right on. Maybe I'd even tell my mom about it when she picked me up. Make her feel a little less guilty for what she put me through.

Tracy pulled her Skanks R Us uniform, actually just a wrinkled white blouse with a name tag, out of her locker and yanked off her own black t-shirt right in the middle of the hallway. "Shield me, would ya?" she asked, which kind of made me feel fat whenever she said it (which is whenever she had to work after school). Would she ask me to shield her if I had less of a protective area with which to shield? Or is that just what friends do, and I am a friend? That's not a question I'd ever get a truthful answer for anyway.

"Thanks, man," T offered. "Today's our seventeenth yearly sale. All bras are buy one, buy another one." She rolled her eyes and stuck out her tongue in a gagging way.

After we said goodbye, we'd call each other later, I walked the halls to my mom's pickup spot. I passed Tucker at his locker and was surprised to see him in a school soccer uniform. As with most soccer players, he had way decent legs. I'd never noticed them wrapped in his skinny jeans, which had the intentional result of making him look just, well, *skinny*.

"Hey," I said, with a touch of confusion in my voice.

He slammed his locker abruptly and shouldered his backpack. "Hey, Anna." He paused and looked down at himself with an expression that said he was as perplexed as I was. Tucker is the smart guy. The *really* smart guy. And the cool art guy. He's not the jock guy.

He looked up again, tilted his head, scrunched his eyes

thoughtfully through his square, black, hipster glasses, and explained, "I play soccer."

"Okay," I offered.

"I like to run. I like to kick. I like to score," he said in his concrete manner. I wanted to laugh, at the scoring and all, but I let him continue.

"Eleanor and Meredith think I'm at an off-site art-enrichment program after school. I would appreciate if you didn't share this information with them."

"Sure. No problem. But won't they see your name or picture or whatever in the sports section of the school paper?"

"Have you ever read the sports section of the newspaper?" he asked.

"Good point." I smiled, and he smiled back. He removed his glasses, as I envision Clark Kent does when he's about to change into Superman, and stuffed them into his backpack. He actually looked quite the soccer player then: lean, surprisingly muscley, with flipping bangs I imagined wouldn't be out of place on some European soccer field. "I gotta motor. My mom's picking me up. Good luck at your game. Or am I supposed to say 'break a leg'?"

"I think that's only in theater. In sports, that's probably more of a curse."

"Oh. In that case, keep your leg intact."

"Will try. See you tomorrow." Tucker jogged off down the hall in his blue-and-orange uniform, number 23. As I turned around to leave, he called down the hall to me, "Anna!" I looked back at him. "Glad you're okay!"

"Thanks!" I yelled, and gave a little wave.

That was . . .

Nice?

HOME AGAIN, HOME AGAIN

I arrived at my mom's car with a spring in my step. The sun seemed to be glinting off the silver of her Honda just for me. I flipped the door handle. Locked. Usually, this completely annoyed me. You know I'm coming, unlock the freakin' door. But today, it seemed a little funny. A little *normal*. That's a word I could get used to.

The click arrived, and I hopped into the front passenger seat.

"Hi," my mom said with such astonishment in her voice I had to check my face in the mirror to see if I had a giant booger or newly formed zit. Neither sighted, I answered back.

"Hi?" with an equally confused tone. We must have sat looking at each other for six hours, when my mom finally said, or more accurately, dubiously asked, "You had a good day?"

"I think what you meant to say was, 'How was your day, dear?' To which I would answer, 'Pretty good, actually.' Then you say, 'I'll take you home and make you a delicious, nutritious snack before you start your homework. No video games until you're done!' " I adopted a black-and-white-television-show mom's perky voice for the occasion.

My mom kind of got it, laughed through her nose a sniff, and started to drive. "Sorry, honey, I didn't mean to imply that you shouldn't have had a good day. It's just a little hard to remember the last time I picked you up from school that you had one."

While she may have been right, she was bringing my good-day buzz down. "Yeah, I know. Hence, you putting me in a mental hospital to get better, remember?" Just like that, the anger came back.

Big sigh from Mom. "We"—Mom always used the royal Dad and Mom "we" even though the Dad piece was obviously just a

44

formality, since he could give a jackrabbit's tiny turd about me—"we spoke with the professionals at the hospital—" I love that she refers to those assholes as professionals, even though all I saw them do was tell the kids on the floor to do things without being remotely constructive or ever having anything to do with our lives outside of the hospital. "And they feel that patients need to continue the work they started even after they leave Lakeland."

Oh God. Where was this going? "I'm not going back to that freaky Freudian bitch," I argued. The therapist I saw—the one who convinced my parents to throw me in Lake Shit—was in dire need of therapy herself. Don't tell me I like to eat donuts because they have a *hole* and a *hole* is like a *vagina*. You know what, crazy lady? *You're* the vagina. How you like that?

"No, I know, she wasn't the right fit for you. But we were thinking"—that "we" again—"what about group therapy?" Was she really asking me? Or was she just telling me in a question format?

"Like going back to Lakeland and doing Group again?" I was both pissed and intrigued. Pissed at having to continue with therapy, but intrigued at the thought of going back to Lake Shit. Justin wasn't in my group, but being there would mean being close to him, and—

"No. A local group. A private one through a private counselor."

"Oh." I looked out the window at the stream of fast food restaurants and car dealers. So many choices of greasy things to eat and enviable things to drive. People appreciate choices. "I'll think about it," I told her.

"Actually, we've already scheduled you for your first meeting tomorrow after school."

Yeah, people like choices. But when you just got out of a mental hospital, I guess you aren't really "people" yet.

———

HANDLING

The rest of the afternoon was spent blasting The Ramones' *Rocket to Russia* and plucking my bass 'til my fingers bled along with it. I suppose I could have put on my iPod and my headphones and emoted strictly to myself, but if there's one thing I learned at Lake Shit, it's that you need to let people know they pissed you off. We even had a whole event at Community meetings called "Confrontation," where people would confront each other about the things they did. Most of the time it was just to get points for participating, but sometimes it was genuine, like when Matt O. would go on a destructive spree and end up in the Quiet Room over and over, Justin stood up to say that he was mad at him for getting in trouble so much because he was sabotaging his chances of ever going home. Justin was sweet like that. I wished he was with me right now, so he could see my actual bedroom. We once had a Play Therapy meeting where this flaky woman with giant hair, who I liked to call Big 'Do (not to her face), made us re-create a safe place using the other kids as representative, inanimate objects, with no touching, of course. If Justin *were* here right now, touching would *so* be allowed.

With that thought, I turned down the stereo enough so that my brain had the tiniest bit of room to think. To remember. My eyes relaxed, and I was back at the Shedd Aquarium on my Lake Shit field trip. The shark reef. Dreamy, wavy blue light illuminated the scene. With no opportunity for touchage back at the hospital, my plan was to kiss Justin as soon as our chaperone, the one and only Big 'Do, was out of our sight. Not something easy to do in a mental hospital where probably every room was bugged. I chewed on gum from Big 'Do's purse for minty-fresh breath. I was ready. But then Justin and I were alone, and the gum stuck to my fingers when

I tried to throw it out, and we laughed. Justin. So gorgeous. His brown hair always dangling in his equally chocolaty brown eyes. So tall I had to stand on my tiptoes to reach his lips. But I reached them. So soft and sweet and a perfect combination of moist and strong.

I lay on top of my bedspread and relived the kiss, the sharks swimming over our heads in the shark tunnel, until the CD I had on ended. I lay there in the quiet, remembering how his hand felt on my back, how his thin, muscley arms held me up when my tippy toes began to wobble. How——

"Anna?"

It was my mom.

"What?!" I yelled, probably a little too aggressively.

"Dinner's ready." Her voice sounded apologetic through my door.

"I'm not hungry," I said, and I wasn't, really. Not for her dinner, at least.

"I made broccoli-spinach casserole." She brandished my favorite dish like a white truce flag. But I wasn't feeling forgiving.

"I'm just going to have Cap'n Crunch. You guys can eat without me," I called coldly through the door.

"Oh," she said, defeated. "I'll save you some if you change your mind."

I almost felt guilty. But what did I do? I'm not the one who ruined her daughter's perfectly decent first day back by putting her in ridiculous group therapy with another bunch of people she's going to have to tell her fabulous life story to and start the whole therapy bullshit ball re-rolling. I'm not the one who totally interrupted her daughter having a spectacular make out session memory with her mental hospital love that she'll probably never see again and wouldn't even be obsessing over if her parents didn't put her in the hospital in the first place.

I tried to get back to the aquarium in my head, to see the sharks swim above me, to feel Justin against me, but all I could think about was how I really did want some of that broccoli-spinach casserole.

DAMN DINNER

Damn my grandma and her hand-me-down recipe for broccoli-spinach casserole. Damn my fat ass for caving to the creamy goodness. Damn my parents. Period.

I crept down the stairs, listening for voices at the dinner table. No Dad sounds, which was good, except it didn't necessarily mean he wasn't there. I listened further, but there were no obvious crinklings of newspapers either. I was safe, or so I thought.

Mara looked hopeful, but all I could produce was a tight-lipped smile. My mom had a nervous, glassy-eyed expression that pissed me off. How was I ever supposed to get better when she was such a mess? I tried to ignore her and heaped a spoonful of BSC onto my plate, waiting politely at my usual seat as though it knew I'd be there. Just as the first bite of heaven entered my mouth, the front door opened and in walked my dad. My parents: the professional buzz killers.

"You started without me?" Dad asked in classically trained dick fashion, as though our eating dinner without him was unusual.

Mom closed her eyes and took a deep breath, something she liked to do to calm herself, and she answered, "I didn't know when you'd be home. You told me not to call."

I didn't need this. I shoved my chair back in a scuff, when my dad said, "Wait, Anna. Did your mom tell you?"

Flashback to the night I was magically transported to Lake Shit. My mom spent the entire day making nice with me, only to have the day end with the exact same line, "Did your mom tell you?"

What she was supposed to tell me was that I was being taken to a mental hospital. Must have slipped her mind.

"Am I going back to Lake Shit?" I snapped. As much as I wanted to see Justin and my other friends, I didn't think anything that happened in my three days home warranted a redux.

"What are you talking about?" my oblivious turd of a dad asked.

"She doesn't know anything, Allen. I didn't think I should have to tell them alone."

"Tell us what?" I was yelling now. I could see Mara sinking uncomfortably in her chair. It made me feel shitty to upset my little sister, but my parents weren't doing anything parental to help ease the tension in the air. That should be the oldest household member's responsibility.

"Well, Beth?" my dad pressed.

"I don't think I should have to be the one to tell them, Allen," she stressed again.

Why were they using each other's names so much?

"Tell us, or we're leaving." I walked behind Mara's chair and put my hands on her shoulders. Not like we had anywhere to go or any mode of transport faster than a bike to get there, but I had to say something. God knows no one else was.

My dad looked at my mom with his explosive stare, but she didn't budge. Tears began streaming from her eyes, which made me want to throw up. Why always the drama?

Finally, Dad spoke in an unexpectedly somber tone for someone who was beet red with anger only a moment earlier. "Your mom and I are separating. I'll be staying in the guest room until I find a place."

"Why?" Mara gasped.

Mom managed a slight explanation. "There's no one reason."

"But," Mara choked, "tomorrow's Tuesday." It seemed like the most ridiculous thing to say, like parents can't separate on Tuesdays because it's a holy day or something. So I laughed.

"You think that's funny?" There was that Dad anger I knew and hated.

"We want you to know it has nothing to do with either of you," my mom interjected with what every parent is supposed to say when they're breaking up. Do any parents ever tell their kids it was their fault?

"Right," my dad agreed, attempting once again to be calm and rational and, dare I say, parental. One-word parenting was generally as far as he got.

Mara's body began shaking beneath my hands, and I knew she was crying. Part of me wanted to hug her, to be the support she couldn't get from either of our parents, but the larger part of me, the one that still had that whole mental hospital grudge, needed to leave.

I walked out the front door.

WALK

If only I had my iPod, I would have put the Pantera song "Walk" on repeat. So angry, yet with such a perfectly marchable beat. Instead, I made it around the block twice before I decided actual music was necessary and headed back to my house.

The dinner table was empty of people but still filled with food. I wrestled with bringing the entire broccoli-spinach casserole upstairs with me, but thought better of the gaseous consequences.

My parents'—my mom's?—bedroom door was closed, the sound of her TV mumbling through the walls. Mara's door was open, so I peaked inside. She looked up at me from the *Archie* comic she was reading, her eyes red and puffy.

"Anna, you're home." She sounded so relieved, and I thought she might start crying again.

"You okay?" I asked. It felt funny to be asking someone else that question.

"No. What's going to happen? Are we going to sell our house? Will there be a custody battle? Do I have to change schools?"

Poor thing. "You're worrying too much. It's not even going to be that different. Dad's never home anyway. He's an asshole, but I don't think he's a big enough asshole to make Mom sell the house and have us live with him." I swallowed hard at the possibility of having to live in a house alone with my dad. He would never, would he? "Why don't you ask Mom if you're worried?"

"I don't want to bother her. She's so sad." How pathetic is it that neither of us wants to upset our parents when it should be them trying to make us feel better? What is wrong with this family?

"Keep reading your *Archie*. I know you have the hots for Jughead."

"I so do not!" Mara yelled.

"Oh, right. I meant Moose Mason."

Mara scoffed, "Shut up!" At least she was smiling.

"I'm going in my room now to listen to some music. Stop by if you need me." I secretly hoped she would not take me up on that, so I could be alone.

Once in my room, I closed the door and looked around. Pink puke.

I sure as hell wasn't going to do any homework on my first day back at school, so I decided to try writing Justin a letter again. At least I'd have something to tell him. But once I started writing stuff down, it began feeling too real. I didn't want to deal with my parents right now, so I screwed my earbuds in and fell asleep to the not-so-soft sounds of Pantera. Anything was more soothing than thinking about my life.

———

WRINKLES

I woke up the next morning with an iPod cord bored into my cheek. Sexy. My face said scarred in more ways than one. How could today not turn into a bowl of ass when my parents are separating and I'm starting a brand-spankin'-new therapy group?

Not only did I have to dress second-day post-mental-hospital appropriate for school, I also had to wear something that said, "Hello, my new gang of therapeuds!" I chose the same pair of jeans as yesterday, since they fit, although somewhat less well due to the requisite Lycra they put in jeans. Or was it spandex? Whatever it was, it stretched my jeans out after one day of wear, so being lazy by wearing the same pair of jeans twice just turned them into saggy and misshapen and ugh. Not that anyone would notice.

For a shirt, I picked an ultra wrinkly one at the bottom of my t-shirt drawer that I forgot existed. It's a Mickey Mouse shirt I got at Disney World when I was nine or ten. Faded red, Mickey all worn off—totally vintage looking. I held it up at my shoulders in front of the mirror. Not being the skinniest nine- or ten-year-old (come to think of it, I must have been ten, because the shirt looks large enough to have accommodated my newly expanded chest), the shirt looked like it might just fit me now.

I pulled off my nightshirt and gingerly worked my way into the Mickey tee. It was more fitted than any shirt I had worn in forever, but it didn't look bad. Except for the wrinkles. It was one thing to wear the same jeans twice out of necessity, but I didn't want to look like a hobo.

"Ma!" I called out my bedroom door as I headed for the shower. "Can you please iron something for me?" I froze in the hall, wondering if I shouldn't have bothered my newly single-esque mom with such a mundane request.

"Sure, honey," she replied through the walls of her bathroom. "Just drop it on my bed." Maybe mundane was what she needed. Were there any fallen buttons that needed sewing? Socks in need of darning?

I walked into her bedroom, a room that shares a wall with mine. I'm happy to say that I have never been unfortunate enough to hear my mom and dad doing *that* (which I highly doubt they have done in the last, oh, ten years or so. Probably not since Mara was conceived. I'm just guessing.). But maybe that would've been better than what I have heard over the years: fights so loud that it's like my dad must have forgotten he had kids who could hear every smack of shouting, every last, angry, unsolicited criticism and complaint about my mom. Maybe my mom's voice just didn't carry through the walls, but I don't think that was it. Yelling at my dad was not my mom's style. Defending herself in any way was not my mom's style. What was she even supposed to say when my dad attacked her? Not in the physical sense, I'm pretty sure. Although I wouldn't put it past him, but I think he's more of just a verbal asshole. All bark and no bite? But when he barked, it was sheer insanity. I always dread the Jewish High Holidays, when we go to my Aunt Marjorie's for Passover or Rosh Hashanah. For some reason, these events always set my dad off. Just being at my mom's sister's house, among her relatives, possibly even enjoying her food (I know I did), made him turn into this psychotic monster. It would start during the car ride home. And he always drove.

"You know, Marjorie asked me about my job . . ." Which to any normal person would be, oh, I don't know, *conversation*. But to my dad it was Aunt Marjorie's way of saying that being a teacher wasn't good enough and why couldn't he be rich and provide for my mom like Uncle Manny and he *should* be rich but he isn't so that makes him a LOSER.

My mom had no response to any of his rants. The car responded, though, swerving in and out of traffic, trying to get home as quickly as possible so he could take his big post-holiday-meal dump, then really let loose on my mom in their bedroom. I tried not to listen because there was nothing I could do to help her. A yelling father was scary, *is* scary, and part of me just wanted my mom to yell back. So I'd pray. I'd get down on my knees, palms together at my chin, and pray for it to stop. I don't know if that's the Jewish way of praying, but if it's just me in my room, I don't think God cares too much how I'm sitting. It didn't seem like he cared much at all because the screaming didn't end until Dad was finished saying whatever he thought was important to say.

Maybe if I had changed my praying position they'd still be together.

Dad always managed to find something my mom did wrong. He's like a vulnerability super-villain; he always knows how to find my mom's kryptonite. If only I could find his.

Wait. Maybe I did. Ugh. Because he's moving out. The upsetting part is that, for at least the moment, I don't feel that upset. Not about that anyway. I set my t-shirt down on Mom's bed to be ironed. Dad was already out of the house, but I don't think he was moved out since nothing looked different. Would it look different? How fast would he take to find a place anyway? I heard the sink running in my mom's bathroom, so I took a minute to check things out. My parents' bedroom only ever brought me comfort when my dad wasn't there. Like when I stayed home sick from school as a kid, my mom always let me lie in her bed all day, eating crackers and Jell-O and watching her TV. It never felt that healing when my dad was home.

The guest room, right off the utility room next to the garage, was easy enough to avoid. Maybe it would already feel like he moved out. Maybe I wouldn't even notice when he did.

I picked my t-shirt off the bed, turned on the iron, and ironed my shirt before my mom came out of the bathroom. It was the least I could do for her.

ANOTHER DAY, ANOTHER LOONHOLE

School was harder today than yesterday. Maybe it was because I didn't have the semi-excited newness of being back at school. Or maybe it's because, while I was excused for most of my missed work, I was there, and, therefore, not able to use that excuse for work currently assigned. And then there was that separation thing. Or perhaps it was the fact that I knew I had to start a whole new therapy group after school.

For those who have never been in therapy, *starting* means reliving every shitbit of crap that has happened to you. Not just in recent years, but, like, your entire life. Because they don't need to figure out how to help you now—they have to figure out why you got all fucked up in the first place. And that's supposed to somehow help you now. Don't know if it works, since the only therapy I've been in was with a) a Freudian skag with a Diet Coke habit who loved to tell me how fat I was, b) the mental hospital psychiatrist who figured out the right doses of my meds and berated me to try to emote (an incredibly ineffective method), and c) my mental hospital group which, once we introduced ourselves and explained why we were in a mental hospital in the first place, essentially dealt only with issues that we had *in* the hospital, like roommate problems, behavior problems, and why the hospital maxi pads were so ginormous.

And now I have to start a whole new group with a whole new group leader who, as my past record shows, will probably be a super-cock (or -cockette). Plus, who's going to be in the group? Are they all ex–mental hospital patients? My mom said they were all around my age, but that's all she knew. And that the group came by recommendation of Lake Shit. Which doesn't bode well.

The entire school day, all I could think about was who was going to be there and what would the room look like and what kinds of chairs would we be sitting in and would there be a points system and would I have to go back to the hospital and if I did would that be a good thing or a bad thing?

My stomach sucked all day, and I even left English twice to go to the bathroom. Of course, Mr. Groban stopped me after class to see if I was okay.

"I'd be a lot better if you stopped asking," I said. Which was kind of mean and totally out of character, seeing as I have pretty much avoided confrontation with authority figures and anyone else my entire life, but I was anxious. "Sorry." I looked down, then up, trying my best to elicit sympathy. "I'm having sort of a bad day."

"Well, we can't let that happen. It's not my choice of books, is it?" We had just been assigned *Catcher in the Rye*.

"No, I'm fine with that. I hear it's a classic, and all."

"Well, you know what Mark Twain said: 'A classic is something everyone wants to have read but nobody wants to read.'"

"Um, reassuring," I told him. "Better get to my next class."

"Righto," said Mr. Groban, and he winked. It wasn't a pervy wink, I don't think, just a weird adult wink. Which I guess a pervy wink could also be, but this was more an old-guy wink. Which also sounds perv-possible. But it wasn't.

Before T and I walked into lunch, I told her about my parents' separation.

"Damn, dude, that's rough."

"Is it? I can't even tell. Dad isn't around all that much, and I don't really like him, so is this a bad thing? It's not even divorce, just 'separation.' Do they have places where kids can send their parents away to get fixed?"

"An eye-for-an-eye type of thing?" Tracy postulated.

"Why does everything always have to be fucked up?" I pouted as we reached the table.

"The lee of the stone, my friend." Tracy patted my shoulder. Her meaningless comfort statement felt strangely helpful. Tracy continued being the best shrink I ever had by spinning a never-ending supply of Sluts R Us stories, my personal fave being the one about the two oversized women who went into one dressing room together fully dressed and came out nearly naked, just strolling around the store holding up bras and undies to their hefty bra- and undie-wearing bodies in the full-length store mirrors.

"Careful. You might give Tucker here a woody," Eleanor warned. Tucker took two seconds from the math homework he was scribbling to give her the finger.

I would have forgotten about the nervousness in my stomach if there weren't that whole supposed-to-be-eating thing going on in the cafeteria.

Art was much better at helping block out my impending therapeutic doom. The Art room was even more overstimulating than usual because Meredith convinced Mrs. Downy that she needed The Descendents' *Cool to Be You* playing in order to guide the new photo painting (a photograph painted over with oil paints) she was working on. The photo was of a Korean hair salon she said her mother forced her to go to.

"Straight perm. You must get a straight perm." Meredith adopted her mother's strict tone. It made no sense to me, since I thought perms were for curling, not straightening hair.

Eleanor explained as she and Tucker escorted me to the dark-room: "Korean hair can be thick and coarse, so a straight perm makes it smooth and silky. Even guys get them." I guess Meredith's hair did look smoother and silkier today. Eleanor's hair was in a chunky, textured bob that may or may not have been straight permed. I couldn't tell if it was a good or bad thing in Eleanor's mind—she is one to go off on cultural stereotypes and standards, and I'm never sure what Korean issue will get her heated. She tweaked Tucker's nipple once when he asked when her mother was going to send more kalgi in her lunch.

"That wasn't kalgi, you twat, it was bulgogi! You probably think you're supposed to eat it with chopsticks, too!"

I loved using the secretive entrance to the darkroom, tucked away in a corner near shelves of paper and paint. The door itself is singular, black, and revolving, in order to not let light in as one passes through. I always liked to pretend it was some sort of tele-portation device and that I'd end up in another country or time period every time I went through it. Alas, whenever my eyes ad-justed to the darkness, I was not in London circa 1978 but in a classroom with machines lined up in carrels along the wall to my right, multiple doors leading to developing rooms to the left, and an extra-long sink down the middle with continuously running water for the printing process. Several trays floated in the sink, along with a few abandoned photos, bobbing along in their lazy river. The room was empty of people, but it wasn't quiet thanks to the trickling water. I felt both relaxed and the sudden urge to pee.

Tucker and Eleanor appeared behind me a few seconds after my journey through the magic door, one at a time, since that's all the small door will allow comfortably. Actually, it's a rule of the Art room that only one person can go through the darkroom door at a time. I heard there were several impregnations in the small space of the darkroom door before the rule was set. Or maybe that's just Art room folklore.

"Ladies first, turdmonger." Eleanor pushed Tucker on the shoulders.

"When I see one, I'll let her go first," Tucker retorted.

"Yeah? Well, when I see a gentleman, I'll—" Eleanor paused for the right comeback.

"Kick him in the nuts. Yes, we know," Tucker quipped.

"Anywho," I interrupted. "So refresh my memory." I had told Mrs. Downy that my after-school hours were pretty full up right now, not knowing how many more loony surprises my parents had in store for me. Would there be group workout sessions planned? Child of separation meetings? Would they sign me up for a group bowling league? So as not to take any wrath-incurring chances, I asked Mrs. Downy if I could have a class-time lesson from my friends. She didn't say yes or no, but answered with "Let me know if you have any questions," which I took to mean that it would be okay. And that I could only blame myself if my final products sucked.

I took Photo I last year, but there are a lot of details to developing film and printing that I needed to bring back to the front of my brain. Our school's photo department has both old-school developing ("to show you where photography comes from," Mrs. Downy explained whenever someone asked why we didn't just go digital), and a set of computers for digital editing. Depending on my mood, I like both formats. Digital was super-satisfying because you can take pictures and see them in the same minute. Plus, you can take way more photos than you need and just pick out the not-so-sucky ones. With real film, there's a level of suspense to the process; you have no idea if your pictures are going to turn out while you take them (well, *I* don't have any idea). I also could get into the whole concrete physical aspect of processing, which you generally do by your lonesome in one of the small developing rooms in the darkroom. There's a magic to a roll of film turning into a roll of negatives. Unless you screw it up. Which I haven't. Yet. It's always so sad when you find a blackened string of negatives lying on the darkroom floor, someone's lost time, money, and creativity developed into nothing.

Tucker and Eleanor gave an abbreviated recap (which is twice the shortness of the real thing) on developing and printing. "I prefer to teach when applicable. If you're stuck during a time when you're actually developing in here, I got your back," Tucker offered.

"Who says that anymore?" Eleanor dissed.

"You'd know if you interacted with more humans and fewer electronic entities."

"You're one to talk, Tucker. Wasn't your last girlfriend a Sim?"

That went on in between scant hints and review, which was fine by me. I loved not being the one to cause or receive any of the tension. After the review, I asked Tucker if he could also help catch me up on physics at lunchtime.

"But of course." He doffed a fake hat and rolled out through the darkroom door.

When the bell finally rang, I sagged. School was over, which ironically meant the true suck of my day was yet to come.

HELP ME

My mom told me I needed to hurry out of school because the group meeting started promptly at 3:45. Which meant spending an extra-long amount of time at my locker packing up my backpack, rearranging my books, and cleaning the pieces of lint and old gum wrappers out of my locker.

It was only 3:29 when I finally made my way outside with Tracy as the little devil on my shoulder.

"Just tell her you can't go. You have a stomachache," she whispered as we approached my mom's car.

"Yeah. We all know how well that worked out for me. I wouldn't be going to this turkey-assed group therapy if it weren't for my big, fat stomach."

"You mean your small, fat stomach," Tracy reminded me.

"Was that supposed to sound good?" I asked.

My mom watched Tracy and I creep along toward the car. I could see her glancing anxiously at the car clock, then her cell-phone clock, and then her watch. Maybe she was synchronizing them. Probably not.

"Stay gold, Ponyboy." Tracy reassuringly put her hand on my shoulder and was off to peddle thongs to eight-year-olds and the creepy moms who buy them. Lucky.

I'd rather be anywhere than starting another round of therapy. If I had to choose between getting blood drawn, running a mile, or going to therapy right now, I'd . . . Well, I'd probably end up doing none of the above because I'd be in the bathroom dealing with my bowels. But if I made it out of said bathroom, I sure as hell know therapy wouldn't be my first choice. (In case you're wondering, it would probably be the mile because in the end I could always walk or shuffle it. No one can force me to run a mile, can they? Oh God. Can they?)

My mom tried to standardize question me in the car, but I wasn't having it.

"How was school?"

Grumble.

"Are you all caught up now?"

Cross my arms.

"I'm sure this afternoon won't be so bad."

That got me. "Oh, you're sure, Mom? And you know this how? Because you have some secret past as a fat, depressed teenager whose parents locked her up in a mental hospital, decided to separate, and then topped her cake of shit with a group therapy cherry?"

The only sounds in the car for several minutes were the thunks the car made every time it dropped into one of the many never-repaired snowplow-produced potholes from last winter. I almost started to feel guilty. Excruciatingly later, my mom said quietly, "You were never this angry at me before."

She was right. I was always so concerned for her, how my dad treated her like crap, that I didn't want to be like him. But all those kids at Lake Shit showed me I had every right to be angry. When I was the only one crying every day in Community and Group meetings, and everyone else was punished for things they weren't supposed to do, I realized that there was nothing wrong with not always doing things right. By the end of my stay at Lake Shit, I managed to get myself locked in the Quiet Room by throwing a plastic baby down the hall.

Maybe talking back to my mom is how throwing a plastic baby translates into the real world. It's got to mean something. Because part of me feels like the language of Lake Shit doesn't translate at all into reality, and I'll always be frantically flipping through my Lake Shit/Real World dictionary to see if I make sense.

At precisely 3:44, my mom pulled into a maze of brown-shingled single-story office buildings. Various doctors and dentists staked their claim with window decals of names and professions. If ever there were a more terrifying maze to get caught in—all those needles filled with novocaine and TB tests coming at you. Maybe a corn maze. Because of *Children of the Corn*. That movie terrifies me. I always imagined that the Children would shun me because they didn't think I was cool enough to join them in the corn. Or maybe it was that I was *too* cool.

A (not so wise) therapist would argue that the *Children of the Corn* bit was me trying to use humor to avoid talking about the reality of my situation, i.e., going to a totally new therapy group. And a (slightly wiser) therapist might even note that the *Children of the Corn* bit was really an analogy for my fear of not being accepted into my new therapy group.

What really is the point of me continuing with therapy, nay, *starting over* with therapy when I can already psychoanalyze the shit out of any situation?

My final destination was a window marked by the white letters of "Peggy Stein," followed by a bunch of letters I'm sure Ms. Stein felt made her look uberimportant to every parent who has ever dropped a terrified kid off to meet her doom. I'm not buying. Any anus can get a degree online these days, as evidenced by the chodes in commercials they air during *Golden Girls* marathons. I wondered if Peggy Stein was a big *Golden Girls* fan.

"When is this over?" I asked my mom as I stared at the crisp, white letters in the window, my stomach bubbling in that old familiar way I thought I maybe left behind.

"Four forty-five," she answered and brushed some stray hairs away from my eyes. "I'm sure it will be fine, honey."

"Why are you so sure?" I jerked away from my mom's touch, as comforting as it was, and exited the car. A door slam may have been appropriate, but I don't know if I was angry as much as I was terrified. I put my hand to my stomach and swore I could feel tiny acid-scarred pieces of granola trying to escape. Why was this my life?

I took several shallow breaths until I arrived at a deeper, more relaxed state of breathing, something I should have learned from all my therapy but actually learned from that Rodney Yee yoga DVD. I tried to picture Rodney in his tiny yoga underwear, his soothing voice telling me, "Let the mind body meld." I wish Rodney were my new therapist. Rodney. Hee-hee.

A little more relaxed, whatever route I took to get there, I walked into the building. The classic therapeutic waiting rooms are wholly bland—little color, no fun magazines where you could find things to upset you (like the tragedy of seeing which celebrities have cellulite), a standard landscape painting in such dull colors it makes you bored just looking at it. This waiting room was a little different. Bright, but worn, rugs hung on two walls, with another particularly trampled one on the floor. There were magazines, albeit of the children's dentist office variety (*Highlights,* anyone? I wondered what Goofus and Gallant were up to these days), and an electric teapot surrounded by a hodgepodge of tea bags in an old wicker gift basket bubbled on a wonky-looking table. The air smelled of incense and fruit tea. No one else was in the waiting room, but an open door and the sound of people talking led me to a square room with that familiar mental hospital arrangement: chairs in a nonthreatening, therapeutic circle. Other than the fur- niture, one thing struck me as being extremely un–Lake Shit-ish: the walls were painted a deep ruby-red color. At Lakeland, all walls were either a grotesque putty color or pastel pink and blue, the col- ors of tranquility and passivity. Aren't red walls supposed to encour- age aggression? Or was it hunger? I must have gone to the bathroom during the color discussion in Sociology class.

As I scanned the chairs, a crying bubble formed in my throat at the thought of having to tell my story again. My pathetic loser of a story. That wasn't the way I wanted to start this. I was a different person now. I'd been through some shit. *Lake Shit.* I threw a plastic baby and kissed someone when I wasn't allowed to and made it all the way to Level III! I was a mental hospital veteran, not some wussy little girl starting therapy for the first time. I didn't want to be the crying girl, the suburbanite with no real problems who couldn't handle anything.

I pictured Rodney Yee again, the serene look on his face, the perfect smoothness of his ponytail, the docile nature of his voice, and I tried to remember who I was now.

Who's that again?

I surveyed the small circle of two guys, two girls, and one adult (Peggy, is that you?). The presumed Peggy Stein stood up and shot out her hand at me to shake. "Peggy Stein," she said, her voice loud and very East Coast for being in the Midwest. "You must be Anna. Please—" She presented a seat to me with her pristinely manicured hand (dark red polish, if you wondered).

The chairs were unassuming, stacking plastic chairs, nothing like the booger-green or vomit-brown pleather chairs of Lakeland. No incriminating fart sound emitted as I sat, and while I looked around the circle a couple people, including at least one cute therapy boy (is it a prerequisite that there be cute guys in therapeutic situations?) smiled small, but welcoming smiles at me. Not at all like my first meeting at Lake Shit where no one could even look, let alone smile, at me for fear of getting points docked or some other bizarrely unsuitable punishment.

"Welcome to the Tuesday/Thursday group." Wait. WTF? This was two days a week? Thanks for the heads-up, Ma and Pa. "As I said, I'm Peggy Stein. You may call me Peggy." Peggy (who apparently liked saying her own name) was older than my mom with a stylish, white bob. Her neck must have hurt from the eighty necklaces she had layered on it. Her clothes were flowy, but not muumuu-y, and she could have as easily been a high-priced fortune-teller as my therapist. Or maybe more easily. What the hell was a high-priced fortune-teller?

As is the standard in the world of therapy and twelve-step programs, Peggy had me introduce myself to the group.

"Just say a few words," Peggy nodded at me.

I considered the few words I really wanted to say, which were, "Get me the hell out of here," but I settled for, "I'm Anna. I'm sixteen. I'm a junior. I'm really into music, live for The Ramones, and play the bass. Sort of."

I looked toward the ceiling, contemplating which chunk of tragedy I should lob at the group, when Peggy halted my contemplation and said, "Thank you, Anna. Now let's just go around so she can get to know each of you a little."

That was it? No weepies? No bad-parent stories? No irritable bowel syndrome confessions? No loony-bin drama? Maybe she didn't need me to say anything else. Maybe she reads minds, you know, because of her high-priced psychic business? Oh, shut up.

The next person to speak was a girl who could pass for a Weasley. She flicked her flaming red bangs while she spoke flatly, "I'm Ali. Fifteen. Raped."

Whoa. Was that what Peggy wanted me to do? Anna. Sixteen. Depressed. Or anxious. Or whatever it is I was. Just pathetic next to a girl who had been raped. It felt like I was never normal enough for the real world or screwed up enough for the world of therapy. And now I made myself sound like a giant douchetool because I didn't even acknowledge why I was there.

My stomach hurt uncomfortably to the point where I was about to stand up to go to the bathroom (where was the bathroom?), when the next group member, a skinny, blond guy with bedhead and puffy circles under his eyes said, "I'm Miles. I'm seventeen. I paint. And I'm a lead singer in a band called Platypuses Are Mammals, Too."

I involuntarily let out a relieved laugh at the fact that he didn't say anything about his issues. And also at his band's name. Miles looked at the guy next to him and stuck his hand out as if to say, *Your turn*.

This guy was the cute one, although Miles registered on the cute scale. (Have I become the therapy horn dog or something? Since my first major grope session with a guy was born from a mental hospital, does that mean I will always have some sort of sick connection to boys with problems, particularly those in mental-health scenarios? What if sitting in a group of chairs like this provokes my Pavlovian response, but instead of the sound of a bell making me hungry, the sight of boys getting ready to spill their gory details in a circular setting gets me hot? What if I'm forced to face this problem in therapy? #mortified.)

"Bart. Short for Bartleby, as in The Scrivener, if you have any idea what I'm talking about." Bartleby (Why would someone whose name is Bartleby shorten it to Bart? That's like if your name was Fartocomous, and you shortened it to Fart. Kind of.) oozed sarcasm and superiority, which subtracted hot points instantly. So did the fact that his brown hair, which I first thought echoed Justin's adorable shagginess, had more of a home-cut feel to it.

I needed to let him know who he was dealing with (um, me?), so I said, "Yeah, I know of that story, 'Bartleby the Scrivener.' Your parents must be some kind of lit freaks or something."

"Or something." He eyed me disdainfully.

I nearly rolled my eyes, but decided to save that for a special occasion. It was one of the few comebacks I had in my wussy arsenal.

The other girl sitting next to me held up a stop sign hand and freely doled out an eye roll.

"Wah-wah, Bart." Then she looked at me. "I'm Nepa. I'm seventeen. I love the shit out of life. That's really why I'm here. Because I love life so fucking much that my family thought I was crazy and needed to suck all the joy out of my ass."

I smiled. She didn't.

"I hope that's not going to be part of the group therapy," I said to her.

"What?" she looked down at me.

"Sucking stuff out of your ass. 'Cause that's not at all what I signed up for." Her lip twitched, and I saw the beginning of a smile. Ali and Miles actually laughed, as did Peggy, who had the laugh of an eighty-year-old male smoker. I looked last at Bartleby, who just looked back at me.

Is it weird that I kind of missed this?

LETTER B

Most of Group was spent helping Ali deal with an upcoming trial she will have against her accused rapist. Not that I helped at all, but I did lots of good, constructive nodding. Ali's situation pretty much sucked. The rapist, a football stud named Brett Starcraw, was assigned to be her lab partner in biology. Before that, he never said two words to her, but when she helped him get an A by essentially doing all of their labs and homework, he finally "thanked" Ali by inviting her to a party on the last day of school, where he also helped her get really drunk. "Ali can't hold her liquor," Miles noted. Because somehow he knew this? I didn't want to ask too many questions because it already felt like I was some stranger prying into this group's personal lives. Instead, I listened and tried to use my keen body-language-reading skills (which are not keen at all, since I couldn't even tell that Justin liked me until *after* we kissed. I do love the hilarious wholesomeness of the word "keen" though).

Apparently, Miles and Ali go to the same high school but do not hang out with the same people. Miles is more the Art crowd, and Ali, from what I could tell, wanted to be popular and now doesn't do anything social. Period.

The end of Ali's story, which isn't technically over, is that she was raped by Jock Brett at the party, didn't report it until the end of the summer after she confirmed that she was pregnant, forced herself to fall down some stairs multiple times, and eventually had a miscarriage, along with a knocked-out tooth and a broken wrist. She confessed to her mother, who, after Ali was a bit more healed, signed her up for various forms of counseling, none of them inpatient. Meaning: This girl, who had way more shit happen to her than pathetic ol' me, had not been in a mental hospital. How did I get there?

"The trial's in six weeks," Ali explained to me in her dark, monotone way of speaking. "And I'm basically fucked because I didn't do anything the morning after. No sperm for the cops to run their lab tests on, no signs of forced entry."

"What are you, a house?" Bartleby chuckled. Nice. The first laugh he makes at Group is a joke on a raped girl's behalf.

"Why don't you shove a house up your ass, Bart?" Ali retorted.

"Couldn't they, like, use the DNA from the fetus? As gross as that sounds, it's there," Nepa suggested.

"Too late for that, too. And a baby doesn't equal rape," Ali pointed out.

"I don't get why you'd put yourself through this, man," Miles said, using multiple hand gestures for dramatic emphasis. "You're going to have to tell the whole story, like, the *whole* thing, at the trial. I've seen it a billion times on *SVU*. And Brett's just going to be sitting in the court with that smarmy-ass look on his face, winking at the judge to butter her up. Licking his—"

"That's enough, Miles," Peggy finally interrupted. She said so little today, I forgot for a second there was an adult in the room. She went on to explain that "rape trials are indeed tricky, but it's important for Ali to have closure. By bringing Brett to trial, she's acknowledging that she is not accepting the rape on his terms. Brett will now have to publicly relive the night, just as Ali has so many times. The hope is that his conscience will win, and he'll admit that Ali was not consenting."

"That's not in the jock bloodstream, Peggy!" Miles really got into his argument, rising out of his seat a bit. "The whole point of his sport is to knock the shit out of other people and then pile on top of them."

"Isn't a ball involved somewhere?" Bartleby placed his pointer finger on his chin and looked up dramatically at the ceiling to drive home his angelic bite. What a dick. A really, really good-looking one.

"More balls than you have," Nepa told him.

Miles wasn't deterred by the interruptions. "It's probably a prerequisite for a football scholarship. Like, they have a box on the application you check for completing date rape." He smiled smugly at the cleverness of his thought.

"Not helpful, Miles," Ali said, but it wasn't as angry as she had sounded earlier. And I detected a subtle smile at the corners of her mouth. Miles and Ali: an item?

The group therapy session ended with Peggy directing us to take three slow, deep breaths. Very Rodney Yee. "This week, think of all you have, not what you have not. Remember who you are and why that is a good thing. Commend yourself for still being here." I almost clapped at the end, but no one else did so I was glad I resisted the urge. "See you all Thursday."

I didn't anticipate the awkward leaving-group-therapy period.

At Lakeland, we weren't allowed to speak in the halls, so leaving anything meant complete silence or a docking of points would be had. Here we didn't have points, and I didn't know what to say. Or if anyone would say anything to me. I was grateful when Ali walked up to me as we made our way outside and said, "Hey. Sorry you didn't really get to talk."

She sounded lighter than in Group. I overcompensated with a too enthusiastic "Don't worry about it. I didn't have anything to say anyway. Not like you. There's nothing really going on in my life." I even smiled like a tool.

"Peggy told us you just got out of a hospital and that you suffer from panic attacks. Sucks. Hope you can talk about it next week. See ya." With that, she stepped into a silver Saab idling nearby.

Was that legal? For Peggy to tell them that stuff about me? So that whole time they knew I'm some weirdo whose parents threw her in a mental hospital? Were they anticipating some big panic-attack moment, like I had anticipated Abby's Satan-possessed seizures at Lake Shit? Did Peggy set me up to be the freak of the group? How is that going to help me?

The other group members filed past me as I waited for my mom to drive up. Nepa gave a small wave as she walked by, and I reciprocated with a half-assed smile. I knew what she was thinking. She was picturing me in a straitjacket, throwing myself against the wall of a padded room. Thankfully, but not surprisingly, Bartleby ignored me. Miles, though, actually stopped and asked, "You need a ride?" He held up his car keys.

"No thanks." I shook my head. "My mom's coming."

"Okay then. See you Thursday." He smiled, which made his tired eyes look even puffier. In a sort of cute way. Not that it mattered. I'd been branded: the Mental Hospital Girl. Peggy should have put me on a platform with a big sign and a sideshow barker calling out to the rest of the group, "Come one! Come all! Look at the Mental Hospital Girl! She didn't see the sun for three weeks!"

My mom pulled up, and I whipped the passenger door open before the car stopped. Then I slammed it shut. My mom, trying hard, smiled at me and said in her most mommish voice, "How was it?"

I crossed my arms over my aching stomach and said nothing at all.

CRUNCH DIET

Mom tried to buy my happiness with deep-dish pizza, but I resisted the temptation of eighty layers of cheese and chunky sauce and headed directly to my room. I pulled out a pair of pajama bottoms and the sports bra I reserved strictly for gym class hell, then tugged my Mickey t-shirt back over it. I propped my craptop on my dresser and shoved the floor junk as far under my bed as it would go before I felt resistance from the other junk that was already there. Sometimes, when I really couldn't sleep, I pictured old dolls and stuffed animals mating under my bed into wicked hybrids. It didn't usually help with the sleep issue.

The yoga DVD's soothing flute (or was it lute?) music began, and I placed my bare feet in the center of the rug my Grandma Belle bought for me, tan and flecked with small flowers and pineapples. Really, it's fancier and lovelier than it sounds, which is why it was tragic that our old, white German shepherd, Boo Boo (RIP), peed on it. You can still see the remnant of the stain if you know where to look.

I tried to clear my mind (a tough task) and focus on the images in the opening credits. It's weird that a yoga DVD has opening credits. How does one direct a yoga DVD?

Focus, Anna.

I was nearly there when a soft knock at my door interrupted.

"What?!" I shouted in a manner in which Rodney Yee would not have approved. I paused the DVD, so Mom wouldn't hear me doing something good for myself. As happy as it would have made her to see me making strides in the self-help department, I wasn't ready to show her that. She was so willing to dole out the annoyance and misery, I was more than happy to give a little of it back. Well, not really happy, because it didn't feel good ignoring her and shunning her dinner offerings, especially in her fragile state. But a loon's gotta do what a loon's gotta do.

"Can I come in?" The voice on the other side of the door wasn't my mom's. It was Mara's.

I ran over to the door and yanked it open. "Mara, sorry, I thought you were Mom."

Mara may have been twelve and, you know, on her way to becoming a woman and all, but she still had this adorably round face with extra-pinchable cheeks. She lucked out in the body department, which would make me hate her if I didn't love her so damn much. Athletic, petite, proportioned—I wondered sometimes if any of my problems would have even started if I were tiny like she was. Or if I never gained weight at all, if I'd maybe look like that.

It took me a minute to notice that she sported a Poms costume "Hey, you made it. Congrats." I managed a smile and futzed with the puffball surrounding her high ponytail. Funny that the one physical attribute we share is our identical long, brown, wavy/curly hair. I imagined what mine would look like as a member of the Poms and then shook the ridiculous thought from my head. Even if I were a skinny kid, no way in hell I would have been some school spirit drone.

"Yeah, pretty much everyone got in. Except for Sunny Knudson. She had zero rhythm. I felt a little bad for her."

"That scabby wench? She does not deserve your pity." Sunny Knudson was Mara's main tormentor from third through fifth grade. Once, and this has not been proven, she peed in Mara's backpack. Which made Mara smell like pee all day. I suppose it could have been a cat or just some rank apple juice, but I wouldn't put it past ol' Sunny. Hell yeah she didn't make Poms. "You should go pee in her backpack and be all, 'Who smells like pee now, be-yotch?'"

"What?" Mara looked at me like I was, well, crazy. God, will terms like that forever make me feel like they're now actually about me?

"Never mind." I shook away the weirdness.

"Are you going to bed already?" Mara looked over my ensemble, which to the untrained eye did resemble pajamas. If people were trained to interpret my clothing.

"No. I was about to do some yoga." I pointed to the computer, Rodney frozen in mountain pose.

"I didn't know you did that," Mara said, surprised.

"Oh, yeah. I'm a regular yogurt."

Mara laughed. "Can I do it with you? Mom is eating the crust off the pizza in that pathetic way." When my mom was upset, she liked to crunch things. She could make her way through an entire bag of Rold Golds without even looking at what she's eating. For all she knew, she could be eating a bag of pretzel-shaped turds. I ate a bag of pretzels, and I got fat, but Mom knew how to do it with control. Like, if you ate an entire bag of pretzels, that counted as your lunch and dinner. Me? In the past I would eat the bag as an accompaniment to lunch and dinner. Or with Nutella. My stomach growled at the thought of Nutella, but I was committed to keeping away from all things parent. If Mom was in the kitchen eating pizza crusts, I wasn't going down there. Another quickie

Cap'n Crunch dinner would have to do. I would sneak down when I heard her in the bathroom or something.

"Well, you certainly are dressed for a workout of some kind. But you're going to have to bring the enthusiasm down because Rodney Yee is all about relaxing your face. And breathing. Breathing is very important," I told Mara.

"I've heard that about breathing." Mara took off her socks and stepped onto my rug. The glint in her eyes said exactly what I was thinking: She was thrilled to be hanging again with her sister.

"Close the door. I don't want Mom to know I'm doing anything good." Mara obediently closed the door with a quiet click.

After we performed our twenty-minute yoga routine, Mara left to do her homework, not a glint of effort on her body. I, on the other hand, sported a classy sweat-bead mustache. The bottom of my t-shirt made for a handy towel, and I plopped myself down in the middle of my rug. The pee stain stared at me. I stared at the pee stain.

Was this how I was going to spend my nights? In a staring contest with a deceased dog's urine legacy? If I was to get beyond my lunacy branding and acclimate to the real world again, I was going to have to do real-world things. Like homework.

I annoyingly remembered I left my iPod downstairs where I took it out of my pocket to charge on the desktop. Guess my music would be heard by all tonight. I selected The Ramones' *Road to Ruin*, a solid album with some relatable songs, such as "I Wanna Be Sedated" and "I Just Want to Have Something to Do." Not their most aggressive album, but the yoga had me feeling mellow.

My homework awaited somewhere under my bed, possibly mingling with the hybrid stuffed dollimals, so I army-crawled to the edge of my bed and fished out a notebook and my copy of *Catcher in the Rye*. On my knees, I considered my options. The notebook's silver spiral, unlike the safety notebooks we had to use at the hospital, reminded me of another bit of self-imposed home-work I needed to complete: a series of letters I had yet to write to my friends back at Lakeland. Why was it so hard?

Maybe if my first letter wasn't to Justin, it would be an easier place to start. With Justin, there was the confusion of where we were as a couple. Or not as a couple. A couple of what? So I started with Matt O. He had been at Lake Shit the longest, thanks to being sexually abused by his mother's boyfriend, and he deserved a piece of mail.

Dear Matt,

Like my spiral-bound paper? Jealous? Yes, I am allowed to use paper held together by dangerous, squiggly metal! I better be careful. One false move, and my wrist could turn into a bloody disaster area. And I don't mean bloody in the British sense of the word.

So what's shakin' at Lake Shit? Is someone reading this letter before Matt O. gets to read it? If so, SUCK IT AND THANKS FOR NOTHING.

Does anyone miss me? Do you guys talk about me? Has Justin already moved on to a new mental hospital galpal? Don't answer that one. Ignorance is bliss, as they say. And "they" are assholes.

My life is weird and awkward and confusing. My parents are separating. Shocking, I know. My dad's still a dick, my mom's still a wuss, and school still exists where I actually have to do work and get grades. I'll bet you totally forgot what that's like. I shall remind you: It sucks.

Speaking of school, I better get started on my homework.

Wouldn't want to jeopardize getting into college or anything. What a travesty that would be.

I miss you guys! Drink a scratchy little juice cup for me, will ya?

Love,

Anna

That wasn't so hard. It wasn't a masterpiece of brilliant writing, but just a quickie note to let him know I'm thinking about him felt like enough. And ensured that he couldn't forget me.

The next letter was to my roommate, Sandy.

Dearest Sandy,

I thought I'd start out this letter semi-romantic, since you are the only person I've ever lived with (not that I'm hitting on you. I'm just being dorky). I'm surprised to say that I actually miss having a roommate. Not your incessant snoring and certainly not your pregnancy faking. Yeah, I'm still a little peeved about that one. You know how much beauty sleep I lost thanks to that fake baby they made you carry around? Maybe I'll drive to Lake Shit late at night and throw rocks at your window just to remind you what it was like to have some night staff member busting in on my precious dreams to yell at you, "The baby's crying! Change her diaper!" Man, that sucked. In a kind of funny way.

So when do they spring you? Being on the outside is as confusing as being at Lake Shit. At least there, you know what's expected of you: Be good, don't talk back but do talk about your feelings, and don't touch anyone. Here, people either don't give a shit at all or give too much of a shit. My mom put me in an outpatient therapy group. I guess my dad did, too, technically, but he's not around enough to garner an active participation mention. Did I tell you they're separating? When would I have told you? But, yeah, they are. Ring a ding ding.

Enough about my crap. So has Justin found someone else already? Has he said anything about me in Group? At lunch? Do you think we have a chance when he gets out? When's he getting out?

Um, yeah, miss you! Hope your new roommate is as awesome as I was. Or almost as awesome. She couldn't possibly be as awesome.

Love,

Anna

By that point I was getting tired. I was assigned to read the first three chapters of *Catcher* in addition to 50,000 math problems (that the teacher never checks, so I decided to put off the math joy until tomorrow).

But I still had at least one more letter to write.

There were other friends from the hospital, people in my group, people from lunch. I could ask Abby if she'd had any seizures lately. Or write a letter to Victor and ask how his mom is doing. But what would be the point? I'd never see them again. We had nothing in common, aside from being locked up together on a single floor of a mental hospital in Chicago. We ate the same flavorless cafeteria food, watched the same Sunday night movies (which in my three weeks equaled the Star Wars trilogy. The first one. Or was it the second?), played card games, and attended various forms of therapeutic meetings. It was awful, and intense, and sometimes even funny, and they, and all the others, were there for that with me. But if you threw us all into a room together outside of the hospital, what would we do? What would we say?

To quote the brilliant musical episode of *Buffy*: "Where do we go from here?"

Maybe if I reminisced about why I liked Justin so much, it would help me write the letter. Before the accident that destroyed his hand, he, too, played the bass; he, too, loved punk music; and he knew depression. More so than me. I never attempted suicide, as much as I thought about it. But he was funny, too, and sweet and smart. And then there was the physical connection. God, he was beautiful. And we kissed. Twice. Touched our legs under card tables when no one was looking.

I closed my eyes and remembered the cab ride we shared on our field trip. A cab, not a bus like on real school field trips, because only the two of us and Matt O. were allowed to go, our chaperone in the front seat. If I could spend the rest of my life in the backseat of that cab, I might do it.

But what if someone had to go to the bathroom? Which would, of course, be me first. And what would we eat?

So ended the reminiscing. The Justin letter would have to wait.

I plopped down on top of my bedspread and clicked on the new lamp my parents bought for the room redesign. It was one of those adjustable, tilting desk lamps with an exposed bulb underneath. No matter how I fixed it, the light shone directly in my eyes, obscuring words on the pages of *Catcher in the Rye* with a blue blob. In order to read, I alternately pushed the light to the far end of the nightstand or flipped onto my side away from the light entirely.

Useful.

Once I finally got past the technical difficulties, I found I couldn't put down *Catcher*. I kind of fell in love with the main character, Holden Caulfield. His swears and his ridiculous hat and his old-fashioned boarding-school life.

The thing my brain got stuck on was, would Holden fall in love with me as I did with him? Or would he just have looked at me sitting at the table next to him and said, "That chubby girl at the table next to me, the one with bags under her eyes, really annoyed the hell out of me. You would have thought I was a goddamn steak sandwich or something, the way she looked at me."

God. I can't even get lucky with book characters.

Delusionally tired, I clicked off the extreme light on my nightstand and worked my way under the covers.

Good night, Justin, I thought, hoping somehow we were so connected that he could read my mind. *I promise to write you tomorrow.*

No one answered back in my head. Which was probably a good thing.

WALKER

I woke up early today. Not on purpose, but my eyes sprung open and everything was in perfect focus. My therapist—*ex-therapist*—once told me that it's a good idea to wake up when your body wants to, instead of just lollygagging (yes, that's what she said) in bed until your brain decides it wants to get up. You can be much more productive that way. As much as I'd like to live my life in the exact opposite direction as that psychotic bitch suggested, I did have some unfinished business to attend to. Mainly, pre-calc and Justin.

The pre-calc was nothing, especially because all of the answers were provided in the back of the book. The sample problems were in the chapter, so all I really had to do was fill in the sample problems with the new numbers in my homework and check the answers in the back. When I figured out I was doing it correctly, I sped through it.

Which should have been great.

Which should have made writing a letter to Justin easy.

I even had a dream about him last night. One of those dreams that seems so real, you can feel everything. The snozzberries tasted like snozzberries, if you know what I mean. The dream should have made me jump into the letter. Tell Justin how much I miss him and how I can't wait to . . . what? Talk to him again? Be his girlfriend? Get married in a Lake Shit ceremony where people throw antidepressants at us instead of rice? What, if anything, was actually possible? We don't even live near each other. And not just now, when he's in the city in a mental hospital and I'm in the suburbs, but when he gets out and he's in some totally random west-side burb I'd never even heard of before Lake Shit. There wasn't any time to talk about where we'd go and what we'd do after one of us, let alone both of us, got out. It was like, *bam,* we kiss, *bliss,* and then *bam,* Anna goes home (with another tiny bliss kiss before I left). No heart-to-heart. No professing our undying, hopeless devotion to each other. No vows of commitment or declarations of boyfriend/girlfriend/just friends labels.

What do I say to someone I liked so much that he inspired me to do things I wasn't supposed to do? Someone I wanted to spend more time with so I could memorize every detail of his sad brown eyes, his inviting lips, and the glossy grossness of the scar healing on his hand? Because right then, Justin felt so far away that I couldn't even remember what he tasted like. I do know it was not a snozzberry.

After my shower, I slipped back into my pajamas until I was ready to commit to another outfit. It was easier when all of my clothes fit, albeit suckier. I decided that I needed some more head clearing—not by therapeutic means, but by releasing this grip my family had on me a bit. I hated that my mom drove me everywhere. As lame as it was for a sixteen-year-old to do, I wanted to walk to school.

At breakfast, which consisted of a piece of toast with raspberry jam and a glass of OJ (followed with an antidepressant chaser), I told my mom, "I'm walking to school today."

There was a pause as my mom processed. She was good at processing, unlike my dad, who just let whatever crap fly that came to his mind first. But he was already out of the house, thank God. As usual.

"That sounds nice, honey. By yourself?" There was a not-so-hinty hint of concern in her voice, which made me start to reconsider. What would I encounter walking to school by myself? Was that an extremely weird and losery thing to do?

"Maybe I'll see if Tracy wants to walk with me." Tracy either took the bus or drove when she had to work directly after school. She lived farther from school than I did, and I thought maybe she could catch a ride with her mom to my house, and then we could walk together.

I left my unfinished toast and half-empty glass of orange juice and walked around the corner to the living room. We never used the living room. Except for photographs we have in crusty, fading albums from baby birthday parties, the room had gone basically untouched. The irony of the living room. There's a puffy, blue-striped, L-shaped couch that's probably pretty comfortable. It's not as though my family is super-fancy and my parents have set this room off-limits. We just don't use it. Maybe it's because there's no TV in it.

I dialed Tracy's cell, which rang six times before she picked up.

"Top o' the morning to ya," Tracy grumbled. Tracy is not a morning person. She's not even a lunchtime person. Tracy's body is in its own jacked-up time zone, so she can't fall asleep until two or three a.m. You'd think being forced to wake up at six every day would eventually change your body's habits, but not T's. Which is fine with her because it gives her plenty of time to catch up on watching her beloved wrestling.

You should see the television in Tracy's room. It's a wall-mounted flat screen that takes up half a wall. Her parents make her save every penny she earns at Sluts R Us for college, but Tracy's aunt loves to give her these giant balloons every year for her birthday and Christmas that are filled with crumpled dollar bills. You pop the balloon, and then you spend an hour running around the room finding all of the money that scattered from the explosion. Some may think it's a weird gift. Why not just write a check or give a gift card? I think it's kind of cool. Tracy wanted cash. Each year her parents would ask T what she wanted for Christmas, and Tracy would hand them a list that said two things:

1. A huge-ass TV
2. Cash

And what did her parents give her? Purses. Clothes. Perfume. All stuff that was so not Tracy. She had a closet full of it. None of it cool enough to wear or borrow. So the cash balloon was thoughtful. And pretty fun. You get a check or a gift card, and it's just this tiny, little predictable envelope. But with the Balloon-o-bucks, you have an afternoon of good, clean, rollicking fun. Well, sort of clean. You don't know where those dollar bills have been.

As soon as she had enough dollar bills rolled up, hidden in the armholes of a pair of Bert and Ernie puppets, she bought the huge TV and a DVR to go with it.

"Good morning, sunshine," I cooed into the phone.

"I make you happy when skies are gray, yeah, yeah. I haven't had my coffee yet." Much clanking ensued in the background.

"You working today?"

"Thank jebus, no. You want to do something?" She slurped what I assumed was the blackest of black coffee. Tracy also likes the blackest of black sunglasses; she bought a pair of retro Ray-Bans and then took them to some optometrist who hand-dipped them in a special coating over and over to make the lenses as dark as possible. "What's the point of wearing sunglasses if people can still see my eyes?" was her logic.

"I have to ask my mom about that one. You could probably come over, though," I told her.

"Why don't they just staple a chip to your forehead and be done with it?" *Slurp.*

"Because then I'd have a chip stapled to my forehead? Anyways, I'm calling to see if you want to walk to school with me this morning. Your mom could drop you off, and we can walk from my house."

Slurp. "Better than taking the bus. Sure."

"See ya in a few." We hung up, and I finished what was left of my breakfast.

Upstairs, I faced my closet of baggy clothes. I slid the door to the right, so the left side was exposed. These were my usual clothes, the ones I'd been wearing all of high school, aside from my three drawers of t-shirts, socks, and underwear. Nothing looked right, so I slid the door to the left. That side was partially blocked by a bookcase and held all of the clothes I'd loved in my life that stopped fitting as I grew up and out. It was like looking at pictures of myself in junior high, back before I really ballooned. Most of the stuff was too small or too dorky or too outdated, but I found a black, stretchy A-line skirt that looked decent. I shimmied out of my PJ bottoms and pulled the skirt over my legs, then my hips. Okay so far. But I refused to look in a mirror at the slight muffin top—effect it created. I needed to find a shirt that was long enough and baggy enough to cover the stomach situation, but nothing in my closet looked right. There was always the jumbo t-shirt option, but as long as I was going with a new/old skirt, I wanted to try something different.

I walked into my parents' bedroom. A quick rifle through my mom's closet proved her clothes were too small and too mommish. So I went to my dad's side. Seven billion button-down shirts hung side by side. One half of my dad's closet was reserved for dirty shirts, which my mom gathered every couple weeks or so to take to the dry cleaners. Why he didn't just toss them onto the floor in a pile made no sense to me. My dad, in general, made little sense to me. But he had some nice shirts.

I flipped though the button-downs until I came to a solid blue one that looked alright. I pulled it out and sniffed it, not too closely because I wasn't sure if it was on the dirty or clean side. Slightly stinky, with the musky scent of his aftershave, and definitely not clean. I switched to the other side of the closet and flicked through the shirts until I found one I'd never seem him wear. It was purple and green checked, almost a cowboy-looking pattern, complete with pearlescent snaps, not buttons. When was my dad a gay cowboy? Lucky for me he was, because as I snapped the shirt on, it fit, and in my parents' full length mirror I looked, dare I say, cute?

Then I noticed my legs.

I shaved the instant I got home from Lakeland, since while there I hadn't been allowed to shave at all (razors, you know). I probably lost another two pounds of weight just from body hair. But it was Wednesday now, five days later, and I didn't think to shave in the shower that morning.

Back in my room, I pulled open my dress-up drawer. No, not a drawer filled with princess and French maid costumes (um, what?), but the drawer with all of the annoying body-accessory-type things one needs when getting dressed up (which is practically never in my life, except for the occasional cousin bar mitzvah). You know— Spanx, pantyhose, slips, and tights. I dug until I found what I was looking for: a pair of blush-pink tights I was forced to buy for my final performance in a dance recital. Yes, I was a dancer. Not a very good one. Not really a bad one, either, but after puberty struck and blew me up, it was so awkward. Wearing skin-hugging leotards and tights in rooms fully lined with mirrors was miserable. In eighth grade I finally convinced my mom that I didn't fit into the skinny, obsessive, competitive group of girls, and she let me quit right after the recital.

I scrunched the tights up and pulled them over my feet, one leg at a time. When I got to my stomach, I sucked it in and pulled the elastic waist over my gut. When I breathed out, the pain wasn't horrible. I could actually breathe out, which was the important part. For survival, and all. When I pulled the cowboy shirt down, the whole outfit wasn't bad, in a quirky way. I added a pair of ultra-worn, black low-top Chucks that I retired last year. Back in my parents' room, I checked myself out in the mirror.

Huh.

Tracy rang the doorbell fifteen minutes later, which would give us twenty minutes to walk to school. Plenty of time for decompression. Or recompression at going back to school, but it was better than being in silence/anger/awkwardness with my mom in the car again.

I was hoping to just fly out the door without any Mom/Tracy interaction, but my mom followed me as I gathered my books into my backpack.

"Don't you look cute?" she asked. When was the last time she uttered those words to someone other than perpetually cute Mara?

"Whoa," Tracy responded when she walked in, eyeing me up and down. "I left my ball gown in the car. Should I get it?"

"Funny." I rolled my eyes. I guess this really was a different look for me. I hope not different enough to get me noticed by anyone. I don't think I'm ready to be noticeable. Still Mental Hospital Girl inside.

My mom approached the door tentatively. I could sense tension between her and Tracy, like when your friends break up and you see the ex that wouldn't have been your friend unless they were dating your friend. Are you supposed to be pissed at them? Are they the enemy? Tracy and my mom had that vibe. I think my mom was a little bit the enemy to Tracy. I hope she didn't think it the appropriate time to bust out a wrestling move.

Gratefully, all that was said was "Hi, Tracy, how have you been?" by my mom and "Hi, Mrs. Bloom. A-OK," with a slightly forced yet congenial smile from Tracy.

With that over, Tracy and I walked on our merry way to school. Without much merry.

"Your mom looks tired," T noted.

"Yeah, I guess."

"Or like she's been crying."

"Maybe she has been. Do we have to talk about this? Once I leave the house I'd like to pretend my parents don't exist for a little while."

"Whatever, Little Orphan Anna. You can tell me all about your new therapy buddies. Should I be jealous?" Tracy asked.

"Jealous?" Why would someone be jealous of anyone forced into group therapy by their parents?

"You know, 'cause they get to hear everything. Like, the gory details of your warped psyche."

"The only warped psyche here is yours, thank you. And, I mean, I tell you everything anyway."

"You did. I thought you did. But then you were gone for three weeks, and I don't really know why and I don't really know what happened because I don't want to push you into talking about shit that you don't want to talk about like everyone else is doing."

We walked in silence for a minute as I processed this. Tracy was right. All of those other people—those total strangers—knew nothing about me except for the deeply personal. And Tracy was trying so hard to maintain best friend status that she wasn't pushing to hear any of the personal stuff, even though she knew everything else.

There was so much she didn't know now. Why I went into the hospital. My friends from Lakeland. My *more than* friend. It was a lot to tell someone, even my best friend. At least too much for right now.

"I'm sorry, T, I didn't know you felt that way," I finally said.

"Hey, I don't want to make you feel guilty or depressed or any other adjective in the negatory department. You've had enough of that, and you don't need it from me. But . . ." She paused to kick a Strawberry Crush can out of her way. It lifted into the air and landed on the road, promptly crushed in a manner fit for its name. "Things feel kind of different between us. Which, you know, makes sense, considering what you've been through. Although, I don't know what you've been through, and other people do. It just feels off."

I started to answer with a lame excuse, but she wasn't finished. "People ask me about you. Teachers, kids we barely know. They ask me how you're doing. If you're okay. And I don't know what to tell them. I'm, like, 'Yeah, Anna's okay. Why don't you ask her yourself?' Because I have nothing to tell them. I don't even know if there are things I shouldn't tell them because you haven't told me things that I should or shouldn't tell people, you know?"

"Yeah," I snuck a word in as she kicked a plastic Coke bottle into the street.

"Why don't you people fucking recycle!" she shouted at no one and everyone.

"Just so you know, Tracy," I said in a serious tone, "I recycle."

"Thanks, bitch." She nudged me with her shoulder.

"T?" I asked.

"Yeah?"

"Sorry I haven't told you anything. I guess at this point there's so much to tell you, I don't know where to start."

"That was such a good book—" I looked at Tracy, confused. "*So Much to Tell You*. Where that girl's in a boarding school and she won't speak to anyone and you don't know why—"

"And then you find out she can't speak because of what her dad did to her. That was good. Why are dads such dicks?"

"My dad's okay." Tracy shrugged. "Just old as hell. Nice and oblivious, really." I nodded. "You were saying?"

"I was? What was I saying?" Tracy and I too often found ways to interrupt each other or ourselves. Hundreds of conversations have been tragically lost in our lifetime.

"That you had so much to tell me."

"Remember that book?" I joked.

"Speak," she demanded.

"Another good book."

"You want your ass kicked in the street like a can of Crush, or you want to tell me something real?"

"Something real," I pondered. We were five minutes away from school at this point. Not enough time for the long stories—the romance, the friends, the what and where of my missing three weeks. So I started from the beginning. "Hi. My name is Anna Bloom, and my parents put me in a mental hospital because I wouldn't go to school and I had panic attacks and I was depressed and I thought about killing myself."

"Who the fuck doesn't?" Tracy asked, slightly enraged.

"Exactly. Not like I did anything about it."

"Thank God for that," Tracy said, looking forward at the school now in our view.

"Yeah," I agreed. "Thank God for something."

"You know that's only a tiny piece of what you owe me, right? I want to hear everything."

"Can I skip the parts where I go to the bathroom?"

"You never did before," Tracy reminded me. "I don't know how many times you told me about that poo you made that you swore was wearing a hat."

"It was!" I yelled.

We finished our walk to school and arrived just as the bell rang.

I don't know about Tracy, but I already felt a little lighter.

When I got to my locker, Tucker was there waiting for me.

Tracy said, "I have to talk to Mr. Grubb about the B he gave me on an oil change. I'm claiming sexism. See you guys," and she strutted away down the hall.

"Good morning, Anna. I trust you slept well?" Tucker sometimes spoke like an alien who came from outer space, landed on Earth, and learned English by watching a million movies on some ancient movie channel. He was a little weird. Maybe he is an alien. Better than an asshole, I suppose.

"I slept alright. You?" Not that I had ever thought about Tucker sleeping. As cute as he was, he was always more the out-of-my-league, smart, art guy. The smart doesn't make him out of my league so much because up until high school, when he fast-tracked into the advanced classes by force-feeding himself toxic doses of summer school, we were always in the same level classes. But Art gives him that super-cool identity piece I'm kind of lacking. I mean, there are things about me that are identifiable, but not in such an outward way that makes people recognize that trait. Or remember me. For example: As you know, I love The Ramones. Their music is my lifeblood; it's what wakes me up in the morning and helps me not sleep at night. I'm sure some people know that about me, seeing as I have a small wardrobe of vintage and reissued Ramones t-shirts that I rotate through. But it's not like anyone *cares*. It's not like I have the balls to wear a leather jacket like the guys in The Ramones did. I don't want to be the fat girl in the squeaky leather jacket. Plus, I'd feel kind of guilty smelling like dead cow all day. Sometimes I want to dye my hair, maybe just a streak, with blue or red, just to say, *Hey, everyone, I like punk music! I like to listen to indie radio stations and find obscure CDs at the library!* But that would draw attention to me. And attention means people looking at me.

Yes, Anna, that's part of the very definition of attention.

Blow me, Anna, I'm making an important point here.

Shit. Have I gone schizophrenic now?

The point that the Annas were trying to make is that drawing attention to my physical being is drawing attention to my chubbiness, which means the possibility of a 4th grade redux in which Brad Schmidt told me I was the fattest girl in the class. Seven years ago, and I could still relive every painful pinch of that degrading moment. If I add anything to myself to clearly identify me as someone with a *thing*, then I'm just opening myself up for more Brads in the world to spot the fat girl, right?

Super-weird, smart art guy Tucker doesn't seem to be thinking about any of the above or have any awareness that I was just degrading the shit out of myself in my head. Which is good, because ever since I got back from Lake Shit, I've been noticing the, shall we say, kissability of more people. Now that I'm a professional in that area (thank you, Justin), I tend to watch people's mouths as they speak. Which is a total step up from dumpy girl staring at the floor, but is not quite at the apparent goal of looking into their eyes. You can't kiss eyes, though. Well, I suppose you can, but, gross.

Tucker's lips are almost a little too much, full on both the top and bottom. Plump. A nice shade of pink.

I shook my head before my brain went in the direction of him using those lips on me.

"Everything okay?" he asked.

"Everything's fine," I answered. Except that I'm a head-cheating perv. There I was worried about Justin hooking up with another Mental Hospital Girl, and here I was thinking about another guy's lips. Another guy who wasn't even a possibility because he had no interest in me. And should he, in some parallel guys-like-Anna-outside-of-a-mental-hospital universe, then what about Justin? What about Justin either way? What kind of maybe-girlfriend was I if I haven't seen him in five days and haven't even tried to communicate with him the one way I could?

Not like I've heard from him.

I flipped open my locker to sort my books for the day. My brain was too full up crazy right now to even consider Tucker's lips anymore. He probably noticed the panicked look in my eyes as my brain battled itself. "The second bell's going to ring soon. Did you need something?" I asked. I hoped that sounded more nonchalant than bitchy. I don't do either very well. I'm more an expert on awkward and depressed.

"Just checking in, really. I wanted to say thank you for operation SCU. That's Soccer Cover Up, in case it's too early for you to decode acronyms."

"It's never too early, Tucker," I said in faux seriousness. He got the joke and smiled, those damn lips reminding me they're there.

"Well, see you at lunch then."

"See ya." I nodded.

"Oh, and I like your tights." He saluted and ran off. Tucker's always running places. Maybe that's how he stays so skinny. I'd try that, but I wouldn't want my boobs bouncing all over the hallways.

HOLDEN

English was annoying, yet at least stimulating enough to keep my IBS at bay.

I shouldn't be surprised that people are this stupid. Ignorance runs rampant all over the place, from sick-ass right-wing hate mongers to people having drunk sex on camera for the *Real World* (think of your poor grandmothers, people!), the world is full of assnubs. But it amazed me how differently people felt about Holden than I did.

"No wonder the guy's home on a Saturday night. He's a pussy. I'm allowed to say that, right? Because Holden's always swearing?" so said Steve Andrews, a guy who must be shockingly dull based on the selection of sports jerseys he wears on a daily basis. Anyone who gives that much of a crap about sports that he has to dress the part even when he's not playing a sport is as interesting to me as a bag of plain, baked potato chips.

"Mr. Groban." Conley Arnatz raised her hand and spoke at the same time. I twinged a bit at the aggressiveness of her hand in the air, flashing back to my Lake Shit no-hand-raising rule. Only two fingers held out at the side. One of the many rules that didn't make sense there, and now made me feel extra-weird outside. We've been raising our hands since kindergarten, and three weeks in a loony bin magically made even *that* uncomfortable for me. "Mr. Gro-ban," Conley repeated herself, even though everyone knew it was Conley's turn to speak. Not that she held some power over our class, it's just that she's one of those people who continues to speak whether or not someone is talking. Like, in regular conversation it's perfectly acceptable to politely interrupt with an interested inter-jection, but Conley just steamrolls right over those interjections. Her class comment was, "I was intrigued, so I read a few extra chapters." Naturally. "And I was just wondering what the story is going to be? The plot? Is it some sort of mystery? I mean, the book itself has no explanation whatsoever." She held up the paperback with yellow lettering and red drawings of horses on the front and back, no words to describe the story, and flipped it back to front a few jerky times.

"The SparkNotes are just as confusing," some guy said under his breath.

"Anyone who reads the SparkNotes for *Catcher* will get nothing out of the experience," Mr. Groban told the class with a slight edge in his voice, reserved for books he felt most passionate about. I guess I can understand. Freshman year we had to read *Lord of the Flies*. Everyone in the class was so busy laughing about the pig's head on a stick that nobody noticed me quietly brooding in a cor-ner. I was obsessed with that book. Actually, with Simon. Which is relatively ridiculous because a) he was a character in a book, and b) he was, like, nine years old or something. But he was so intro-verted and pensive and seemed like the wallflower of the island. I got it in my head that he was this gorgeous loner who was my ideal guy. When the tragedy in the book (of which I shall not even speak. *Sniff*Sniff*) occurred, I couldn't even go to school that day (this was before I couldn't go to school for other, crazier reasons, al-though, when I think about it, this does sound a wee bit crazy, too) because I didn't want to hear all the gross comments everyone was going to make. I'm (mostly) over the book now, but I get how Mr. Groban can feel so strongly about a book. I'm quite attached to Holden already.

That didn't mean I was ready to raise my hand and talk about it. One thing about being gone for three weeks was that I still wasn't sure the other students knew where I'd been, even if they knew who I was. My fear was that I'd raise my hand to speak, and some asshole, probably someone I'd had class with since freshman year but who'd never noticed me, would whisper just a little too loudly to his seat neighbor, "Who the hell is that?" to which the person next to him would explain who I was, or at least my name, and then they'd try to figure out why they never noticed me in class this year. Eventually someone who knows someone else who knows of me would tell them that I was in a mental hospital. So then I'm not really blendy, chubby girl but crazy, chubby girl. That's just someone I'm not ready to be. Plus, I was worried that my feelings toward Holden might incriminate my crazy even more. So I pressed the mute button and listened.

Thankfully, Jenna Simpson had something good to say about the book. Jenna always seemed sophisticated to me as we've gone through school together. She consistently dressed more like a businesswoman than a teenager. She wore *pumps*. In every English class I've had with her, she referenced some fat book that she just happened to be reading for fun, like *The Fountainhead* or *War and Peace*. I preferred her pretentious approach to English over sports jersey Steve's. "I found Holden's voice refreshing, really. It's as though he's explaining who he is by the way he views other people."

"Yesss!" Mr. Groban hissed excitedly. And then he was off and running. Any time he asked a question and someone bothered to answer it, you could see him vibrating like a cold Chihuahua, waiting to interject his own theories about the book. It was nice to see a teacher so interested in what he did after already doing it for six thousand years. He almost inspired me to raise my hand when he asked about Holden's hunting cap. But by the time I decided I was considering it, two other people already had their say and it was time for more Groban blathering. I was surprised when the bell rang; the class actually flew by without a stomach incident. If school were this interesting all the time, maybe I would never have been hospitalized in the first place.

¡QUÉ LÁSTIMA!

After math class, where I took one bathroom break and then berated myself the rest of the time (Was it a panic attack? Was I going back to Lake Shit because of it? Or did I just have to go to the bathroom?), physics was a pleasant respite with a movie called *The Secret Life of the Crash Test Dummy*. "Pleasant" might not have been the right word, but at least it wasn't "panic."

Spanish was a different scene. Señora Schwartz assigned a skit where we had to pretend we were traveling through time, thus cleverly utilizing the many verb tenses we learned. In my previous Anna life, this would have brought me both joy and trauma. I loved writing and acting out absurd skits in Spanish. It's like you're five years old again, playing store. *How much is an apple? Five cents, please. Thank you. You're welcome.* And I'd always made sure my skits were punctuated with some over-the-top Spanish expression. Like, my character would take an apple from the bottom of the (imaginary) fruit display, and all of the apples would spill all over the floor. Then I'd dramatically yell, "*¡Ay dios mio! ¡Qué suerte!*" And put my hands on my face in shock. But I didn't quite love being in front of an entire class. Because as funny as I was, I was also forced to be the center of attention in all my chubbed-out glory. Which flashed me back to a Spanish class in 8th grade when we had just learned the word for "pig," *cerdo,* and that same douche-tastic Brad Schmidt, lovely boy that he was, would do that obnoxious cough-talk thing every time I spoke (what dick invented that?) and barf out *"cerdo!"* He has since moved on to the proud and the few at military school, but *cerdo* has stuck in my head.

Creating a skit also meant that I'd have to talk to other people in class on a more intimate basis, instead of just facing forward while the teacher spoke. An opportunity for mental hospital exposure. My stomach started to churn. The panic began to swell. Was I ready to be *chica de la hospital mental*? How did the mental hospital adults expect me to act all regular once I got out when everything we did at Lake Shit was so *irregular*?

Speaking of irregular, my stomach was really roiling. What if the skit group asked me where I'd been for three weeks? What would I tell them? Would they ask me a lot of questions? Would they ask me in Spanish? Would I start to cry? *¡Qué mal!*

As I worked myself into an anxiety ball, Alyssa Compball came over to me and asked if I wanted to be in a group with her and Madeline Bower.

Relief.

Alyssa and Madeline were extreme smarties, always in my classes, and what you would call identifiable nerds. Which, in my opinion, is a very cool thing. And they were always nice. They were very down to business and open to my goofy suggestion of pretending we were Don Quixote, Sancho Panza, and Dulcinea traveling through time. That way, we could make lots of stupid windmill remarks. Not only would the skit be funny, but we'd get bonus points for referencing a classic Spanish novel, or at least the movie musical we had to watch in class.

By the time the bell rang, my stomachache had dissipated and I was feeling pretty good. Saved by the nerds. I should get a t-shirt with that printed on it. Or at least a commemorative mug.

As we stood up to leave, Alyssa casually remarked, "You look really good, Anna. How did you do it?" which caught me off guard and confused me at the same time. Did she want to know how I got hospitalized? I was slightly relieved when she asked, "Diet? Exercise? A combination?"

"Diet, I guess," I said because it was true. I mean, it wasn't a *diet,* but it was *the* diet I ate. Combined, of course, with crappy mental hospital cafeteria food, depression, anxiety, and segueing nicely into not wanting to eat with my family and being too nervous to eat at school. So, yeah, diet.

"You'll have to share your tips sometime. I'm trying to lose a few pounds before Homecoming," Madeline admitted.

Nerds never ceased to amaze me, with their oblivious haircuts and their always active social lives. I forgot about Homecoming. Not that I wanted to go. Or have ever wanted to go. Tracy and I have always ordered pizza and watched *Degrassi* marathons whenever there's a school dance. Because who wants to get all dressed up to uncomfortably dance with a guy to shitty music?

Not me.

But that was sort of because I never had a guy to dance uncomfortably with. What if Justin gets out before Homecoming? It's totally conceivable, since it's a month away. Would we go together? Who would ask who? How would we tell people we met? Why would he go anywhere with me if I haven't even written him a letter? My next period was lunch. I would write him a letter then.

———

OR NOT

So I didn't end up writing Justin a letter. It would have been too bizarre, sitting around a table with Tracy, Eleanor, Meredith, and Tucker. I'd have to explain who I was writing to, and then the whole story, and maybe there'd be more mental hospital questions, and I wasn't ready for that conversation yet. Plus, I hadn't even told Tracy about Justin, so how cruddy would it be for my best friend to hear about my first boyfriend at the same time as my random Art-class friends?

Instead, Tucker and I worked on physics. Boring for a lunch period, but I told myself that my reward would be the time I'd then have at night to write my Justin letter. And for some reason, physics with Tucker was fun. That guy's a robot. You should see the veins on his arms when he's calculating. *You* should see them. I shouldn't. Because that would somehow be disloyal to Justin, me noticing the veins on some guy's arm.

MAIL CALL

I hadn't thought to tell my mom that I wanted to walk home after school, so there she was waiting for me at our usual spot. Tracy and I decided at the end of lunch that we wanted to hang out after school. "Like in the olden days," she called it, and I recognized the hesitant look on my mom's face when she saw both me and Tracy walking towards the car. What could she say with Tracy already opening the car door? And what would be the problem anyway? If my mom wanted my life to be back to normal, then I had to do normal things like hanging out with my friend. And if I wanted to be really normal, I'd tell my friend—my *best* friend— that I was having boy trouble. With a boy in a mental hospital. God, that sounds freaky. Like those women they write about in *People* magazine who thought their guy was sweet and romantic and special. He was special, all right. And in prison. He was so special that when he got out of prison he found you, flayed you alive, and then ate your flesh while watching the horrific new version of *The Price Is Right*. That dud Drew Carey could make anybody want to eat someone's flesh. He doesn't even get excited when people win.

Where was I?

Oh, yes. Does the fact that Justin resided in a mental hospital make it wrong to talk about my issues with him as though they were normal?

Just for one tiny iota of a second, I spied Tucker in full soccer gear, boarding a school bus. For an away game, I guess. Wish I could get away. Where the hell would I go? Where the hell did I *want* to go?

We pulled into our driveway, and my mom asked if I would get the mail. Upon leaving the car, I spied a heap of used tissues on the seat next to my mom. I'm guessing not due to seasonal allergies. Do I say something? Wait until Tracy leaves? Not say anything, since Mom is the grown-up and I'm the fragile, recently-released-from-a-mental-hospital kid? Which reminded me of the mail, and I decided to skip the daughterly concern for now.

I only sent my two letters off this morning, so there was no joyous anticipation as I opened the mailbox. When I was a kid I subscribed to *Ranger Rick* magazine, and getting the mail was the most exciting moment of my day. Would a giant green insect with bulging eyes greet me when I creaked open the mailbox door? I could only hope! The most I expected today was my mom's subscription to *Entertainment Weekly*. That, or Mara's *J-14,* which I will admit to reading on occasion. Although it's truly frustrating how even young girl's magazines never have fat girls in them. They probably claim they're promoting fitness, but all it promotes is discrimination against chubbos and nowhere for heavy girls to look to find some-one like themselves to aspire to be. Maybe that will be my career someday: starting a magazine for young, hefty girls. God. Why does a word for being overweight have to be the same as a brand of gar-bage bags?

I flipped through the stack of envelopes I extracted from the mailbox. Bill. Bill. Bill. I wonder how guys named Bill feel when people complain about getting bills. Bill. Bill. Justin.

Whoa.

What?

In the upper left-hand corner of a plain, white envelope was Justin's name in his chicken scratch handwriting. I stared at my name, *Anna Bloom*, written by Justin's marred hand and remem-bered the first time he wrote it. We were in Lakeland school, look-ing over an architectural project he had worked on, sitting too close for Lake Shit's rules and relishing the lack of supervision dur-ing school hours. Looking back, if I understood guys at all, I totally should have seen that he liked me. And now I had a letter from him that I so desperately wanted to read by myself, away from the rest of the world that I didn't fit into. But I couldn't. Tracy waited for me at the top of the driveway, and my mom's voice called from somewhere in the garage, "Anna? You coming?" I didn't realize I was frozen to the patch of grass next to the mailbox, contemplating Justin's letter.

As nonchalantly as I could, I folded the letter while I walked slowly up the driveway. First in half, then in half again, until it fit flatly into the back of my tights, but on top of my underwear. I didn't want Justin's letter to go *there*. "Shall we?" I asked Tracy when I reached her.

"We shall," she replied, and we walked into the house.

"Do you want a snack?" my mom asked. Funny, she never asked

me about snacks before. Because snacking meant eating more, and I was already eating too much for my mom's comfort. Maybe this was part of her treatment plan to show me that weight isn't really an issue for her. Or perhaps she was worried because I had barely eaten a meal with her and the family since I've been back. "I bought some chips," she said as she rifled through the pantry to produce a mega-pack of individually bagged chips. They were the low-fat kind: Baked Lays, Baked Cheetos, and Baked Doritos. I felt sad for those fake chips, but at the same time I was curious.

"Why not?" I shrugged, and I grabbed one of each. My mom's expression shifted slightly to one of wide-eyed horror at the prospect of me eating three different bags of chips, baked or not. "Don't worry, Mom, I just want to sample them. I've never had these kinds before. I want to try them all to see how they compare to the originals. Because I am an expert on those."

"She kind of is," Tracy concurred. Tracy's allowed to concur with things like that because she has never been afraid to pack the food away with me. The annoyingly lucky-for-her difference is that she also never packed on the weight. Maybe it's all those wrestling moves she practices when she's up late at night.

Upstairs in my bedroom, Tracy and I shut the door, kicked off our shoes, dropped our bags onto the floor, and resumed our usual spots, me on my bed and her splayed out on the pee rug. It seemed odd to "resume" something that hadn't been done in over three weeks, but it felt like a continuation of our old lives. Which was a good feeling. Not quite good enough to talk about Justin and show her the letter, which I know seems absurd. But I ran this discussion over in my head, and this is what it sounded like:

"So . . . I met a guy."

"No. Really? Who?" Tracy would be overly excited for me, since Justin is technically the first guy who has existed in my physical realm, as opposed to the hours when my eyes are closed and my subconscious does most of the work.

"His name is Justin."

"Ooooh. Cute. What does he look like?" She'd start with the important questions.

"He's tall, really tall, and he has dark brown eyes and brown hair that covers them. Really cute."

"What's his story?" That's where things would get tricky. Because then I'd have to say,

"I met him at Lakeland. He's there because he tried to shoot himself after he cut off a bunch of his fingers—by accident—trying to reroof his parents' house to please his dad."

"Uh—"

"And he used to play the bass and like The Ramones, too, but now he won't play or listen to them because of his hand. He'll only listen to The Doors—I know, gag, right?—because they don't have a bass player."

"Uh—"

"We kissed! I forgot to tell you. We kissed!"

"Really? At the hospital?"

"Well, no, at the Shedd Aquarium in the shark reef when we were on a field trip because we were the only Level Threes. I mean, Matt O. was there, but he only went because he was on some special plan. But he occupied Big 'Do, our chaperone, so we could kiss without her seeing—"

"Your chaperone's name was 'Big 'Do'?"

"No. That's just what I called her. Lake Shit was big on the nicknames. Another example is that my doctor was called Dr. Asshole."

"You called your doctor 'Dr. Asshole'?"

"Everyone did. Not to his face. And he wasn't a doctor doctor. He was a psychiatrist."

Blank look from Tracy.

"We kissed one more time, too. Me and Justin. Not me and Dr. Asshole.

When I was leaving the hospital. I almost didn't do it because I didn't want to get him in trouble. But I did it anyway. Such a rebel, no?"

"For kissing someone?" Tracy's face would be all scrunched up in utter confusion.

"Because that was against the rules."

"Riiiight."

"But now Justin's still at Lake Shit, and I don't know when he'll get out and we never got a chance to say whether we were really boyfriend and girlfriend and what if he hooks up with someone else and forgets all about me?"

Another blank stare from Tracy.

"You want to try those new chips?"

And scene.

So instead of talking, Tracy plugged her MP3 player into my stereo, cranked up her favorite Metallica album, and we did our homework. Just like in the days of yore. Mara even stopped in to give us both a wave (too loud to say anything). And all was as it once was. If only that letter wasn't burning a hole in my ass.

Tracy stayed for dinner, which was pretty funny. You never saw someone speak so animatedly about men in spandex, throwing each other off a bunch of ropes. My mom made a couple Tombstone pizzas with a side of frozen spinach. Is mine the only family in the world forced to eat frozen vegetables with their pizza? Classy.

My mom offered to drive Tracy home, but T already called her mom. Lucky for her, we heard the telltale driveway honk at the exact moment my dad walked into the house. He wore his referee's uniform: white pants, black gym shoes, a jailhouse-striped jacket, and black cap. He looked like an idiot. Apparently, there was good money in after-school refereeing, so that's why he subjected himself to looking like a reject from *Jailhouse Rock*. "Oh, hi, Tracy. Nice to see you," he said as he wiped his feet repeatedly on the doormat.

"Likewise," Tracy said, which made me laugh. "Thanks for dinner, Mrs. B. Good luck on the squad, Mara. See you tomorrow, Anna. Mr. Bloom——" Tracy bowed her head to my dad in false reverence. She didn't like him very much either, based mostly on what I told her about him. He was around so little, she barely knew the man. I barely knew the man myself.

Once Tracy left, so began the most excruciating moment in Bloom family history since my mom forced me to tell my dad when I got my period. His response? "Congratulations."

"I have to go call Kendra. She has the practice schedule." Mara bolted up the stairs to her bedroom. She always thinks of perfect, legit excuses.

I was about to make up some lame-ass excuse about my own schedule, when my dad spoke, "How is everything going, Anna?" You could see the pained look on his face, trying to be fatherly and concerned and not having any clue how to do so.

"Not bad." I gave as little as I got.

"And your new group therapy?"

Like I'd tell you. "Fine."

Was I supposed to ask him probing questions, too? Like, how's that house-hunting thing going? Getting along now that you're leaving the family and all?

"Well, I gotta go do some homework. Lots of homework. Yep." Without waiting for more of our charmingly uncomfortable conversation, I ran upstairs and closed my bedroom door. Should I have stayed for my mom's sake? I'll answer that question with: Should they stay married for me and Mara's sake?

Shouldn't life be less complicated sans institution?

Breathing heavily, I lay down on top of my bed. I waited until my breathing settled down a tad, and my heart stopped pounding in my ears, then I pulled the folded envelope out of my tights.

Then, naturally, I sniffed it.

No discernible Justin-y clean-boy smell. Maybe that's hidden inside like the nougaty goodness of a 3 Musketeers bar. The envelope *had* been dangerously close to my butt for the last couple of hours. Perhaps me should rethinks the sniffage.

I carefully peeled open the gluey flap, trying to retain its pristine form, just as Justin would have seen it. How archaeological of me. The letter inside was a single folded piece of lined paper, the same paper I was allowed to use at Lakeland. No holes from a dangerous metal spiral, with the hint of gumminess at the top where it was attached to the floppy pad.

Slowly I unfolded each crease until a page filled with Justin's pencil marks sprawled before me.

" 'Dear Anna,' " I read.

And then someone knocked on the door.

"What?!" I screamed like a competitive eater forced to abandon a hot dog.

"Just seeing if you needed anything, honey." It was my mom. She sounded hurt.

"Sorry, Mom," I yelled through the door, not wanting to move, to separate my hands from the piece of paper that was last held by Justin. I wanted to *be* that piece of paper. "I'm journaling."

Journaling. I laughed to myself at my excuse, exactly what a parent of a kid who just got sprung from loonytown wants to hear. Emoting without anyone having to intervene. A parent's dream.

"Oh! I'll leave you alone then."

"Thanks."

I waited a few seconds to make sure she didn't pull a second act.

Now, piece of paper, where were we?

"Dear Anna." Yes, dear Justin? I was so fixated on those words, that tangible piece of Justin in my hands, that it took me a good five minutes to relax my eyes and brain enough to read more than the greeting. Then I read it seventeen times.

Dear Anna,

How's life after Lake Shit? I can't wait to get out. They're telling me maybe two more weeks. Forever, in Lake Shit terms. How much Cap'n Crunch and crappy burgers can a man stand, I ask you?

The floor's really crowded now. Six people came in over the weekend. Four girls, two guys. Mostly assbags. This one guy, Tom, is okay, and this girl, Dania, you'd like her. She's into music like us. They made her take out her lip piercing, and it's already closing up. Sucks.

Not much else new. Oh, did I tell you I'm writing to you from a desk in the hallway? Our, you know, goodbye got me in trouble for a few days. Hall restriction. It's okay. Was worth it, you know?

What are you doing right now? I picture you sitting in your room and listening to The Ramones and playing your bass. Eating pizza or something else we didn't have at The Shit. Oh, yeah, we've started calling Lake Shit "The Shit." That was Dania's idea. I can't take credit.

Well, better go pretend to do my schoolwork. Hope you're not too busy to write me back.

Justin

Before I could reply, I had to fully analyze the letter.

The first paragraph: He asked how I was doing, which was nice. Then he told me when he'd maybe get out, but he didn't say anything about getting together when he did. What did that mean?

Second paragraph: Dania Dania Dania. Am I right?

Third paragraph: I got him in trouble! I kissed him, probably the most rebellious thing I've ever done, but it was our last goodbye and the moment took over. He didn't actually say "when we kissed." Because he didn't like it or because he was too embarrassed to write it? He did say it was worth it, which implied he liked the kiss, but asking "you know?" is a bit wishy-washy in the conviction area. I wish he'd said something about wanting to do it again. With me, I mean, because . . .

Fourth paragraph: Dania Dania Dania. And something about what am I doing right now, but not that he cared much about that since he ended the paragraph with a sentence about Dania. I hated this girl already. And why was he picturing me eating? Did that mean something?

Fifth paragraph: "Hope you're not too busy to write me back." Is that really him saying don't bother writing me back because we're over? Or was he saying, "Anna, please write me back and show me you haven't forgotten about me"? Or was he just saying that I might be busy and I won't write him back. Because it's not like I've actually written him a letter yet or anything.

Maybe I'm a letter-sending phobe. Does that exist? I wrote that hugely long, detailed letter to Tracy about every moment I spent while at Lake Shit, and I never sent it. If I did, she'd know about all of the stuff I'm not ready to tell her. Which means I wouldn't have to be ready to tell her anything because she'd know it already. I told myself I didn't send the letter because I needed to keep a record that I was there, so I wouldn't forget.

I don't think I could forget Lake Shit if they gave me a lobotomy as a parting gift.

The letter to Tracy is tucked into my desk drawer, under a stack of birthday cards I've collected over the years.

I should have sent it.

Maybe it really is a phobia. I could look it up online, but I can't be bothered getting up to turn on my computer. By the time it runs its lethargic security scan and I manage to get online, Justin would be out of Lake Shit and married to Dania.

He didn't even sign "love" or "sincerely" or "from." That would have sucked if he signed it "from." Did it mean he was confused about how to sign it? Did he not want to sign "love" and lead me on? Did he not want to sign "love" because he didn't feel that way toward me at all?

Did I love Justin?

Why isn't there a letter signature that's sort of romantic but not so intense. *Written by a person who likes you a lot but hasn't known you long enough to write "love."* A bit clunky. And revealing. It should be shorter, with the one-word punch of "love" without all the baggage.

I spent (i.e., wasted) a good hour trying to think up a new word that would fill the not-love-but-not-just-a-friend void. Pathetically, this is what I came up with:

Snooks
Huggins
Squeezums
Kissens
Luvish

Mortified by my disturbing dictionary, I picked up *Catcher in the Rye* to complete my reading for the night. I bet Holden thinks I'm a goddamn phony for my asscake attempt at word creation. And for what I was really doing: avoiding writing a letter to Justin. Again.

Too tired and disappointed with myself to write, I fell asleep the moment I finished my *Catcher* assignment. There was always tomorrow to write Justin a letter. It's not like he was going anywhere. Except maybe with Dania.

DON'T ASK, I'LL TELL

I don't want to talk about Thursday. Thursday was a piece of shit on a cake made of poo, frosted with crap, and baked in a turd oven.

First was my old friend, panic attack, who showed her bowely face not once but twice. Once in Mr. Groban's class, which means I'll be getting another pat-on-the-shoulder "we should talk" talk from him tomorrow. The other time was in Pre-calc, during a pop quiz, which I would have done perfectly fine on if it weren't so fucking quiet in the room that everyone could hear every minute sound my stomach so generously decided to expel.

I spent the rest of the morning in the nurse's office, who rubbed salt into my ass by saying, "I didn't think I'd see you back here, Anna."

I lay on the sterile, plastic bed, praying she got a scorching case of ringworm.

Tucker wasn't at lunch or Art, and Meredith was on some Blink 182 diatribe that bored the wang out of me both periods. In Art, I overexposed the blurry still-life picture I was attempting to develop, wasting a butt-load of uberexpensive photo paper and pissing off Mrs. Downy.

Then came Group Therapy Part Poo (my Freudian ex-therapist would have a field day with all of these excremental references. Which doesn't make a whole lot of sense, since I thought Freudian therapy was all about the sex. Maybe her sex is all about the crap. Jesus, I'm going to need more therapy hypothesizing about my therapist). My hope was to skate by without having a panic attack, or talking about having another panic attack, but I was rewarded for good behavior with neither.

We went around the circle at the beginning of Group with a recap of our week, how it was going, anything we needed to talk about, the rare success story. Peggy insisted Bartleby go first, which was the only silver lining on the cloud of shit (eeeew—does that mean it rains diarrhea?) of my day. Bart grumbled and shifted uncomfortably in his chair. Nepa kicked him with a stiletto boot after a minute of nothing passed by. "Fine," Bart conceded. "I failed my SATs."

"You can't fail your SATs, Bart," Miles pointed out.

"No shit, bro, but in my parents' perfectly twinkled eyes, I did. Which means another wasted series of Saturdays in SAT prep class."

We sat around and waited for him to expound, but he looked up at Peggy and demanded, "Next."

"Feel free to discuss this more, Bart, after our weekly recap," Peggy offered.

"I'll get right on that."

Bluck. I almost don't think he's hot anymore.

It was Nepa's turn next, and sitting next to her made me envious of how perfect her skin was. Not that I had bad skin, but there was just a lot more of it. "Not much to tell today. My dad bought me a new car," she said matter-of-factly.

"Damn! What kind?" Miles asked.

"Prius." She spoke as though it weren't a big deal, not gloating, but not embarrassed by the obvious spoilage.

"Tiny backseat," Bart noted.

"Perfect for your tiny—"

"Anna," Peggy interrupted, "why don't you tell us how your week is going?"

Fugfugfug. My knees starting to bounce as my stomach cramped. I tried steadying my breathing, but that hadn't worked the two times I attempted it already today. Before I could stop myself, I stood up and announced, "I have to go to the bathroom!"

Bartleby laughed and applauded, but that's all I caught as I booked out of the room and into the waiting area. There I was greeted by the only other door in the place: to the outside. Was there a bathroom? Was this not only a therapy group but a supernatural therapy group where no one used the toilet?

Peggy sidled up to me and eased a hand onto my frantic shoulder, asking "Do you need something, Anna?"

I shrugged her off. The last thing I wanted when I felt like pooping in my pants was someone touching me. Did I even really have to go? Or was this the way my panic attacks manifested themselves, in the most mortifying form they could think of for a girl who already hated her stomach?

"Why don't you step out for some fresh air, and come back when you're ready?" Peggy suggested. I didn't bother to answer her and walked outside. The air was still, no wind, no heat, no cold. In a way, it was suffocating. But then a bird chirped from a tree on a parking lot median, and a slight breeze moved my hair. My breathing slowed and deepened, and I finally managed to calm my brain and my stomach.

I had hoped that by the time I returned to the circle, someone else would be in the middle of an important issue and whatever happened to me would be brushed aside. Instead, the group appeared to be awaiting my return. The moment I settled back into my seat, Peggy continued right where we left off. "So, how has your week been, Anna?"

Damn. I didn't want to talk about my panic attacks or my stomach. It was fucking embarrassing to not be able to sit and listen and focus like a normal person. So, instead, I spoke about one of the other shitty things going on these days. "My parents are separating."

Strange. I didn't realize that was something I wanted to talk about.

"Oh, the horror" was Bartleby's response. That guy deserved his nuts to be crushed. Or at least a ridiculous name.

"Shut up, Bart," Ali scolded. "Just because, like, everyone else's parents are either divorced or hate each other doesn't make it nice and pretty when it happens."

"How do you feel about this?" Peggy asked me. Blah blah feelings. I was so tired of feeling things. Why couldn't I just be insanely stupid and ignorant and, thus, blissfully happy? Intelligence is so overrated. "I don't know. It sucks, I guess. They are my parents. But, it's not like they ever got along. For a decent period of time anyway. It's just . . ." And then I realized what was bothering me about them, more so than my parents being out of love, which I was almost used to, "Why are they doing it right after I got out of a mental hospital?"

"Because they couldn't handle your crazy ass," Bart said.

"Out of here, Bart." Peggy pointed a finger at the door.

"Ooh." He waggled his fingers obnoxiously. "Are you going to tell my parents? Let me know if you can find them. They're both away on business," he spat as he walked out.

"Sorry, Anna," Nepa offered.

I shrugged. "Not your fault."

"I can see why that would be troublesome, Anna. Be assured it has nothing to do with you. Overwhelming experiences, such as your hospitalization, can bring things to light, but that doesn't mean you're the reason for their separation. Maybe your parents recognized a change in you and thought it was time they experienced one for themselves."

So glad I can inspire loathing in my parents. Was that supposed to make me feel better? "Can we move on, please? I talked, but I'm done now." I leaned back in my chair and crossed my arms over my chest. This was a gesture not allowed at Lake Shit, as it was either considered combative or gang-related. Guess which one I was.

While everyone else spoke, I glazed in and out. My panic attack was over, so that was good, but now that I had brought my parents' separation out into the open it felt more real and depressing than I wanted to admit before. Another thing to deal with after too many weeks of already dealing with things. I hated to admit that my thoughts were turning to death again—not suicide, but accidental, lucky death—to end all the misery of life's complications.

Three weeks in a mental hospital to end up here.

You would think that was the worst part of my day. You'd be wrong.

The delightfully crappy end to my day—the turd de résistance—was when my mom informed me on the car ride home that tomorrow we would be going to my Aunt Marjorie's house for Rosh Hashanah. With my dad.

"Why is Dad going?" I whined.

"Because we're still a family, he still lives in this house, and we have yet to discuss the matter with anyone but you and Mara. High Holidays are not the time."

Which will mean a delightful fight between my parents on the drive, to be continued when we get home while I try to fall asleep.

Guaranteed.

Happy Effin' New Year.

Dear Justin,

Life is a hairy anus outside of Lake Shit. If I came by with a battering ram, will you help me get back in?

I'm probably the only person in the history of Lake Shit who wants back in. Pretty sexy, huh?

So thanks for writing and telling me all about life back at The Shit. Great new nickname. This Dania sounds like a real catch. Did you touch her legs under the card table, too? Make out with her at the aquarium? Are you sneaking kisses when the teacher isn't looking during school time? We never even got to do that. Would we if my insurance hadn't run out?

Tell everyone I said hi. I do miss you guys. Living with all of you was better than living with my parents any day.

Love (that's how you sign a letter),

Anna

Yeah. I didn't send it.

THOROUGHLY IRRITATED BOWELS

My stomach was truly bunged up this morning. I played the mental hospital guilt card with my mom, and she let me stay home. "But we're not starting this again," she informed me. Mom sounded defeated, like she knew she had to say that but didn't have any fight in her voice. She looked a bit bedraggled, too. Instead of blow-drying her hair straight, it hung in damp, wavy clumps. Was my stomach taking advantage of her fragile state?

I considered throwing out a snotty retort to light a fire under her tearstained feet, but then I thought, *why?* Did I want to start this again? Did I want to have stomachaches every day and freak out during classes and get fatter again and have to start seeing another awful therapist who makes up crazy shit about my dreams and then when I can't go to school anymore and my parents don't know what to do with me they'll throw me back in Lake Shit? I bet Matt O. would still be there. Maybe it wouldn't be so bad.

While I nibbled on a piece of raisin toast, my mom said, "Don't tell your dad I let you stay home. He already blames me for things getting out of hand because I let you stay home so much before." Mom sipped her orange juice and flipped through our local newspaper. She preferred it to the *Chicago Tribune* or *Sun-Times* because its stories of teenage sports heroes and county-fair beauty pageants were much less bleak than big-city corruption. Depends on who you ask.

"As if I'd talk to him. But if it comes up, you want me to lie?" I was intrigued by the sneaky suggestion.

"Well, it's not lying if he doesn't broach the subject, but if he happens to ask how school was, then, yes."

In her passive-aggressive way, this was Mom standing up to Dad. A side of her I didn't get to see often while growing up, but a side that seemed to be blossoming since the separation announcement.

"About Rosh Hashanah tonight . . ." I started.

"You're going. It's the Jewish New Year. I think we could all use a fresh start."

"Yeah, but it's the New Year whether I go to Aunt Marjorie's house or not."

"Please, honey, it will be relaxed and fun. Aunt Marjorie told me she made the Yum Yum Coffee Cake you love."

Yum yum was right, but food wasn't going to work as a bribe this time. "Can't you just bring me back a piece? It's going to be so awkward, Mom. All those cousins looking at me, asking me how I'm doing. And they'll all know I was in a mental hospital because Aunt Marjorie probably invited them over for a clan meeting beforehand to prepare them for my impending visit. You know her. I'm guessing there won't even be any butter knives on the table, just in case."

My mom laughed at the dig at her older sister. "Maybe, but it's only because she cares about you."

"Which is all good, but can't she care about me at a non-holiday event when seven hundred relatives won't also be attempting to 'care' about me?" I shoved some finger quotes in for emphasis.

"Can I think about it?"

My mom asked me if she could think about letting me out of a family commitment. Was it my newfound power of persuasion or her newfound lack of husband? If I wanted to go back to Lakeland, could I convince her of that, too? Would I make it back before Justin left?

Do I really want to go back?

I sat in my room for most of the day picking out songs on my bass. My mood wasn't aggressive enough to play along to The Ramones or The Descendents, so I flipped my crusty stereo to a classic-rock station. The same station we used to listen to during Free Time at Lakeland. Before the hospital, I couldn't stomach freewheeling, jam-feeling, peace-love-and-drugs crap. Now, I was transported back to the farty pleather yellow and green chairs, the games of Hearts, the friends and gossip and on-floor drama I was a part of. It felt better than anything I'd experienced in the past week.

A week.

I've been out of Lake Shit a whole week. One week since I kissed Justin in the hallway. One week since I was Sandy's roommate. One week since I actually felt . . .

At home.

———

A WIN AND A LOSS

A part of me believed my bass playing would magically improve having not played in over three weeks. Improving from barely knowing how to play and only plucking along to songs, I have cranked up really loudly while my bass isn't even plugged into my amp (a completely useless investment) was asking a lot without the help of magical intervention. Alas, the bass fairy did not decide to pay me a visit whilst away. Playing an instrument is a little annoying. You want so badly to just be amazing at it instantly, that the royal suckage that excretes from said instrument on most days while you attempt to reach a semblance of goodness is enough to make you stop playing altogether.

I have my own magical daydream of how one could play an instrument without learning to play. I'm sure we've all done this, but sometimes when I'm fantasizing about, you know, living at Hogwarts (where I am not Harry, Hermione, or Ron—although he and I do hook up. It's a constant battle between Ron and the Weasley twins for my affection—but myself: magical, adorable, and completely thin), I have this story line where I'm an American witch who only went to wizarding day school back in the States because Chicago didn't have a boarding school like Hogwarts. Then my mom (because in this fantasy, my parents are already divorced) gets a job as a professor of knitting at Oxford, so we move to England. Which is how I end up at Hogwarts. Everyone there is blown away by what a kick-ass witch I am and how hilariously American I can be, and I am wide-eyed and enthusiastic about everything because I can't believe the wizarding world can be this *magical*. The Weasleys take me into the Forbidden Forest to show me all of the creatures I'd never seen before (I cry when I meet the unicorn, which is probably when Ron and I first kiss. *Muy romantico*), and I even manage to kick Draco's ass in a dueling challenge, totally warranted after the perv makes an assumptive pass at me in the library. The coolest thing I do, though (besides going jogging every morning with Cedric Diggory), is share this spell I created whereby I point my wand authoritatively at any instrument, command some Latinesque words such as *Musicus playbius,* and if you "play" that instrument you will be able to actually *play* the instrument. I, of course, will already be a master of guitar, drums, and cello and, therefore, don't need the spell, but it comes in handy when I decide to form a band, RIP Scabbers, with me on lead guitar, the Weasley twins on either side as bass and rhythm guitar, and Seamus Finnigan on drums. Surprising everyone is Neville Longbottom, who more than holds his own as a screaming lead vocalist. Ron, naturally, watches me adoringly from the crowd that gathers during practice.

I'm sure everyone thinks that stuff, too.

At least my bass playing stays the same in reality and delusionment. For my birthday last year, I asked for a bass and bass lessons. My mom took me to a music store that sells new and used instruments and gave me a price range. I quickly realized that I would need to only look at the used basses, unless I wanted the kiddie starter bass that not only sounded like crap but made me look extra-huge when I played it in front of the store's full-length mirror. And yes, music stores tend to have full-length mirrors, so you can see how you look holding an instrument, which is just as important, if not more, than how the instrument sounds. I tried several styles: a brown, wood-paneled bass that was a little too au naturel for my taste; a shiny black one that made me feel disgusting every time my nervous fingers left their prints on the glossy surface; and a nail polish–red beauty that was a bit too sexy for me. My bass ended up being all white, but not shiny and pretty, and a tad dinged up. The previous owner obviously had affixed a sticker or two to the pick guard, and then ripped them off in order to sell it, leaving behind some sticker residue. My mom pointed out the gunk to the guy behind the counter (long hair, long earring, long goatee, who seemed more interested in my mom than me. This was during the beginning of my panic attack/depression/heaviest era, so I wasn't as beauteous as I am now. Or, at least I looked worse than I currently do. Not like I wanted his attention or anything), who gave us a great deal and threw in an amp for a small amount more.

The second I got the bass home, I rummaged through my desk drawers until I found my old collection of fuzzy stickers. I selected a cluster of hilarious animals: a pig, a cow, a hamster, and—my favorite—a Siamese cat, and placed them all carefully over the gooey remnants of stickers past on the bass. Now, instead of sticker leftovers, anyone watching me play bass (which is no one) will witness a delightful animal menagerie.

As I awaited my mom's verdict on the Rosh Hashanah Heist (not the appropriate word selection, but it sounded good), I fingered my bass strings to the beat of a Wire CD called *Pink Flag* that I borrowed from the library before I went to Lakeland (which should make it really overdue by now, but I checked it out on my mom's card, so it's kind of a mini–FU to my mom, no?). Wire's a punk band from England that played around the same time The Ramones were getting big. A completely different sound, more complex, sometimes slower, and very British sounding. Not bad. My bass playing sure jazzed it up. I found a sort of zone, playing and listening to music, phasing in and out of my Hogwarts musical fantasy, that it sucked a cornucopia full of ass when my mom simultaneously announced, "Knock knock" and physically knocked on my bedroom door.

Why does she do that?

"Come in," I huffed.

Mom peeked her head around the door as she slowly pushed it open, and when she saw I was decent (is that what she was looking for?), she opened it all the way and walked in. "You're playing your bass." She beamed. I think my mom had high hopes when she bought the bass that it was somehow going to cure the maladies that ailed me. I heard her tell my dad the day we brought it home (my birthday, mind you), "Allen, this could be good for her. Maybe if she focuses on playing music, she won't focus so much on other things."

"Like what?" my dad asked, utterly clueless because of course he had little knowledge of what was going on except that I had started having trouble sitting through my classes, and I was about to begin seeing a therapist. Neither he, nor any of us really, had any idea what it would turn into.

"If she's committed to playing the bass, maybe her self-esteem will blossom. Maybe she won't eat as much and she'll be able to sit through her classes. Let her at least try."

"Makes sense, I guess," my dad said, and I could practically see the memory cloud above his head reminiscing about the olden days when he was in a band with his stoner friends. Or so he likes to bring up every few months in a tragic attempt to relate to me.

As we all know, the bass failed me. It failed all of us.

But it did give me a connection to Justin.

Damn. I had managed an entire Hogwarts-filled afternoon without thinking of Justin. What was I going to do with that? Make up a new spell that would turn him blind to all girls but me?

Nothing crazy about that idea.

"So, honey"—thankfully my mom interrupted my internal insanity—"I've been thinking about what you said, and I see how uncomfortable the dinner may be for you. You can stay home tonight."

Yippee! No obscenely awkward interactions with my relatives. No attempts to make conversation. And absolutely no horrid drive home where my dad berates my mom for everything she has no control over.

Happy New Year to me!

I smiled hugely at my mom, which made her smile warmly. The sound of the front door opening and a shout of "Hello? I'm home!" from Mara downstairs cut me off.

Shit.

Now Mara had to endure the car ride alone.

THE GUILT AND THE FIGHT

Poor Mara. Not only does she have a crazy for a sister, but she's got an asshole for a father. Or should I reverse those things? Which sounds worse?

My dad wasn't always such a jerk. Or maybe he was, but as a kid I really loved him. I remember this one time I went over to my friend Katie's house to play, and when I came home my dad was gone—he had left for a week-long fishing trip with his buddies. For some reason that devastated me. That I didn't get to say goodbye. While my mom gave me my bath, I sobbed uncontrollably. Looking back, shouldn't my dad have wanted to say goodbye to *me*? There I was, a six-year-old feeling like a bad person because I didn't say goodbye to my dad, the adult who was supposed to love me and take care of me. Kind of like how now I'm the one having to deal with my semblance of a life after my parents (again, the adults) threw me in a mental hospital and thought I'd come out all better.

I don't want it to seem like my dad is all bad. No one is (except maybe Hitler). My dad's funny, or can be when he's around. I think maybe I inherited my sense of humor from him. He can also be randomly sensitive, like when I was in preschool, and I gave him a handmade plaque that read "I love my dad because he lets me sit in the front seat of his car" for Father's Day. He ate that shit up and started choking up right in the audience of all the dads obligated to attend. Or maybe he was crying because people found out he was endangering the lives of children by putting them in a seat with incorrect restraints. Whatever, he was man enough to cry in public. He's also man enough to wear pink shirts and not feel less manly because of it. And he'll watch any movie, even chick flicks. I hate when you hear guys complain, "I don't want to see that. It's a chick flick." Do you know what a dildo you sound like when you say that? All it does is show that you're threatened by a) women and b) the possibility of enjoying something that may actually cause you to have some emotion. Therefore, not watching chick flicks because you'd rather watch penis-shaped cars drive really fast through tunnels (suck on that, Freudian ex-therapist!) actually has the opposite effect. I don't even know specifically who *you* are that I'm referring to who's getting my polka dot underwear in a twist, but what I'm saying is, it's not my dad.

As sensitive as my dad is (in his preschool-audience, chick-flick kind of way), he can also be incredibly frightening. There are his predictable, one-sided arguments, which are what I was hoping to avoid by not going to my aunt's for Rosh Hashanah, but even worse is his unpredictability. You never know when you're going to say something to annoy him or set him off. It can be anything, and it can come from anywhere. I'm not talking physical abuse–type stuff, though, which thankfully hasn't happened. The only time I remember my dad being physically angry is when he and my mom came home from a night out. The babysitter went home, and I decided to lie on the couch and pretend I was asleep so that my dad would have to carry me up to bed. Sweet, right? Instead, my parents came in, my dad yelling at my mom about something that I either blocked out or didn't understand at such a young age. The two of them shouted (or, should I say, my dad shouted at my mom) for the next half hour, eventually culminating in him violently slamming the dishwasher and breaking several dishes in the process. And there I was pretending to be asleep. I finally stood up and faked a groggy half-sleeping walk up the stairs past them to my bedroom because I was afraid the anger in the room would be displaced onto me, instead of how it should have been—my dad being mortified that he could get so angry and aggressive in front of his sleeping daughter.

He has that way about him. To this day, when he gets angry or annoyed or disgusted with something one of us does, I feel in the wrong.

And he scares me.

Tonight while my family got ready to go to Aunt Marjorie's, I could already smell the tension in the New Year's air. It reeked like the awful aftershave that my dad saved for such an occasion, and it triggered a stomachache in me faster than a Steak 'n Shake Double Chocolate Fudge Sippable Sundae and Triple Steakburger combo.

I wanted to go into Mara's room while she dressed, to apologize for leaving her alone with our psycho dad. But I was also afraid that if I left my bedroom, there would be some sort of Dad/Anna communication/confrontation, and I wasn't up for that.

Maybe it doesn't sound like much to have your dad get angry a lot of the time when you don't expect it, which then makes you always kind of expect it. Yelling is better than hitting, right? I guess. Probably. It may be less physically painful in the obvious outward sense, but inside it eats away at me. The constant hesitation around him, the loud, cutting way he drops an insult or threat, and the worst piece: the way he doesn't seem to care about anyone around him at all (who would yell like that when they saw their little girl asleep on the couch?) makes him much more likable to me when he's not around than when he is.

Drawers slammed louder than normal, and I knew the annual Rosh Hashanah explosion was starting its predinner build. It's a wonder I haven't renounced my Judaism, what with the horrific association my dad has given me. Every year there's a glimmer of hope that my dad will get sick or decide not to go at all. But every year he goes, as if he's doing my mom some favor. Not because it's a celebration and it's family and you just go to these things and you sort of dread it but then you like it because it's fun to see people you don't see very often and it's interesting to practice rituals that our people have been practicing for thousands of years and because *this is what people do.*

Unless that person is my dad. Tonight promises extra weirdness considering, with the separation and all, my dad technically *shouldn't* be there.

A tiny knock on my door made me jump, but my dad would never knock in a tiny way. Mara peeked her head in, and I waved her into my bedroom. She wore a hand-me-down dress of mine, a wrap dress I bought with my birthday money one year because someone on *Project Runway* made a wrap dress, and I had to have one. Weird to think of me ever having to have a dress, but this one was pretty cute. Plum purple with three-quarter-length sleeves, edged in the same lavender as the coordinating belt. Mara's hair hung down around her face in long, loose curls, and I detected a dab of lip gloss.

"You look really nice," I told her.

"You don't. What are you going to wear?" She skipped over to my closet. I almost said there was nothing in there so don't bother. Was I changing my mind? Could I go and endure the humiliation of the relative inquisition along with the unbearable, inevitable agro car ride?

"This is . . . okay, right?" Mara pulled out a god-awful dress that made me look like a box wrapped for a 90th birthday gift.

"Not so much." I cringed. Mara continued to sift through my slim closet pickings. "God, no offense, Anna, but you don't have anything nice to wear. I'm not saying you don't look okay when you just get dressed for normal, but there's nothing in here that says 'Rosh Hashanah.'"

I wanted to tell her that I was thankful that none of my clothes said "Rosh Hashanah," but because, well, how dorky would that be? But I let her enthusiasm to help go on long enough. It was time to be a crappy big sister.

"Hey, look, Mara, can you get out of my closet for a minute?"

"Maybe if you put this with this?" I couldn't see what glamorous findings she contemplated, but I knew there was nothing in there Mara could salvage on her own. It made me think I'd be an excellent candidate for a makeover show, except that I'd probably heave all over the preppy plaids and blazers the hosts picked out for me. Plus, then I'd have to go on TV and tell my story.

So far I've lost over twenty pounds, and none of my clothes fit me anymore.

That's wonderful, Anna Bloom. How'd you do it?

I spent three weeks in a mental hospital!

Uh . . .

That's also how I got my delightfully ghostly glow. Not seeing the sun will do that to you.

Right. Well, hmmmm. What do you think of paisley?

Maybe not.

"Hey, Mara, really, come over here for a second."

Mara finally popped out of my closet, a determined look on her face as she eyed my dresser. "You need to put some nicer clothes on. We're leaving in ten minutes, and I don't want Dad to get all pissy."

I envied Mara for the way she dealt with my dad's moods. She didn't seem to internalize it like I did. She could make fun of it easily (not to his face, but to me after the bomb finished detonating), like cracking jokes about him having his period and how we should get him some Aleve. She was even able to stand up to him in a juvenile way, with an eye roll or an annoyed sigh, which sometimes could make him angrier, to which she would just respond with an even bigger eye roll and louder sigh. Me? My dad starts to elevate his voice, and my gut flips on its side.

"He'll no doubt find something to get pissy about whether I'm ready or not. It's a Jewish holiday, after all," I said.

"What is it about the High Holidays that gets his nuggets in a knot?"

"Nuggets in a knot?"

"I read it in a book."

"Nice. Anyway, I have no idea what gets Dad's nuggets all knotty about the Jewish holidays. Or everything else."

"Maybe he's a Nazi," Mara contemplated.

"Are there also Nazis in this nugget knotting book?"

"No. Just cute boys and intrigue. Unless one of the cute boys is a Nazi . . ."

"Come here, please." I patted the corner of my bed, indicating Mara should sit instead of continuing to edge toward my dresser. She leaned on a corner, just barely, and smoothed her dress. This was Mara's way of communicating that she was not giving up on finding my perfectly Jewish holiday–suitable outfit somewhere if I just gave her free rein of my bedroom. "I have to tell you something."

"Are you pregnant?" Mara expelled loudly and stood up, both terror and fascination in her voice.

"You need to turn off ABC Family once in a while," I told her as I edged my way off the bed and rested my bass on the floor against my nightstand.

At that moment, before I was able to tell Mara I was abandoning her for the night, my door swung open. There stood my dad, wearing an argyle blue-and-yellow sweater vest over a blue button-down shirt. His cologne wafted into my sanctum.

"You're not ready, Anna?" His voice was on edge, but I was surprised to hear a little hesitation. Was he trying to be a more decent human being? Did he realize he was soon to be officially less a member of our family? Or was he afraid to set off his recently crazy daughter? Or, worst of all, was he saving his wrath for the after-dinner drive?

And why didn't my mom already tell him? Why was it put upon me? Just because they're separating doesn't mean she's not still my mom and obligated to do mommish things.

I panicked and reacted in the way my body chose (I have so little control over this mushy shell): I started to cry. Surprised at myself for the unexpected emotion, I put my hands over my eyes to mask, yet add, to the drama. In the psychedelic darkness, as I pressed my fingers tighter into my eyes, I knew these tears weren't sincere. Sure, I was upset—sad that Mara had to go it alone, scared of my dad's reaction once I told him I wasn't going, but my usual defense mechanism was to internalize it all. Pack the terror in my tummy and hate myself and everything around me in my head.

Those tears were a gift. A tool to make my dad feel guilty, or at least confused. I spoke quickly, so words spilled out in one long, tearstained sentence, "I can't go because I don't have anything to wear because I've lost all this weight and nothing fits and nothing looks good on me and all of the relatives are going to be there looking at me telling me how nice I look but also thinking I'm a freak because I just got out of a mental hospital and what are they going to say about that so they won't say anything and I'll just feel like shit all night."

I never swore in front of my dad, I don't think. He never seemed to hold back the profanity during his tirades, but it was different coming from my mouth. Even though I was a blathering, blubbering fool, I didn't feel like a terrified, blathering, blubbering fool. It felt like I was channeling my Lakeland friends.

Get some points, Anna.

All you have to do is cry, and they give you a shitload of points.

If they think you're expressing your emotions, you'll be a Level III in no time.

At Lake Shit I was a Level III. I actually expressed real emotions because I was doing so in front of people, my friends, who genuinely cared about me.

In real life there are no Levels.

But instead of crumbling inside, I used my emotion to my advantage. I expressed true sentiments—who could argue against my reasons?—and combined them with an overdramatic emotional outburst, sure to melt the hearts of even the most horrid fathers.

And it worked.

"Well, fine. Okay. Mara, five minutes." Dad tapped his wrist, where there wasn't actually a watch to tap, and closed the door, quieter than how he entered.

Mara pouted at me.

"I know," I said, waterworks instantly over. "I suck. I'm a sucky sister. I can make it up to you."

Mara looked at me incredulously. "How?"

"You can have anything in my closet." She smacked me on my arm. "Ow! But deserved."

Now Mara fully sat down on my bed, and I nudged next to her so our arms touched. "Maybe it won't be so bad. You'll get to sit at the kiddie table."

"Yeah, I guess. And Eric's pretty funny." Eric is one of the cousins we like. He's a freshman in high school and a total screwup. Not in the I-just-got-out-of-a-mental-hospital way, but in an I-can-barely-make-Ds, class-clown, regular-fixture-in-the-principal's-office way. Why did that sound so much cooler?

"What are you going to tell them about me?" I asked. I hadn't thought about how Mara might have to explain things with me gone.

"What do you want me to tell them?"

Good question. I sat for a minute and weighed my choices: honesty, half truths, or full-on lies. Did it even matter? I probably wouldn't see most of them until Passover in the spring. "Why don't you tell them that I didn't feel well tonight. And about the hospital, if that comes up, say you don't want to talk about it. Do you want to talk about it?"

"Not really. I wasn't there, so there's not much for me to talk about anyway."

"Cool. And what about the car ride? What are you going to do?"

"I'll bring my iPod and turn it up as loud as it goes. And close my eyes so I can't see Dad almost hitting a million cars."

How did Mara come out so well-adjusted, and I some overweight basketcase?

Through the door, my dad called, "Let's go."

I put my hand on top of Mara's and said, "Godspeed, my child." She whipped her hand away, but smiled and bounded out of my room.

After the sound of the automatic garage door buzzed through the house, I knew they were gone.

I was free for the next two hours at least. I texted Tracy, but no response meant she was working. I thought about calling Eleanor or Meredith or maybe even Tucker, but what would I say? They were probably out. Plus, I'd have to explain why I wasn't at school again, and I wasn't up for that.

I decided to finish my collage, the one I started before I went to Lake Shit, worked on minimally while at Lake Shit, and might as well complete now that I'm home from Lake Shit. This should be some amazing, symbolic, inspiring piece of art, but it still looked like a bunch of random people with poorly drawn noses interspersed with even more random objects, culminating in one giant, noncohesive and, if I do say so myself, butt-ugly mess on the page.

I needed music for inspiration, but I don't like listening to my iPod when no one else is home, just in case someone breaks into the house or the smoke detector goes off. My CDs just confused me; I'm sure I still love the same music I loved before I was institutionalized (God, have I used that word before? That sounds horrible), but none of it felt right for my current mood. Was I really different? Wrong? Weird? Off? The goal was to *get well,* right? And now I was acting to get out of family plans, abandoning my sister, hiding things from my best friend, and avoiding writing the first guy I might actually have been in love with.

I clicked my stereo over to the radio. Instantly (annoyingly? Prophetically?) a Doors song aired, one I knew by sound but not by name. Justin would know it, would envy the independence of a moment where I could listen to his favorite band, be in my safe place, and have the freedom to eat better food than hospital slop.

Then why is it that I envy him? And everyone locked up with him?

My unfinished collage stared pathetically from my desk. It was like someone else made it, chose the subject, designed the layout. It wasn't me. I mean, of course it *was* me, but it wasn't the me I am now.

Who that is, I don't know.

It was like my bedroom: What once was mine really proved to never be mine because my parents could choose at any moment to do with it what they wanted. And they did. They pink-washed it. As many posters as I put back on the walls, it's still not my old room with the circus border and the lived-in-for-sixteen-years feeling that couldn't be replaced. Although, it *was* replaced with a coat of Pepto-Bismol paint and a careless rip of my posters. The message was loud and clear: We own you, Anna, and we'll do what we think is best for you whether you like it or not.

I grabbed the stapler off my desk and started slamming staples into my half-finished collage. Actors' faces became replaced with metallic bars, legs held together even better than with a chastity belt. This wasn't their beautiful world where they told everyone how to look perfect; this was me telling them to stay put and leave me the hell alone.

After the stapling, I scooped up a sickly-green colored pencil from the dregs in my drawer and started scribbling. The addition turned these lovely starlets into gashed-up zombies.

That wasn't enough.

I was finished with the collage, though. The assignment was fulfilled, where I could see it was *art*. So what next?

I took the colored pencil over to the hugely blank pink wall next to my bed, the wall that used to be so complete with my posters, magazine clippings, and randomly found Anna crap that it was like the wrapping paper for my soul.

Scribble. Scratch. The green pencil left an undetectable smudge on the new impervious pink, less so than even the pee stain remainder on the carpet. Colored pencils wouldn't do.

I jumped up, fueled now by the rush of creation, and dug through my desk drawer until I found a fresh, unopened box of thick black Sharpies. I had bought them during that killer back-to-school time, when you're sick to your stomach at the back-to-school ads that have to start in July, but can't resist the amazing deals.

Now I had a reason to use them.

Pop! The cap tugged off with a satisfying yank, and the familiar whiff of permanence wafted at me. This wasn't your thin- or medium-grade Sharpie. We're talking fat, industrial strength, wide tip with a metallic holster. I could probably have sniffed that marker until my brain fried and my parents had to put me in a—

I cleared the useless thought and hopped onto my bed. In a prime spot in the dead center of my wall, I started to draw. A slow, deliberate line at first—this was permanent marker after all—but when I felt how easy it was, how the Sharpie would actually go where *I* wanted it to go, I controlled it, my hand moved faster. In a grand, sweeping motion, I managed a pretty decent four feet tall circle. With three quick slashes, I scrawled the iconic A.

And then it was Anarchy.

Truthfully, I didn't have a clue about the principles or the political beliefs of an anarchist or what life would be like under anarchist rule. But what did that matter? I'd seen the symbol on enough punker t-shirts and old punk albums that I knew it had something to do with how I felt tonight. Maybe I couldn't be controlled as much as people wanted to control me. Maybe if I let go of my fears more, of stomachaches and food issues and what my dad's voice sounds like when he's angry, of being a "punk" or an "art kid" or a "fat kid" or a "mental hospital kid."

Maybe if I could just let go of those expectations and disappointments, life wouldn't be as complicated. The tub of Manic Panic's After Midnight Blue called to me from beneath the sink, where it hid ever since I bought it last year on a whim. I've always been too wussy to use it, and I considered dyeing the blue streak I'd wanted tonight.

But, no. Not quite ready. Maybe one anarchist step at a time.

After I contemplated anarchy a little longer (I felt like I should write a college essay: What Anarchy Means to Me), I decided—what the hell—to write Justin a letter.

Even the chaos of anarchy couldn't keep Justin out of my head.

Dear Justin,

Sorry to hear our little tryst got you jammed in a desk. Hope it wasn't too boring. It sounds like you've got some cool new people there to hang with. Pretty soon the Shedd Aquarium will be but a distant memory.

My life is…ah, you don't want to hear about my life. There are way fewer rules, real pizza, and a lot more homework. I'm reading *Catcher in the Rye* for English. I like it a lot. I think you'd like it, too. Maybe. We never really talked about books, did we? I'd recommend it anyway.

Hope you get out soon. Maybe you can call me when you get out, and we can meet for coffee. Even though I don't drink it.

Signed,

Anna

I didn't send that one either.

———

I spent the rest of the night before my family came home reading *Catcher*. I was way ahead of the assigned pages, but Holden captivated me and I wanted to make sure everything turned out for him better than it did for my boy toy Simon in *Lord of the Flies*.

Holden talked about the Museum of Natural History in New York, which I assumed was like Chicago's Field Museum. The way he described it, how it always smelled like it was raining outside, even if it wasn't, almost made me cry it was so true. Museums had such a magical quality for me as a kid, but now I get hung up on the fact that those bones or pots or stuffed animals are so old and were once used by actual living people. I think Holden and I would have a good conversation about that.

Then Holden started talking with this lame girl, someone I couldn't understand at all why he liked because she was just some snob who only cared about her appearance. This lucky girl had Holden going on and on about how they should just go away together to a cabin in the woods and get random little small-town jobs and then get married and chop wood together. And this moronic girl was, like, are you kidding? How could she not see that this was the most romantic proposal anyone could possibly offer? The chance to be alone with another person, without the constraints and preconceptions of society . . . And not just with any person. With Holden Caulfield! I was getting borderline obsessed with this fictional dreamboy.

Then he said something that was a little too real.

He was going on about how much he hated movies, which I could kind of understand, even though I love them. And then he said that he was glad the atomic bomb was invented and that if there were another war he'd volunteer to sit right on top of it.

Holden was talking suicide.

Or was it just death? Was it the way I thought passively about dying, how sometimes I wanted to die so badly that I'd just wish for it, but I wouldn't seek it out?

Is that how Holden felt?

Either way, it hit a little too close to my anarchy-encrusted home.

I heard the door open downstairs and loud voices (well, voice), which caused me to jump off my bed and whip through my stack of posters lying on the closet floor in poster purgatory. The largest one I owned was a Clash *London Calling* print, probably six feet by six feet. While I was disgusted that my parents didn't bother to remove the Fun-Tac from the backs of my posters before they decided to turn them into a sad poster sandwich, it made it easier and faster for me to throw the poster up onto my wall.

I may have been ready for a little anarchy, but I wasn't ready to share it with anyone.

Running footsteps, Mara's, bounded up the stairs, and I thought they'd make it to my door. They didn't. Instead, her bedroom door slammed with a rattle. The yelling from downstairs was muffled enough that I couldn't hear the context, but it didn't matter. Every fight was the same: one-sided and pointless.

With people back in the house, I switched off my stereo and twisted my earbuds into my ears. To match my new/old poster, I found The Clash on my iPod and allowed them to block out the post–New Year's celebration below.

After I finished my other homework (rockin' Friday night), I lay in bed and flicked through my shuffle, clicking uncommittedly from song to song.

That's when the party brought itself upstairs. They didn't even share the bedroom anymore, yet they still had to fight there. Just like the good ol' days. Between songs, my dad's shouting sounded its fullest, but even during the loudest, fastest songs I could find, I could still feel the vibrations of his voice. I unplugged the buds from my head and switched to my full-sized can headphones, complete with squishy protective barrier ear cushions.

I could still hear my dad.

I flung the headphones off and listened through the walls. It really was the same fight, about my mom not supporting him (at Rosh Hashanah dinner?) and how her sisters are bitches. Really juvenile. In fact, when I thought about it, my dad was kind of like a little kid, repeating over and over what he wanted in the most obnoxious way possible.

But why didn't my mom say anything? If he was just a big little kid, why couldn't she stand up for herself? Why, after all these years, couldn't she just shut him up? Especially now that their demise was official?

I was tired of both of them. The sound of my dad's voice shook through me, but the silence of my mom shook just as hard. He was the same uninterested father, shitty husband, and selfish man he'd always been. And she was the same, too sweet, too passive victim that she'd always been.

I was different.

Before I could stop myself, I pounded my fist hard on the wall. One good, solid, loud punch.

The noise stopped.

I waited for some backlash, for my dad to start screaming about me, and then charge into my room and let me have it. That didn't happen.

Silence.

Some movement.

Their bedroom door opening.

Footsteps out and down the stairs.

The end.

Because of me.

I slipped the headphones back over my ears and put on some re-laxing music to help me fall asleep. I'm pretty sure I heard a knock on my door, but it wasn't loud enough or desperate enough to war-rant getting out of bed.

Sleep took over, and I dreamed I was doing yoga with Rodney Yee at a Passover seder.

DON'T SAY I NEVER GAVE YOU ANYTHING

I woke up the next morning with a start. Nothing actually woke me up, but I sat up in bed quickly, knowing something was differ-ent. Instead of putzing around in my room hoping to avoid my family members at breakfast, I pulled on some pajama bottoms and answered the call of clinking cereal spoons downstairs. There I saw my typical family formation: Mom and Mara, which I was semi-relieved about. I may have had a moment of wall-pounding clarity, but it was still easier to not deal with my dad. I wasn't re-ally up for confrontation, just change.

The breakfast mood was somber, as it often is the night after a dad explosion. Mom's eyes were particularly shrunken by the swollen crying puffs that surrounded them. Mara didn't even look at the cereal she shoved into her mouth but kept her eyes firmly planted on a Robert Pattinson article in her *J-14*.

As much as I expected a surprised, yet delighted, greeting from my mom, at seeing my bright and shining face at breakfast, I would have also settled for a weak "good morning." I got neither, so I started the breakfast niceties.

"Good morning. Did you guys bring me some challah?" Mara looked at me with wide, serious eyes and shook her head no in a tight, rapid manner, like a warning not to ask stupid questions.

I looked over at my mom, and saw the only part of her moving were the tears streaming down her face and into her coffee cup. If someone else drank that coffee, would they forever be sad?

"You okay, Mom?" I asked.

Another voiceless headshake, and I glanced over at Mara to see if she had any answers. "What's going on?" I asked them both, looking from Mom to Mara, then back again.

"It's . . . your dad," my mom began.

"Oh my God. Is he dead?" Was it sick that was the first thing that popped into my head? Was it sicker that part of me felt relieved that we'd never have to talk about last night—or any other night—ever again?

"Anna!" Mara gasped. So, not dead.

"No, thank God." My mom looked up at the ceiling, possibly to actually thank God, or maybe to squelch the flowing tears. "He's, um"—she cleared her throat—"moving out tomorrow."

I had waited for those words for a good chunk of my life, after I started having friends with divorced families. It seemed ideal to me, to only live with my mom and sister, not wonder when my dad would be home, and if he were, what his mood would be, what one of us would do to upset him, to not live on the edge like that but have the comfort of home that the word suggests. I shouldn't have been shocked. We knew it was coming.

But finally hearing those words felt differently than I expected.

My dad was moving out.

My dad.

My dad who let me sit in the front seat of his car. Who went on the highest water slides at the Wisconsin Dells. Who brought me to R movies way before the appropriate age suggestion. Who could make me laugh when I hit my knee and ask if I had "knee-monia." Who would go to Toys R Us before Hanukkah and come home with a garbage bag—sized shopping bag filled with lumps of unknown toys that we didn't ask for, and Christmas wrapping sticking out from the sides because it was more plentiful than Hanukkah paper.

My dad who I kind of looked like when he was a kid.

My dad.

Who I kind of hated most of the time but kind of loved, too.

I wrapped my arms around Mom's back. She stood up to face me and enveloped me in her mom arm cradle. Mara scooted her chair out, ran around the table, and joined the circle.

As good and right as it always felt with just the three of us, it still felt wrong for my dad to go.

After the initial shock wore off, I went upstairs to call Tracy.

Her voice sounded groggy, the blast of wrestling from her enormous TV deafening over the phone.

"Turn the TV down, T!" I yelled.

"What? What time is it?" She smacked pasty, gross sounds with her tongue.

"It's, I don't know, ten?"

"In the morning?" From the TV came a guttural scream and a "holy cow!" from, I suspected, the announcer.

"No, T, it's ten in the afternoon. Yes in the morning! What are you doing?"

"I was having a marathon of my favorite Steve Austin moments, and I guess I fell asleep." How she could sleep with that shouting and pummeling is beyond me.

"Hey, can you turn it down?" Much fumbling and swearing ensued, until all I heard on the other end was more morning mouth noises. Not the most pleasant trade. "I need to talk to you. My dad is moving out."

"Yeah, I know, you told me. Sucks," she sympathized.

"No, like officially tomorrow."

"Whoa. Is that a good thing or a bad thing?"

"I know! I don't know! Can you come over? My mom doesn't want me to go out today. She said she needs her girls around, which I guess I get. You can be one of her girls."

"Dang. I work at the Slut Shop all day—their Biggest Boobs Yet Sale, or some shit. But I can come over tonight."

"You could sleep over, if you want. I don't think my mom would mind."

"Sounds good. Hang in there."

"T?"

"Yeah?"

"You're going to turn the wrestling back on as soon as we get off the phone, aren't you?"

"Yeah." And before we even hung up, I heard a scream and a crunch.

THE REVEAL

Mara and I spent most of the day on the couch watching old Disney movies together. I tried not to be in my teenaged brain, to let the kiddie memory innocence and nostalgia take over, but it was hard not to notice how skinny all of the so-called princesses were and how fat or ugly the baddies looked. And what's with all the butt chins on the guys? Mara and I counted seventeen butt chins in *The Little Mermaid, Beauty and the Beast,* and *Pocahontas* alone. There may even have been one in *Finding Nemo*.

"Remember that time"—Mara began through chomps of microwave popcorn. She handed me the bag as she continued—"we were at Disney World and we were on the Peter Pan ride—"

I finished the story for her, "And you dropped Jim Bob in the middle of the bedroom scene?" Dropping Jim Bob in the bedroom scene probably sounds salacious, but Jim Bob was Mara's beloved stuffed bear and the bedroom scene opened up the Peter Pan ride, where Peter comes and takes Wendy and her brothers to Never Never Land. "You screamed like a psycho the whole ride about how Wendy was going to steal Jim Bob and give him to the Lost Boys, and you kept trying to jump out of the flying ship."

"I was five!" she yelled and threw a piece of popcorn, hitting my cheek. I picked it up and popped it in my mouth.

"Then Dad went up to one of the workers while Mom and I tried to console you. Remember how I was, like, 'We'll buy you a stuffed Pooh,' and I couldn't stop laughing because I said 'stuffed poo.' Why would they name a bear after a turd? And then two minutes later Dad came back with Jim Bob."

"I wonder how many times a day that happens at Disney World."

"I wonder." Our day was peppered with memories, most of them somehow involving Dad. For as little as he was around, he still made it into our kid story brain vaults.

At around 4:00, I decided to peel myself off the couch and take a shower. Refreshed, if not a little logy from loafing all day, I knocked gently on my mom and dad's—or was it just my mom's now?—bedroom door to see how she was doing. I didn't hear her answer, but I didn't hear any sobs, either, which I took as a good sign. Gently, I turned the knob and peeked inside. My mom was on top of her covers, sleeping with a wrinkled expression around her eyes. I crept out of the room backwards and closed her door unnoticed.

Downstairs, Mara sorted through the mail she had just re-trieved, searching for a new magazine. Today's bounty included

Mom's *EW* and Mara's *Seventeen*. Mara's thing is she likes to preview each magazine page at a rapid pace, and then she reads every single page from cover to cover, even the ads. Then comes the dismantling, where she carefully cuts out her favorite pictures and applies them to a) her walls, b) her assignment notebook, or c) her locker. All in a very orderly fashion. She's a real wiz with a pair of funky scrapbooking scissors.

"You got some letters." She held them out to me as she whipped through the magazine pages.

There were three letters, all with the Lakeland return address in the corner. One from Matt O., and not one, but two from Justin. He took the time to write me three letters, and I had yet to send even one. In my defense, I had *written* several letters to Justin, but they were on their way to the recycling center to reincarnate into a new cereal box or a 70–80 percent postconsumer-fiber notebook. Why not 100 percent, I ask you.

Not wanting Mara to read over my shoulder, as if she could peel her eyes away from her beloved mag, I carried the letters to my bedroom and closed the door undetectably. I felt like Gollum trying to keep people (or, you know, hobbits) away from his Precious. So which Precious, I mean *letter,* should I read first?

To add to the drama I created in my head, I naturally began with Matt O.'s.

Dear Anna,

You're never going to believe this, but I'm finally getting out of this shitstain in a week or two. They're moving me into placement, which is kind of like a boarding school for fuckups. But I'll actually get to go outside and walk around and go to real school (joy of joys), and I still have the added bonus of only seeing my parents at the holidays! The assy thing is that it's downstate, and they're taking me straight from here so I won't be able to stop by and say hello to you. But maybe they won't have such strict phone rules, and I can call you. Justin said you gave him your number, so I'm putting it in my address book in case.

Life sure is going different for me. Hope you're doing good and you haven't forgotten us yet.

Love,
Matt O.

Wow. Lake Shit without Matt O. would be like Hogwarts without Hagrid. I wonder if he'll miss it like I missed it, or if he'll just be so grateful to be out that he'll never look back. That would be so sad. Not for him, but if a guy who's been there for six months can get over it just like that and I was only there for three weeks and I can't figure out how I fit in here or there . . . Pathetic.

Why was I thinking about going back again? Ah, yes. Justin.

The two letters teased me to open them. But which one first? The postmarks were the same date, so there was no order in which to read them. Maybe it was one of those things where the person writes at the top of one letter, "Read this first" and "Read this second." I eeny-meenied until I picked one. Carefully, I ripped open the gummy flap, trying to envision Justin's tongue licking the envelope closed. But when I pulled out and unfolded the piece of paper inside, I recognized the bubbly, girly handwriting. Sandy.

Dear Anna,

I am so sick of Lake Shit. If it were not for my new roommate, Dania, I'd kill myself. How, I don't know, since we don't even have springs in our beds, but I'd find a way. Dania isn't as great as you, of course, but she's funny and not boring and not completely crazy, which here makes a good roommate.

The kick-ass news is that I finally get to go home. I might even be out by the time you get this letter. Man, I can't wait to eat pizza and see Derek. Hope you weren't confused by Justin's name on the envelope. Remember how I'm not allowed to send letters as part of my "treatment" because I lied about being pregnant and everything? Assholes.

Maybe we can get together when I get out? Reminisce about looking out the window and shit ☺

Gotta go. Community time! Gag.

Hugs,

Sandy

Even Sandy loves Dania. If she does, then of course Justin does. There's a reason to go back to Lake Shit: Kick Dania's ass. Not that I've ever kicked anyone's ass or had the desire to kick ass or have my ass kicked. It's just, why does an Anna replacement have to be there? I haven't replaced them in my real life, have I? It's not like I've gone out and found a new roommate with big hair and really ugly overalls.

Annoyed, I ripped open the second letter, assuming it was a PS from Sandy. But there was the scratchy Justin font, and my annoyance melted away.

Dear Anna,

I haven't gotten any letters from you yet. Maybe they're still holding my mail since the big hallway showdown. I did get a couple letters last week, though, just not from you.

Maybe they're only holding the ones from you? I'd really like to know how you're doing. Matt O. said he heard from you and you weren't doing so great. I don't know how you couldn't be when you're not here. This place sucks. Obvious, I know, but I want out. They keep telling me soon, but . . .

Nothing new here. Same old/new people. Too crowded at lunch, so we have to wait in line longer and get less time to eat. There are so many girls now, not like when you were here, that they've segregated the cafeteria tables. I'm so glad you were here when you were here.

Sorry to get sappy. I'm climbing the walls here. I have an appointment with the Birdcage (in case you have forgotten any Lake Shit lingo, the Birdcage is my shrink. Your shrink was Dr. Asshole. Although, I hope you have been able to forget him. Erase him from your mind now!)

They just knocked for me to go.

Justin

PS I had an idea. You can write me a letter through Sandy or Matt O., and then they can give it to me like Sandy had me do. Just a suggestion.

God, he was so cute and sweet. Why wasn't he real? It's as though he was a character in a book that was somehow communicating directly to me. Or maybe more like a person in a parallel universe where we existed simultaneously but never in the same space. Because even though we were once together, we will never be like that again.

I thought about writing him back in a letter sent to Matt O.— to make it look like maybe it was just the crappy Lake Shit system and not the crappy *me* not getting letters to him, but I still didn't know what to say. Everything I tried to write came out so defeated.

We'll never be the same together.

You'll forget me as soon as you return to your real life and realize I was just the slim pickings you get in a mental hospital. Chubby girls don't fit with gorgeous, tall, perfect guys like you.

Feeling hopeless, I left the letters on my bed and opened my door. My mom, swollen-eyed, left her bedroom at the same time.

"What a day," she said, and she managed a small smile. As we walked down the stairs, the doorbell rang.

It was Tracy, holding a massive sheet cake from the grocery store with "Happy 46th, Bob" written in frosting across the top.

"You have the wrong house, ma'am," I told her. "It's my forty-seventh birthday."

Tracy pushed her way past me and dropped the cake onto the kitchen table. "I got this for five bucks! The guy at the bakery counter said the people never came to pick it up."

"Their loss is our cake," I enthused.

My mom smiled at that one, and Mara managed to pull her eyes away from a cheeseball pinup to admire Tracy's find.

"So what should we have with our cake?" my mom asked, and she rustled through our menu drawer until she came up with six menus for various pizza, Chinese, and Thai restaurants.

I watched my mom, Mara, and T weigh their choices and recapped the day in my head: Dad leaving, Disney movies, Matt O., Sandy, Justin. Then I shook my head as hard as I could in an attempt to erase and reboot. At least for dinnertime, I wanted to pretend that my life was normal.

BEDTIME CONFESSIONS

After some Pad Thai, a piece of cake, and a viewing of *Willy Wonka*, the four of us walked upstairs. Mara, instead of turning into her own room, asked, "Mom, can I sleep with you tonight?" which both warmed and broke my heart.

Tracy and I spent the next half hour laughing hysterically while trying to use the foot pump to blow up the air mattress. No matter how many times we stamped the pump up and down, the bed didn't seem very full. Then Tracy decided, "Ssshhh. There must be a leak," and she crawled around each side of the mattress until she found the tiniest hissing sound. We were thrilled to be able to use the repair patch included with the bed, and I carefully peeled off the adhesive backing and pressed the patch onto the miniscule hole. After that, Tracy pretended she was Stone Cold Steve Austin and yelled out absurd affirmations, like "I'm a machine!" and "You can't mess with the pecs!" while she pumped the bed to its fullest state.

At about eleven o'clock we settled into our respective beds and turned out the lights. Not that we were going to sleep, but there is something about the lights off and lying in close proximity to each other that makes you want to talk. And not about the normal things you always talk about. Deeper philosophical issues and questions about the future and brilliant observations, such as Tracy's, "It would really suck if farts came out in little colored rainbows, depending on what you ate."

"What would your fart look like right now?"

"I didn't fart. Why, do you smell something?"

Which reminded me of the chairs at Lakeland in the Day Room, the ones that made an embarrassing fart sound no matter how depressed you were or how serious the situation. So I told Tracy about them.

"What else?" she prompted. And because the nighttime can make your mind fuller and your mouth looser, I talked. I told her what happened when I got to the hospital, how I was stupid enough to tell them that I sometimes thought about killing myself and when they asked me when was the last time I thought about it I answered sarcastically, "Right now because my parents just put me in a mental hospital." I told her how that statement screwed me, how because of it I had to wear pajamas 24/7 and sleep on a bed in the hallway and have someone with me at all times, even when I tried to go to the bathroom. I told her about my day, my schedule, the different meetings: Community, where we covered floor business; Group, where we had group therapy; School, where we were supposed to do the work they sent us from home, but some people just made out; Physical Therapy, which was working out on exercise equipment without getting a chance to shower afterward; Free Time, where depending on what level you were, you could control the channels on the TV or radio, but mostly you just played cards; and Play Therapy, where the lady with the giant hair, Big 'Do, made us pretend things to supposedly help us get better. I told Tracy about the rules, none of which I learned until my fellow patients told me about them: no touching, no talking in the halls, no relationships of the romantic sort, no dropping your pillow in Relaxation, no raising your hand. I demonstrated the two fingers out, not up, way we were supposed to get people's attention, but it was dark and I think T was too intent on listening to notice.

"What were the other people like?" she asked, but she didn't have to. Describing every piece of Lakeland brought me back to those halls and rooms, and I could see all of my friends and inmates waiting on the farting brown and green chairs of the Day Room for me to introduce them to Tracy.

I named each person I met while there: Sandy, my roommate, whose fake pregnancy and subsequent fake babydoll meant I was forced to wake up every night for feedings and changings ("Did you hate her?" Tracy asked. "Nah, she was a good friend," I answered. I hope that didn't somehow make T feel bad); Matt O., the lifer who has his very own treatment plan because he'd been there so long; Sean, with his scum-stache and ability to escape from boarding schools ("Sounds kind of interesting," Tracy mused. "Think I would like him?"); Victor, who sold drugs to help pay for his mom's cancer treatment; Tanya, the bitchy girl in the adjoining room who was always in trouble, so she never gained privilege to eat in the cafeteria ("Was that a big deal? Eating in the cafeteria?" Tracy asked. "It was kind of fun, actually, one of the only places where we were allowed to talk to one another like normal people." "Was the food any good?" she asked. "Not at all," I answered); Phil, who we called Shaggy because he looked like a miniature version of Shaggy from *Scooby-Doo* ("I think Shaggy's kind of cute," Tracy said. "You wouldn't think that about this one. He was a perverted pyromaniac." "And those are bad things?"); Bobby, who was super young and reminded me of Mara; Abby, Tanya's roommate, who had seizures and supposedly sometimes talked as though possessed by the devil ("No!" Tracy whisper-yelled. "Yes," I whisper-yelled back. "Did you see it?" she asked. "A seizure? Yes. Demonic possession? Afraid not." "Bummer"); Lawrence, the giant freak of a Satan worshipper who managed to become obsessed with Abby and wanted to make her his bride ("Are you making this up?" "I couldn't if I wanted to"). Then I listed some of the workers and some of the kids I didn't know as well but were on the floor with me.

At around one a.m., my mouth dry from storytelling, my mind wondering if Tracy had heard enough, she asked quietly, "Was that everyone?"

I focused on the halo around my window shades made from the street lights outside. Why hadn't I told Tracy about Justin? Was I afraid that if I did, any of the magic that still remained would poof away into reality? That she'd see how we have absolutely no chance for a future and how part of me desperately clung to the idea that we do? That when he gets out, he'll come straight to my door and we'll embrace like long-time movie lovers, and then we'll kiss for three days straight, only coming up for air for some Cap'n Crunch to restore the energy needed for kissing?

Because part of me truly wished for that. Maybe even believed it a little.

"Who's Justin?" Tracy, barely audible through my conflicting thoughts, asked.

"Are you reading my mind? How do you know about Justin?" I sounded accusatory and panicked.

"Calm thyself. I don't *know* about Justin. I saw his name on an envelope on your dresser. But I obviously now need to know about him, so dish."

And dish I did. I described the way his hair always sat in his perfect brown eyes, how he hid his fingers because he cut them off trying to help his dad with roofing and now his hand looked all shiny and fake as the stitched-on fingers healed, how he liked music like I did before his accident but couldn't listen to it anymore because it reminded him he couldn't play the bass so now he only listened to The Doors, how he tried to kill himself but failed because his hand was too screwed up to pull the trigger. I told her how beautiful he was to look at and how he smelled like soap and deodorant and how he liked when I talked about how women are betrayed by the media. He liked the way I looked and I didn't realize it and how I hatched a plan to kiss him on our field trip to the Shedd Aquarium and it turned out he had the same plan. I told her how when I left, I jumped up and grabbed him for one last kiss, not knowing if we'd ever kiss—or see—each other again. And I told her how he wrote me letters, and I didn't know what they meant and how I hadn't written him back yet because I didn't know what to say to him now that I'm out but he's still in.

"I don't really know where I belong anymore, Trace."

"I don't think any of us do, Anna. We just have to try and be happy that we're here. I am."

"You're what?"

"Happy I'm here. Right now. With you."

"Are you getting mushy on me?"

"I couldn't possibly be as mushy as you and Justin." She emphasized his name in a middle school, lovey-dovey way.

I repeated his name with a pin-up dreaminess. "Justin."

"I can see pink flowers and hearts floating out of your mouth when you say that, you know."

"Uh-oh. I hope they don't send me to a hospital for that."

"I won't tell if you don't."

"Did you know that people actually sent me get well soon cards when I was at the hospital? How freakishly inappropriate."

"People can be pretty fucked up, Anna. Even those of us who have never been in a mental hospital."

We were quiet after that for a long time. I whispered, "Good night, T," into the silence, and it was answered with steady breathing. I nestled into my blankets, happy to be here for the first time since forever ago.

———

152

GOODBYE, BIG SCREEN

Tracy woke up early in order to work the Boobs Sale again. I rolled around in bed, pretending I could fall back asleep, but a welling sadness wouldn't let me. At first, I couldn't even remember why I was supposed to feel sad. It's like when you wake up after your grandpa dies, and you have those first few moments of normal, everyday thoughts, like, what am I going to have for breakfast? Did I study for that test? Am I getting my period soon? And then you realize, oh, my grandpa is dead. Then your gut clenches and you remember why your eyes were crustier than usual because you fell asleep crying last night.

This wasn't exactly that bad.

No one was dead in this scenario. Dad was just moving out, and my parents were separating. Last night while I helped Mom do the dishes, I asked her what that meant, separating, and why not just divorce. Does anyone really get back together when they separate? She looked as though I smacked her.

"The point is that it's a chance for us to try and work things out while not having to be in each other's faces all the time."

"What's to work out? The guy's a psycho. And he's never around enough to be in our faces. Except when he is."

"Anna, don't talk about your dad that way."

"I'm siding with you, Ma."

"This isn't about sides. This is about two people wanting to work things out."

She kept saying that: "Work things out." I couldn't understand what they could do, though, when my dad had some unpredictable anger management problems and my mom had wuss issues. Would they all of a sudden be different people, problems solved? I doubted it.

153

Maybe I should throw them into a mental hospital, so they could come out fixed. Like me. Right.

While my mom and Mara ate breakfast, I continued my chi or whatever with my boy, Rodney. I wonder if anyone ever calls him Rod? So phallic. And there he was in his tiny little yoga undies.

Once I got my brain to stop focusing on Rodney Yee's crotch, I began to relax and "let the mind-body meld," as he says. I think.

After I finished and dressed in slightly less pajama-like clothes, my mom decided we all needed to get out of the house. Since I still needed a better-fitting wardrobe and Mara always needed something that everyone else had, we went to the mall.

It was a beautiful fall day, the kind where everybody in Chicagoland should be outside grabbing every last bit of sunshine and warmth before the six months of winter hit. Then why was the mall so effin' crowded? Mom circled to find a close parking spot, but I suggested we give up and park in one of the secondary lots. The walk wasn't that far, and it made all the others look lazy as they drove around desperately trying to find the shortest distance between them and the gluttony.

Mara wasted no time finding a new pair of boots and some t-shirts at Field's, and I managed to find a pair of jeans and some black skinny-type pants that were unexpectedly flattering. My eyes were drawn to an obnoxiously fluorescent pink zip-up hoodie with randomly placed patches commanding people to "Have a nice day" and "Smile." I tried it on, and something about the loudness and color of it seemed to brighten up my face. Maybe the fluorescence reflected off the oiliness of my forehead that collected during the experimental jeans marathon, but it looked good in a pink, ironic kind of way. "Hey, Mara, what do you think of this?"

"You look totally cute!" she squealed.

Me? Totally cute? That was a switch. "Mom, can I get this?" She nodded with a forced smile, as if her mind were elsewhere. Which it probably was, what with the dissolution of her marriage and all. Maybe she'd feel better if she read one of my patches.

As we walked out of Field's, I noticed a couple leaning against a store window, the guy running his fingers through the girl's hair. I knew them. Just barely, but I was sure it was Bartleby and Nepa from Group. That sarcastic dickhead and the smart Indian girl who told him he didn't have any balls were standing very closely. And then they kissed. Soft, sweet kisses that turned into harder, more passionate ones, and, God, I was really staring.

Bartleby and Nepa? I guess nothing brings people together like good, old-fashioned psychotherapy. They were too busy groping to notice little ol' me. Which I was grateful for. If we started up a conversation at the mall, what would we have to talk about in Group? I kid. When I managed to peel my eyes away, I packed the vision into the back of my brain to ruminate on at another time.

After I picked out several nicely fitted t-shirts and harassed Tracy in the Boob Store's sale madness ("Excuse me, miss, do you have this in forty-six triple Q?"), we schlepped our way to the secondary lot, arms satisfyingly sore from lugging so many shopping bags. My mom's face even looked a little lighter, less consumed by thoughts of my dad and more consumed with being a consumer. The three of us sang and bopped along to an old B-52's song in the car on the ride home. A good time was had by all.

Until we arrived at our house.

First was the U-Haul truck we passed on our street with a familiar figure behind the driver's seat. Next was the gaping hole in the family room where our beloved big-screen TV once lived. Lastly, after my mom dropped all of her shopping bags and bounded up the stairs, was the open closet door, where all Dad had left behind was his formal wear and a few outdated button-downs.

My mom collapsed on her bed and sobbed. Mara and I, having followed her up the stairs, looked at each other with gulps and shrugs. How do you comfort your mom when your dad just moved out?

I warily sat down on her bed and reassuringly told her, "It'll be okay, Mom. We're still here."

Mara joined us on the bed and patted my mom's leg while she said, "We're better than Dad any day, Mom. He was barely here anyway, right? We'll never notice he's gone."

That made Mom cry harder, so Mara and I just sat there and tried not to say or do anything else insensitive. Finally, my mom sat up to grab a tissue and said, "I appreciate what you girls are trying to do. And of course I still have you." She stroked my cheek, and then Mara's. "Let's go downstairs and start dinner. I want to see if he left a note."

We helped Mom off the bed and walked down to the kitchen. After searching every counter, table, door, and wall, we concluded that Dad did not, indeed, leave a note.

"Why wouldn't he at least leave a note?" my mom asked, on the verge of breaking down again. She plunked herself into a kitchen chair, defeated.

"Maybe he didn't know what to say," Mara consoled her.

And right then I shivered. Me and my jerk dad had something in common.

I ran to my room and started writing.

Dear Justin,

Sorry it's taken me so long to write you. It hasn't been for lack of trying. I could re-wallpaper my room with the letters I haven't sent. Not really, but they would help cover up the crap paint job my parents did while I was at Lake Shit. Beware that you may have a new bedroom when you get home. Not that I talked to your parents or anything. Speaking of parents, did I mention my dad moved out? I don't really feel like talking about it, though.

So how are you? Yeah? Glad to hear it. Or not, depending on your answer.

Life outside of The Shit (nice new name, btw) is random. I'm better sitting through classes most of the time, but not all of the time. I'm in a new group that I've only seen a few times, although I did see two of the members making out at the mall (I don't think they saw me). Brought back some memories...

Let me know when you get out so we can hang or go for coffee or something. I think about you a lot. I miss you and, strangely, everybody else at Lake Shit. But you most for sure.

Better go do my homework. They actually expect that in real school.

Yours,

Anna

ENOUGH WITH THE STOMACH ALREADY

I woke Monday morning with a nervous stomach, and I considered fabricating some elaborate scheme where I told my mom I didn't want her to be alone and I'd come to work with her at the knit shop in case she needed a break. But I'd already missed (okay, skipped) school on Friday, and if I wanted some semblance of a regular life, I didn't want to spend it catching up on homework.

Besides, it's always kind of fun to wear new clothes. I yanked the tags off my new skinny(er) jeans, and a royal blue v-neck tee. The color brought out my dark brown eyes, which I think was a good thing. Although brown is the color of poo. Why do my eyes and hair have to be the same color as poo? Blonds and redheads, blue- and green-eyed people, they don't have to worry about someone writing a sonnet about their eyes and rhyming "I am so into you" with "your eyes are the color of sparkling poo."

I settled my mind into agreeing that bringing out my eyes was a good thing, that chocolate is also brown, and then I decided I needed earrings to complete my chocolaty, not poo-y, look.

I have this thing where if I *feel* the earrings in my ears, it makes me puke. The tugging of the ear holes all day as the dangling metal swings hither and yon is most disturbing. I seriously gag sometimes when I see Beyoncé wearing a pair of hole-stretching behemoths. Therefore, my earring collection is relatively lacking in anything remotely funky and consists solely of studs of varying colors and shapes. Red stars! Pink hearts! Blue diamonds! My jewelry box is a veritable Lucky Charms of boring earrings.

Except for one pair that I've never worn: a pair of silver aliens, the classic kind with a bulbous head and overexaggerated eyes, rested in a dusty corner of the box. I bought them on an alien high when my family visited Roswell, New Mexico. I picked them up, slipped the hooks through my ears, and swung my head. The pull was definitely there, but not quite to gagging proportions. I looked in the mirror. Somehow, just adding silver aliens to my ears framed my face and made me look different. If you ignored the fact that they were alien heads, one might say I looked a tad sophisticated. For me. It looked good. *I* looked good.

If you say you look good, is that like a jinx?

Breakfast was quiet, since it was just me and Mara. Dad was gone, which shouldn't have felt different since he was always gone at breakfast, but did feel different because I didn't know if he was ever coming back. Mom stayed in her room. I knocked on her door before I descended the stairs. "You okay, Mom?" I didn't want to open her door, with the selfish fear that I'd have to say something meaningful and encouraging. She answered through the door, "I'm fine," in a creaky voice. "Have a nice day at school." I wondered if there would ever be a moment of happiness in my life that wasn't punctuated by a pile of shit.

Mara was slightly blubbery at breakfast, heaving in rickety sighs between spoonfuls of Count Chocula. Again, I just wanted to deal with my own crap. It seemed so unfair that a week after I got out of a mental hospital I now had to be the mommy to my sister while my real mommy broke down behind closed doors.

And I'm the one on meds?

Mara tried to convince me that she needed to stay with Mom, but I told her the Poms squad needed her more. When I finally managed to get Mara to her bus stop, I decided I just wanted to be alone. But not in a lonely way. My Chucks were comfy, the sun was shining, and I had aliens in my ears.

I popped in my earbuds and shuffled my iPod. "Judy Is a Punk" assaulted my ears (in a good way) and added a dancy skip to my step. Before long, I was halfway to school and feeling light as a feather.

A tap on my shoulder forced me to pull the buds out of my ears. Alyssa from Spanish class walked next to me, breathing heavily, and said, "I called your name a bunch, but you didn't hear me. You were hauling ass."

"I was?" I didn't know my ass could haul.

As we walked, Alyssa and I had your basic we-only-know-each-other-from-Spanish-class convo, which consisted of us rehashing Great Moments in Spanish Class History. It passed the time, and we arrived at school in a few minutes.

It all felt so freakishly normal.

Tracy waited by my locker armed with an arsenal of hilarious stories of Boobs R Us. Before she could regale me, I informed her,

"It's official. Dad moved out. You will be devastated to learn he took the big-screen TV."

The contemplative look on T's face said it all.

"Don't say anything more, Tracy. I'll give you a minute." I patted her shoulder.

"Do you want to talk about it?" she asked.

"Not really."

"Good, because I have a tale of Glenda the Good Bitch." Glenda the Good Bitch* (*not her real name) was Tracy's workplace nemesis because she was always trying to take Tracy's sales. If Tracy helped a woman find twenty bras and spent an hour doing so, Glenda would say, "Oh, we have nail polish on sale for one dollar" and then swoop in and take the commission. A similar sitch happened yesterday, but Tracy wasn't having any of it.

"You should have been there, Anna. I went right up to her, stood on a kick stool because I needed to be in her face and that bitch is like eight feet tall, and I growled at her, 'Those tits are mine.' She surrendered, and I got the sale."

" 'Those tits are mine.' Brilliant."

The first bell rang. "Crap. I need to find something in the library," I said.

"Go during lunch," T suggested. I nodded. Seeing Bart at the mall made me curious about the story he was named after. I knew people referenced "Bartleby the Scrivener," but I didn't quite know why. I thought if I checked it out from the library and read it, maybe it would give me some insight into his life. And why Nepa would be into such an asshole.

In English, Mr. Groban assigned an in-class essay on "support." "Holden didn't realize he had people supporting him, and he tries to make it on his own. Who do you look to for support in your life? What do they do for you? How do you thank them?

"All of the computer labs are full." Mr. Groban elicited a room full of groans. "So this is one of those situations where spell-check won't help you. No shortcuts or abbreviations allowed. I want your minds to expand, not contract. Oh, and write legibly enough so someone besides you can read this. Meaning me."

Mr. Groban had done this before, where he has us handwrite in order to retain our spelling and handwriting abilities. He doesn't always collect the essays, even when he asks us to write legibly, and usually uses the class time to catch up on his grading. I wasn't too concerned about the possibility of his eyes on my paper. What I was concerned with was the chance I'd choose something so agitating that I'd start crying in class. Or my stomach would go haywire and I'd have to bolt.

Ugh. What a sucky assignment for a Monday. My tummy burned as I tried to focus on someone or something that made me feel supported. To divert the churns from the obvious, possibly painful essay I could have written about my mom or my sister, I opted for Tracy and how her job at the Boob Hut *supported* my breasts, which was true. The title: *Those Tits Are Mine*.

I have a friend, we'll call her Lacy, who works at a mall lingerie store, a store that promotes slutism and stereotypes of the worst kind to all men and women who walk by. Lacy refuses to buy or wear anything from this store, claiming that by working for them, she is only taking their money, not contributing to their success. Except that she is extremely competitive and has the need to outsell everyone else in the store.

Thus, she supports me by finding me the very best-fitting bra possible. She graciously takes me into the fitting room with at least six or seven different bras of varying shapes, colors, and coverage. Then she leaves me to my modesty while I find the bra that best fits, separates, lifts, and hides. Once I choose my over-the-shoulder nunga holder, I tell Lacy the exact style number. Later that day, she will purchase the bra as a gift to me (to be paid back when I see her) using her oh-so-generous employee discount.

To recap, my friend Lacy fully supports me by helping me find the best-fitting bras, which offer my chesticles an even greater support, and by giving me a discount. I thank her by buying her coffee and not making fun of her too much for liking professional wrestling.

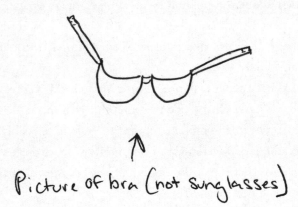

↑
Picture of bra (not sunglasses)

There. A complete essay and 100 percent avoidance of anything that would make me tear up in class or need to leave for toilet-using purposes.

Thank God we weren't forced to read the essays aloud.

Just to turn them in.

Ruh-roh.

Did I just turn in an essay with the word "tits" in the title?

Can I plead insanity? Or has that been played out?

———

When I placed my essay on Mr. Groban's desk, he gave me that weird-guy wink and said, "Glad to see you back, Anna." I gave him the slightly obnoxious quick smile, the kind where you're not really smiling and you do it so fast that the recipient sees both the start and end to the smile. Like you're giving a smile and taking it back in the same second. I didn't need the extra guilt of a teacher checking in on me. All those other kids in school are allowed to be absent without a welcome parade.

Then, as I left the class, I heard Groban say, "Feeling better today, Callie? Glad to see you back," and I felt bad about the non-smile.

My stomach started acting up within the first five minutes of physics. Why couldn't I be in chemistry where we have an experiment every day and lots of noise and moving around? Instead, it was lecture and note-taking time, complete with a rousing joke of "Physics Are Phun" from Mr. Fripp. The room was so quiet quiet quiet that there were several instances of *Did that guy just fart or did his foot scrape on his chair?*

I bounced my knee in my anxious prelude to a bathroom break. But I didn't want to go. I didn't want to leave the class like a freak, and I didn't want to spend any more time in a school bathroom than it took to pee, wipe, and wash my hands, and I sure as hell didn't want to spend any more time on that godforsaken plastic nurse bed. And I really didn't want my mom to have to deal with any more *tsuris,* as she called it, the Yiddish word for "trouble."

That's when Rodney Yee's calming voice popped into my head. *"Relax your eyes,"* so I did. *"The skin of the face relaxes deep to the bone. The bridge of the nose widens, spacious for the breath. The tongue is relaxed. The root of the tongue relaxes deep in the mouth."* All of which sounds super-flaky, and possibly a little gross, to someone who has not lived the Rodney Yee experience, but along with some deep, even breathing, Rodney managed to bring my anxiety level down in a few minutes. My leg even stopped bouncing.

I realized my eyes were closed, and I worried that Mr. Fripp was going to call me out, but he scribbled busily on the whiteboard without notice to anything going on in the classroom. I looked around and saw three or four other kids with closed eyes. Instead of looking like some weirdo relying on yoga breathing to get me out of an uncomfortable trip to the bathroom, I looked like a teenager catching up on sleep during physics class.

In other words, beyond normal.

Tracy met me at my locker before lunch with a full-sized brown grocery bag, scrunched up at the top where she held it closed.

"Whatcha got there? Doing a little mid-school shopping?" I asked as I stuffed the eighty pounds of morning textbooks into my locker. "I think my arms are getting longer from carrying these things."

"I like to do curls with mine on my way to class," Tracy noted. "And this is my lunch. Leftover sushi. My mom didn't have any smaller bags."

"I still find it very surprising that your mom makes your lunch," I said. "My mom finally stopped making mine when she realized I wasn't taking them."

"You can share my sushi." Tracy hefted the bag in offering.

"No thanks. Not a fan."

"Your loss is my roll."

"Hey, I have to stop at the library to get a book before we eat. You wanna come?" It wouldn't take me too long to find "Bartleby the Scrivener."

"You mind if I meet you in the caf? I've been dreaming of California rolls all morning."

"California rolls are unforgettable," I noted.

After I closed my locker and spun the lock, I walked to the library. Our school library was never the most welcoming room, mostly because when I was the *before* Anna and totally lost my shit at the end of last school year, there was a period of time when I went on what the school referred to as homebound, where I stayed home most of the day and came back to school periodically to work with a tutor. The multitude of suck that came with homebound was a) the tutor was as stupid as a graham cracker, and thus a total waste of my valuable, panic-attacking time, b) being called homebound made me sound like an old person who had soggy meals delivered to his house by some Good Samaritan, and c) whenever I came back to school and worked with my tutor we had to work in these tiny rooms in the back of the library that were wildly infested with earwigs.

I would have been better off being tutored in the school's bathrooms.

When I walked into the library, my nerves kicked in until I made myself remember that I was there of my own volition. And I had a mission: to find "Bartleby the Scrivener."

I typed "Bartleby" into the computer catalog that balanced precariously on an ancient, tall wooden table. The dark wood that made up the library's décor screamed 1976 academia, but the dainty sentiment of "EB sucks cock" scratched into the wood brought a modern feel.

There were several Herman Melville short story books that contained "Bartleby," and as I scrawled the call numbers onto scratch paper with a tiny library pencil (so cute! So pocketable!), I felt a tap on my shoulder. I was about to defend myself for stealing the pencil (I only took it to assist me with the Dewey Decimal System!), I realized the tapper was Tucker. "Hey!" I said, happily surprised.

" 'Bartleby the Scrivener,' huh? How depressingly pretentious of you," he said, which I thought perfectly summed up what I knew about Bart from group, but I didn't want to get into that with Tucker.

"So nice of you to notice while creepily reading over my shoulder," I told him.

"Touché. You want help finding your book?" I shrugged a sure, and Tucker led me into the stacks.

"Why are you here and not at lunch?" I asked as we passed through a surprisingly stocked graphic novels section. "Hey. I didn't know they have graphic novels here." I slowed down and fingered the spine of *Out from Boneville,* the first book from one of my favorite series during middle school. "They have *Tales from the Crypt*?" I pulled an anthology of the old horror comic off the shelf. "This is, like, brand-new. Why doesn't anyone check these out?"

"Did you know they were here before now?" asked Tucker. I shook my head no. "That's why."

I tucked the anthology under my arm, and we continued on to the fiction section. I stopped again when I saw *The Neverending Story.* "I used to love this book. And the movie."

"The book is much better," Tucker said confidently.

"I don't know. I think it's just different. There was something about the movie that made me so in love with that world."

"I guess the special effects weren't too bad for being that old."

"I don't think it was the special effects as much as Atreyu's flowing hair." I shook my head in dramatic hair fashion. Tucker laughed and pulled the book off the shelf. He flipped through it, while I looked over his shoulder. Well, not his shoulder really, since I was much shorter than he was. More like his elbow. I leaned in enough to see the pages and for us to touch arms. Part of me wanted to flinch, the idea of touching someone I wanted to touch was against the rules. But those rules were gone with my discharge from Lakeland, and— Did I just say I wanted to touch Tucker?

"Oh my God. It's beautiful." I gushed with reverence at the hard-cover copy of *The Neverending Story* Tucker held. The text was printed in bright green, and when Tucker flipped past several pages to the next chapter, those pages were printed in red. I reached over Tucker's arm to feel the book. "Probably one color for each character." In the paperback I have at home, they used plain and italic fonts to differentiate between perspectives.

He turned to the copyright page. "It says it's a first edition. I wonder if it's worth anything."

"Probably not with all the library stickers and stamps. Still really cool, though."

"Did you want to add it to your stack?" He gestured toward my *Tales from the Crypt*.

"Nah. I can read my crusty paperback if I'm in the mood." He reshelved the book, we walked toward the Ms, and I asked, "Is it technically a stack if it only has one book?"

"Well, I just meant that it would be a stack, once you had 'Bartleby.'" Tucker tried to cover his intellectual tracks and fumbled like it was a big deal.

"I'm just kidding," I assured him.

"Right," he conceded, and added, "are those aliens in your ears?"

"Indeed," I answered.

"Nice."

We found "Bartleby" without trouble, but when we went to check out the books, I learned that I needed my school ID to check them out. Which, of course, I didn't have on me. "You can check them out under mine." Tucker pulled his wallet out of his back pocket and showed his ID to the library clerk. "Just don't lose them."

"Thanks, and I won't," I said.

Tucker walked with me to my locker where I stored the books, and I asked him how soccer was going.

"Surprisingly well, actually. We're four and oh."

"Oh?" I asked.

He smiled. "I'd ask you to come to a game, but then Eleanor might ask if you want to hang out after school one day, and then you'd have to tell her you're busy and then she'd ask why and then you'd have to dance around the subject—"

"Dance around the subject?"

"Avoid talking about it," he explained.

"I know what that means, Tucker, but who says that?"

He adjusted his thick-framed glasses in a frustrated manner. "Are you hungry?"

"A little."

"Then we should get to lunch before they close the lines."

After I bought a bottle of water and a soft pretzel from the cafeteria snack counter, Tucker helped me pump mustard into a little cup and carried it with his plate of spaghetti to the lunch table. Eleanor dominated the lunch conversation with a loud story of her latest beholder conquest, while Tucker and I sat down relatively undetected except for an incriminating eyebrow raise from Tracy. I shook my head, as if to answer an unasked question about me and Tucker. Truthfully, I didn't really know what the question was. Or what the answer meant.

In gym class I began to read "Bartleby the Scrivener" on the sidelines while everyone else played a game called "Pickleball." Giant paddles, a low net, and tiny balls made it look like everyone had shrunk and now stood on a Ping-Pong table. I thought about joining them because it didn't look that un-fun, but the story wasn't the super-short three-paged deal I had hoped for, and I wanted to get a head start so it didn't usurp my actual homework tonight.

The language of "Bartleby" was a bit Ye Olde for me, but I figured out that a scrivener is essentially a human copy machine. Two pages in, a ball hit the book, and I looked up to see Jock X coming towards me. "Hey, can you throw that back?" I threw the ball, he caught it, he said thanks, the end.

I wondered if he knew I was in a mental hospital. If he heard about it and thought I was a freak. But then I thought, I've gone to school with this guy for three years, and he looks exactly like five other jock guys I'd never bothered to tell apart, let alone know a single morsel about their lives inside or out of school. So why would he give a crap about me?

It was a comforting thought. If I didn't expose my mental hospital side to people, did it really exist anywhere but in my head?

My head could maybe be fixed. It was my heart I still had trouble with. I couldn't leave the Lake Shit piece of me behind because that would mean leaving Justin.

Where was Justin while I sat on a gym floor, reading a story I got in a library with another guy, watching jocks with no names play a game called Pickleball? Was he thinking about me, too?

In Art, Mrs. Downy introduced a photo narrative assignment using natural lighting (as opposed to setup studio lights) to be due in two weeks. Tucker, Eleanor, and Meredith buzzed with ideas while I approached Mrs. Downy with my new, metallically enhanced collage. She was, of course, in the middle of berating a freshman for his weak still-life drawing. When she finished, and the freshman was thoroughly mortified, I presented her with my collage.

"What's this?" she asked bluntly.

"It's my collage. The one that was due at the beginning of the year, but I was in a men—"

"Right, right," she interrupted, more as though she didn't have time for my trivial explanation than her not wanting me to have to admit such a thing aloud.

She turned the picture sideways, then upside down, then spun it right side up. She nodded. She said, "Mmmhmm." Then she took her red pencil from somewhere in the back of her hair and wrote a grade on the back. She thrust the collage at me and said, "Excellent work, Anna. I see you've found some inspiration in your situation. Always a good thing in Art." I flipped the collage over and saw the letter A written in the top corner.

I never get As in Art.

"Do you mind if I take this back? I think it would make an excellent addition to the Fall Art Show," Mrs. Downy commended.

"Um, no, sure." I handed the collage back to her and walked proudly to where my Art friends sat.

Eleanor pounded her fist on the table and shouted at Tucker, "What are you, a fucking moron? You wasted your money on regular chain mail? You were supposed to hold out for the elven chain!" I sat down with quizzical eyebrows.

"Eleanor is forcing me to play World of Warcraft. As you can hear, it's delightfully joyful. I don't know when I've had nearly so much fun," Tucker explained with a bite in his voice.

Tucker and Eleanor continued to do battle, so Meredith and I discussed our photo assignment ideas. "I'm considering my life through music," Meredith shared. "Maybe pictures of my concert t-shirts as they've evolved. Ticket stubs from shows, that sort of thing. What do you think?" she asked.

"Sounds really good. Actually wish I thought of it first." I didn't have a clue what I wanted to do.

"You know what would be cool?" Meredith asked, picking some paint off the table with her blue fingernail. "If you could do a series on your hospital. You know? Hallways and straitjackets and stuff? I mean, I don't know what it was like, but I'd really be interested."

That took me aback. "Really?"

"Yeah, I mean, was it like *One Flew Over the Cuckoo's Nest*? Or *Girl, Interrupted*? Was it like an episode of *Intervention*?"

I laughed uncomfortably. "We weren't addicts, just . . . troubled." I tried to sound funny because I didn't know how I felt.

On one hand, someone, a class friend, was interested in what happened to me instead of not acknowledging that it existed. On the other hand, it was less about what happened to me and more about the glorification—or freakification—the mental hospital evokes.

"It wasn't like either," I explained. "It was like being at an exclusive hotel for teenagers with fucked-up lives, where you weren't allowed to leave, weren't allowed to communicate with the outside, weren't allowed to touch, and the food and service sucked."

"So, no straitjackets?"

"No. Well, one, but not for me. They moved that guy to the really messed-up floor."

"What about sexy stuff?" She was really interested then, and I noticed that Tucker and Eleanor stopped arguing and inserted themselves into the listening end of our conversation.

"What about it?" I asked.

"Were there any cuties?" Meredith nudged me.

I looked at Tucker, who looked at me intently, then I looked back at Meredith. "Possibly," I answered coyly. The bell rang, oh so helpful in its saving.

"You are so not done with your story," Meredith warned me.

My life as a story? Meredith may have had something there.

When my mom picked me up from school, I detected a mood shift. Happier would be too optimistic, but hopeful seemed right.

"Hi, honey, did you have a good day?"

"*Asi, asi,*" I said, although it was probably more accurately *bueno* than so-so. Can't let Mom in too much on my life improving so quickly after incarceration. I still liked having the guilt card at my disposal. Plus, would it be rude to say I had a good day when hers probably sucked?

"I talked to your dad today," she started while she pulled out of the parking lot. I said nothing. "He asked about you." Doubtful, but okay. "He's seeing a therapist."

"Like, couples therapy? With you?"

"Well, no, but talking to someone alone could still help us." Mom sounded unrealistically positive. My dad was much too old a dog to learn new, nice tricks. Plus, wouldn't a marriage counselor be the answer to work on *a marriage*? Of course, I couldn't say that, so I joked, "Guess I'm not the only one in the family with mental health issues, huh?"

Mom wasn't laughing. "It could be genetic, you know. Just like regular health problems."

"Whoa. Hell no. I am nothing like Dad. The guy is a miserable butt-hole who isn't even dealing with his marriage problems. And he's *mean*. I'm nothing like that."

"No, of course you're not. I just meant—"

"I don't care what you meant. That's not cool, Mom. You just knocked my day down from *asi, asi* to *mal*." I shouldn't have said that because it was so stupid that it made me laugh. And then my mom laughed, nervously, but still laughter.

"All I meant," she tried again, "was that maybe all of the hard stuff that's happened with you isn't your fault."

I wanted to tell her no shit, it wasn't my fault. That my parents didn't care enough about me to figure out what was going on, so they dumped me off on someone else. But I stopped myself. Because if my depression *was* genetic, then it *was* nature instead of nurture. And it wasn't technically my mom's fault except for her choice of breeding partners. Did that make me feel better? Having a possibly concrete reason for being the way I am? Was it the same as feeling better knowing the reason your throat hurt for a week was because you had strep, and all you needed was an antibiotic to take the pain away? Because having an official reason for being messed up is better than just being messed up?

What *was* official was that I was nothing like my dad. Even if we did both see therapists.

Before bed, I finished "Bartleby the Scrivener." The first light it shone was that all parents are fucked up, genetics or no. Bartleby, the character, has no redeeming qualities. Basically, the weirdo gets this job scrivening, tucked into a corner of an office with a crappy window facing the side of a building. When the boss, who narrates the story, starts asking Bartleby to complete tasks, Bartleby says, "I prefer not to." Like, over and over again throughout the entire story. Which drives the narrator boss crazy. Not literally crazy, just ultra bothered. Then he tries to fire Bartleby, who *prefers* not to be fired, and eventually it turns out Bartleby has been living at the office, surviving on snacks called ginger nuts. When he's finally ousted from the building and sent to what I assume was a prison, he *prefers* not to eat and dies (I think). The narrator learns that Bartleby once worked at, and was fired from, the Dead Letter Office, which is where letters go when they aren't addressed correctly or the person who once lived somewhere moves and can't be found. Quite possibly the saddest place in the world to work. Surrounded by all those letters that no one will ever get, and you're still not allowed to read them. Or are you? And would that just make you sadder? Knowing that thank-yous and apologies and proclamations of love would never reach their intended? The story ends in rather dramatic exclamations: "Ah Bartleby! Ah Humanity!"

What were Bart's parents thinking? Were they just pretentious college kids when they had him and thought any literary reference would make them sound intellectual? Did they admire Bartleby's commitment to his *preferences,* thus hoping to instill the same level of commitment in their son? Or were they just miserable people who wanted their son to turn out as miserable as a character in a creepy story, as miserable as they themselves were?

Not a single good answer. At least I might have Nature to fall back on. Bart seems to have gotten the short end of the Nurture stick.

THE REAPING

Tuesday morning, Tracy picked me up for our walk to school. I texted her first thing to hopefully gain some perspective on the Bartleby name conundrum. Two hours of cruddy sleep between three and five a.m. gave me no extra clarity on the matter.

While I sat on the porch waiting, I tied a purple scarf that I found in my mom's jewelry drawer around my hair like a headband. It complemented the pink in my new shirt and exposed the alien earrings, which I decided were going to be my trademark from now on. Until I grew the balls to dye a stripe into my hair. Then I can be stripy hair girl. Not that anyone would notice. Although Tucker might.

As we walked, I filled Tracy in on Bart vs. Bartleby, and asked her opinion on why a parent would name their kid after him. "For the same reason I'm going to name my kid Hulk, after the legendary twelve-time World Heavyweight Champion Hulk Hogan: because I think it's cool." God help poor Hulk. Although, I guess he'd know what line of work to get into.

174

"I kind of need to talk to you about something," Tracy unexpectedly interjected, interrupting my vision of a Tracy-made baby wrestler. Uh-oh. What was she going to ask me about that was so important that it usurped my Bartleby discussion? Group? Mental hospitals? Divorce? "So, I sort of"—Tracy looked over her shoulder suspiciously, as if to check if anyone were in earshot—"made out with Arthur Bernard outside of Auto Shop."

"What?!" I yelled, making earshot a lot farther away. "Wait. Which one's that?" Auto Shop is filled with a lot of characters I have never shared class space with, mostly because our classes are leveled and those who take Auto Shop are usually more on the trade road of education than academic. Plus, they're way better at gym than I am, so I don't even have gym class with them. I feel classist or elitist or something saying that, but you know it's true. That's what makes Tracy so awesome and random.

"The kind of short one." I threw up my hands and made a that-didn't-help face. "The buff one." Still no clue. "The short, buff one who we once called The Assman because his jeans were so tight." Aaahhh. The Assman.

"You made out with The Assman? And his real is name is Arthur? Right on." She told me the story of how she and The Assman were partnered up for this oil change speed competition last Friday, which they won. So naturally when partners were needed for lubing or whatever (I just said that because it sounded perfectly pervy), he chose her. During the lubing process, The Assman invited T out of the shop for a smoke. Tracy doesn't smoke, but she was intrigued. When they went around the corner, out of the class's sight, The Assman pinned her up against a wall and kissed her.

"It was like a scene in a movie. Man, it was hot," she reminisced.

"So, are you gonna, like, marry The Assman and have little assbabies?" She smacked my arm. Hard. "Ow!"

"I don't know. I mean, no, we're not getting married or having babies, but, maybe, like, a movie wouldn't be out of the question."

"Cool," I approved.

"Cool?" she double-checked.

"Definitely cool."

We walked into school as the first bell rang, and I was aglow with the sweet, assy romance for Tracy. Just as awesome was that, instead of talking about me and craziness, Tracy told me something about her. Something funny and kind of wonderful and not at all about me and Lake Shit and family and crap. It felt really good.

Until I walked into English and got the stare-down from Mr. Groban. I guess he didn't like my essay?

As soon as the second bell rang, Mr. Groban started class. "I read your essays last night"—collective groan from everyone who thought maybe he just collected them for quick checks—"and I have to say for the most part I was very pleased. Most of you understood that there are people out there supporting you, even if you don't always recognize it, and that you can learn something from that. But some of you"—he glanced my way—"took the opportunity to, I don't know, mock the assignment. Maybe you thought you wouldn't have to turn it in." He pinched the bridge of his nose, as though speaking pained him. "I can't say I'm not disappointed." I think he was trying to jab me with that, as adults often do. As if disappointing him is worse than a bad grade. Check yourself, Groban.

Class was spent listening to those students who wanted to share their essays. It was totally voluntary, and I, of course, did not volunteer. But Mr. Groban's accusatory words welled into a knot in my stomach. What did he want from me? Did he think I was going to write an essay appreciating my hippie English teacher for offering me his office in case of emergency? Did he want me to *EMOTE* (big, giant, dramatic letters) about my recent experiences and talk about all of the wonderful, helpful, insightful "professionals" of the mental health field who magically returned me to my pre-crazy state? Did he want me to appreciate all that my parents did for me by putting me into a mental hospital because they loved me?

Fuck him.

I stewed in my seat for the rest of class, barely hearing the half-assed tales of coach love, grandpa inspiration, and, of course, teacher worship. It was all so phony, as Holden would say. You don't thank people with a class assignment. You thank people by being there for them, in sickness and mental health, and by not judging them, and by laughing when they say something funny. Or even not that funny, but you still laugh because it makes them feel good. It makes them feel normal to sit down in a classroom, which they couldn't even do for a really long, uncomfortable time without having to get up and leave to go to the nurse's office or the bathroom or ditch. It makes them feel normal to laugh about something, to have something to laugh at, to remember laughter when so much shit has been thrown their way that they weren't sure if they'd ever be the life-filled person they once were.

Class ended, and just as I expected, Mr. Groban called my name as I walked past him. "I'd like a word with you, Anna."

I stopped, turned, looked at him with laser beams of hate shooting out of my eyes, and drolled, "I prefer not to," and walked out.

THE ASSMAN COMETH

I had a bounce in my step all morning, and when lunch rolled around I couldn't wait to share my story with the lunch table. As

Tracy and I walked to the cafeteria, she confessed, "We made out again."

Tracy's girlish excitement was so uncharacteristic, I had to give her crap. "You made out with who again?"

"The Assman," she whispered, looking around suspiciously, as if anyone knew who The Assman was. Or cared she made out with him.

"I'm kidding. How was it?"

She sighed in such a girly, romantic way, I thought she might have sniffed too much lube (I need to stop using that word, and yet I cannot). "He's a really good kisser. Beyond. And there's something about being up against the back of the Auto Shop wall . . ."

"It's like he's been reading the bad boy handbook," I joked.

"Exactly," she agreed. "But still, maybe don't say anything to the lunch table."

"Yeah, for all you know he has some skank stashed in Woodshop."

"You think?" she asked, concerned.

"Don't worry, T. I'm sure you're the only skank The Assman needs."

The lunch table completely appreciated my Bartleby punch-lined story. Tucker even added, "I picture Mr. Groban after you stormed out of the classroom, crying out, fists clenched at the ceiling, 'Ah Anna! Ah Humanity!'" Everyone laughed.

Two minutes before the bell rang, The Assman himself approached our lunch table. I'd never looked at him close up, but there was something ruggedly attractive about him. Like maybe he was really twenty-eight but flunked a million times. He had good skin, too.

He stood behind Tracy, so she didn't notice his (not so looming, since he's so short) presence until he tapped her on the shoulder.

"Can I talk to you for a sec?" he asked her in his gruff, smoker's voice.

"Um, sure?" Tracy's look said confused, about both why he wanted to talk to her and if she should be mortified that he did. I watched the back of T's head as The Assman asked her a question, and she nodded. They did look pretty cute together: Tracy with her tough shortness and The Assman with his, well, tough shortness.

Tracy came back to the table with a goofy smile on her face.

"Well?" Meredith pressed. "What did that guy want?"

"His name is Arthur," Tracy scolded. Was she blushing? "And he just asked me to Homecoming."

"No way!" I gasped, excited. "And?"

"I said yes," she informed us with more confidence.

Arthur the Assman is taking Tracy to Homecoming. Now there's something to appreciate.

GROUP GASP

I wasted most of Art class attempting to come up with some brilliant narrative to tell using only natural lighting. I couldn't see how I could tell my story about the hospital when I lived so far away from it, so I played around with another idea I had, to visit the local pet cemetery and take pictures of sad headstones people had inscribed for their beloved, deceased animals. Oddly, the pet cemetery is relatively near my house. It's not some homemade wooden crosses staked into the ground like in the Stephen King story, but a real pay-lots-of-money-for-engraved-elaborate-headstones cemetery. Tracy and I went in there once after passing by the gate one too many times. Who could resist?

But how did a bunch of pet graves tell a personal narrative about me? I scribbled on my art pad, but nothing remotely artsy came to me. So I wrote the name "Bartleby" in the only style block letters I knew. I always envied people who could write in fancy letters. Finding a cool font on Word never had the same impact.

"Still dwelling on the scrivener?" Tucker sat down next to me, his huge brown art pad of paper under his arm.

"I have Group today, and I feel like I should acknowledge that I read the story. But I have no clue what it tells me about Bartleby the person, nor do I think he'll even give a ball of squat if I did. So why did I bother?"

"I don't know. I think it was thoughtful of you. Personally, I'd be flattered if you read a story my name was based on."

"Your name was based on a story?" I asked.

"Well, no, it was actually taken from the movie *Innerspace* about a guy who gets shrunk down and injected into another guy's body. Kind of like goofy sci-fi. The character's actual name was Tuck, which my dad liked, but my mom said it rhymed too easily with 'fuck.' So I'm Tucker."

"Which still kind of rhymes with a variation, no?"

"Yeah. Parents can be pretty naïve in the ways of the adolescent mind." As he spoke, he scratched his name onto my Bartleby page in perfectly funky letters. Damn him.

"If it's any consolation, I like your name. It sounds kind of cozy, like 'I'm plain tuckered out.'"

"Better than 'I tuckered my shirt into my pants,' I guess." Tucker then wrote "Anna" in the same edgy font. Flashback to Lakeland, when Justin told me the story of his hand, and in his messy, uncontrolled script he wrote my name. What would Justin think of my sitting here with Tucker, free to bump shoulders without consequence, our names sharing the space on a page written in forbidden pen?

The bell rang, surprising me. "Wow. Time to go already? And still no game plan for the scrivener."

"I'd offer you a ride home, but we have an away game today."

"No problem. My mom drives me straight to Group after school anyway."

"Well, good luck." Tucker stood up, and I saw he had removed his shoes while sitting next to me. He shuffled his gray socks into his tattered black-checked Vans, and I smiled at the oddness.

"Good luck to you, too. Kick some ass. Get it? *Kick?*"

"I've heard better, but thank you anyway." He secured his art pad under his arm and left.

I half expected a Dad report when I got into the car with my mom, but she was in full knit-shop mode. I guess it was good she extracted herself from her room.

"You wouldn't believe these women," she complained. "They scrunch the yarn back into nothing near the semblance of the original skein, and they try to return it as if it was never used. Who's going to buy a lumpy skein? I'll only make back a tenth of the original price when it goes into the sloppy skeins basket."

I let her ramble about old ladies and felting because it was a lot better than me having to talk about me. I'd have to contend with that once I left the car. Unless, of course, the other people in Group had more important things to talk about again, and I'd be left nodding my supportive nods until next week. So is the beauty of group therapy without a points system.

"Sorry, honey, I didn't even get to ask you about your day." My mom patted my hand as we sat outside the therapy office. Miles slumped by wearing a green peacoat, far too warm for the early fall weather. "Who's that?" Mom asked, then corrected herself, "unless you don't want to tell me. Or you can't tell me, for privacy's sake. I don't want to intrude on other people's healing processes."

I'd hardly call Group a "healing process," but it was nice for Mom to be considerate.

"Don't worry, Mom. There's not much to tell yet anyway. That's Miles. He said he was in a band. I don't remember much else."

"He's sort of cute in a sleepy, sluggish way."

"I'll tell him you said so," I joked and left my mom in the car to fantasize about underage guys, you know, now that she was sort of single.

Weird.

My plan for Group this week was to pretend I was normal. Which is a tough thing to do when you're in group therapy. But what I meant was that a) any time I got nervous enough to want to leave, I'd practice some of Rodney Yee's breathing exercises until I calmed myself down, and b) if asked, I'd share some stuff about me that made me sound not crazy, like my Art assignment, and c) if pressed to address my issues, I'd talk about my parents getting divorced because that sounded like the type of thing people talked about in therapy. Not like, oh, I had a stomachache and I had to poo in the middle of a pop quiz on the Pythagorean theorem.

Inside the group room, only Peggy, Ali, Miles, and Nepa were there, which isn't really an "only" since the "only" one missing was Bart. But since I had done my homework on Bart and was sickeningly intrigued by him, what with his secret make-out mall session with Nepa and his annoyingly attractive therapeutic good looks, he was the one I actually hoped to be there.

I sat down in a seat between Miles and Ali and gave a small wave to both of them. "Hi," they both responded, neither enthusiastically nor snobbily. Peggy looked at her watch, extremely red and over-sized plastic, and declared, "We'll wait three minutes and then get started, okay?"

Three minutes until Group meant three minutes of forced socialization with my group mates. Would the awkwardness force a stomach explosion? Or was I past that phase? Before the evil butterflies had a chance to assault my tummy, Miles spoke, "So, anyone else get in to the Fall Art Show?"

"Which art show would that be?" Nepa asked. She seemed a little on edge, her words pinched.

"The all-district one. You know, like all the high schools in the area pick works and display them all together at the Shriners building? You had a piece in there last year, didn't you? That distorted nude photo you took of Bart?" Miles waggled his eyebrows.

"Oh yeah. You were totally obsessed with that picture. A little *too* obsessed."

"I was not. It was just a surprise that you and Bart were, you know . . ."

"Yes, I know. Don't remind me. That guy's such a cock-knocker. He doesn't give two shits about anyone but himself. My friend Sital told me she saw him making out with some trash at their school by her locker."

Ali and Miles simultaneously groaned. "Here we go again," Ali proclaimed, head tipped back, eyes up at the ceiling in an exhausted pose.

"What?" I asked. It was an involuntary response to their reaction, but I felt so out of the loop that it was either sit there like an ignorant nub or get into the conversation.

Miles explained, "Nepa and Bart have this tragic on-again, off-again thing going. Very passionate when it's on, very icy when it's off. Peggy actually made a rule that we are no longer allowed to talk about their relationship issues in Group. Isn't that right, Peggy?" Peggy nodded as she scribbled on her clipboard.

"Just because it's happened before, doesn't mean it still doesn't suck," Nepa said. "Can we move on, please?"

"I've got a piece. Of art. In that show you're talking about," I said, in hopes that Nepa really did want to move on, and I wasn't just blathering about art.

Miles perked up. "Really? What medium?"

"Well, it's sort of a colored pencil collage with, um, staples."

"Interesting. I'll have to check it out." Miles looked at me intently, the bags under his eyes still as puffy as ever. He had a sparkle in his blue eyes and intense focus that was unnerving and appealing at the same time.

Damn sitting in a circle!

"Do you have something? In the show?" I asked.

"A few things, actually. Painting is my medium mostly. Although I do have a photo, too." Miles crossed his thin legs towards me and explained using his hands. "It's me in bed trying to sleep, except my eyes are wide-open, and behind me, superimposed in Photoshop, is the night sky in time lapse."

"So the night is going by you all fast while you remain awake," I understood.

"Exactly! I call it *Ode to My Insomnia*."

So those bags under his eyes weren't some cultural attribute, like all the Romanian gymnasts in the Summer Olympics.

"You're not much of a sleeper?" I asked.

"I haven't had a full night's sleep in over a year now." Wow, he had really blue eyes. And great lips. Why was I always thinking about lips? Better than thinking about my stomach.

"That sucks. More hours a day to be stuck with your thoughts."

184

I regretted saying that the millisecond it spilled out. Maybe Miles liked his thoughts. Maybe Miles was a perfectly content guy, and I just pounded another nail into my crazy coffin.

But then Ali said, "I know. I'd go insane if I didn't have my good pal, Ambien."

"It's not so bad anymore," Miles said to me. "I get a lot done. Paintings, writing songs, blogging, chatting. If you're ever up in the middle of the night, hit me up for a chat. I'm always on. Sleepless Platypus. That's my screen name."

"After your band. What's with you and platypuses?"

"You remember." He smiled, then Peggy interrupted.

"It's been five minutes. Let's begin without Bart today. Hopefully he'll show."

"Hopefully he didn't fall into the bathtub with a toaster," Nepa grumbled. Peggy looked at her with reprimanding eyes. "Sorry. I know we don't joke about that here."

That's when I remembered "here" was group therapy, where we were because something was wrong with us. "That," which we didn't talk about, was committing suicide because as normal people are allowed to throw around words like "toaster" and "bathtub," we, as mental health patients, are not.

The comfort was that there was a "we" involved.

I started to get it.

Without Bart there, and with Ali proclaiming that she didn't want to talk anymore about the rape or the trial, at least not this week, I felt more open to talking about myself. When Peggy asked, "Anna, is there anything on your mind this week?" it was all the invitation I needed.

"My dad moved out on Sunday." I paused for what I expected might be a "so what, BFD" type of reaction. This was no rape, after all, but Ali was the first to say, "Well, that sucks."

I went on to explain their fights, my dad's temper, how I managed to avoid him during Rosh Hashanah, but he still came home and raged. I told them about how I pounded on the wall ("Right on," was Nepa's response), how he moved out, and how he's going to see a therapist.

"Ah, yes, because shrinks can fix everything," Miles sniffed.

"I know," I commiserated. "My doctor in the hospital was a dick."

Oh. I brought up the hospital. I hadn't meant to.

Mental Hospital Girl shows her freakish head once again.

But nobody seemed to notice or care.

"I had this guy," Miles enthused, "who would prescribe anything to me. I'd be, like, 'I'm depressed,' and he'd give me drugs. 'I can't sleep,' he'd give me drugs. I considered telling him I couldn't get my junk up just to see if he'd give me some Viagra. Not that I need it."

"Oh God." Ali rolled her eyes. "What is it with you guys and your dicks?"

"I can't help it if I have this appendage."

"Appendage? Very sexy, Miles. No wonder you're the only one who's ever touched it," Nepa shot.

We all laughed, and like that my problems became a shared experience instead of my own burden. They still existed, but that didn't mean I had to dwell on them constantly. There was more to me than crazy and depressed. Even if I did need a therapy group to prove it.

BUZZKILL

We left Group on a high note and Peggy's deep breaths. I bounced to my mom's car and waved goodbye to my group members. "Hello," I sang as I stepped into the car.

"Hi, honey." I could tell my mom was psyched that I was smiling because she looked at me in that satisfied-mom way, like, maybe she did something right. "All went well, I suspect."

"You suspect correctly, Mother."

"I have some more good news for you: Your dad is coming over for dinner tomorrow night."

Sag.

Deflate.

Suck.

That meant I'd have to look at my dad and listen to my dad and talk to my dad. I'd have to watch my mom and dad uncomfortably interact and deal with the aftermath, whatever that may be.

"Why?" I asked.

She huffed as though it was an unheard-of question. "Because he's your dad. And he's still my husband. And he'd like to talk with us."

"Happy happy, joy joy."

Why can't life ever just float above the clouds for more than five seconds?

I spent the rest of the night in my room, door closed, music loud. I played my bass until a blister popped, and I had to get a Band-Aid. When I went into the hall, Mara was out there in her pj's.

"Sorry if I was loud. Are you going to bed? I can turn the music down."

"Thanks. I guess you heard about Dad?" Mara looked at me like little kid Mara, like she needed her big sister and I just shut her out of my room for three hours. I walked over and gave her a big hug. She leaned into me and held on. "Do you think they'll get back together?" she asked, hopeful.

"I don't know. They barely just separated" was all I could say. She wanted her parents back together, which I know I should, too, but when life felt easier with them apart, I didn't know what I wanted.

I let go of Mara, and we walked to the bathroom together. While she brushed her teeth, I pulled a Band-Aid out and wrapped it around my blister.

"Mara?" A question came to me. "Are you happy?" It was a stupid, generic question, one I'd probably punch someone in the face for asking me. But I needed to know her answer.

She spit into the sink and turned off the faucet. "Yeah. Are you?"

I shrugged. "Sometimes," I answered.

"Sometimes is better than what you were before." She wiped her mouth on a towel. "Good night."

I stood in the mirror, hit by what Mara said. *What you were before*. I hated to think about what I must have looked like to Mara before. Before what? Before the hospital? Before losing weight? Before, when I couldn't even sit through a class and hated life so much I wanted to die?

I looked at the bathtub, moist with water from Mara's shower earlier. And then I smiled.

Because I didn't want to get inside of it with a toaster.

BOOBS ARE PEOPLE, TOO

I woke up too early with Dad on the brain. To clear the noggin, I booted up the ol' Rodney Yee yoga DVD. Rodney and I were becoming fast friends, and I can honestly say none of my other friends wore tiny exercise shorts as well as Rodney did. Not that I knew of, anyway.

Tracy had to get to school early for some math extra-credit work, so I was on my own for the walk. My outfit was relatively classic Anna: jeans (that fit), a t-shirt (dark purple, not too baggy), and Chucks. I didn't bother with a festive headband, since my anticipatory mood for dinner was not festive enough to warrant one. The alien earrings remained part of the look. Maybe they'd give me some sort of extraterrestrial powers to help me cope.

My nerves dictated my thoughts as I walked. Would my dad be angry and throw things across the table? Would he be medicated and thus not at all like himself? Could meds work that fast? Was he cheating on my mom? Gay? A woman?

I hated the unpredictable.

Thankfully, Spanish class Alyssa popped up next to me again. We attempted our conversation *en español,* but it was too slow-going for Alyssa when she had to stop every few words and ask, *"¿Cómo se dice?"* I was impressed with myself that I did actually know how to say most of the words she was asking about, but it was like having a pop quiz before school even started. "How about we just *hablamos* in *inglés?*" I suggested.

"Okay," she agreed. "So who are you going to Homecoming with?" Thankfully, she didn't give me time to answer. "Scott Webster is taking me. Can you believe it? I used to think he was so cute. I mean, I still do, but it's like I've had a crush on him since third grade. God, he was cute in third grade! And all of a sudden here we are going to Homecoming together. It's like fate, you know?"

"And he's just as hot as he was in the third grade," I noted.

She missed the joke. "My dress is wicked. You know I never go all out slut, but this is reaching. It's red, like, really red, and satin so it makes me feel all slinky, with a halter to hold up Thing One and Thing Two."

"You call your boobs 'Thing One and Thing Two'?"

"Mark Tussel made it up when we were going out, and it stuck with me. Cute, no?"

That wasn't quite the word that came to mind, but, "Sure . . ."

We reached the school with Alyssa describing in lurid detail how the shoes she chose were an integral part of her Scott Webster seduction.

"Oh!" she realized. "We didn't even get a chance to talk about your date." The bell rang. "Next walk!" she promised, and I gave her a thumbs-up in agreement.

Gah. That was odd. Hearing about Alyssa's boob-naming boyfriend and her plan to expose Scott Webster to her Things was not how I thought my day would start.

But it wasn't such a bad thing (1 or 2). She had confided in me, which made me seem like a friend. She assumed I was going to Homecoming, which made it sound like a guy would actually ask me. Plus, all of the above had nothing to do with me being crazy.

Now how was I going to get through English class after giving Mr. Groban the Bartleby snub?

Mr. Groban wrote on the board as I entered class, and I sat down stealthily. Or at least undetected. The final bell rang, and Mr. Groban jumped right into teaching mode. "Motifs. What's a motif?" A few lazy hands raised into the air, and I decided, what the hell, to raise mine.

He didn't call on me.

Which then made me wonder if it was me. Was he mad at me? Would he never call on me again? If I asked him why he stopped calling on me, would he answer, "I prefer not to"?

After Kenny Monahan blathered on far too long to explain what a motif was, Mr. Groban assigned the class a group project (audible class groan), dealing with motifs and involving a—you guessed it—skit. Well, not a skit so much as a reenactment (interpretation?) of a scene we choose to represent our motif. Maybe it would be more fun if we did it in Spanish.

Since I'm not friends with anyone in English, I worried about that uncomfortable *can-I-join-your-group?* moment, but Mr. Groban actually did something right by making us count off by fives. Maybe he did it to help me avoid stress. Because Mr. Groban's decisions all revolve around me, of course.

My group consisted of one jock guy, one dork guy, one brainy girl, and one random girl who I knew nothing about. We had until Monday, and luckily all of the work would be done in class. I'd hate to have to hang out with this motley crew somewhere other than the safety of the classroom. Mr. Groban did that teacher-hover thing a few times, and I thought he might say something about my little outburst from yesterday, but he didn't.

I was safe. Or so I thought.

On my way out of class, I heard those arm-hair-raising words "Anna, can I see you for a minute?" Maybe life would be easier if I never left his classroom.

I walked over on the defensive, ready to tell him exactly how his overly-caring-teacher persona kind of sucked, but he threw me when he said, "You're reading Melville?" He nodded to the Bartleby book in my pile. "Do you think the class would benefit from a little 'Bartleby'?"

And they said *I* was crazy. "I don't know. I read it for a specific reason," not that I'd tell him that reason, "and I thought it was too long and a total downer. It's your class, though, so assign away if you like."

Mr. Groban paused in overly thoughtful silence, long enough where I had to interrupt his brain whirrings: "I kind of have to get to my next class."

"Oh, sure, sure, absolutely. Thank you for your insight."

I walked to Pre-calc, relieved that the bra assignment thing had blown over, confused as to what Mr. Groban wanted from me, and annoyed that I'd possibly just influenced our class's curriculum.

And I still had an entire day of classes before dinner with my dad.

By the time lunch rolled around, my stomach was so tightly wound, there was no room for any food.

"You have to eat something," Meredith pressed. "Your metabolism slows down when you don't eat, you know. So then when you do go back to eating, you gain weight twice as fast."

"I'm not *not* eating, Meredith. I'm too nervous to eat. Not all of us can have the gift of the iron stomach that was bestowed upon you."

Meredith destroyed a double serving of the cafeteria's boneless ribs sandwich (aren't ribs technically bones?) and would certainly maintain her stick-like figure. In the past, I would have been jealous, but I was realizing that one can look good without the complete lack of any curves on their body. Plus, who would want to eat boneless ribs?

"You could have a salad," Eleanor suggested.

"Roughage really isn't my thing." I shook my head.

"It goes right through me, too." Tucker offered up that TMI tidbit.

"Can we stop talking about me eating lunch for a minute? Why don't we talk about what Tracy's going to wear to Homecoming?"

That got the lunch table abuzz with plans for girlifying Tracy for the big night. Eleanor and Meredith described how their moms forged a union and found both of them Korean dates that they had no say in choosing.

"Your moms picked your dates?" I asked.

"It was either go Korean, or don't go at all. If the guys are lame, we can just ditch them when we get there. No biggie." Meredith bit into ribless sandwich number two, and I decided I needed some air.

As I stood up, Tucker stood up, too. "I'm going to get a shake. Want to join me?" he asked.

The two of us walked over to the cafeteria snack counter, where all of the good food resided: hot pretzels, shakes, candy bars, and popcorn. A faux rib sandwich did not entice me, but the menu board's suggestion of hot chocolate sounded soothing. When Tucker ordered his shake, he asked me, "Do you want anything? It's on me. As long as it's under"—he counted the change he dug out of his front jean pocket—"four dollars and eighty cents." I don't know how he fit that much change into his skinny jeans, but I decided to take him up on the offer.

"A hot chocolate, thanks."

"One chocolate shake and one hot chocolate, please." The lunch lady said nothing and went about her chocolateering.

"Does it bother you at all that Eleanor has a date to Homecoming?" I pried.

"Nah. Let her abuse someone else for a while." The lunch lady handed over two identical Styrofoam cups, one with rising steam. "Thank you," Tucker said to her. "Careful, it's hot," he warned me as he handed me the cup. "I always hoped that the violence of her gaming would somehow dissipate her anger in the real world, but it just seems to exacerbate it."

We sipped our respective hot and cold chocolate drinks on our way back to the table. While we walked, I noticed a small hole in the toe of Tucker's worn Vans. For some reason, the tiny tuft of his purple sock that peaked through seemed really sweet. So did him getting me away from the lunch table during a non-inclusionary Homecoming conversation. Because I think a part of me really wanted to go to that stupid dance, wanted that night of teen normalcy and pretty dresses and different hairdos and uncomfortable shoes.

I wondered if Eleanor's and Meredith's moms could hook me up, too.

The afternoon minutes sped by surprisingly fast, making me more anxious as the Dad dinner approached. When the sanctity of Art arrived to end my school day, I was a mental mess. I was supposed to work on my photo shoot plans, but I had yet to think of anything beyond the pet cemetery idea.

Tucker was already finished with his photography and had moved on to processing, so instead of dwelling inside the drama of my brain, I joined him in the darkroom.

The trickling water and extremely low lighting had a calming effect similar to Rodney Yee's voice. If only I could do my yoga *in* the darkroom, I could possibly achieve complete serenity. That, or I'd be shipped back to Lake Shit for being a loon (isn't it weird that I have a specific mental hospital to reference? Instead of just saying, "I could be shipped off to a mental hospital," I actually have a return address. Will a mental hospital be a staple in my brain's dialog for the rest of my life? Is it because my brain *has* a dialog that the mental hospital was there in the first place?).

Tucker's photo essay was composed of intricately written SAT Power Words placed amongst the beauty of nature—hiding in logs, under rocks, floating in a stream. He used the natural lighting of a forest preserve beautifully, and I understood how this really was his story. Even in the solitude of nature, Tucker was forced to think about his brainiac future. Could they somehow fit together to make him a whole person, or would they tear him apart and destroy his love for both? I asked him if I read his idea correctly.

"Pretty much," he said, as he dipped a newly developed photo into the bath. "I was going to do a series of me climbing a tree and mount them in one giant, vertical display. But while I was in the forest preserve, all I could think of were these huge words that described everything around me. Annoyingly large, yet precisely defining words. So I went back to the car and got out some paper and a pen and voilà. I think they turned out pretty well. What about you?"

"What do I think?" He nodded yes, looking down at me through his glasses while he stirred the photograph around with a set of tongs. "I think it's brilliant, of course. Which is exactly what you are, so it tells your story perfectly." After I said it, I realized how it sounded. Yes, it was meant to be a compliment, but was it too much? Was I flirting?

"Really? Huh" was Tucker's response, and he quickly looked down to finish developing the word "pragmatic" on a tree stump. I sat down on one of the high metal stools near a developing station and dragged the rubber of my shoe along the foot rung.

Eleanor stumbled through the darkroom's rotating door, breaking the hole in the conversation with, "Holy shit! I just got a text from this girl Betty I know from WoW, and she said this guy Rex told her that my Homecoming date is Napalm!" Tucker and I looked at each other in confusion, then back at Eleanor. "Napalm is his game name. He's a member of the rival guild whose ass we wholeheartedly ripped open last week!"

"Vivid imagery there, Eleanor," I pointed out. "What does that mean?"

"It means I'm going to be sleeping with the enemy. Well, not sleeping with him, but, you know, going to Homecoming with him!" she yelled, too loudly for the peace of the darkroom.

"Is that a good thing or a bad thing?" I asked.

She walked over to a developing station and set down her negatives. "I'm not sure yet. There's something kind of kinky about it. If he's into that."

"Are *you* into that?" I questioned.

"I'm not sure yet about that either." We laughed, although I couldn't tell if Tucker joined us. It must have been awkward hearing your semi-ex talk like that about another guy. How would I feel if Justin told me down and dirty details about that girl Dania at Lakeland? How would he feel if I told him about Tucker's socks?

Would we ever feel anything together again?

DINNER FOR DOUCHES

I called my mom from my cell about halfway through Art to tell her I didn't need a ride home. She protested a bit but seemed somewhat reassured when I told her I'd be doing homework and promised I wouldn't bail on Dad's dinner. Not that I would (although, why not?), but it was what she wanted to hear.

Tracy met me at my locker after school, a non-work day for her. Instead of going home to one of our houses, we decided to hang out at one of the study nooks in the halls.

"We could go to the library," I suggested.

"We could, but then I'd be assaulted by the librarian who swears I borrowed the S volume of the World Book and never returned it. To which I always have to say, 'Look, Crusty, I never checked out your encyclopedia from 1982, since we have access to World Book online. But if I did have the S volume, I'd turn it right to the page that says 'Suck My Balls.' "

"So no library then?"

Tracy and I worked in silence with the occasional interruption for help with a math problem or asking for a piece of gum. Fifteen minutes into our hallway homework hullabaloo (makes it sound more exciting), Tucker came sprinting down the hall in full soccer regalia (makes him sound fancy). "What up, Tuck?" I called to him as he passed. He came to a stop and walked back to our table.

"Oh, hi, Anna. Tracy."

"Big game today?" I asked.

"Just Apple Heights. But I forgot my lucky rabbit's foot in the locker room, and I had to run and get it before the bus left." He hopped in place, not wanting to decelerate completely.

"Lucky rabbit's foot? That's gross." I blanched.

"It's not real." He dug his hand into his pocket and pulled out a dyed green fluffy foot on a gold-balled key chain.

"Does that mean the luck's fake, too?" Tracy asked.

"Possibly. It's all a matter of suspension of belief. And I choose to suspend mine."

"Suspend away. Don't let us keep you," Tracy pushed.

"Good luck!" I yelled after him as he reaccelerated down the hall. Tucker held up the green foot as he ran to show that he, indeed, had his luck in the palm of his hand.

"That guy's weird," Tracy proclaimed as she dug back into her homework. I almost spat, "Hello, Assman?" but then she said, "I didn't know he was on the soccer team. Arthur's on it, too."

"He is?" I was shocked.

"Goalie," she gushed.

"Hardcore."

"Would you be interested in coming to a game with me Friday? I kind of told Arthur I'd be there." T scribbled black circles around the binder holes in her notebook paper.

"Home or away?"

"Home. Does it matter?" She looked up.

"Nah. But that's pretty much all I know for high school sports terminology. That and 'ball.'"

"What about 'kick'?" Tracy asked.

"'Kick'?" I overpronounced the word like a tourist trying to speak a foreign language.

"So will you go?" She ignored the brilliant hilarity of my non-answer.

"Sure. Just don't say anything around Eleanor. Tucker doesn't want her to know he's on the team."

"Is it because he doesn't want her trying to get back together after seeing his sexy soccer stud legs?"

"You think he has soccer stud legs?" I asked, surprised.

"Don't you?"

"Um, maybe?" Did I?

"You can watch them for two whole halves Friday afternoon and make your decision accordingly."

Pre-calc finished, Spanish vocab studied, World Cultures chapter read, it was time to pack up and face the inedible, I meant inevitable, dinner with Dad. Tough under normal circumstances, and these circumstances were anything but normal.

Tracy offered me a ride home, but I declined, not wanting to get there any sooner than I had to. Besides, the walk might help clear my head. Or fill it with even more dread. I twisted in my earbuds and found *The Ramones* by, who else, The Ramones. There was comfort in the familiar, joy in the speed, and drowning of thoughts in the volume. I almost forgot that at the end of the walk would be my dad who had moved out, scared the crap out of me, treated my mom like dirt, and somehow made me feel guilty for hating him.

Why didn't the volume on my iPod go any louder?

I arrived home at 5:30 with my dad expected to make his grand appearance at 6:00. Would he ring the doorbell? Use his keys?

Drive his car through the living room? Would he be late? Early? Cancel and prolong the agony another day?

I felt like I was about to get a shot at the doctor's office. The waiting and buildup would drive me insane, the experience would totally suck, and hopefully when it was all over I could say I made it through. But what if this was like a tetanus shot, where I not only had the buildup and the suck but the entire week after of a giant, gross bump on my arm and pain and stiffness so freakish I have to call the doctor to make sure I'm not the one in 7,500 who has an adverse reaction?

To my dad.

When I arrived home, the driveway offered no sign of my dad's car. That didn't mean it wasn't lurking in the garage, but a quick "Hi! I'm home!" through the front door greeted with hellos from only my mom and sister told me we were safe. For now.

My mom wore a swingy skirt, low heels, and a shawl she knitted but rarely wears. Mara had on the Rosh Hashanah wrap dress, apparently her favorite item to wear to a meal where my dad's unpredictability dominated. "Do I have to dress up or something?" I asked, annoyed. Why should I wear anything nice for him? Why should I put any extra effort into my clothing for something that should just be an everyday, average event? You know, for most people having dinner at their own house with their own parents isn't some occasion to transform into the fancy version of themselves. It should be relaxed and comfortable and uneventful enough to warrant only jeans and a t-shirt, possibly a bathrobe. Napkins optional.

"Only if you want to," my mom said as she pulled a turkey out of the oven. What was this, Thanksgiving?

"I don't." I dropped my backpack, which I still clutched in my hand, with a thud on the floor.

"Can you put that thing in the hall closet, honey?"

Who was she kidding? That we were a family that dressed up? That we ate turkey other than from the deli counter at the grocery store? That we put things away?

I kicked my backpack along the floor until it found its place in the closet, then I stomped up to my bedroom and closed the door. I didn't slam it because I wasn't in a slamming mood. But I also wasn't about to set the table for Dad. I stepped my shoes off and lay down on top of my covers. The Clash poster barely contained the anarchy symbol underneath, so I thought, why hide it? Standing on my bed, careful not to rip the poster any more than my parents had during the room makeover, I peeled it from my walls. The rashness of the anarchy symbol made me chuckle to myself, and I placed The Clash poster onto the bare wall space next to it. The punky pink blared through the spaces in the anarchy symbol, a perfect juxtaposition of my new life trying to contain the new life wanted for me by my parents. The very new life that they completely shot to shit by dissolving their marriage.

Pink walls couldn't help that.

But maybe blue hair could.

If not, at least it might help pass these anticipatory twenty minutes or so.

I dug an old towel out of the linen closet and locked myself in the bathroom. Under the sink was my jar of Manic Panic's After Midnight, a radiant deep blue that I thought would stand out nicely from my dark brown hair. Once, when Tracy and I were walking around Chicago, I saw this girl with curly black hair interspersed with curls of bright blue. I hoped mine would turn out similarly.

The directions suggested using gloves, and I thought it was a good idea to not go to dinner with Smurf hands when I would already be going with a Smurf head. I fished around under the sink until I found some big, yellow, rubber cleaning gloves. Those would have to do. The clunkinesss of the fat finger holes would make the application of the color less precise, but I was going for a wide blue stripe and thought it shouldn't be too hard. I dipped two fingers into the blue goo and smoothed it onto a strip of hair at the front of my head. It just looked wet. So I added some more and made the stripe a little wider. Maybe it would look different when it was dry.

I sat on top of the toilet and let the dye sink in. Mara had left one of her magazines in the bathroom, so I passed the time looking at pictures of young stars with zits. I loved how they had zits, in a sort of evil bitch way, like, ha-ha, beautiful people, not looking so beautiful now, are we? Then I felt bad, which was ridiculous since they couldn't hear what I was thinking. Nor would they care if they could.

The doorbell rang downstairs. My stomach leapt.

I dove to my knees and rinsed my hair under the bathtub faucet. Blue water trickled off my hair and down the drain. When the water began to run clear, I squeezed the excess water out of my hair and rubbed it with the old towel. There was no time to blow my hair dry, which I didn't do normally because it makes curly hair turn 'fro. As of now, my hair looked pretty much the same as it always did wet, with maybe a tiny glimmer of blue where the light hit. Maybe I did something wrong, but I'd have to figure it out later. I heard the familiar deep voice of my dad coming from downstairs, so I crept out the bathroom door to the edge of the stairs. My mom frittered in the hallway, while my dad spoke to her in his conversation-starting voice, the voice he used before things began to annoy him, before we had to figure out which things we said were wrong. My mom walked by the stairs, then my dad, who must have sensed my presence, and looked up at me. Was that a genuine smile? Or was it the fox smiling at the gingerbread man before he bit his head off?

I think I was hungry.

"Hi, Anna. You look nice."

I do? My hair is wet, and I didn't even change my clothes.

"Have you lost some more weight?"

I hate that question. It's such a backhanded compliment, like, *You needed to lose weight and now you've lost some so you look better than you did before because you couldn't possibly have looked as good while you were fat.*

"I don't know. I haven't weighed myself lately." My answer felt cold, but I hoped it wasn't cold enough to set him off.

"Time to eat!" my mom called from the kitchen, so I was forced to walk down the stairs with my dad waiting for me at the bottom. With each step, I wondered what we would do when I reached the ground floor. Hug? Shake hands? Bow to each other, Japanese style? Dad answered that by engulfing me in his wide embrace, my arms pinned to my sides, unable to hug him back, even if I wanted to. Did I want to?

After too many excruciating seconds, my dad let me go and we sat down at the table. Mara had taken the time to construct place-holders for the four of us, each with a fuzzy animal sticker from her own collection (I was represented by a narwhal. They make narwhal fuzzy stickers?). Thankfully, she sat me between her and my mom, although that put me directly across from my dad. This was possibly the only time in my life I ever wanted a gigantic family to help diffuse the situation.

Dad watched as Mom bustled bowls and plates onto the table, heaped high with things she never made before to showcase what effort she put into this sham of a meal. We were never the pass-the-food type of family. We're a go-to-the-counter-and-make-your-own-plate group. Maybe that's how I managed to chub out as a kid; giving all that freedom to a child is dangerous. But so is giving them a stressor in their life that makes them eat to comfort themselves because their mom is too busy cowering from their dad to be the comforter.

I glared at my dad across the table, but subtly just in case. Steamed green beans, candied sweet potatoes, rice with various rice colors and styles intermingling, all made their way around the table. I mean, bowls of them were passed. How creepy would that be if green beans walked around the table? Or the rice? They would look like maggots. God, maggots are gross.

Obviously, I occupied my mind with anything that would find its sick, little, writhing white head inside, just to avoid the tension of the table. Nobody spoke at first about anything of importance. *How was school?* Who gives a shit? *How's cheerleading going, Mara?* Who gives a shit? *Business at the knit shop good, Beth?* WHO GIVES A SHIT?

I didn't.

So I just said what everyone was really thinking.

"Why are you here?" I asked my dad, point-blank.

He set down the spoonful of maggot rice that he was about to shovel into his mouth. I thought maybe we'd get into a circular conversation, like, I'm your dad, why wouldn't I be here, blah blah blah. But instead, my dad looked at my mom, cleared his throat, then spoke to all of us. "Your mom and I have been married a long time. And we both love you very much." I turned my view from my dad to my mom. She watched him with anticipation. The brightness had faded somewhat from her faux polished face, like she wasn't quite sure what was coming next.

"After much discussion, your mom and I are going through with a divorce."

Dropped fork and blank stare from Mom. That was not what any of us were expecting.

Dad waited for a response, as if one of us would clap him on the back and tell him he made the right decision.

Finally, Mom spoke, "Allen," but she wouldn't look at him. "I don't understand. We didn't discuss that. Not recently. You told me you were working things out. With your therapist."

"And I did, and we decided that divorce was the right option."

"You decided? With a person you've known for a month?" My mom's voice quivered.

"You're the one who set me up with her. Don't blame me."

Was he kidding? He just announced that he and my mom were getting divorced—surprise!—and somehow it's my mom's fault because she got him to see a therapist. God, were therapists good for anything except screwing people up? What if Dad was seeing my Freudian ex-therapist, and she told him to get a divorce because that's what Freud would do? If I ever saw that woman again, I'd pee in her Diet Coke.

I could barely contain the anger from this "conversation." My parents, the same two who thought I needed fixing, were the most fucked-up adults I'd ever known. And I didn't have to sit around and listen to their lopsided marriage dissolve.

"Come on, Mara. Let's get out of here." I stood up, knocking my chair back. Mara's frozen face said traumatized, so I grabbed her hand and yanked her behind me as I walked down the stairs and out through the utility room door, not before I grabbed the keys to my mom's car.

I punched the glowing garage-door button, and the heavy door jerked open. Mara was too glazed to question my next move. I opened the driver's door to the Accord and inserted the keys into the ignition. Before I closed the door, I stuck my head out and asked,

204

"You coming?" Mara didn't hesitate, her only answer was the physical act of joining me in Mom's car.

I had very little driving practice. With all of the missed school and panic attacks and irritable bowels, I skipped the sixteen-year-old's right of passage of Driver's Ed. But one of the few things that Lake Shit taught me was that I learned best by experience, and there was no better time to try than now.

Jerkily, I chugged the car out of the garage and down the driveway. As an ultra-novice, I checked right left right left before feeling comfortable enough to inch my way onto the street. My mom and dad appeared on the front porch, and I could hear my dad yelling through the thick car window. I slammed my hand on the radio knob, not caring what I heard other than the sounds of *not* my dad. Even talk radio was better. I kicked the car into drive and overdramatically jammed onto the gas. Mara and I screeched away from the ruins of our once-complete home and turned the corner and out of sight.

When I finally relaxed enough to recognize I was only driving twenty-five miles per hour and on a residential street, I turned to Mara to witness her reaction: heaving tears.

I'm guessing I had a little to do with that.

"Hey, hey, Mara." I wanted to pet her head or something, but I wasn't confident enough to take my hand off the wheel. I pulled over less than two blocks from our house and put the car in park. "Everything will be okay," I told her, hating myself the second the generic reassurance left my lips. What did okay even mean anymore? Was that the void that lived between good and bad, the space where most people lived? Yeah, it was bad that my parents were getting divorced, but it was good that they wouldn't be around each other to fight. It was bad that I was in a mental hospital, but good that I met some amazing people. It was bad that I took my mom's car, but it was good . . . um, that I didn't hit anything? Yet? Was life meant to be lived in that okay space because it was a hell of a lot better than living in the bad one? Is that what people mean when they say, "It's going to be okay?" That it might not end up good, but something surely will surface to drag it out of bad?

"I don't want to live with Dad," Mara snuffled.

I laughed a little, that Mara's first fear was not the impact the divorce had on our parents but on her life. And why shouldn't it be? If they were thinking about us they would have worked things out. So why should we think about them?

"Hell no is that going to happen. You think Dad wants us to live with him? He doesn't even spend time with us on the odd occasion he *is* home."

"So are we never going to see him again?" Mara looked at me with full-on saucer eyes, like those creepy beanie animals that look so desperate for love.

"We'll see him. Maybe they'll have some every other weekend deal or a week in the summer or something. Before you know it, you'll be in college and it won't even matter."

"Nuh-uh. Before *you* know it. I still have five years to go."

"Yeah, that kind of sucks. But you can milk it for all kinds of goods and services."

She laughed and looked at me sideways. "Goods and services?"

"You know, if your wagon ever breaks down and you need some oxen. Or a cure for your dysentery."

"You're weird." She smiled. "Do you think Mom and Dad are shitting because you took the car?"

"Probably. Let them shit awhile. They've given me enough shit for a lifetime."

Mara and I sat in the car and talked for another half hour, some about our parents but mostly about school and boys. Mara did most of the talking, and I was happy to hear of her popularity and successes. At least someone in this family was doing something right.

As I cruised into the driveway at a staggering eight miles an hour, my mom watched with arms crossed on the front porch. I put the car in park, pulled out the key, and left the car on the driveway. My first solo mission wasn't the venue for a garage landing.

I thought maybe Mom would yell, like, because she couldn't seem to get the fight up for my dad, she saved it for the (very rare) moments like this. She didn't. Mom turned on her heels, whipped open the screen door, and disappeared inside the house. Dad's car was gone. When Mara and I walked into the house, Mom was texting someone. She looked up at me and Mara and said, "Your dad's driving around looking for you. I told him you're home."

"Is he coming back?" Mara asked.

"No. He isn't." Mom was on the verge, so she tripped her way up the stairs and slammed her bedroom door.

You know your life is fucked up when you just stole your parent's car, and your mom is acting like the overly dramatic teenager.

SKIRTING THE ISSUE

I awoke the next morning feeling hungover. Or what I assumed hungover people felt like. My head hurt, my mouth was pasty, and when I looked in the mirror, I stared a bit at the circles under my eyes. Not to mention the faint halo of blueness that barely registered on my hair. I thought for a minute that maybe Rodney Yee would help me out, but looking at a man in tiny undies didn't sound appealing. Instead, I showered until the hot water turned into warm water turned into unbearably cold water that forced me to get out.

When I left the bathroom, pruny but less face punched, my

mom met me outside the door. I had so many questions, yet I didn't really want to hear the answers. Can't I ever start the day with a Pop-Tart and a cup of happy?

I asked, "Sleep okay?" It seemed like a relatively benign question.

"Yes," she answered, bedraggled.

Was it really my place to comfort her? To get her up and out and ready for her day? Was I not the child of parents of divorce? Or was I just being selfish?

We stood in silence for a minute, neither of us budging on the coddling. Not wanting to be late for school nor to be standing at a stalemate in the war of who deserves the attention, I said, "Sorry I didn't save you any hot water."

"Oh. Well, I don't open the store until eleven today, so that should give me some time for the hot water to grow back." So no coddling then? "I see the blue didn't completely wash out of your hair," she noted with a hint of agitation.

"I didn't think anyone noticed."

"It's subtle." She touched the barely there color. "I noticed the stained towel you left on the floor even more."

"Yeah. Sorry about that. I picked an old one, if that helps."

Silence.

"I guess I'll be going to school now. And you?" I prodded.

She looked wistful. "Maybe I'll do a little yoga to clear the ol' noggin."

"Rodney Yee?" I asked her.

Mom looked at me quizzically. "You know Rodney?"

"Not personally. I mean, we're not sharing codpieces or anything."

"Codpieces?"

"You know, those tiny underwear he wears."

"I think they're workout shorts."

"I prefer to think Rodney likes to exercise on the beach in his banana hammock, and a roving camera crew just stumbles upon him."

"Is that why you watch him?" She raised an eyebrow.

"Mom! The guy is like forty. And has a ponytail. And did I mention the crotch cuddlers?"

"But you do watch him, right?"

"Yes, I have been doing a little yoga lately. It helps me relax," I admitted. Something about both exercising and trying to relax made me feel like I was admitting to my mom that I had needed improvement, which then was somehow an admission that mental hospitalization had been necessary and she, and Dad, were right.

She clapped a small victory clap but saw my look of hesitation and toned it down. "Would you mind if I borrowed the DVD?"

"It's yours, so technically I'm the one doing the borrowing. I'll get it." I popped the DVD out of my craptop and delivered it to Mom. At the handoff, she surprisingly and desperately hugged me. The hug felt full of praise and love, and like she'd break if I let her go. "Better get dressed," I told her, still in hug. "School and all." She hesitatingly let go, and I skedaddled to my room.

In an effort to combat the home yuckiness, I wanted to dress up a little. Rifling through my drawer, I found a Ramones t-shirt that my Aunt Gilda bought me for my birthday two years ago. It was a seriously generic Target shirt, which felt so wrong to me at the time—a Ramones shirt at Target!—that I promptly threw it on the bottom of my drawer. No, that's not true. The first thing I did with it was try it on. Just to see how it fit. And the annoying thing, besides it being from Target, was that it had a really tiny neck hole. Why would they make an extra-large shirt with a tiny neck hole? Not that extra-larges necessarily have big heads, but this was like microcephalic tiny. So what I did was step into the neck hole first with one leg and then the other, and I spread my legs apart as much as I could to expand it. When I was finished, the neck ring was almost as large as the hem on the bottom. *Then* it went into the bottom of my drawer.

I stepped into the super-sized neck hole again, this time pulling it up around my hips, where it fit in a snug but not muffin-squeezing manner. I pulled out one of my new t-shirts, a solid red v-neck, and put it on. The tee covered the misshapen neck portion of the shirt/skirt but the sleeves on my hips caused some unflattering lumpage, so I tugged the shirt/skirt back down, found my scissors, and lopped off both sleeves. When I pulled the shirt/skirt back on, the holes where the sleeves once were now provided a lovely window onto my polka-dotted underwear, as well as a portion of my lily-white thighs. That wouldn't do. Rummaging through my tights drawer, I found a royal blue pair and pulled them on, creating a blue circle that barely peeked out from underneath my red t-shirt. It almost had a superhero-like feel. I loved it.

Anna Bloom: able to leap divorcing parents and do-gooder English teachers in a single bound!

I finished the look (I had a look!) with my black Chucks, alien earrings, and a black stretchy headband.

My mom paused the Rodney Yee DVD as I bounded down the stairs. "Don't you look cute?"

"Yes. Yes, I do." Not that she was really asking.

"That skirt is cool!" Mara complimented me between cereal shoves. "I'm going to make one."

"Not out of one of your shirts, you're not," Mom warned.

"Whatever, Mom. Go back to your sun salutation," Mara commanded.

My walk to school was uneventful, as was, gratefully, much of my day: just your average school day after your parents, or should I say, *your dad,* announced their divorce: group work, pop quizzes, lessons where no one else gets anything, lessons where everyone but me gets everything. The exception to the average was that I hadn't had average on a regular basis for so long that I guess it wasn't technically average. I was so busy at school that my body forgot to have a stomachache.

Plus, I don't know how many compliments I received on my shirt/skirt. At lunch, Meredith suggested I turn it around, so The Ramones were on the back instead of the front. " 'Twould be sacrilege for me to sit on Joey Ramone's face," which I regretted saying before I finished the sentence.

Eleanor blurted out, "You would totally sit on Joey Ramone's face!" way too loudly so that the adjacent lunch table of freshmen looked over at us.

"Joey Ramone is dead, Eleanor," I noted somberly.

"Oh, man, sorry."

"No worries. He's not my dad or anything." Why did I say that?

"I bet his face looks way too nasty to sit on now anyway." Eleanor found some consolation.

"Nice, Eleanor." Tucker looked at Eleanor with steely eyes, but she ignored him and started up another conversation about her game-crossed Homecoming date. Tucker's steel turned into roll, so I suggested, "Want to go get a shake?"

He stood up as a yes, and we snaked our way around tables to the snack counter.

"Why does she still bother you so much?" I asked. "I thought you were over her."

"Is it obvious? And I am over her."

"First you shot her the eat-shit look of the century, and then I

211

thought your eyes would seriously roll out of their sockets and land on her Pocky."

"Graphic."

"But apropos."

"Apropos?"

"Please continue avoiding my question until I'm old and withered and only have one tooth left with which to chew."

"I don't think one tooth would be enough with which to chew. Wouldn't you need a second tooth to break up the food?"

"Walking away now . . ." I turned abruptly back towards the way we had come, but Tucker grabbed my shoulder and forced me to look at him.

"Sorry. I'd like to pretend that she doesn't piss me off, but she does. I don't get how anyone can be such a stone cold bitch. Pardon my French."

"Is that really French?" He smiled. "It is a little scary sometimes. But she must have some redeeming qualities that make us stick around. For instance, she shared a piece of her Pocky with me today. Albeit the end without any chocolate on it."

We walked until we reached the snack counter. "Hot chocolate again?" he asked.

"Sure," I replied, about to dig into my pockets. But I didn't have pockets. "I forgot I was wearing this skirt. My money's in my locker. I can pay you back tomorrow. At the soccer game." I said the last bit subtly, to see if the occasionally socially oblivious Tucker would notice. At first, he didn't, ordering our chocolaty beverages and leaning against the counter to wait. Eventually, though, the bulb illuminated. "And what soccer game would that be?" The lunch lady handed our drinks over the counter. Tucker warned me, "Careful, it's hot," and we started the journey back to the table.

"Thanks. You know, the soccer game? The one you're playing

in? Not that that's why I'm going. Tracy's new stumpy Auto Shop lover is on the team, too. So we're going to watch him. Or, she is, and I'm just going along for moral support."

"I see." Tucker spooned some shake into his mouth but didn't look at me.

"Would you like me to cheer for you? Since I'll be there anyway?"

"Is that what you'd prefer to do?" I watched as his smirk started between spoonfuls of shake.

"Absolutely. I can make up clever little cheers, like"—I used my most bubbly cheerleader voice—"Tucker, Tucker, he's no sucker. You can't beat him, you little—"

He interrupted, "Nice. Very nice."

"I do my best." I smiled. But shouldn't I be doing my best for that guy who might be waiting for me at Lakeland? Crap.

The bell rang, and Tucker and I said quick goodbyes to avoid the ridiculous crap that had just spewed forth from my mouth. I guilt-whipped myself all the way to Gym, then I spent all of World Cultures scribbling Justin's name over various notebooks, binders, and book covers in funky fonts in penance. I attempted Tucker's font from his photo essay, then recognized that I was again thinking about Tucker instead of Justin, and promptly changed to 3rd-grade-type bubble letters. I'm even a cheater in my doodling.

Somehow I managed to doze off during the last fifteen minutes of class while we watched yet another historically accurate film (which luckily wiped the guilt from my brain, if not the drool from my desk).

Art was time to get serious. If I was going to have enough time to select, develop, print, and mount any of my photos for the narrative, I'd actually need to take the pictures soon. With Tucker and Eleanor in the darkroom and Meredith working diligently on frames she was creating for the project, I finally managed some focus.

The pet cemetery idea was kind of cool, right? But still didn't really have to do with me, I guess. If only I had a dead pet! I mean, my pet dog was dead, but that was like more than five years ago and I have no idea what the vet's office did with the remains. I could make up a story, pretend one of the pet graves was mine . . . I worked with that idea for twenty minutes, then scrapped it when I realized it was crap. I kept coming back to that one day in class, when Tucker, Eleanor, and Meredith asked me about Lakeland. And how Tracy did, too. And all the stories I could tell but hadn't. Slowly a narrative idea came to mind, and I got that feeling in my stomach, the good kind, that's warm and buzzy and excited because it knows that it finally got something really right.

AND I'M THE ONE IN THERAPY?

I happened to leave Art at the exact time as Eleanor, so we walked down to our lockers together. Eleanor used to be on the debate team, back when she cared about school appearances. Now her only extracurricular is first chair in the orchestra, which essentially took all her time that wasn't usurped by World of Warcraft. I liked the dichotomy of that: the romanticism of the musician vs. the dorkism of the gamer. But they both involved intense commitment and focus, not to mention a competitive streak that Eleanor brought to everything she did. I admired her for that. While it did up her intensity and administration of fear, it also rocked a girl power vibe I should probably rock myself more often.

I wish I knew her enough to understand what went down between her and Tucker. Were they actually boyfriend/girlfriend? Did they hook up? Have sex? I shook my head, trying to erase the budding image of the two of them together. Which should not have mattered. But I had never seen them kiss or even hold hands, and the contact I had seen usually somehow involved a palm or fist transfer from Eleanor to Tucker. Being just in-school friends with people meant I never got to know the real, no-holds-barred version of them.

Funny, then, as Eleanor and I said our goodbyes that I was on my way to seeing *only* that version of a group of people I barely knew.

Which meant I didn't really know them either.

And said a lot about how they, and I, aren't only defined by one facet of our lives.

So, like, was I not necessarily Mental Hospital Girl?

Let me figure that out while I sit in group therapy. Sigh.

Mom picked me up, and I was relieved to see her slightly less of a mess than this morning. While she wasn't as polished visually (her bob was half pulled back into a barrette), she still managed to match her clothes and wear a little makeup. Lip gloss at least. She definitely could have used some under-eye concealer, though; I'd never seen her look so puffy. Or maybe I'm just looking to see if things are wrong.

I didn't have to look very far.

Mom didn't ask me how my day was. She had NPR blasting and drove hunched over the wheel like a granny trying to read street signs.

Ugh.

I was on my way to *therapy*.

Therapy she (along with another guilty parental party) put me in.

Again with the confliction: Do I ask how she's doing, or should she be asking how I'm doing?

"Mom, do you need me to drive? You look tired." I wanted to say, you look like you might run a red light and drive through a 7-Eleven window, but I thought that was going a bit far.

"What? No. I'm fi—" She couldn't even get the word out before the tears dropped and the shudders began. Luckily, we were only a block away from my group when this happened, and she somehow managed to find her way to the office.

If only eyes came with windshield wipers.

I had nothing useful to say to her, and I didn't want to have to say anything even if I did. So I bolted.

"I have to go. Don't want to be late." And that was it. Out the door.

Did I feel guilty?

Yes.

A lot?

No.

How many things was I supposed to be working on here?

"What's your problem?" Bart asked me when I walked into Group, an annoyed sneer on his face. I didn't deserve that. Not from him.

"Fuck off." I blurted the first thing that sprang from my head to my lips.

Whoa.

I had never told anyone to fuck off aloud before. It felt both scary and empowering, especially after I noticed the tiniest wounded expression on Bart's face.

And then I felt bad again.

Why did everything have to make me feel bad? What was the point of having parents if they couldn't take care of me because they were incapable of taking care of themselves? What was the point of being in therapy if it made me feel like shit? And what was

216

the point of going to a mental hospital if now I was out and my life still wasn't better?

Even if maybe it sort of was.

"Sorry, Bart, didn't mean to snap at you." He shrugged it off as though he could give a turd, but I felt better. I flashed back to Apologies at Lake Shit. Did they actually have something productive to teach me?

Peggy started Group per usual by going around and having us share our moods. Ali went first. "It's been a decent week, actually, I got a B on a trig test I thought I was going to fail, and Brett has been absent the last few days. I checked the attendance sheet."

"I thought there was a noticeable lack of Axe in the air." Miles chuckled to himself.

"And what about you, Miles?" Peggy prodded.

"Not much to report. Mom threatened no band practice if I didn't sleep, so then I didn't sleep for fear of lack of band practice. I worked on a new installation piece using broken guitar strings and a pop-can lamp." He looked at me as he said this. Was he trying to impress me? Was I impressed?

"Anna?"

How much did I want to tell? Was I ready for actual therapy here? Did I need it?

"My parents' divorce is official. I mean, not signed, sealed, and delivered, but my dad moved out and told my mom he wanted a divorce. We were thrown totally off guard, so now Mom spends all her time crying or trying not to cry and I feel like a bitch because I have no interest in any of it."

"That doesn't make you a bitch," Bart surprisingly interjected. "It makes you selfish. Just like your parents are selfish. Just like everyone else in the world is."

"Except you, right, Bart?" Nepa blinked.

217

"I learned from the best." He stared down Nepa. "By that I mean my parents, of course."

"We all blame our parents to some degree, don't we? For everything?" Miles looked around the circle.

"For everything. For their damn sperm and egg and placenta and shitty genes and depressing house and bourgeois rules." Bart was on a roll, and Miles and I looked at each other with held-back smiles. Bourgeois?

"I don't blame my parents for my rape," Ali piped up.

"Ah, but you should," Bart continued. "If they didn't fuck you up to where you wanted to be liked by some jock bro, then you wouldn't have been so needy. You wouldn't have gone to the party, and you wouldn't have waited so long to tell someone what happened."

Ali crossed her arms and glared at Bart. "You miserable prick."

Peggy tried to add an adult perspective to the building momentum of blame. "It's very common for teenagers to discover that their parents have faults which, in turn, can lead to distrust, disillusion, or disappointment . . ."

"Peggy, no offense, but you're playing for that team," Miles pointed out.

"True, but if I just sat here with my mouth shut the entire time, I'm afraid we'd have a mass parental lynching on our hands."

"What about you, Anna? You started this," Bart accused. "Do you blame your parents for making you this way?" He flapped his hands at me, indicating "this way" had something to do with the way I looked. Or the way I was. I couldn't tell, and I wasn't about to give him the satisfaction of asking.

"I do and I don't. I'm sure the genetics are there that predisposed me to depression. The environment, while not ideal, was still not horrible compared to some people I know." I thought about my friends at Lakeland, dealing with sexual abuse, absent, sick, or dead parents. "They put me in a mental hospital, and yet here I am doing a million times better without relying on them emotionally because I can't rely on them right now due to the fact that they are just as emotionally inept as I am. I think it's too easy and cowardly to just blame our parents because if we do that," I looked at Bart as I spoke, "then we aren't taking any responsibility for our own actions. And we're not giving ourselves any credit for what control we do have over our own lives. I don't want to end up like my parents, so I'm going to choose not to."

"Amen to that." Nepa produced a hand for a high five, and the whole circle was high-fiving, excluding Peggy. And Bart.

"You prefer not to," I jeered at him. He offered a delicate middle finger.

Peggy wrangled the group back. "Anna, would you like to speak anymore about your feelings on the divorce?"

"You know, not really. I think my parents should talk to someone about it. I've got enough of my own stuff to think about."

After that, Nepa talked about her parents pressuring college decisions, and everyone gave their two cents. Including me. There I was, a part of the group. And not the part that felt like the mental hospital freak either.

Was I moving beyond Lake Shit, or had it merely become another facet of me?

MAIL CALL

As I waited outside of Group for my mom to pull up, Miles approached to offer me a ride again.

"My mom picks me up. Sort of her way of keeping tabs on me."

"Well, if she ever wants to take her tabs off you, tell her I'm willing to give you mine?" Miles confused the both of us with that one, and we laughed.

"Thanks. I'll be sure and let her know there's a tab trade offer out there."

"Cool. Well, see ya."

"Bye."

He looked back. "Very cool skirt, by the way."

"Thanks." I hoped I wasn't blushing.

My mom pulled up an uncharacteristic five minutes late. While we sat in relative silence on the drive home, I thought about my mom's mom and dad, neither alive anymore, and if she blamed them for where she ended up. Was there a cycle going back to the beginning of time of kids blaming their parents? Are we all doomed to turn into the same people as our parents, or are we, as I so eloquently tried to convince myself earlier, in control of our own lives? What if everyone on Earth is really just a slightly tweaked version of the people who made them and we're all living the same lives over and over again but in different period clothing? My brain thoroughly warped by the time we arrived home, I decided to check the mail. I lugged my weighted backpack out of the car and onto my shoulders and headed towards the mailbox. By the time I reached it, I felt like the two straps were permanently embedded in my shoulders. I gingerly slid the straps off one at a time and let the backpack flop onto the grass. Inside the mailbox were bills with both my parents' names on them (God, what a mess that's going to be), mailer things that are most definitely contributing to deforestation, and a letter inked with familiar handwriting. "Justin Waters." Except that it wasn't in the *from* corner of the envelope, but in the middle where the *to* address was in *my* handwriting. In perfect script, on an angle to the left of the Lakeland address, was written, "Return to sender."

Return.

To.

Sender.

That was me.

What the fuck? What happened? Did he write that? No, because there was no way his handwriting would be so neat. Who, then? Did they stop giving him his mail? Was he caught having sex with Dania in the middle of the Day Room, and so now he is on no girl contact whatsoever?

Or did something happen to him? What if . . . ?

I couldn't think about it. I couldn't think about him trying again and succeeding at the thing that brought him to Lake Shit—to me—in the first place.

I sunk down into the grass and laid my head on my rock of a backpack. Tears snuck out of my eyes at first, and I willed them to go away with a swipe of my palm. That just made it worse, and they flowed freely. Sobs and shudders joined the tears.

Did I lose Justin? Had I already lost him when my insurance ran out? Is this what they mean when they say it's better to have loved and lost than never to have loved at all? Are *they* freaking crazy?

After crying on the grass next to our mailbox for ten minutes, I started to worry that my neighbors might alert the authorities that there was a lunatic girl wearing a shirt for a skirt sprawled out on the grass at the Blooms' house. I worked my way up onto my knees, then pushed with my hands until I stood. There was no way in hell I was lifting that backpack again, so I kicked it with my Chucks. Big mistake. There was no longer a crazy girl lying on the grass because now she was hopping in a circle and screaming every obscenity she could think of, plus a few choice ones she just made up (chodecruncher, anyone?).

I reached down for the handy handle on the top of my backpack (so that's what it's for) and dragged it up the lawn and through the front door. Mara and Mom looked at me as I stopped right inside our front hallway, with the saggy, flushed face of a girl who'd just been crying for ten minutes straight and the hair of a girl who did it in the grass. At first, I read my mom's look of frozen panic. The is-she-depressed-again? expression that combined sadness, disappointment, and annoyance I saw so many times when my parents thought I would go back to normal by myself before Lake Shit. But Mara, who was my sister, thank god, and not my messed-up mom saw more than that. "What happened, Anna? Are you okay?"

That completely did me in. I couldn't have stopped myself from crying if someone glued my eyes shut by accident with Krazy Glue. Or on purpose.

Eeewww.

And with the tears came my story. I told them everything. About my friends at the hospital, about the weirdness of trying to be normal again, and about Justin.

My mom and Mara sat with me through three hours of tears and laughter and disbelief. We huddled around the kitchen table, the Bloom women, and they consoled me and let me know that whatever I felt, wherever I was, it was okay. Mom assured me that she'd get to the bottom of the returned letter and suggested I write to some of my other friends at the hospital to see if they could tell me anything.

While I wrote short, urgent letters to Matt O., Sandy, and even Abby, I was fueled by the possibility of hope. It was just a mistake, and I had to believe that until I found out the truth.

It almost felt like my mom was taking care of me for a while this afternoon when I fell apart. Imagine that. I only noticed her eyes glaze over to that far-off divorce place three, four, maybe five times, as I talked. And she managed to say yes to pizza when she completely forgot that we needed to eat dinner.

I was trying not to blame her in my head, but I really wanted her to be uninterruptedly there for me. Was that selfish? Were we all really selfish, like Bart said? I didn't want to turn out like my parents. Or Bart.

After a few pieces of pizza, I went up to my room. I couldn't concentrate on my homework, so I read from *Catcher,* which was homework but didn't feel like it. I read all the way through to the end. And then I reread the last page about fifty times. Was Holden where I think he was? Because the implication was that he told his whole story, the one I completely fell for, from a hospital. A mental hospital? It's not like he mentioned a broken leg or appendicitis. Jesus fart. Even in books, I fall in love with the crazy guy.

I didn't want to dwell on it, since I was sure we'd analyze the piss out of it in Groban's class. When I finally managed to shut my brain off and fall asleep, visions of Day Rooms and textured, pastel walls danced in my head.

TEN GALLONS

The next day, I wasn't in a dramatic fashion mood, so I threw on a new pair of jeans and a Big Steppin t-shirt I ordered from this guy who walks all over the world taking really big steps. The shirt shows a silhouette of a big stepper. Kind of funny. I had never worn it because I ordered the women's large, and it was nothing of the sort when I originally tried it on. Now it fit decently. On my shoes, I experimented with some fluorescent duct tape I acquired back in the day when I was into making wallets. Instead of plain, black shredded Chucks, I now had shredded Chucks with happy, hot pink and orange mouse eyes, ears, nose, and whiskers on the toes. That way, every time I looked down, my shoes would make me smile. In theory.

Once down the stairs, I assaulted my mom with, "So you'll call Lakeland?"

"I'll see what I can do." She sighed as though put out. Forgive me, Mom, for asking for your help. "There are a lot of rules and laws and all sorts of things protecting your privacy, which is a good thing, Anna. For your sake, it means other people can't call them and get information on you." She sipped her coffee to let me ruminate on her point.

"Thank goodness. Now no one will know my sordid mental hospital secrets of playing too many card games and eating Cap'n Crunch," I joked. Maybe I was being too hard on her.

"I'm only saying that I'll call, but I don't know how much it will help."

"Will you please mail these letters for me?" I stood up after my bowl of the Cap'n and handed my Lakeland letters to Mom. I know it means, if my mom's sleuthing attempt fails me, I'll have to wait a minimum of four days to hear anything from anyone through snail mail. With today being Friday, that means Tuesday at the earliest. My mom better hear something or I might go crazy. Again.

Mom took the letters and laid them next to her half-eaten egg white omelet. "Do you want a ride today?" she asked.

"No thanks. Tracy's coming to get me. And is it okay if I stay after school today? There's a soccer game T and I want to go to."

"You want to go to a soccer game? Who are you, and what have you done to my sister?" Mara cracked.

I gave Mara the old scratch my cheek with my middle finger.

Mom hesitated. "I guess that's okay."

I tried to move my mom's brain away from wherever it was headed. "Did I tell you guys Tracy's going to Homecoming?"

"No way!" Mara choked on her Golden Grahams.

"Yeah. With a guy she met in Auto Shop. He's the perfect size for her."

"What about you?" Mara asked.

"I'm also nicely sized for her." I knew what she was really asking.

"I meant are you going to Homecoming?"

"No. I mean, no one's asked me. I just kind of assumed it would be like every other dance in my life, and I'd either go with my friends or not go at all. And since all of my friends appear to already be going with actual dates, I guess that means I'm not going." I didn't realize the subject of Homecoming was a topic of contention for me, but by the end of the answer to Mara, my voice was noticeably louder and icier.

"Sorry I asked."

The doorbell rang, and I booked out of there before my mom could impart some depressing words about how love doesn't work out anyways so why bother? Not that she would, but I felt guilty talking about anything romantic even if it had nothing to do with me.

It was five minutes into our walk that I realized Tracy was wearing a soccer jersey. Assman's soccer jersey.

"Whoa. You are wearing school-spirited clothing, T." I stopped walking, crouched low, and scanned the horizon with my hand over my eyes.

"What the hell are you doing?" she asked.

"Looking for the apocalypse. This is a sign, right? It's coming?"

She shoved me, but not hard enough to break my ready stance. "Shut your bag, okay. I like him. He asked if I wanted to wear his uniform shirt. It seemed kind of romantic at the time."

"That's not the shirt he wore yesterday, is it?" I waved my hand in front of my nose to waft away any potential smell.

"Yes, and it's steeped in his sweat. I drank the majority of it with my breakfast." I gave her my grossed-out tongue face. "It's his away-game shirt. See, opposite colors."

"But of course. Looks good on you. In a weird, jockish girlfriend way."

"Thanks, in a kind of backhanded compliment way."

"No problem." I smiled overly sincerely. "Well, I'm totally ready for the game. I brought my vuvuzela," I joked.

"What the hell is a vuvuzela?"

"You know, those really loud horns they blast at the World Cup? Not that I watched it, but I read a news story that people kept complaining about how annoying the sound was."

"Did you really bring one?"

Blank stare.

"Okay, that's a no. I like your hair, by the way. Didn't notice it earlier"

"Yeah, you can barely see the blue. I feel like it just made my hair look darker."

"It did mostly. I can actually only see it when the sun shines directly on it." I frowned. "If you want it to really show up, you have to bleach the hair underneath the blue first. I can help you do it sometime. My aunt makes me bleach the shit out of her hair whenever I visit. I'm an old pro at sucking the pigment out of hair."

"I may take you up on that. I never thought I'd say that to you about something having to do with hair coloring, but cool."

While we walked I told Tracy about the returned letter from Justin. As suspected, Tracy had a plan. "You know what we have to do?" she asked. I waited for some scheme involving auto parts, giant asses, and wrestling moves. "We have to go down to the hospital and find him."

I hadn't expected that.

"Like, go to Lake Shit?"

"I can borrow my mom's car tomorrow, and we can leave first thing in the morning and——"

"Whoa, T. I don't know if I'm ready to go back there. I'm just getting used to being out."

"How else are you going to know what happened?"

"My mom's going to call. I wrote . . . letters."

"They're not going to tell your mom jack shit, and the mail is so Oregon Trail, Anna. We need to take matters into your own hands."

"You've been watching cowboy movies on your big TV again, haven't you?"

"Maybe. But cowboys wouldn't puss out, so you shouldn't either."

I was no cowboy. But after being in a mental hospital, making it through and coming out the way I did, which was at least better than I was before, I was no puss. "Let's saddle up, then. Tomorrow. High noon."

"A bit much."

"You started it."

"Your shoes are cute, by the way."

"Thanks, pardner."

"Shut it."

WHO KNEW?

As my English group tried to pull motifs out of our asses, I asked if anyone else finished *Catcher*. Ed Muntz, the brainy one, had of course, as did Ella Santos, the girl I hardly knew.

So they finished. Which meant they knew that Holden was in a mental hospital. Did they know I had just been in one, too? Did they think it was a freakish coincidence that the character of the book we just read *and* this girl in their group were both hospitalized?

I felt sweat forming on my upper lip, and a tingle in my stomach. Luckily, a classroom full of people in their final day of group work on a Friday maintained maximum volume. Even if I did manage to work myself into a panic attack, I knew I could calm down with my Rodney Yee breathing without anyone noticing.

I had to understand what I read, though. I had to get why this character who I thought was sweet and romantic, a little selfish and arrogant, directionless but in a charming way, was hospitalized like me.

Mr. Groban sat at his desk grading papers. I stood next to him, expecting him to look up when he recognized a student standing nearby. He did not, so I cleared my throat and said, "Mr. Groban?"

He looked over the tops of his glasses at me, a hint of surprise in his brow when he realized who it was. Then he said pleasantly, "Anna. What can I help you with?"

I sat down at a chair next to his desk. "Did you know when you assigned this," I pointed to his copy of *Catcher,* "that Holden was in a mental hospital?"

"So you've read ahead?" He looked pleased, and I wanted to slap that smarmy look off his face.

"Not the point, Groban." I never called teachers by just their last name, at least not to their face. That seemed like such a jock thing to do, like the next step was to smack his ass and scrimmage, whatever that meant. Funny word, "scrimmage." "Do you not think it at all weird that the second I get out of a mental hospital, you assign a book where the main character is in one? Do you not think—"

He interrupted me. "Anna, my syllabus is the same as last year. Would you have wanted me to change it because of you? If I had told the students to disregard their calendars and forget *Catcher in the Rye,* do *you* not think at least one student would ask why?"

"I wasn't saying we shouldn't read it, but, I don't know, a little warning would have been nice," I conceded.

"Anna, that was partly why I was so, shall we say, overprotective of you when you first came back. On top of what you already had to deal with, I felt some sense of responsibility to guide you through your reading in case you had a negative reaction to it."

"That was kind of thoughtful, I guess. But not Mr. Antolini thoughtful, right?" Mr. Antolini was one of Holden's teachers in *Catcher*. Holden called him up in the middle of the night to ask for help and a place to stay. As Holden was about to fall asleep on the couch in Antolini's apartment, he found the teacher petting his head. Holden freaked out and left abruptly.

"What was wrong with Antolini?" Mr. Groban asked, intrigued.

"The guy was an obvious perv."

"You think so, huh?" I nodded emphatically. "That's definitely one interpretation. We'll talk about that chapter in class on Tuesday."

"So you don't interpret him as being a little creepy?" I asked.

"A little drunk, maybe, but teachers can be very protective of their students, Anna. Sometimes it's like I have ninety children of my own. Maybe Mr. Antolini was treating Holden in that way."

"Maybe," I mulled, amazed at how quickly a teacher can twist my mind. "I guess I better get back to work then."

I started to stand up, but Groban had more words of wisdom to impart. "Anna." I sunk back down in the chair. "Mr. Antolini had some advice for Holden. On page"——Groban picked up his copy of *Catcher*, licked his finger (which grossed me out fully), and flicked until he found his page——"one eighty-nine. Here . . ." He thrust the book at me, and I began to skim. It was a big, long paragraph where the teacher was telling Holden about how he's not the only one going through crap, and then he basically tells him to get an education.

"So you want me to stay in school. I get it." I put the book down.

"No, no. I mean, yes, but that's not what I wanted you to see." Mr. Groban opened the book back up for himself. "Mr. Antolini says that many people are just as troubled as Holden is and that, happily, many of them have kept records of their troubled times. Holden can learn from them, and if he chooses to write some of his thoughts down, someday others can learn from him. I see a lot of you in that, Anna. I think you have a potential for greatness. This blip in your life of being hospitalized might help inspire some of that to come out, which in turn might inspire someone else."

I didn't know what to think of Groban's speech. Whenever someone says I have potential, it makes me feel like I'm not living up to it. But he also made me feel like maybe there was something more to me, something I could share of myself to better the world.

The bell rang with me still sitting near Groban's desk. Everything he told me was probably spouted directly from the What Every Teacher Should Say Manual, but it made me think differently about the book. And myself.

What to do with those thoughts, I had no clue.

SLEUTHING IT UP

At lunch I decided I couldn't just sit around and wait for the Pony Express to deliver my mental hospital mail, so instead of going to the lunchroom I went to the library. The network was on my side for once, but when I sat down on the butt-abusing wooden chair, I didn't know where to begin. Social networking sites were blocked, which didn't matter anyway since Justin already told me that he didn't believe in Facebook or Twitter or any other site where you posted pictures and up-to-the-minute information about yourself. As he so eloquently put it, "No one needs to know when I'm taking a crap. Besides, my real friends know how to find me." At the time, I thought he was dreamy cool for bucking the system that everyone else is so addicted to, but now I had one less place to seek him out.

I had an email address, memorized because of how it said so much with so little: bassnomore@gemmail.com. Here we go again with having to think of clever banter when all I wanted to do was grab hold of him and never let go.

With the time constraint of the lunch period and having already exhausted so much of my emotional self recently, I went with simplicity:

To: bassnomore@gemmail.com
From: gabbagabbaanna@dotmail.com
Subject: Exodus from Lake Shit
Justin, I wrote you a (real) letter, and it came back returned.
Where are you? You better be ok.
<3
Anna (Bloom, from Lake Shit, in case you didn't know)

After I hit send, I wasn't satisfied with my complete lack of answers.

I typed *Justin Waters* into Google as a start.

Thirty-three million results stared back at me.

"Mother effer," I said aloud.

From behind me, a voice said, "It might work better if you put quotes around the words, like this." Tucker stood over me, looking at my computer screen. I whipped around in my chair and hissed, "What are you doing? Here? Looking at my computer screen?"

His eyes widened beneath his glasses, surprised by my protective reaction. "Hey, sorry. You weren't at the lunch table, so I thought I'd see if you were here. I'll go." He began backing up, but I stopped him.

"No, it's okay, sit down. You can help." Tucker dragged a heavy wooden chair next to mine. "Nearsighted," he explained, as he lifted his glasses on top of his head to get a better look at the screen. "So what are we searching for?"

How much should I tell him? He didn't need to know everything, since I certainly wouldn't want to hear about a romance he had in a loony bin. Why not, though?

I looked at his hazel eyes turned blue from the reflection of the computer screen. "Who's Justin Waters?" he asked, breaking the pixilated spell I was under.

"Oh, a friend. From the hospital I was in. I wrote him a letter, and it got returned to me."

"Did you try resending? Maybe it was just a glitch in his email."

"No, like a real letter. We couldn't use computers at Lake Shit."

"Curious," he said. "Do you mind?" He commandeered the keyboard and surrounded the *Justin Waters* with quotation marks. "That way, it searches for the two names together instead of every website that has either the word Justin or Waters."

"Right. I forgot about that." I also forgot about Tucker being such a know-it-all. As we scrolled through thousands of pointless listings with Tucker asking almost an equally thousand number of times "Is that him?" I wanted him to go away.

"Tucker?" I said through clenched teeth after he somehow managed to click on a website for a dentist named Justin Waters for the fifth time. "I got this, okay? There are only"—I leaned back to read the clock on the library wall—"five minutes left in the period, and I have nothing. Don't you want to eat lunch or something?" Which, no matter how it was said, sounded bitchy.

He scooted back his chair and mumbled, "I just wanted to help you," which somehow annoyed me even more.

"I don't need help, Tucker. I'm perfectly capable of many things. And look, you didn't help me because I still don't know what happened to Justin!" My voice was raised well above acceptable shushing levels, and the evil librarian eye fell upon me. Tucker lowered his glasses back into place and looked at me seriously through them.

"Do you need to talk?" he asked.

Wrong question. "Tucker, as much as I appreciate your help, this is sort of personal. No offense. I'll just—"

"No problem. I get it," he said sharply. "Maybe I'll see you in Art." With that, Tucker turned on his ratty Vans and marched out of the library.

So now I get to feel like double ass because I knew nothing else about Justin and I hurt Tucker's feelings even though I didn't even ask him to be there in the first place.

I closed the browser and walked into a far back corner of the library. Hidden by the nonfiction stacks, hopefully out of view of the leering librarians, I pulled out my cell phone and crouched down, pretending to look at a book on the bottom shelf, and pushed and held 3, my mom's cell on speed dial. It rang until it hit voice mail. The lunch period bell rang, and I knew I needed to get to Gym on time considering the only thing contributing to my Gym grade anymore was my attendance. I quickly pounded 7, the number to my mom's knit shop, and on the fourth ring my mom picked up. "Mom?" I whispered, panicked.

"Anna? Are you okay, Anna?" She repeated my name, like we were taught to in health class during trauma situations. Was this a trauma situation?

"Calm down, Mom. I'm fine. I'm in the library and the bell just rang and I'm not supposed to be on the phone. I just wanted to know if you called Lakeland."

Pause.

Very annoying pause.

More silence.

"Hello?" I pushed.

"I kind of forgot, honey."

"Forgot? What the hell, Mom!" I whispered a little too enthusiastically. Phone confiscation by librarian was growing nigh! "This is, like, everything to me. I have to go to class. Will you please call now?"

"Sure. Yes." Mom sounded like she was scrounging for something on the desk, hopefully a stapler to affix a note to her forehead.

"I'll call you back after this period." I hung up without a goodbye to go along with all the drama.

I trudged to gym class, deflated from lack of information. I watched a particularly lame game of badminton (even the word "shuttlecock" wasn't funny today). When what seemed like six-hundred shuttlecock jokes later, Gym finally ended. I ran to a bathroom stall and dialed my mom again. The second she picked up, I hissed, "Did you call?"

"Oh, um, yes. Yes, honey, I did." That didn't sound good.

"What did they say?"

"I'm sorry, dear."

"Oh, shit. He's dead, isn't he? He's dead and they returned the letter and they didn't even tell me. What kind of therapeutic bullshit is that?" I wasn't able to keep a whisper going, but I didn't care.

"Anna, let me finish. They wouldn't tell me anything. I mean anything. They couldn't even admit to having a patient by that name because of privacy issues."

"But didn't you tell them we knew he was there, and that I was there and I just needed to know—"

"I tried everything, honey. You're just going to have to wait and see what your friends write back to you."

If they write me back, I thought.

"I gotta go, Mom."

"I love you, honey."

"Yeah, you, too."

As I trudged to Art, I tried to look on the bright side. No information still meant everything could be okay. And maybe Tracy and I would find something out at high noon tomorrow.

In Art, Tucker was already in the darkroom when I got to class. I knew he deserved an apology of sorts, but I was having trouble coming up with one that didn't sound like "Tucker, sorry you were so annoying and didn't help me AT ALL today." Then I flashbacked to Community at Lake Shit, where we handed out Appreciations. What would I have said to Tucker if this happened at the hospital? How would I have gained maximum points?

I rolled through the darkroom door. There were three other people, Eleanor being one of them, developing photos, but the trickling water provided a nice sound buffer to the room.

"Tucker." I tapped his shoulder, and he jerked and pulled a black earbud out of his ear. "Sorry, I couldn't see the wires in this darkroom. You'd think someone could have come up with a cleverer name for a room where you develop pictures. I mean, it is a dark room, but that doesn't need to be its official name."

Tucker put up a curt stop sign hand in the air. "I'm in the middle of something, Anna, do you need anything? Oh, wait, I can't help you, right?"

Was I that rude in the library? Or was he just oversensitive? Appreciation, Anna. Appreciation.

"Tucker, I'm sorry. I appreciated that you tried to help me this afternoon. It was the best you could do with the little amount of information I gave you, and it wasn't your fault we didn't find anything. I probably wouldn't have done any better on my own."

Long pause. The room was so dark that I couldn't tell if he was looking at me, glaring at me, or crossing his eyes under his glasses.

"Apology accepted," he finally offered, even presenting his hand for a shake. I shook it, which seemed to erase any anger he held. For once, something easy. "So have you figured out your project?" He turned to work on his developing, but he let the earbuds dangle around his neck.

"Yeah. You actually really helped with that. In fact, would you like to help me even more? Like, as a model?" I hadn't thought of how I'd execute my brilliant idea for my narrative until now. To make it work, I'd need at least three people. Tracy and Mara were the first two, and they didn't even know it.

"What kind of model? A nude one?" I swore I saw some dancing eyebrows in the shadow under his glasses.

"Not so much. Are you free Sunday? I'll explain everything then. It'll be easy, don't worry."

"I'm not worried. What's your number?" He pulled out his cell phone and typed my number into it, then I did the same with his. I told him I'd call around ten on Sunday morning. "You know we have Monday off, too, for Yom Kippur. If you need me then, I'm free, too."

"Yeah, I kind of celebrate Yom Kippur. Well, not really celebrate. Partake? Slightly observe? But thank you."

As I walked through the revolving door, I caught Eleanor watching me. In the darkness of the darkroom, I couldn't read her expression.

———

KICK ME

Tracy met me at my locker after school with a rolled-up piece of giant red construction paper. I stuffed my backpack into my locker to be picked up after the game, and asked, "What've you got there?"

"Just, you know, a poster I made to hold up during the game."

"Say what now?" Tracy was rarely meek, so I relished the thought that whatever hid in that paper was appropriately mortifying.

"I made a poster for Arthur."

"Let's just take a gander, shall we?" I grabbed the paper tube and used my three-inch height advantage to hold it high in the air until it unfurled and revealed, "Kick Their Balls, Arthur!"

I busted up laughing, not able to hold back even a little to soften the blow to Tracy's tough-girl façade. When she looked as red as I'd ever seen her, I said, "No, T, it's really sweet. And yet, violent at the same time. Very you. He'll love it."

"Think so? I wonder if he'll even be able to see it in the bleachers." She rolled up the paper and gripped it in her fist.

"Most definitely. And I'm sure it will inspire him to kick many balls, soccer or otherwise."

As we walked, I looked down at my mouse-made shoes. Still funny. When I looked up, I ran smack into a solid mass bolting down the hallway. The impact was enough to knock me back onto my slightly less-padded butt. Above me stood Tucker, sans his usual horn-rims, holding out a hand to help me up.

"Sorry, Anna, I was running around a corner and I didn't see you. Are you okay?" Without his glasses, the hazel in Tucker's eyes reflected a twinkle of gold that I'd never noticed. Did I just say twinkle?

I reached for his offered hand, and Tucker helped me up off the floor. For a second, I panicked that he wouldn't have the strength to heft me up, but the way he did it felt effortless.

"Is this part of your pregame warm-up? Running through the halls of the school in your uniform?"

"No, I just forgot that I left a picture in the stop bath. I didn't save it in time, in case you're wondering. I can print another tomorrow." He looked at his watch. "Not to be rude, but I have to get to the field."

"Break a ball, or something," I encouraged him. Tucker ran off, and I smacked my forehead at the ridiculous sentiment.

"We seem to have balls on the brain," I noted.

"Well, it's better than on our—"

"No need to finish that sentence, T."

"Your call."

The game was a blur of boys in shorts with nice legs running back and forth after a ball. Whenever Arthur or Tucker came near our bleacher seats during play, Tracy and I shouted such cheery inspirations as, "Rip off their shin guards, Tucker!" and "Kick 'em where it counts, Assman!" which Tracy approved of because it sounded more competitive than "Arthur."

Oddly, no one else seemed to share in our violent spirit, but that didn't stop us from trying to start stomping psych-outs for the other team. I'd like to believe our four feet's worth of stompage had an effect on the outcome of the game, since our team won 2–0, but I suppose we should give a little credit to the actual players.

Tracy wanted to hang around after the game to congratulate Assman, but I thought if I waited around for Tucker it might be a bit too fangirl. So I collected my loaded backpack from my locker and tried to walk home without turning into a hunchback at the ripe old age of sixteen.

Mom and Mara left a note on the kitchen table that they were out seeing a movie based on some bestseller about middle-aged people remembering their youth. No thanks. I helped myself to an Amy's microwave mac 'n' cheese but didn't finish it. My stomach was punched up from the anticipation of the Lakeland visit tomorrow.

To quell my nerves, I tried watching a marathon of *Ghost Adventures* on the Travel Channel, but even Zak getting his butt grabbed by a Civil War ghost couldn't exorcise the fact that tomorrow I may or may not see Justin. Way scarier than ghosts.

WELCOME BACK, BLOOM

What exactly does one wear when returning to their alma nutter? I felt like somehow I should look better than I did when I went in, all pasty and depressed, wearing only the socks and sandals I had with me until my parents dropped off my Chucks. I don't mean I *only* wore socks and sandals. God, I was nervous.

I thought about wearing the Ramones shirt/skirt again, but after wearing it all day and stretching out Marky's face, it wasn't exactly in mental hospital debut mode. Instead, I went with a pair of my new jeans, fitted in all the right places (What does that even mean? Like, yeah, they fit in the right places, otherwise how would I wear them? If they only fit the wrong places, like my head, that would just look stupid), and my Mickey Mouse shirt. I slipped in my alien earrings and chose a red scarf of my mom's to roll into a headband, offsetting Mickey's red shorts nicely.

I decided against telling my mom where T and I were going. First off, I didn't think she'd be okay with it. Or maybe she would have because it's not like I was checking myself back in. But maybe she'd think it would be too traumatic and bring back horrific memories of public showers and Satan worshippers.

Thinking about the satanic absurdities of Lakeland made me laugh to myself. How is it that in one small mental hospital floor there was one Satan worshipper, one girl who sometimes had seizures and spoke in demonic tongues, and one boy who believed he heard Satan in his head?

And would I get to see any of those people today?

The other reason I didn't tell my mom I was going back to Lakeland—back to a place I was dragged to against my will and kept for three weeks in some bizarre alternate, yet slightly romantic universe—was because it felt very personal and powerful. I didn't want to have to explain to my mom the Why. Although she knew about Justin, going back wasn't just about him. It was about seeing how this place fit into my real life, my life now. And how *I* still fit into it.

My excuse was effortless and not even that much of a lie. "Tracy and I are going out to plan my big photo narrative essay assignment. Then she's going to come over tomorrow to shoot it. So is this guy Tucker from school. Is that okay?"

My mom gave me the curious and slightly perverted mom eye that asked who this Tucker character was, but I didn't bite. I had one boy on the brain today, and he needed all my focus if Tracy and I were going to get to the bottom of the Justin mystery.

The bottom of the mystery. Who really says shit like that? And what are they referring to? The mystery's ass?

Mara shuffled downstairs, bleary-eyed and hair wildly sprigged, while I fueled up with the Cap'n. "I need you, too, tomorrow."

"Need me for what?" she yawned.

"I have a big assignment for Art class, and I want to use you as a model."

"Okay. As long as I don't have to be naked."

Why is that where everyone's head goes? People need to get their minds out of the gutter. Which is apparently where naked people hang out.

Tracy texted me to let me know she was outside. I grabbed a bottle of water for me and a Code Red Mountain Dew for Tracy. They were technically Mara's, but her eyes were still glued shut with crusties so she didn't notice.

"What time will you be home?" Mom asked.

"By dinner. Tracy has to work until close tonight."

Before I left, I ran up to my room and grabbed my digital camera. I was supposed to be working on a photo assignment after all, and maybe there would be something—or someone—photo-worthy.

I could hear and feel loud and heavy—and did I mention loud?—music emanating from Tracy's car. When I opened the door, Metallica assaulted my ears.

"It is too early for Lars, thank you," I yelled as I reached for the volume and turned it to a more bearable level. Metallica was one of those bands that I liked when I was in the mood but grated on my innards when I wasn't. With the anticipation of what or who I may encounter today, my innards were already thoroughly grated.

We drove for a while with only the speed metal as our soundtrack and the wind flying through the open windows. When we hit the highway, T closed the windows and spoke over a never-ending guitar solo, "I saved directions on my phone just in case."

"Thanks for doing that. I don't know why I didn't. Maybe I thought that chip they implanted would lead me directly back to the hospital."

She glanced at me to check the seriousness on my face, saw I was kidding, then asked, "So what do you want to do first when we get there?"

As simple and obvious a question as that was, I didn't yet have an answer. When Tracy originally came up with the idea of visiting Lakeland, I had visions of a romantic reunion with Justin, complete with slo-mo running towards each other down a long corridor and an even longer make-out session. But number one: We didn't even know if Justin was still there. Or still, you know, *there*. And number two: How exactly would we get close enough to the floor to see Justin or any of my other friends?

"The plan may have a little snag," I eked out.

"Which is . . ."

"Well, it's not exactly a plan, is it? All we said was that we were going to Lakeland to try and find Justin. But Lakeland is this four-story building with a lobby and heavy security in their elevators."

"What, like big dudes with Uzis?"

"Uzis, T?" She shrugged. "No big dudes in the elevators. But there was some elaborate key system. We couldn't go down to the cafeteria without someone sticking a key in a hole."

"That sounded dirty." She chuckled.

"*Anyway*," I stressed, "we couldn't even push a button to call the elevator without a key. How are the two of us going to get anywhere near the floor?"

"I—" Tracy started, but I interrupted.

"And let's say we did get to the floor, which we won't, then what? The elevator opens into a hallway right in front of the check-in desk. What if the instant the elevator door opens, they call security? Or worse—what if they think we're some escaped psycho teens and instead of kicking us out, they lock us up and no one knows where we are and we have to wear the same clothes every day and you miss Homecoming with The Assman!"

"Anna!" Tracy finally barged her way into my spewage. "You must chill. I didn't think we would really get anywhere near the floor. Did you? You already told me how tight security was while you were there."

"Then why are we going?"

Tracy looked at me with guilty eyes and then back at the road. "I hadn't really thought that far ahead. But I got directions."

"T!"

"What? You were all mopey about Justin, and there wasn't anything you could do, so I though this was being proactive. Something to give you hope."

"But what is this even? All we're going to be able to do is look at the outside of the building. Maybe if we're lucky, the lobby. It's not like we're some super-sleuths who could figure this shit out by a fingerprint and suspiciously gnawed pencil."

"Speak for yourself."

"Dude, as much as I appreciate your thought, there was no thought." I sagged down in my seat.

"So what you're saying is that you don't appreciate any of this."

I thought on it, then said, "Guess so."

"That's a load of rhino testicles."

"What do you mean?" I looked over at her, pissed.

"You don't appreciate at all the fact that a) you're no longer stuck in the mental hospital we're trying to infiltrate, b) you look and act a million times better than before you were in there, and c) you have a kick-ass motherfuckin' friend like me to take you back just in case we find Justin." She paused with recognition. "Get it? Just-in case?" Tracy smiled at her obvious pun, and I couldn't help but smile, too.

She was right, of course. If this were Appreciation time, I'd rack up the points for all the things I could appreciate.

"Sorry I was so unappreciative. Ugh—can we use a different word?"

"How about buttsnicker?" Tracy suggested.

"What? I meant a synonym for appreciate."

"Who says buttsnicker isn't a synonym for appreciate? I just made it up."

"Fine. I buttsnick you, T, for taking me to Lake Shit. Even if we don't find anything."

"That's my little buttlicker."

THE EYES AND THE SOUL AND WHATNOT

After we exited the highway, I played navigator with Tracy's phone and shouted out rights and lefts until we were only a block away from Lakeland. The building itself, really just a short, brown, unassuming building, looked barely familiar, since I only saw it on my discharge day. When I was admitted, it was dark outside, and I was a blubbering mess who wouldn't have recognized Johnny Ramone if he were the guy giving me the Rorschach test. I did, however, recognize the building across the street, my view for three weeks whenever I was sequestered in my room. Which was quite often. I knew every window, with its hanging laundry, and the number of parking spots on either side. My getaway cars were gone, which was probably how it should have been. Those cars weren't meant for driving; they were fatefully parked there to give me hope of getting out.

And there I was.

Out.

"There's a spot on the street over there." I pointed to a parallel-parking spot on the opposite side of the street from the hospital. When Tracy turned off the engine, silencing the Metallica song she had playing, the reality of where we were hit my stomach like an extra-large stack of blueberry pancakes.

I was sitting outside of Lake Shit.

My friends, maybe even Justin, were living inside.

I was so close to them, but I couldn't touch them. Although, I couldn't touch them while I was inside according to the rules.

A choke settled in my throat, and a tear slid down my cheek. Tracy looked over at me.

"Aw, man, I didn't think this would upset you. Do you want to go?" she asked, shoving her keys back into the ignition.

"No. Not yet. It's just weird. I don't even know how I feel. Proud that I'm out? Sad that I can't even say hello to my friends inside? Totally freaked out that I'm here with you, and yet there are these other friends"—I waved my arms to indicate somewhere nearby— "and you guys will never ever meet. This spot where we are right now is just the complete intersection of my two lives. Are we even supposed to be here?"

Tracy opened her car door, but I hesitated another minute. Out the window, a homeless man pushed a shopping cart filled with pop cans down the street. At the next corner, little kids screamed on a jungle gym at a playground. Two more worlds that were so different, yet existed simultaneously. The world can be so fucked up, yet we're all living in it.

If we choose to.

I opened the car door and stepped outside. Another beautiful, not-too-hot, blue-sky, sunny, Chicago fall day. I joined Tracy on the sidewalk directly across the street from Lakeland. The signage on the building was subtle, nothing like "Lunatic Crossing" or "Beware of Crazies" to indicate who dwelled inside.

"What do you want to do?" T asked.

"Well, we're here, so we might as well try to go inside." I surprised myself by saying that, but it's what my heart told me to do.

My head was telling me I was an assmunch, and I should be grateful I got out of this place when I did, but I tried not to listen. It was my head's fault I got admitted in the first place.

I crossed the street with authority, and Tracy followed. If I stopped, I might have wussed out and not made it over the threshold, so I powered through the automatic double doors. Obediently, they opened.

I stood about ten feet in. Nearby was the room where they first interrogated me upon admission. Ahead and to the left were the elevators that took me upstairs to my floor. Between me and the elevators were a lot of people, some waiting in black pleather chairs, others looking busy in doctor coats, and a few standing behind various desks with signs dangling overhead indicating "Billing" and "Admissions."

"This is not at all what I expected the inside of a mental hospital to look like," Tracy said from behind me. "It looks more like a bank."

"You won't find any patients on this floor. Once they figure out what level of insanity you are, they ship you off to the correct floor."

"No shit," Tracy whispered in awe.

"As long as we're here," I said, and walked towards the Admissions desk. In my most adult voice (which was really just my voice with a serious look on my face), I spoke to the sullen, middle-aged woman wearing wire-frame glasses behind the counter. "Hi. I'm looking for a patient that was here. My mail to him has been returned, and I—"

The skag interrupted me, and not in a very pleasant manner. "Are you family?"

"Not exactly." You never know. Maybe I was his future wife.

"Then I can't release information."

"But I know he was here, and all I want to know is if he's okay."

"I'm sorry." No, she wasn't. "We are not at liberty to release that information."

"How would you feel if you didn't even know if your friend were still alive?"

"And how would you feel if you were hospitalized and any Tom, Dick, or Harriett could walk in off the street and gather information about you?"

"I *was* hospitalized, and I sure as fuck would want my friends to know if I was still alive!" I yelled, definitely too loudly for a mental hospital lobby. Or a bank.

"I cannot help you."

"You're right about that," I quipped and turned dramatically on my heels. I walked angrily down the hallway and out the double doors, Tracy following closely behind me.

"Bastards!" I yelled when I got outside. "That's just how they were on the floor, too. Rules. Fucking rules that don't make any sense. Oh, don't drop your pillow, or the world might end! Don't touch anyone or you might explode into molecules! Don't smile because that might mean you're happy and then how would we make our money!" I yelled loud enough that the homeless guy, who was now coming up our side of the street, looked my way.

"Sorry, Anna. This wasn't the best idea." Tracy started toward the car, but I grabbed her arm and stopped her. As I looked across the street to my Lake Shit window view, it came to me.

"No, T, look up." She followed my eyes, which were focused on Lake Shit's fourth-story windows. "I think that was my room." I pointed at a window on the front right of the building. Behind each window was the heavy mesh screen that prevented us from escaping. I counted with my pointer finger. "If that was the Day Room window, then that was Justin and Matt's, Colby and Lawrence's, Abby and Tanya's, my room, and the Quiet Room." That covered all the windows.

I shivered with excitement at the discovery, but I didn't know exactly what to do with it.

"So you want to scale the walls or something?" Tracy asked.

"Why, do you have a grappling hook in your car?"

"Left it at home."

I looked around the ground until I found a nice array of decorative white stones bordering some bushes at the base of the building. I picked one up, stepped back, and lobbed it at my old window. Missed. When Tracy realized what I was doing, she came over and grabbed a rock, whipping it and hitting my window on her first try. We stepped back and waited.

What was I expecting? Sandy to come to the window with a wave and a smile? To let her hair down so we could climb up and gain entry? Or was there part of me that thought I might see myself up there looking back at me?

Nothing happened.

"They're probably at Community. Or maybe lunch," I told T.

"Why don't we try the other windows, just in case." Tracy and I gathered a handful of rocks and started chucking them at all of the bedroom windows. After each hit, we waited, but no one came. "We could hang out and wait until they're back," she suggested.

"We could," I said, but I wanted to try one more window. "Let's go to that window. That's the Quiet Room. Maybe someone's in there."

Tracy and I each threw a stone, and they both tanged off the window perfectly. I shaded my eyes with my hand and waited. Two seconds later, a familiar face appeared.

Leave it to Matt O. to be in the Quiet Room when I needed him.

SIGN LANGUAGE

Matt O.'s pudgy face looked down at us. I jumped up and down excitely and waved my hands as if trying to attract a plane on a deserted island. It was hard to read the expression on his face through the thick screen, but there was no mistaking the overexaggerated waves of joy he expressed.

Now what?

I tried yelling to him. "How are you?" Which came out as an aggressive shout in hopes he could hear me.

His questioning hands told me he couldn't.

"Do you have paper in your car? And a pen?" I looked to Tracy.

"I'll go get them." Tracy ran to her car while Matt O. and I attempted our crazed form of sign language. Which meant me screaming things and him pressing his face against the screen. Given Matt O.'s propensity for talking about his ass, I was lucky he wasn't trying to moon me.

I thought about all of the universal symbols I knew, and they all screamed either hateful, the finger or the chin flick, or romantic, blowing kisses or drawing a heart in the air with my fingers. Even if I did know actual sign language, I doubted he could read it from this distance.

Tracy arrived with a notebook and a Sharpie, and I wrote in giant capital letters, HOW ARE YOU? When he shrugged in confusion again, I realized that in order for him to see I'd have to write one word per page.

HOW ARE YOU?

Matt O. flashed a thumbs-up from the window, then pointed his finger out to me. I returned the thumbs-up, along with a mega-grin.

I didn't know how much time we had, since someone was bound to notice Matt O. interacting with—gasp!—someone on the outside, so I didn't want to waste a moment. I wrote,

WHAT HAPPENED TO JUSTIN?

I wished I could read Matt's expression, but all I saw was a lot of hand waving and finger moving.

"What the hell is he saying?" I desperately asked Tracy.

"No clue. For all I know he's ordering a cheeseburger."

Just then I saw another head pop into view and look down at us. It was Eugene, one of the pathetic excuses for a counselor at Lake Shit. I wondered if he recognized me. I wouldn't have minded never seeing his bloated face again.

And just like that, Matt O. was out of my sight.

I was about to give up, to turn away and admit defeat, when Matt O. appeared in the window again. It was only for a second, but I could have sworn I saw a thumbs-up.

Then he was gone.

"Did you see that?" I looked at Tracy.

"Yeah, but what did I see?"

"There was a thumbs-up, right?"

"I think so. There definitely was some thumb movement."

"So that's good, right? He means Justin's okay?"

"Or did he mean he's okay after he got in trouble for talking to you?"

"No. Did he? Shit."

As we stood on the sidewalk attempting to interpret Matt O's thumb usage, Eugene rolled through the automatic doors. I froze like a bunny in a garden. Was I in trouble?

Then I thought, what the hell could he do? I wasn't under his rules anymore.

"Hello, Anna. Nice to see you," he said in a way that said it wasn't nice to see me at all.

"Likewise," I said, which was hilarious since I never said like-wise, and obviously, I didn't mean it either.

"You know you can't hang out here, right? This is private property, and the floor needs to be isolated for the program to work properly."

A) We were on a sidewalk, which was public property, and b) program? You call sitting at a desk in a hallway for three days straight because you kissed someone a "program"? Who was he kidding?

But I thought about it, and as much as I wanted to see my friends, I didn't need to get them in trouble. They were still trapped under Eugene's regime.

"We were just leaving. Going to eat some pizza or something." That was my attempt at a dig, since they were always baiting us at Lake Shit with the lure of pizza if we were good.

"Well, nice seeing you," Eugene repeated.

"You said that already," Tracy told him, and I smiled at her protective nature.

After he waddled his way back inside, Tracy asked, "Who was that dildo?"

"Eugene," I said in my whiny nerd voice. So glad he had a name like that to make fun of.

"So what now? Are we going?"

"In a few," I said. "I need to get my camera." We walked across the street, and I retrieved my camera from Tracy's car. From across the way, I began snapping photos of each of the windows of floor four of Lakeland. The sun was bright enough that I couldn't see the images very well on my small view screen, but I had a plan evolving for how they'd fit into my photo essay.

When I was finished, I took one last look at Lake Shit, first the building, then the windows to rooms that once housed me and still held some of my friends.

"Goodbye," I whispered because it felt like the thing to do, then I waved in case anyone, even someone I didn't know, was looking. Couldn't hurt to get a wave from a stranger when you're trapped in a mental hospital.

Tracy and I got into the car, no looking back, and drove off towards home, away from Lakeland for the last time in my life.

ZOOM SNOOP

I waited until Mara and my mom were asleep in their rooms before I went downstairs to view my photos on the decent computer.

As I crept down the hall, I peeked into my mom's room and saw her asleep, sitting up, a book splayed across her chest and a classic black-and-white movie on the TV still at full volume. Maybe she was trying to replicate the loud sounds of my dad's voice.

Before I examined the photos, I checked my email for Justin's reply. Nothing, except a forward from my aunt about the dangers of pumping gas at night. Nothing means nothing. He might not be home, he might not have access to a computer, or he might not be alive. All delightful choices. Moving on . . .

I plugged the memory card into our PC and clicked until a genuine Lake Shit window filled the screen. I photographed them sequentially, from left to right, which meant, based on the lowest JPEG number, I was looking at the Quiet Room. The framing of the window, perfectly aligned with the border of the photograph, begged for something to fill the dull, empty space. Tomorrow when Tucker and Tracy came over, I'd make that happen.

The next few pictures looked very similar to the first, except for the placement of a tree or the faint white drip of bird crap to the side of a window (Abby and Tanya's, not mine). I clicked past Colby and Lawrence's window, expecting to see a cloud of the devil distinguishable in the lines of the screen, like on the cover of the *Weekly World News*. The thought made me laugh, remembering Lawrence and his towering height and imposing deep voice, professing his love for dainty Abby and denouncing Satan for his lover. When she didn't love him back, he returned to Satan-worshipping and even vowed revenge. Then he was discharged to go home and take care of his little brothers and sisters.

At Lake Shit that felt so real.

Outside, it sounded bizarre. Cartoonish. Fabricated. Unreal.

But it was all real. Just a little weird.

Was it any weirder than Tracy dating a guy called The Assman?

Was it any weirder than Eleanor and her devotion to computer-generated violence?

Was it any weirder than Tucker the Brain hiding from his friends that he was also Tucker the Jock?

And was it any weirder that I once lived there, comfortably adjusted, and I now live here, feeling almost the same way?

I clicked to the final picture, Justin and Matt O.'s room, and that's where I saw something different. A silhouette—or was it two silhouettes?—stood like a shadow figure from *Ghost Adventures* behind the screen. The bright sun outside made everything inside the room unidentifiable. Was that Matt O. again, back from the Quiet Room, watching because he knew I was out there? Was it Justin and Matt O. together because Matt O. told Justin I was there? Was it Matt O. and his new roommate because Justin was . . .

. . . gone?

Or was it Justin, standing alone, looking out his window at the exact time I happened to be outside, because he was meant to see me?

I zoomed in, but the image only became more pixilated and less human as I closed in on the figure. Our assignment was to use natural lighting, and the sun was working hard to make that happen. Annoyingly, my camera decided to pick up more sun than shadow, making it impossible to see whoever was behind the screen.

If I had used a regular camera instead of digital, would I have been more careful manipulating the shutter speed and aperture so the image would have been clearer? I kicked myself for choosing the digital quick fix, adding another element of maybe and what-if to the puzzle of Justin.

After I shut down the computer, I brought the memory card upstairs to my bedroom. Inside my desk drawer was a small candy tin, a souvenir from a fishing trip my family took to Minnesota.

There, I met a girl who I spent most of my days fishing with on a pier. When the week was up, we exchanged email addresses. For a while, when we were younger, we wrote each other every day. As we grew older, turned into our teenaged selves, the emails slowed to holidays and birthdays. I put the paper with her email address inside the candy tin for safekeeping. Even though we rarely wrote each other anymore, I still knew I could find her.

I gingerly opened the candy tin and placed the memory card on the piece of paper like a tiny bed. Maybe somehow the magic of the candy box would connect with the pictures of the hospital and help me get in touch with Justin. My brain can go crazy places at night, but it made me feel better and helped me fall asleep. I couldn't remember what my dreams were, but I woke up feeling hugged.

CAMERA READY

When I asked Tucker if he wanted to help me with my narrative project, it didn't occur to me that meant he'd be hanging out in my bedroom all day. Not that we'd be alone, and not that it was *like that,* but my bedroom was sort of sacred, which was why I was using it for the project in the first place. I straightened up best I could, pushing stray objects into my closet, dresser, and underneath the bed. The Clash poster went back on top of the anarchy symbol because I wasn't quite ready to explain it to anyone other than myself. Tucker arrived promptly at 11:00 as I had requested when I called him, and we shared a lovely moment of awkwardness where he met my mom, she smiled a little too much whilst wearing her bathrobe (couldn't you bother putting on some clothes?), and I had to say we were going up to my room. Before my mom could offer up snacks or a promise ring, I also invited Mara to join us.

The blinds in my bedroom were raised all the way in order to let in the optimum amount of natural light. While I set up my tripod and camera, Tucker and Mara made small talk. I fished the memory card discreetly out of the candy tin in my desk.

"You're on the soccer team?" Mara asked Tucker. He nodded. "Cool. Do they have cheerleaders for soccer? 'Cause I'm on the Poms squad at my middle school." Was she flirting?

"No cheerleaders for soccer," Tucker answered directly.

"I wonder why?" Mara pondered.

"Cheerleaders are a skanky American institution, Mara," I explained. She looked at me with offense, but I corrected, "You're a Pom, not a cheerleader. Soccer is more of a European sport, so they don't go by America's sexist, booty-shaking, woman-objectifying rules."

"Really?" Tucker asked. "I thought it was just because soccer and football are the same season, and everyone associates cheerleaders with football players."

"I was totally just pulling that out of my butt, but now the question is if you would rather the cheerleaders be associated with the soccer players."

"Is this some kind of a test? Like if I answer one way, you'll never speak to me again, and if I answer the other way, you won't believe me?" Tucker asked, looking stoic. "Know this, Anna Bloom. I have as much interest in cheerleaders as you do in football players."

"Point taken," I said, adjusting the lens so it focused on my bed.

Tracy walked through my bedroom door gnawing on some beef jerky cradled in a wrapper. "Sorry I'm late. I had to stop for a snack." She raised the jerky into the air as a proclamation.

"We have snacks here, you know," I told her.

"Do you have any jerky?" she asked, sitting on my bed.

"No," Mara scoffed.

"Then you see why I'm late."

"Enough with the dehydrated meat talk. Let's get started. Mara,

Tucker, have a seat, please." I gestured towards my bed and stood behind my camera. "Today we are partaking in Play Therapy. It's something we did at the hospital where this totally flaky woman with gigantic hair asked us each to choose our safe places, and then we had to show everyone, setting up the other people essentially as human LEGOS, to build our safe place. Make sense?"

"In an explanatory way? I suppose. In a therapeutic way? I'm still trying to wrap my head around the concept," Tucker mused.

"That's the messed-up beauty of Lake Shit, Tucker. We may never understand its methods, but we clearly recognize its madness. Case in point: When we did this in the hospital, we weren't allowed to touch anyone. So let's say I was re-creating my bedroom as my safe place, which is what I did at Lake Shit, and I wanted you, Tucker, to be my bed. I could not adjust you in any sort of way—"

Tracy snorted with the obvious, "You said 'adjust' him." Sarcastic stare from me. "Sorry. I'll just quietly tug on my jerky."

"You do that. Anywho, what I was trying to say was that it was a very off experience to not be able to touch a person in *any* capacity"—I eyed Tracy with a "shut up" look—"for three weeks, and this Play Therapy exemplified that. So today I'm going to set you guys up, as my bedroom, just as in Play Therapy, and I'm going to use the self-timer and be in the pictures with you."

Mara raised her hand. "I don't get it."

"Here's an example. Get off the bed, you guys." I shooed them. "Now, Tucker, you lie down on my bed, on your back, and pretend to be a bed."

"How does one pretend to be a bed?" Tracy asked.

"Just lie there. Arms by your side, feet straight out. That's what Justin did." I cringed at myself for revealing that. I don't know if I imagined it, but I swore I heard a quick intake of breath, as if everyone was waiting to hear what I'd say next. Thoughts flooded my head at that moment: the closeness I felt to Justin during Play Therapy while we pretended to be in my bedroom; standing outside of Lake Shit, not knowing where Justin was; and me being there, now, in my real bedroom with my best friend, sister, and another guy who was not at all Justin.

I concentrated on breathing deeply, trying not to let any tears escape. When I decided on this subject for my narrative, I knew it would be personal. The idea of reliving a moment from Lakeland seemed like an interesting, unique, and powerful subject that would fulfill the assignment and earn an A. What I didn't realize was that it was truly reliving that moment for me, and being back inside Lakeland with my outside-of-Lakeland state of mind, not to mention my outside-of-Lakeland people, was a lot harder than expected.

"You okay, Anna?" Tracy asked.

I looked around at my actual bedroom, with an actual bed, actual stereo, and actual posters on the wall. I looked around at my window, sun streaming through without the blurry, darkening screen. I looked at Tracy, Mara, and Tucker, who I could speak to, laugh with, and touch whenever I wanted without getting in trouble for it. And even though Justin wasn't there, and the rest of my Lakeland friends weren't there, and I didn't have the consistency of my Lakeland schedule to rely on, I knew this was where I wanted to be.

"I am freakishly better, T, thanks for asking. Now, where was I?" I finished setting Tucker up as my bed on my bed, Tracy as my stereo in front of my stereo, and Mara as my bulletin board in front of my bulletin board. "I'm going to take pictures of each of you alone, and then I'm going to set the timer and take pictures of me interacting with each of you because that's what the whole Play Therapy deal was about." I began shooting pictures of Tucker as my bed while I spoke. "We were supposed to play, or pretend, I guess, that we were in our safe places."

I assessed the pictures of Tucker on my camera screen. Something wasn't quite right. Behind him was the giant Clash poster I used to cover up the anarchy sign I scrawled on my wall. I jumped up on my bed, standing over Tucker as I pulled down the poster, careful not to tear the corners any more than my parents had during their room rejuvenation project. "Excuse me," I said to Tucker, as I jumped over him onto the floor. "Can you roll this up, T? Try not to get any jerky residue on it." I handed her the poster while I reframed and shot the bed pictures again. With the anarchy sign on the pink wall behind Tucker, I had the picture I wanted.

"Did your parents draw that when they repainted the room? I never thought of your mom as an anarchist. A knittist, maybe," T pondered.

"Yes, and they scrawled 666 under my bed for extra pizzazz." I erupted into jazz hands.

I was about to turn the tripod to capture my Tracy stereo next, but Tucker suggested, "Why don't you do the shots with you in them while you still have the picture framed? That way, both shots will have the exact same framing."

"Oooh. Good point," I said. "At ease, stereo and bulletin board." Tracy and Mara dropped their arms from their mechanical poses and stood behind the camera to watch. I set the camera timer, knowing I could easily have asked Tracy or Mara to take the pictures, but I felt that would make it less my project in some way. When I hit the button, I knew I only had ten seconds to get into my position on the bed next to Tucker before the automatic shutter went off. I dove onto the covers next to him, curled onto my side and closed my eyes. In the ten seconds before the camera's click, I imagined Justin's face, the patches where he was starting to grow hair and the patches where he couldn't. His fuzzy ears. His sweet smile. I opened my eyes and saw Tucker, his sharp features, his hazel eyes, his tempting lips.

Click. Click. Click. Click. Click. Click. Click. Click. Click. Click.

"I had it on repeat mode. In case we moved or something," I spoke quietly into Tucker's ear. Being on a bed together made speaking at full volume seem wrong.

"Can I make a suggestion?" Tucker looked at me out of the corner of his eye, still unmoving as a bed. "Take some pictures from above the bed, looking down at us."

It annoyed me a little that Tucker was always making suggestions, and that they were always good. But when I stepped back and thought for a second, it was cool that such a personal project could illicit collaboration. Which hopefully meant that when the final project emerged, other people would get it. "Good idea," I commended him.

When I attempted to set the tripod up for an over-the-bed shot, I realized that my tripod wouldn't go high enough when on the floor. So I tried setting it up on the bed, which proved way too unstable.

"I'll take the pictures," Tracy offered. I hesitated at the thought of someone else holding the camera, and Tracy never having taken photography, but I didn't see a way around it. I showed her which buttons to push, to which she responded with a delightful "Really? I thought I was supposed to lick the lens to make this thing work."

I lay down next to Tucker again, and Tracy snapped a few pictures. "Open your eyes, Anna. Now move your leg closer to Tucker. Nice." I wasn't sure if Tracy was trying to make the pictures look better or hook Tucker and me up, but the beauty of digital was that I could delete and reshoot instantly.

"Let me see." I held up my hand for Tracy to relinquish the camera. Flipping onto my back, I scrolled through the pictures

Tracy just took. Tucker slid closer to me on the bed, his shoulder touching mine, and we looked at the pictures together. It was a surreal, meta moment. Tucker and me looking at pictures of Tucker and me, all while on my bed, touching. What is it about pretending to be with someone on my bed that is always so freaking romantic? Imagine the possibilities if we weren't pretending.

"These are pretty good, Tracy," Tucker complimented.

"Did you think my button-pressing skills would be subpar? I'll have you know I'm an expert at Wii Golf."

"What he meant was they're framed really well. Thank you."

"You're welcome. Are you done having your way with each other on the bed because I'm ready to be a stereo now." A blush welled up on Tucker's cheeks, which struck me as super-adorable. It took knowing that my little sister was watching for me not to kiss that cheek. Instead, I was all business, firing through the stereo and bulletin board shots in fifteen minutes. When I finished, I suggested we celebrate over lunch. "Can't," Tracy declined. "I told someone at work I'd cover for her two-to-six shift."

"I can't either." Tucker looked at his watch. "I have this huge calculus assignment to finish. I would, though." His face was all disappointment.

"No big thing, Tucker. We eat lunch together five days a week."

"I suppose you're right." He brightened.

We all walked downstairs, Mara to the kitchen for some food and me, Tucker, and Tracy to the front door. As Tracy left, she told me to "Text me if you get bored later. I'll send you the boob report."

I thanked her for her help and promised to text her whether I was bored or not. After the screen door closed behind Tracy, Tucker lingered in the front hall.

"Thanks for everything today, Tucker. I feel really good about this project."

Tucker looked at me seriously, as though he were preparing something important to say. His brow scrunched under the tops of his glasses, and his lips tightened. I looked down to see his hands clenched in fists. Then he released a deep breath, and his hands relaxed open. "Anna, I wanted to ask you something."

"And I want to hear your question, Tucker." A smile twitched on my lips at the concentrated seriousness of Tucker's presentation.

"Anna," he said and cleared his throat. "Anna," he started again. "Would you go to the Homecoming Dance with me?"

Well.

My twitch of a smile turned into a huge grin. "Homecoming?" I asked. "With you?" I never thought I would even go to Homecoming, let alone have someone actually ask me.

"So that's a no, right?" Tucker looked annoyed.

"What? No. I mean, no, it's not a no. Yes."

" 'No, it's not a no, yes'?"

"Delete the nos. Keep the yes."

"So you're saying yes?" He looked down at me through his glasses, a smile budding in his eyes.

"Affirmative. It is a yes. I would love to go to Homecoming with you."

"Well, alright." Tucker looked pleased with himself, then presented his hand to me. I confusingly took it, and he shook my hand once to seal the deal. "I look forward to going to Homecoming with you."

"And I with you, Tucker." I wondered if he knew I was semi—making fun of his formality.

Did it matter? I was going to Homecoming. Anna Bloom, ex—mental hospital patient and fat girl, was going to Homecoming.

THE CALL

The second Tucker left I checked my email again out of guilt. Still nothing. I considered sending another email, threatening to go to Homecoming with someone if Justin didn't write back, but that didn't make any sense. I wanted to go to Homecoming with Tucker. But did I want to see Justin even more?

That night after dinner—an overlapping din of screams from my mom and Mara trying to decide where we needed to go to find the perfect Homecoming dress—I cleared the table. At random intervals, I caught myself smiling about certain memories from the day: lying close to Tucker on my bed; the total surprise of being asked to Homecoming; the handshake. I couldn't believe something so good and so normal was happening to me.

Then the phone rang.

I assumed it was Tracy on her way home from work, calling to discuss the Homecoming text I sent. I answered without looking at the caller ID. Therefore, you probably know it wasn't Tracy on the other end.

"What tittie tragedy do you have for me today?" I asked my caller.

Uncomfortable pause.

Male voice: "Is this Anna?"

Oh my god.

It was him.

Justin.

I ran out of the kitchen into the living room for some privacy. "Yeah. This is Anna."

"Hey, this is—"

"Justin. I know. Oh my god. Are you okay? Your letter came back to me."

"My letter?"

"The one I wrote you. Someone wrote 'return to sender' on it."

"You wrote me? Because I never got any letters."

"Yeah, sorry about that. I tried writing a bunch, and they just sounded really stupid so I never sent them. And when I finally did, it came back. I thought something . . . happened to you."

"Something did. I got out."

"I figured, with the phone call and all . . ." I tried to sound light, when all I wanted to do was scream.

"Yeah." It was hard to gauge his expression over the phone.

"So. How've you been?" I asked, not knowing where to start or what to talk about.

"Not too bad. Listen. I have to go in a sec. My parents are keeping me off all forms of communication, but I was wondering if you want to meet for coffee tomorrow. Even though I know you don't drink it."

"Yeah. I'd love to. We have the day off for—"

"Yom Kippur. I figured. My parents aren't sending me back to school right away, so I can sneak out while they're at work. Do you know where Dagwood's is in Stansville?"

"No, but I can look it up." I ran back into the kitchen, and scrambled for a pen in our junk drawer.

"Does two o'clock work?"

"Sounds good." It sounded more than good, but his phone voice was so cool, I didn't want to sound as crazed as I felt.

"See you tomorrow, Anna." The sound of Justin saying my name melted me to the floor.

"Bye," I managed.

I was going to see Justin. And I had a Homecoming date with someone else.

Fishpaste.

———

264

I spent the first chunk of the night plugged into my iPod with the volume turned up to tune out any thoughts. It didn't work. So I played my bass for an hour. That didn't work. I even tried doing my Rodney Yee yoga DVD, but all I could focus on was fantastical conversations with Justin. Thank god Tracy called me when she got home from work.

"Can you come over?" I blared the second I picked up the phone.

"It's kind of late, what's up?"

"Late? You stay up all night."

"I know, but there's this WWE match on I kind of wanted to watch."

"That's what your DVR is for. I need you here now."

The urgency in my voice must have been apparent because she changed her wrestling tune and said, "I'll be over in ten."

"And Trace?"

"Yeah?"

"Can you bring over the hair bleach?"

When Tracy finally arrived, a painful twenty minutes later, we locked ourselves in the bathroom. I alternated between only wanting to talk about Justin and not wanting to talk about him at all. Either way, my brain was on overload. Like a mad scientist, T snapped rubber gloves over her fingers while she applied a nostril hair–melting liquid to my skull.

"Are you sure this isn't going to make a hole in my head?" I winced.

"No."

"Your bedside manner is appalling."

"Do you want a nurse or do you want fast and cheap?"

"Oh, Tracy, you make it sound so dirty."

"Your brain went there. I merely supplied the innuendo."

While my scalp fried, I relived every moment of my phone call from Justin and the terror, elation, nausea, and confusion I felt. She promised it would work out how it was supposed to work out (whatever that meant), and that she could drive me to Dagwood's. What seemed like three hours later, Tracy helped me rinse the bleach from the front chunk of my hair. "Damn, I'd look awful as a blonde."

"For sure. Let's see how you'll look as a blube."

"A blube?" I laughed.

"Do you have a better name for someone with blue hair?"

We plastered what was left of my Manic Panic's After Midnight Blue to the orangey-yellow stripe that clumped on the front of my head. Tracy left me to do the final rinse, as she had a kinky phone call to make to The Assman before bedtime. I didn't ask a follow-up question.

After I rinsed the blue dye from my hair and the bathwater ran clean, I could still very obviously see bright blue, even with wet hair. This is what I had wanted to do for years but was too scared. Too scared of the attention it might attract. Too scared to look like a poseur. Too scared to do something in case it was doing the wrong thing.

But who's to say what's right or wrong anymore? Nothing feels right in my life, and yet, nothing feels that bad either. However tomorrow goes, I'd have very blue hair while it happened.

MY DAY OF ATONEMENT

Yom Kippur is the Jewish Day of Atonement, one of the holiest days of the year, where God seals your fate for the next year in His Book. One of the atoning pieces of the day is fasting, something I've always been conflicted over. Not eating for an entire day is hard, which of course is the point. I still hadn't decided what I wanted to do on the eating front. My mind could use the cleanse that fasting brings, but my body was already grumbling for some Cap'n Crunch.

I trudged my way down the stairs to find Mara deep in a bowl of Golden Grahams. "Your hair is blue." She spat Grahams, but didn't sound surprised. I envied her easy Yom Kippur eating. My mom didn't allow Mara to fast after she tried it four years ago and passed out during a short walk around the block. I resisted the urge to join her and threw myself facedown onto our couch. "Where's Mom?" I asked, muffled in the pillow.

"She went to temple with Aunt Jackie." I could hear every crunch and swallow Mara made, and my stomach gurgled. But I made up my mind. This year of my life: the hard-core depression, leaving school, three weeks in a mental hospital, making it out, working my way back to the land of normal—it was a lot to think about. A fast, showing my commitment to God and my religion, felt like something a normal Jewish person would do. Of course, not eating would make the wait to see Justin excruciatingly longer than if I had food to take him off my mind. Maybe the hunger pangs would take care of that, too.

To torture myself, atonement style, I worked on my homework most of the morning. I desperately wanted to turn on the TV and kill the next three hours, but another part of attempting to be a good Jew was to not turn on the TV today. I'd already broken my self-imposed Jewish laws (because, ultimately, it's me who decides how I want to participate in Yom Kippur) by going online to print out directions to Dagwood's (I refrained from checking email, which I thought was very good atoning strength on my part), and texting back and forth with Tracy a few times to confirm her chauffeur gig this afternoon.

Being the good Jew that I was (which is laughable because if I were actually the good Jew, I would have been at temple with my mom. Although, I liked to argue with myself that devotion to God and religion comes in all forms and is a personal choice between the devotee and God, so I wasn't really a bad Jew. Annoyingly, that argument only took about five minutes of my atoning time), I decided, atonement style, to reread *Catcher in the Rye*. Perhaps I missed something or got it wrong about Holden being in a mental hospital. Or maybe the clues were more obvious, and I was too blinded by my love for boys in complicated therapeutic situations to recognize the signs.

Atoning and fasting put the kibosh on my second read. Before I even opened the cover, I fell asleep on the couch.

Mara woke me up around 12:30, which was lucky since Tracy was supposed to pick me up at 1:00. I still had to choose the perfect outfit in which to reunite with Justin. That didn't feel very atoney. Part of me thinks the more I use the word "atone," the more I am atoning. If that were true, I would kick ass in the atonement department.

I quickly showered and brushed my teeth, both no-nos for conservative Jews (which I am not) on Yom Kippur. Luckily, along with my relaxed and Anna-created atoning methods, my family were reformed Jews and thus allowed to brush our teeth. I think. All I knew was there was no way in hell I was meeting Justin for the first time since Lake Shit without brushing. For clothes, I went with a newer pair of jeans and a red t-shirt. Then I changed to black, thinking red was too showy and happy, and I didn't want to send the message to God that I wasn't thinking about the somberness of my clothing on Yom Kippur. Plus, with my blue hair the red shirt made me look too patriotic.

I slipped in my alien earrings (because I knew God had a sense of humor), and a bobby pin to hold my blue streak in place (because I think God would want me to look nice for Justin), and put on my black low-top Chucks (because God put Converse All Stars on this Earth), and I was ready to go.

Tracy texted that she was in my driveway at 1:05. I grabbed the old, white beaded bag of my grandma's that I used on occasions when I didn't lug my backpack with me, yelled goodbye to Mara, and walked to the car.

"Hey. How goes the atoning, Blubey?" Tracy greeted me with a question and an uncharacteristic soundtrack of some guy singing over an acoustic guitar.

My stomach growled loudly. "Does that answer your question?" I pulled out the directions to Dagwood's. "It should take us about forty-five minutes to get there," I told her.

"I know. I already put the coordinates into my phone."

"Ah, yes. The coordinates." Tracy slugged my arm.

"Damn!" I cried. "What is this crap music we're listening to?"

Tracy hesitated, then confessed, "Arthur made me a mix. It's not that bad, right?"

Whoever was emoting on the stereo sounded like a dying giraffe. But it was sweet of The Assman to make her a mix. I'd kill for a guy to make me a mix. Really, is there anything more romantic than someone choosing music they either think you'd like or makes them think of you? "It's not that bad," I offered.

We spent most of the forty-five-minute drive listening to The Assman's selection of songs for T, which consisted of mostly singer/songwriter slow jams mixed with singer/songwriter country songs. Very far from our realms of music, but my light head from lack of food didn't mind. The drama of what song would appear next, combined with the directions Tracy's phone strategically announced, kept my thoughts off my stomach and the fact that in a short time I would be seeing Justin, the guy who only two weeks ago was the first and only love of my life.

Then I couldn't stop thinking about it.

We pulled into the parking lot of Dagwood's fifteen minutes early. I directed Tracy to a spot away from the front door so that I could see all cars and people exiting and entering the parking lot. The pit in my stomach, which was now completely empty and really angry with me about that, filled with nervous butterflies drowning in stomach acid. So not a good feeling.

"Holy shit, T. What is going to happen today?" The tension of the moment was given the soundtrack of a gag-worthy John Mayer song, so I turned off the stereo. "Seriously, if I had to listen to that, you would be seeing my bile on your dashboard."

"John Mayer does suck balls, doesn't he?"

"I am so freaked out right now."

"He sucks, but don't let it get to you, Anna."

"I'm not talking about John Mayer, T. I'm going to see Justin." I spoke his name with reverence, remembering how that felt on my tongue. "We were in a mental hospital together. We kissed. Twice! And then—we didn't see each other or talk to each other. All I had was a couple letters from him, and he never got any from me at all. So where do we stand?"

"Where do you want to stand?" Tracy asked.

"I hadn't thought about that." I hadn't.

I was so concerned with where we were supposed to be, that I forgot to think of the *how* we're supposed to be. There weren't any books in the self-help section about this: Girl meets boy (in a mental hospital). Girl falls in love with boy (in a mental hospital). Girl kisses boy (in a mental hospital). Girl leaves mental hospital while boy stays there. Boy writes letters, not of the overly sappy Nicholas Sparks variety. Girl can't even get herself to send a letter until she does and it gets returned. Now boy and girl are both out of mental hospital and are about to see each other. And did I mention girl now has a Homecoming date?

"What do I want?" I said aloud, and on the last word, the *want*, I saw him. His roughed-up black Chucks, his lanky legs in worn jeans, his long torso in a black t-shirt, and his open, sweet face, now completely exposed underneath a newly shaved head.

I gasped involuntarily.

"That's him," I breathed to Tracy, pointing only with my eyes.

"He's purty," she noted.

"Beautiful," I concurred. The taste in my mouth could have been better, a side effect from not eating all day. "Do you have any gum?" I asked T. She pulled out a pack of mint, and I shoved a piece into my mouth, chomped it a few times, then spit it out into the wrapper. I didn't want to look like some cud-chewing cow when we met again.

"Are you going to get out?"

"Can't I just look at him and leave?" I asked.

"And then what?" Tracy sounded annoyed. "Don't you want to know what's going to happen next?"

I did. I needed to know. I opened the car door and called, "Justin?"

DAGWOOD'S

"Justin?" I called a little louder. He turned away from his old maroon Volvo, the one we pretended to be in in Play Therapy, and looked towards me. The car was real now, and Justin looking at me was real. There were no hospital boundaries or rules for us. That felt scary as hell.

I walked towards his car, and he walked to me. We met in the middle of the Dagwood's parking lot. My heart beat so hard there was no way he couldn't see it through my fitted t-shirt. We were close enough that I could smell his soapy boy smell, see the glossy scar on his hand, look up and see the first lips that I'd ever really kissed.

I smiled up at him, the kind of smile that comes with tears, not just happy, but a little confused, and a little sad. He warmed up with a closed mouth, crinkly-eyed smile, then slowly brought me into his chest for a long, needed hug. I wrapped my arms around his back and fell into him, tears streaking his black shirt and making my nose all snuffly. When I pulled back, embarrassed by my snot collection, I noticed his eyes glistened with tears, too. I dug through my beaded bag until I found a tissue, then turned around to not-so-discreetly blow whatever was left out of my nose. When I felt sufficiently boog free, I turned back to face Justin.

"So," I said casually, "how've you been?"

"Oh, you know, in a loony bin, out of a loony bin, that kind of thing."

We laughed, and I felt a little of our ease return. I turned around and waved to Tracy, our signal that she could go. The plan was for her to hang out at a nearby bookshop (she found a cute little indie on her GPS), and I'd text her when I needed her.

"Who's that?" Justin watched as Tracy drove off.

"My friend, Tracy. My ride."

"Oh, yeah. I remember you talking about her. She's into wrestling, right?"

"That's her," I said.

We stood outside and waited for Tracy's car to drive completely out of our view, then Justin gestured towards the door of Dagwood's. "Shall we?" he asked.

"We shall."

As we walked to the restaurant, Justin brushed the newly blue section of my hair with his warped hand. "Nice hair," he complimented.

"Thanks," I smiled. "Nice non-hair." I normally wasn't into the shaved look, too reminiscent of skinheads or the lice epidemic of third grade, but it made Justin's already warm face even more welcoming. I noticed a small scar above his right eye that I couldn't see before.

Justin held the door for me, and I walked through into a brightly lit, old-time diner. Thirty-three flavors of ice cream were written in chalk on an ice cream–shaped board, and the walls were adorned with black-and-white photos of foods gone by.

"Have you ever been here?" Justin asked as a waitress in a pink uniform dress led us to a table near a window. "They have the best ice cream."

"No, I don't live anywhere near here, so I haven't been. And I can't have anything to eat because it's Yom Kippur." Nice going, killjoy.

"Wait, don't you live in Deer Park?"

"No. Deer Grove. They sound the same, but they're like forty-five minutes apart."

"Dang. Sorry I made you come all the way out here. I didn't think, I guess." Justin looked down and rubbed the fuzz on the top of his head.

"It's okay," I assured him.

"And I'm the one with the car. That was rather assholian of me." He reached for a sugar packet to play with. "Did I know you were Jewish?" he asked.

"I don't know if it ever came up. Is that a problem?" I tried not to sound too aggressive. It was a concern, with the buzzcut and all.

"No, of course not, I just should have asked if today was an okay day to meet." The look on his face said he was beating himself up inside.

I put my hand on top of his scarred one, the one he was using to play with the sugar. "Don't worry, Justin. No matter where or when we did this, it was bound to be kind of strange, don't you think?"

He relaxed back into his chair with a puffing breath. "I'm so glad to hear you say that. Would you believe I was actually freaking out about what I should wear today?"

"I'd believe it, and I'd match and then raise you some in my freaking out."

He held on to my hand now, and looked at me with those dark brown eyes that made my stomach butterflies dance. As much as we were together at Lakeland, there were very few times we could sit opposite and just look at each other. In addition to the newly discovered scar, I found an adorable pimple next to his left ear. God only knows what Justin was finding on my face.

When the conversation didn't flow, I pondered where we should go. To the past? The present? What's to come? Justin answered my unasked questions with, "Remember Lawrence?"

"Yeah," I chuckled. "Did he really exist?"

"Of course. What do you mean?" Justin looked perturbed.

"I only meant that he was so into Satan, and then he was so into Abby, and then he was so into Satan again. Seems kind of bizarre when you think about it."

"Yeah, I guess." Now Justin looked confused.

"I wonder what happened to him when he left."

Justin scrunched his brow seriously.

Thinkingthinkingthinking.

"What movies did you guys watch after I left?"

"The next three Star Wars." Justin's face lightened a little.

"You're kidding."

"I wish I were."

"Remember the Tater Tots?" I asked, kicking myself for such an inane question.

"I think I still have a mountain of them eroding in my stomach." Justin laughed. "Remember Play Therapy?" he asked, and then he was serious again.

Our eyes locked. Was this supposed to be a romantic moment? It would have been, once upon a time, but here we were reminiscing about our time together in a mental hospital. My mind struggled with the guilt about my most recent adventure in Play Therapy with Tracy, Mara, Tucker . . .

"Why is this weird, Anna?" Justin asked, first dropping his eyes, then looking back into mine. "Is it because *we're* weird?"

"What? No. We're weird, for sure, but so is that guy." I pointed with my free hand towards a round, bald man holding a ketchup bottle three feet above his French fries and squeezing red drops down onto his plate in a pulsating rhythm.

"And what about that guy?" Justin pointed to a man in a fancy suit with a cell phone in his ear, who shouted, "I can't hear you!" between mouthfuls of ice cream.

"See, weirdness all around us. We're no weirder than they are."

"That's not really all that comforting." He laughed. "Do you think this is weird?" he asked me, serious face again.

"Yeah." I looked at his kind features. I reveled in the fact that I could look and look. "You know what the weirdest part about this is?"

"What?"

"I think it would have been less weird if you and I were sitting together in a mental hospital." He scrunched his eyebrows in confusion. "It's like we were trapped on a royally screwed-up deserted island, and we, you know, fell in love-ish." I looked down as I said this, thus missing any telling expression he may have given up, "but now we're off the island and we're actually on islands that aren't even close to each other and there are lots of other people on these islands and homework and Homecoming dances and—"

"Homecoming? Man, I totally forgot about that," Justin said. I studied his face. Did he know?

"And that's another thing. I've been out of the hospital for a couple of weeks, which is like a lifetime for you being *in* the hospital. So, in essence, you and I aren't even living in the same time period. It's like you were caught in a time warp, and now you have to catch up, but I'm already far ahead of you . . ."

"At the Homecoming dance," Justin filled in the blank.

Did I look guilty? "I guess. Along with other, non-dance-related places that you still have to get to."

The waitress in the pink dress came by and asked through tacky chomps of gum, "You ready to order?"

"Can you give us a few more minutes?" Justin asked. The waitress shrugged like she could give a crap since she'd be there for the rest of her life, and walked away.

Justin and I still held hands when he took his free hand and surrounded both of my hands with them. "I think part of me really loves you, Anna."

God. If time could freeze right there, that was all I ever wanted. But people were still moving around the restaurant. Time didn't stop for us. "A part of me really loves you, too, Justin." It was so easy to say, and yet I knew it didn't mean what I had wanted it to.

"But I think that part"—he swallowed—"is stuck on that island. I mean, it's still here." He tugged our intertwined hands towards his heart. "But I don't know if it can work off the island. You know?" He looked at me with sad hope, and I nodded.

"I know." It was like my favorite movie ended after seeing it for the first time. I could watch it again, but it wouldn't feel the same.

We watched each other, hands intermingling, until the waitress returned. "How about now?"

Justin didn't take his eyes off me, but said, "Just a coffee."

"Water for me," I told her, eyes on Justin.

The waitress huffed, then returned to her chomping and stomped off.

"I think the waitress hates us," I whispered to him.

"She just doesn't know us." Justin winked at me. His wink broke the intensity of the mood, and I threw my head back and laughed, a wonderful, contagious, uncontrollable laugh that Justin soon joined. We were still laughing when the waitress returned with our drinks. She gave us a glare that said we were crazy, and as I looked at Justin through a haze of laughing tears, I thought, if she only knew.

Justin and I sat and talked through four cups of coffee and a bowl of ice cream, three scoops, that I couldn't help but sample. He told me about everything that had happened at Lakeland since I left, how it wasn't the same without me and yet everything was the same. He updated me on the old people, as well as the new. I particularly liked the story about how Dania got a room restriction for making out with another floormate. A girl. Now that he's home, his parents are making him see a therapist twice a week and may send him to military school if he can't regain his focus.

"Is that why you shaved your head?" I asked, reaching up to run my fingers over the short, dark fuzz.

"No. I just needed a change."

"It looks good," I told him.

"You look good," he told me. And if it weren't Yom Kippur, I would have eaten him right there.

When all the ice cream was finished and after too much coffee made Justin jittery, we decided it was time to leave. I reluctantly texted Tracy to pick me up in five minutes.

Justin paid the bill at the counter, left an overly generous five bucks for our surly waitress, and we walked outside to his maroon Volvo.

"Do you think," I started, "if circumstances were different, like, if we lived closer to each other and didn't have all this baggage—"

"Like being in a mental hospital together?"

"There is that," I concurred. "And just trying to get our lives back to normal. Do you think . . . ?"

I didn't finish my thought, which could have been anything from, "We'd go to Homecoming together?" to "We'd get married someday?" although I probably would have averaged the two with, "We could have been a normal couple?" when Justin answered for me.

"I think so. I think maybe we could have stayed together. Maybe next time around?"

"God forbid there's a next time." I shuddered.

"Maybe there'll be *another* next time. Maybe somehow if I get my shit together and apply myself as my dad says, we could go to the same college."

"Yeah, or live in the same city after we graduate," I suggested.

"Or randomly run into each other at the grocery store after we both just broke up with our future significant others when we're, like, twenty-five."

"That could totally happen," I agreed.

"You think?" Justin looked skeptical.

"Why not? What were the chances of the two of us ending up in a mental hospital together? A random grocery store run-in seems a lot more realistic, if you think about it. There are way more grocery stores than there are mental hospitals.

"But does that mean it will be harder to find you?" I mused.

Justin smiled warmly at me and cupped my face in his hands. I moved my hands on top of his and looked up into his chocolaty eyes. "If life gets hard," he said, "you can always call me. Shit, you can call me even if it's really easy."

"Same for you, okay?" We both said it, but I didn't really believe I'd hear from him anytime soon. Or that I'd call him. Our lives were so far apart now, geographically and emotionally. We'd never get back the forbidden, rule-breaking romance we had at Lakeland, the tension of sitting next to each other at a table, the intensity of being forced to share our feelings twenty-four hours a day. But we could never be casual friends, either, asking how your day is and what you're wearing for school pictures. We knew too much to go back.

Annoyingly, a tear slipped from my eye again. Justin leaned down and gently kissed the spot on my cheek where it landed. I tilted my face up for one last kiss, this time without fear of consequence or punishment. It wasn't a kiss full of passion and urgency as our previous ones had been; it was a kiss goodbye. A strong, slow, deliciously ice cream–tinged kiss goodbye.

We let go reluctantly, and Justin folded himself back into his Volvo. He started the engine and rolled down the window. As he pulled away, he gave one last wave and smile. I could hear The Doors playing through the open window.

Tracy's car sat in a far-off parking spot, and I mechanically made my way to it. Drained from the lack of food and abundance of everything I hadn't known to expect, I collapsed into the passenger seat without a word. The Arthur mix played again on the stereo, but I was too tired to turn it off. Besides, these were songs I'd probably rarely hear in my life. Maybe one day, when I'm sitting at the student center in college, a crappy John Mayer song will come on the radio. At first, I'll cringe, but then I'll remember this day, when I saw Justin again, and the song won't be so bad.

"Do you want to talk?" Tracy asked cautiously.

"Maybe later. Right now I just want to listen."

That night at home, I helped my mom make the break-the-fast dinner. Fasting had made us both lethargic and grumbly. Eventually I would tell my mom about my bittersweet meeting with Justin, but for now I wanted it all inside of me. Before bed, I would write about it. There was so much to process, so many moments and looks and touches that I didn't want to forget.

My mom worked on a pasta salad, and in mid-stir she dropped her spoon, then her shoulders, and crumbled to the floor.

What now? I wanted to ask. It had been such a huge day for me, so important, I didn't want to lose it all by having to take care of my mom.

"Mom?" I started hesitantly, then gained momentum when she couldn't even answer me through her sobs. "I know this sucks, and Dad kind of sucks, and it's really shitty that your marriage is ending. But you're my mom, my parent, and I need you to pull it together. I don't want to be the one to pick up the pieces of Mom that are scattered all over the kitchen floor. If you'll recall, I just got out of a mental hospital, and I am dealing with stuff. Maybe you need to get yourself some help that doesn't involve someone twenty-five years younger than you who once actually lived inside your body." I just grossed myself out. "Because I'm trying really hard to make my life better now, and the last thing I need is my parents mucking it up."

I stopped the diatribe, wondering if it was too harsh, if the lack of nourishment in my brain made me go overboard.

My mom put her hand to her temple and stood up. She ripped a paper towel off the roll and dabbed her face, then walked over to me and placed her hands on my shoulders. "Anna, I am so sorry. I'm too tired and hungry"—we both laughed as much as our empty stomachs and heads would allow—"to say anything more, but I won't put this on you again. You are very right, and I'm incredibly proud of how far you've come. I really admire you, and I won't burden you with my problems anymore. I'll ask Aunt Marj for some suggestions for therapists tomorrow." Mom gazed out the window. "Is the sun down yet? Jesus, I need something to eat." She yanked open the freezer and pulled out a pint of Chubby Hubby. "Oh, the irony." She shook her head and dug in a spoon.

"Just don't see a Freudian therapist, please," I begged her. No one needed another therapist who believed the world revolved around her vagina.

While Mom licked her spoon, I dug into an apple sitting on the counter. Food tasted and felt so good that there was no more talking for a while.

Mara plodded down the stairs in her pj's.

"You didn't even get dressed today?" I asked through chomps of apple.

"That was my form of atoning." She shrugged.

We all had our own ways of reaching out to God. Today, for the first time in a long while, I felt He was reaching out to us.

IAMNOTCRAZYIAMNOTCRAZY

I had the strangest dream about Justin last night that bordered on the TMI, so I won't go into too much detail. But when I woke up, I felt a sense of relief. Almost that feeling after someone close to you dies, like a grandparent, and you dream about them and the dream feels so real that you know they aren't truly gone from your life. Not that Justin is dead, or even dead to me, but it made me happy to see him still hanging around.

My walk this morning was solo, after Tracy texted to report she was skipping her first few classes until the Aleve kicked in and her mega-cramps subsided. I felt a little anxious about seeing Tucker for the first time after he asked me to Homecoming. Not because of Justin; our meeting was between the two of us (and Tracy's ears). It was more that I wasn't exactly sure what our going to Homecoming meant. I think there was some flirtation over the last couple of weeks, although Homecoming could totally be just a friend thing. The guy did shake my hand. But the guy is Tucker, who is not exactly the king of obvious social cues. Was Homecoming to be our first date? Would we go on a date beforehand? Do people even go on dates anymore? What would I know, considering my only date consisted of a card game and under-the-table gropings in the Day Room of a mental hospital.

Before I could get myself completely worked up, but just after I got myself to the point of stomach agitation, I arrived at school. No one waited by my locker to greet me, except the familiar duo of Julie Ganty and Chris Panlin dry humping against their lockers. Glad I could count on them, even though they did make me want to break out the Clorox wipes.

We aced our group presentation in English, and along with an A on a math test, and an experiment involving marbles (and the pee-in-your-pants funny quote from Mr. Fripp: "Science never sucks. It vacuums!"), my morning classes did an excellent job of taking my mind off things. Which is to say, I actually focused on my classes while in school. Wacky concept, I know.

Tucker remained unseen at lunch, which I thought put me in the clear of having to explain things to Eleanor. Except that, naturally, Homecoming was all Tracy, Eleanor, and Meredith talked about. It was like my lunch table had gone through some Wonka Wash that magically transformed its stereotype-busting inhabitants into giggly, girly drones. Instead of joining the talk of dresses and limos, which is what I was completely dying to do (perhaps I went through the Wonka Wash with them), I decided to take my time while buying a granola bar from the vending machine.

Fail. When I returned to the table, the first thing Eleanor said was, "We have to get you a date, Anna. Then we can all go together!" I had never heard such enthusiasm from Eleanor, at least not towards something completely lacking in blood and violence. Tracy played wingman and didn't turn me in. I wasn't sure if Eleanor would actually hurt me if I told her Tucker and I were going together, but, well, yes, I was.

I summoned up my newfangled Lake Shit courage and inquired, "Can I ask you a semi-personal question, Eleanor?"

"Sure!" She was oddly cute and personable, sipping milk from a straw.

"What exactly happened between you and Tucker?"

"What do you mean?" Did this Wonka Wash also have an effect on memory?

"Why did you guys break up?" I broke my granola bar into itty-bitty pieces, hoping it didn't somehow predict what would soon be happening to my bones.

"Break up? We were never going out." She gave an incredulous snort and continued sipping.

"Wait. I'm confused. You have that love/hate thing. You went to Homecoming together."

"Not like you have to like the person you're going to Homecoming with, case in point." She pointed at Meredith. "Meredith hasn't even talked to the guy taking her. Her mom has."

"And Mom says he's nice." Meredith stuck out her tongue. "And you're totally full of it, Eleanor. You liked Tucker at one point. You even told me. Remember, after he did that portrait in Art, and you were all—" Meredith didn't have the chance to finish her sentence due to an elbow from Eleanor connecting with her ribs.

"Dammmmnnnn." Meredith pouted. "You're a butt."

"Harsh words, Meredith. I may need to wash your mouth out with soap. I think I have a bar of Zest around here somewhere." Tracy pretended to rifle through her lunch bag.

Conversation over. So, did that mean Eleanor did like Tucker, or once did, or never did? Still so confused. And her saying, "Not like you have to like the person you're going to Homecoming with" didn't help the matter. I think I liked Tucker. So did he like me?

I could so use a Scrumdiddlyumptious bar.

When I finally saw Tucker in Art, our interactions were minimal and friendly. He experimented in the darkroom with some sepia technique while I spent class uploading my pictures to the school server and starting to play around with combining the home Play Therapy pictures with the actual mental hospital windows as frames. A jagged test cutout of a photo of Tucker and me on the bed proved striking against the mesh of the screen.

"Ooh la la," Meredith commented as she peeked at my computer. "What would Eleanor say?"

What *would* Eleanor say? It was so hard to tell from lunch. I hoped she was too into that online role-playing Korean setup from her mom to care. Or to act out some violent gamer fantasy involving a katana and some chain mail on me.

Was there anything even to worry about? Besides her elbow.

I let myself get reabsorbed into the glow of the computer screen, and by the time class was over, I had successfully, I hoped, created two of the nine pictures in my narrative. Tomorrow I'd print one up to see how it translated from pixels to photo paper. For now, the memories of the process, from visiting Lake Shit, seeing Matt O. in the window, to sharing a bed with Tucker, made the narrative already a great story. If only I knew where Tucker fit into it.

AH BARTLEBY!

Part of me dreaded going to Group, as if I was beyond the need for group therapy at this point. The other part of me didn't mind so much, since it was sort of the real-world link to my past life at Lake Shit, and at least the people weren't so bad. Tracy, cramps wrangled by sixth period (no period pun intended), invited me to join her at another home soccer game.

"Can't," I told her at my locker. "Group."

"Oh, yeah. I forgot about that. Turdballs. Am I going to have to sit alone?"

"I'm sure there'll be other girls in the footballers' wives section," I joked, and received the expected punch in the arm.

"I just don't want to have to look like some sort of pathetic groupie."

"As long as he wants you there and you're his only groupie, I see nothing wrong with that."

"Oh! Speaking of groupies, Wrestlemania is coming to Chicago. You said you'd go if it ever came to Chicago again."

"I said that?" I asked. "Was I high?"

"On hot, buttered wrestlers! Tickets go on sale Saturday. I'm going to have three computers going at the same time to get the best seats. We'll be wiping their sweat off our faces."

"Not quite the selling point, is it?"

"Well, too bad, because you're going. And, if it's okay with you, I asked Arthur to go, too."

I shrugged. "The more, the sweatier."

She eyed me suspiciously. "Anyone you want to ask?"

"To Wrestlemania? Hardly." I stuffed my books into my backpack and checked the time. "I gotta go. My mom's probably idling outside already."

"Think about that fourth ticket. You might change your mind. You have until Saturday to decide."

"I'll get right on that." We started walking towards the front doors. "And you best be getting into groupie position. You don't want The Assman to find another Asslady." Tracy smacked me on my butt and ran off.

My mom waited in our designated therapy pickup spot. The second I entered the car, she assaulted me with Homecoming dress delirium.

"I was at the mall today, and I saw this adorable blue dress. I almost bought it, but I have no idea what size you are anymore. We'll have to go back this weekend to try it on." It was awesome seeing her so excited for the first time in weeks, but I had no idea what I wanted to wear to Homecoming. Maybe I'd just make a dress out of an old t-shirt and duct tape.

We pulled in front of the Group building. Miles shuffled up the sidewalk, hands in the pockets of his mustard yellow hoodie, eyes puffed as ever, and gave me a tiny wave as I got out of my mom's car.

"Hey, Anna. I like your hair. How's the rest of you?" That sounded pervy. Was it meant to?

"Pretty good. You?" I asked, trying not to sound suspicious.

"Oh, you know, the usual: not sleeping, playing too much music when I should be doing homework. Here." He dug into the back pocket of his jeans and pulled out a folded, green piece of paper. I opened it to find a flyer for his band, Platypuses Are Mammals, Too. "We're playing this Saturday at the Whedon Bowl. Maybe you could come." Hope shone through the tiredness in his eyes.

"Sounds cool. I'll see if I can go. My mom still keeps kind of a tight leash, but she's been letting up."

"Sweet." He looked pleased, but I didn't want to read too much into it.

Inside, the only people in the circle were Peggy and Ali. Instead of her overly pleasant welcome, Peggy looked somber and ushered us to our seats with, "Sit down, Anna and Miles. We need to talk abut something." For a minute, I thought she was going to say something Lake Shit–esque, like Miles and I aren't allowed to be in a relationship, to which I was ready to protest, since we weren't. But instead she said, "Bartleby attempted suicide last weekend." Ali exhaled a gasp, and I heard Miles breathe, "Damn."

"Attempted?" I pressed.

"Yes. He's going to be okay, but his parents decided to have him hospitalized," Peggy explained.

"Where?" I asked too quickly.

"Actually, he'll be at Lakeland next week, Anna." Her words felt like a punch in the gut, but I wasn't sure why. Maybe the tiniest part of me wished that for just a second I could go there, too, to say hi. But then that tiny part got whipped by the rest of my brain, when I remembered that Justin was out, Matt O. was leaving, and life outside of the hospital was feeling more and more comfortable every day.

What would it be like for Bart at Lake Shit? Would he cry like I did when I first got there? Would he barely eat any food, like I did? Would he fall in love like I did? Then I remembered: "What about Nepa?"

Peggy paused solemnly.

"She's not dead, is she?" Miles asked, wide-eyed.

"No, Miles, thank goodness. Nepa was the one who found Bart."

"Found him, how?" Ali asked.

I wanted to know, too. It's a little sick how when someone dies, I always want to know how. Like in obituaries, when people are really young and it doesn't say how they died, there's something very unsettling about it. With Bart's attempted suicide, I needed to know how he did it. If it was with a gun, was he all disfigured now? If it was his wrists, did he do it in a bathtub like in the movies? If he hung himself, how did he tie the knot?

Peggy continued, "Nepa was supposed to visit Bart at his house, and when she rang the doorbell he didn't answer. She called him and there was no answer there either. She somehow knew where the spare key to his house was hidden—"

Miles interrupted, "Somehow because they've been screwing for the last several months."

"Miles!" Ali reprimanded.

Peggy spoke over Ali's slapping of Miles's arm, "So she went into the house and found Bart lying on the floor, surrounded by some prescription drug bottles. The ambulance arrived soon after, and they were able to pump his stomach."

I could see the waves of relief on Ali's and Miles's faces, the same relief I felt, knowing both how he attempted it and also that he'd fully recover. At least physically.

"How's Nepa?" I asked.

"Pretty broken up, as expected. Her mother told me that Nepa will be taking a break from Group for a short while, during which she'll seek individual help." She paused. "Would any of you like to share your thoughts?"

I did and I didn't. Part of me instantly wanted to go home and call Justin, but that seemed wrong since he had attempted suicide himself. The other part of me wanted to share the news with Tucker, but I didn't really know him well enough to know how he'd deal with that kind of thing. I felt so beyond where Bart must have been emotionally that I didn't even know how to feel sad for him.

Several minutes of silence passed. Peggy eventually spoke, "Are we all still processing? Miles?" she pressed.

"Um, actually I was thinking about my show on Saturday," Miles admitted.

"And I was thinking about my trial again," Ali confessed. "I know it's enough already."

"How is it enough?" I asked angrily. "That's a huge deal. And so is your show, Miles. The fact is we're here, and Bart pussied out. We're dealing with our shit, and he couldn't. Should we waste our one hour of group time for the day dwelling on an attempted suicide that was obviously a call for attention? The guy knew Nepa was coming over. He knew she'd find him. He knew they could pump his stomach."

"True," Miles agreed. "And he never said anything constructive in Group. It was always some dickwad comment and then a smirk."

"Or a sneer," Ali added.

"And what's with his hair—" Miles went on, but Peggy stopped him.

"Guys, hold on. I understand your feelings on Bart's situation may be manifesting in anger, but this is still sensitive and Bart's not here to defend himself."

"Whose fault is that?" I muttered. Ali and Miles snickered.

Peggy looked at each of us with a concerned brow, then suggested, "Why don't we practice some deep breaths, and then we'll move on to things you need to talk about this week?"

I watched the others close their eyes and breathe. Before the second breath was up, Miles's eyes popped open and he looked directly at me. I smiled, closed-mouthed with my breathing through my nose. Miles winked at me.

A cute boy in a therapy circle and a wink. I closed my eyes, and breathed in deeply, unable to turn off the smile on my face.

At the end of Group, after Ali talked some about her trial next month and I got some feedback on my parents, I brought the talk back to Bartleby. "Sorry I got so bitchy about Bartleby's suicide attempt. I know it's not anything to make light of. It's just so annoying that people think suicide will make everything better, when all it does is make everything suck for everyone around them."

"I'm sorry, too," Miles conceded. "I still think the guy needs a serious attitude adjustment, but he must have felt pretty horrid to do this."

"Well, I'm still mad. Nepa didn't ask for any of this," Ali added.

"I'm glad you all came around a little," Peggy told us. "Unfortunately, our time is up."

"When do you think he's going to Lakeland?" I asked Peggy as we all stood up to go.

"His father told me probably this Friday."

"That's crazy," I told her. "Three weeks to the day that I got out. Do you think it would be okay if I sent him a letter?" I asked.

"I think he'd like that." Peggy smiled.

"Really?" I doubted.

"Perhaps," Peggy waivered.

Outside, my mom hadn't arrived yet. I imagined her frantically flinging fancy dresses off racks at Nordstrom. I must have laughed without knowing because Miles appeared from behind me and asked, "What's so funny?"

"Long story," I said, dismissing with a wave.

"So, Anna, I was wondering"—Miles rolled a pebble around with his shoe and dug his hands deeper into his hoodie pockets—"do you want to go to Homecoming with me?"

My head shrunk back with shock, and I replied with a "Really?" that sounded a little too dubious.

"Never mind." He shook his head and ran his fingers through his sandy hair.

"No, Miles, I wasn't sure if you were serious is all." He looked at me with the demeanor of a puppy. "Thing is, I'm kind of already going with someone."

"I though you might say that." Miles brightened, enough to take his normally animated hands out of his pockets and raise a finger. "So I looked on your school's website, and our Homecomings are on different weekends."

"You looked at my school's webpage?" I asked, but what I really meant was, you put out that much effort for little ol' me?

"Yeah. So what do you think? It can be just as friends. At least come see my band this weekend. Maybe it'll help make up your mind."

My mom pulled up, her running engine pressing me to answer quickly. "Okay. I mean, I'll try to make it to the show. And I'll think about Homecoming," I told him, turning towards my mom's car.

"That is all I ask." He tucked his hands back into his pockets. "You can tell me at Group next week. Or this week, if you already know the answer. Or at the show, if you are so moved." He bounced on his heels and watched as I ducked into my mom's car.

"What were you two talking about?" my mom questioned with a goofy grin.

I looked at her with pleasant confusion. "He just asked me to

Homecoming." I shook my head in disbelief. We passed Miles as he unlocked his car door.

Less than three weeks ago, I was in a mental hospital. Before that, I couldn't even sit through my classes. Now, not one, but two guys had asked me to Homecoming.

Who the hell am I?

ON SECOND THOUGHT

It wasn't until I tried to fall asleep that night that the reality of Bartleby hit me. I had felt bad in my life, really bad, bad enough that I was beyond hope. But I never outright tried to kill myself. Bart was for sure a douchebag, but he must have been nice enough for someone as smart as Nepa to see something in him. What was his life missing that he tried to end it all? Was it really just a cry for help, that he knew Nepa would find him there in time to save him? Had he thought about what would have happened if she didn't?

I guess it wouldn't have mattered to him by that time.

Instead, soon he'd walk the same sterile halls I had, drink the throat-burning juice in the too-small plastic cups, take showers in the communal stalls, sit in the farting pleather chairs, and maybe meet some of the same people.

I choked up at the thought of him eating breakfast with Matt O. or Sandy or Abby. As my eyes brimmed with tears, I silently said a prayer.

> *Dear God,*
>
> *Please watch over Bartleby. He didn't have much of a chance, really, with parents who'd give him that name. Make it so he comes out okay. Better than okay. And please make sure Nepa is okay, too.*
> *Amen.*
> *PS Watch over Justin, too, please.*

It wasn't much of a prayer, but I figured God would sense the sincerity.

JUST CHECKING

Tracy and I walked to school, and I told her about Bartleby's attempted suicide.

"Whoa," she exhaled. "Should we have a moment of silence for him or something?"

"He's not dead."

"I know, but I feel kind of bad. I totally made fun of his name."

"I'm sure you're not the first person," I assured her. "Besides, he has no clue that you even exist, so I'm sure he's not feeling bad because of you."

We talked the rest of our walk about Homecoming outfits, which was random because a) Tracy never talks about clothes unless it's wrestler spandex and b) we had no idea what the logistics of her going to the dance with The Assman would be. Was he going to rent a limo? Drive her on the back of a Harley? In one of the practice cars they used in Auto Shop? And would Tucker and I go with them?

Being a normal teenager was confusing.

Even more confusing was Tucker waiting by my locker when Tracy and I arrived at school.

"I'll catch you later," Tracy said when she saw Tucker, who gave her a two-finger salute before she walked away.

"Good morning, Anna. You're looking well."

"As are you," I told him, emulating his odd formality.

"Before the bell rings, I just needed to check something with you," he started.

"What's up?" I asked, discarding books from my backpack and grabbing needed ones from my locker.

"Are we still going to Homecoming together?" he asked in the same manner someone would ask a waiter, "Can I get this with onions?"

I slammed my locker and looked up at him, his glasses creating a glare that covered up any hint his eyes may have shared. "I thought we were. Is something wrong?"

He pretended to wipe sweat off his forehead. "Phew. I just thought since we hadn't mentioned it again, and I hadn't really seen you that you might have been avoiding me."

"Not at all. It's just that Monday was Yom Kippur, and yesterday you were gone at lunch and then I had Group," I explained.

"Well, good. Then we're still on. Good," he repeated.

"Good," I concurred.

His lips twitched into a smile. The bell rang, and he quickly leaned down and kissed my cheek. A peck if there ever was one, but a kiss nonetheless. "See you at lunch," he called as he bounded down the hall.

I floated to English, confused but content, and sat down dazedly in my seat. I mostly managed to ignore the class's discussion of *Catcher,* the same scene Groban and I discussed the other day where Holden visits his teacher in the middle of the night, and the teacher gives him all that advice. And then gropes his head. Most of the class fixated on the teacher being a possible pedophile, with the minority defending him. Groban looked over at me several times, obviously hoping I'd add something enlightening to the discussion. But I'd had that conversation already. More importantly, I had just been kissed.

On the cheek.

But I hadn't even been expecting that.

———

AWKWARD MUCH?

At lunch no one could get a word in on Eleanor blabbering about her gamer hottie.

"We met. Like, in person, and he was ripped. Straight out of the game, full on Level Eighty. The backseat of his car gave us barely enough room, if you know what I'm saying." I wasn't entirely sure, since Eleanor has told us before that she plans on being a virgin until marriage, but I nodded along with everyone else. "Too bad you're not going to Homecoming, Anna, or we could all share a limo."

I choked a bit on the carrot stick I was munching. "Um, I am going, actually." I don't know why it was a big deal. Tucker and she were so last year, plus Eleanor gave full disclosure of her gamer backseat shenanigans. But obviously it was somewhat of a big deal, or she would have already known. Before I had a chance to explain, Tucker, who had been silently enduring Eleanor's whore-ific tales, piped up, "She's going with me. I'm taking Anna to Homecoming. And, just so you know, I'm also on the soccer team."

It was as though the entire lunchroom stopped talking at that moment. Or maybe I just imagined it. Our lunch table's collective inhale was palpable.

"Oh. That's cool," Eleanor dismissed, twisting her plate lunch spaghetti with a spork. When we realized that's all she had to say, our lunch table exhaled a united sigh of relief. Then came the eternal silence.

Thank God for The Assman. He strode over to our lunch table, squeezed in next to Tracy, and spent several minutes unloading the most food-filled, crinkliest brown lunch bag in history. I noted every item, just in case I ever needed to build up my ass. He and

Tracy sparked a hilarious conversation about HDTV and wrestler testicles. Made for each other, really.

When lunch ended, Eleanor caught me as everyone left the table. "I'm really happy for you, Anna. Tucker deserves someone like you," she said with such a serious expression that I almost laughed. "Just know this: If you hurt him, I will stab you through your spleen."

"With a real sword or a computer one?" I asked her, half kidding and half concerned for my safety.

"I hope we'll never have to find out," she deadpanned and walked away.

Crazy Eleanor. I liked how she made it seem as though she didn't even know what she'd do.

THE GAME IS AFOOT

Since I only used digital photography for my narrative project, everything was moving pretty quickly. Near the end of class, I already had ten of the twelve pictures ready to print. Tomorrow I would finish the other two, print, then mount them for Monday's critique.

Mrs. Downy stood behind me as I adjusted the contrast of the Play Therapy photo of me and Mara, the bulletin board, framed by the window at Lakeland.

"Is that your sister?" Mrs. Downy asked.

"Yeah."

"Who is she supposed to be?"

"My bulletin board. It's part of this thing called Play Therapy from the hospital." When Mrs. Downy didn't say anything else but continued to stand behind me, I explained to her the concept of my narrative: Play Therapy of my bedroom in my real bedroom with my outside friends all contained within the hospital windows.

296

I looked up at her, and she did that art voyeur head tilt, said, "Very nice," and walked away.

I beamed, knowing that a "very nice" from Mrs. Downy was a guaranteed A.

I popped up from my seat and skipped to the darkroom door, stepped into the rotating blackness, and came out on the other side. In a few seconds, my eyes adjusted to the reddish tinged light to find Tucker and a sophomore working. My skips returned and brought me to Tucker, who I had to tap on the shoulder to get his attention. He tugged out an earbud, and a shout of music came from the dangling circle.

"What are you listening to?" I asked.

He looked down at me through his glasses and warmly said, "Platypuses Are Mammals, Too. They're local. Someone told me I might like them. They're playing this weekend—"

"At the Whedon Bowl! I know! One of those guys is in my group."

"You're in a band?"

"No." I laughed. "My therapy group."

"Oh, yeah. That one." I smiled up at him, still glowing from Mrs. Downy's review.

"So why'd you come in here?" he asked suspiciously.

"To tell you that Mrs. Downy loves my project. She said it was very, and I quote, 'nice.'"

"That's an A for sure."

"I know!" I hopped in place with excitement.

"Is that all?" He seemed eager to get back to his photography perfectionism.

I paused, then remembered something else I wanted to ask him. "I have a question for you," I began dramatically.

"Yeah?" He looked intrigued.

"Would you be interested in attending Wrestlemania with me?"

"Unexpected. I think. Sure. Why not?"

"That's about how I feel. But it's cool you'll come."

"Now I have to ask you something. I wanted to know if you'd be my cheerleader again Friday. We have a home game."

"Sweaty dudes with tiny nipples made you think of me being your cheerleader?"

"No. I was already thinking about you being my cheerleader. The nipples were extraneous."

The bell rang, and together Tucker and I squished into the small darkroom door and spun around into the brightness of the fluorescent bulbs. I'm pretty sure I didn't emerge pregnant. As we walked to our lockers, Tucker asked, "So yes to the cheerleader thing?"

"That sounds so skanky. How about I be your athletic supporter?" I asked.

"I think that's what people call jock straps," he replied.

"Oh. So, essentially, I just offered to hold your balls." I blushed.

"Here." He dug into his bag until he found his lucky rabbit's foot. "Maybe you can hold this for me instead. You can be my good-luck charm. You are very charming, after all."

I cringed with delight at the compliments. After another kiss on the cheek from Tucker, he left to change for his practice. I leaned back against my locker and rubbed the lucky rabbit's foot. It wasn't necessary, though. I was already feeling pretty lucky.

MY LUCK RUNNETH OVER

I was in such a good mood when I got home that I immediately bounded up the stairs and flicked on the radio. The only station besides classic rock that came in was boppy dance crap, but I couldn't help noticing that Ke$ha wasn't all that bad. Am I a glass-half-full person now?

I dove onto my bed and snuffled my nose into my pillow. When I came up for air, I gasped. I hadn't noticed that my door had opened, and standing next to me was my dad.

When was the last time he was in my room? Besides the recent destruction of my wallpaper and posters? When was the last time he was there *with me*? I seriously could not remember. All I could picture was an old photo of him holding a tiny baby version of me up in front of newly installed wallpaper. The very wallpaper he and my mom ripped down to make me feel better, different. Was that the last time we were in my room together?

I didn't say anything, didn't feel the need since this was my territory. He walked over to my stereo and turned the music down to an inaudible volume. I almost protested that he had no right to touch my stuff, but he began to speak in a nonthreatening manner. I sat up on my bed to listen.

"How have you been?" he opened with.

I wondered if now that my parents were divorcing, I would be forced to see my dad more than when they were married. Again with the parental punishment!

"Fine. You?" I tried not to have an attitude because I certainly didn't need one back from Dad.

"I've been okay. I miss you and Mara." That's a underhanded thing to say. Like, dude, you and Mom were married forever. Let's not pretend that never existed. I didn't respond with more than a light shrug, since I couldn't reciprocate the sentiment. He looked at the floor, seemingly disappointed.

Did I miss my dad? No, because he was never around anyway. But that didn't mean I didn't love him. He was my dad after all.

"I don't want you to worry about anything," he finally said, and he used his rare caring-father voice. Instantly I was transported to vacations where our family magically worked as a unit instead of a dismantled stack of LEGOS. "You're going to live with your mom in this house. I want to see you, but I don't want to force anything with custody visits. So I'll leave it up to you." He looked at me and tried to smile warmly through his closed lips.

I didn't know how to take it all. Yeah, it was great not to have to move or see my dad more than I wanted to, but it was also a little too lax in the parenting department once again.

"Here's the deal, Dad," I told him with confidence, but not anger. "You call me when you want to see me. You set up a dinner or a movie or a trip to the circus, I don't care. Because you're the parent and that's your job."

He had a look that read possible explosion, but it softened into resignation. "Okay, you're right. I'll call you. What are you doing Friday night?"

That soon? I think not. "I'm going to a soccer game. Maybe we can hold off on the dinners and things until stuff cools down around here with Mom. How did you get past her anyway?"

"I had Mara text me when your mom was out picking up dinner," he admitted.

"Ballsy."

There was that uncomfortable silence that only comes when your newly estranged dad's sitting on your bed.

"I better get started on my homework," I said, standing up.

"Great idea." He stood up, too. "Wonderful to see you thriving, Anna." He leaned in for a hug, and I granted it.

My conversation with Dad was just another thing I got to tick off my Post–Lake Shit Anna Checklist. Just a couple more things and . . . what? I graduated to normalcy? I received a commemorative mug? Pretty soon I'd be scaling Mount Kilimanjaro and writing the next Great American Novel, or at the very least going to college. I hear college is awesome because you can leave class to go to the bathroom without needing a hall pass. Among other awesomely collegiate things.

OUTING MYSELF

For some reason, I awoke really hungry the next morning. So I poured myself a bowl of one of my mom's healthy cereals. As delish as Cap'n Crunch was, there were only so many days in a row I could take the sugary, sticky, gummy mass it became by the time I reached the bottom of the bowl. To add a little joy to the healthy cereal, I dropped in a handful of blueberries from the fridge. My mom appeared in the kitchen about halfway through my bowl. She looked at it and scrunched her forehead in the way that said, *Should I say something?* Her forehead decided against it because we ended up just chitchatting about what I had going on in classes today at school and what kind of classes she had at the knit shop. When you think about knitting, you picture a bunch of old ladies sitting around in rocking chairs at my mom's shop. You'd be half right. A lot of them are old, but they're also feisty and competitive when it comes to their knitting prowess. I can't stand visiting my mom during classes at her shop because the women are so obnoxious about one-upping each other on the complicated techniques they're applying to their new grandbaby's booties or whatever.

"I was thinking it might be cool for you to knit me a little shawl type-thing to go over my Homecoming dress. When I find a dress. *If* I find a dress."

"Oh, you'll find one." My mom sounded determined. "If I have to keep you home from school one day, you'll find a fantastic dress."

I chuckled at the thought. "Isn't it weird that three weeks ago, all you wanted was for me to go to school like a normal kid, and now you're saying you'll take me out of school to buy a dress?"

My mom blurted out a laugh, and then her expression transformed to one of reflection. "Amazing, isn't it?" She fixed herself her own bowl of healthy cereal, complete with blueberries, and a sprinkling of flax powder. As I rinsed my dish in the sink, I barely heard my mom say over the rush of the water, "I'm sorry."

I shut off the faucet and turned to face her. "What? I couldn't hear you."

She cleared her throat and looked at me sincerely. "I'm sorry," she said. Her eyes looked glossy, and tears were at the ready to overflow.

I tried to blow it off with a joke. I didn't want to see any more tears from Mom. "Don't worry about it. We'll buy some better cereal next time we go to the grocery store."

She wasn't to be deterred. "I'm sorry we put you in the hospital. I'm sorry we couldn't help you. I'm so sorry it had to happen in the first place." She put her head in her hands to hide the waterworks.

I didn't know what to say. It's an apology I could have used three weeks ago, or more, while I was at Lakeland, confused as to why my parents did that to me. But now? I was out, I was different, I was better. Maybe it was because of Lake Shit. Maybe it was because of meds. Maybe I just needed my life to hit bottom before I found my way up and out. Who knows? But I realized I was over-blaming my parents for it. They had enough problems of their own that maybe they were incapable of helping me with mine.

"It's okay, Mom. It's water under a powder blue bridge." I laughed at my reference to the bridge I once read about where people kept jumping off to their deaths. The jumping stopped when officials painted it powder blue. It was something I thought about when I looked at the blue and pink walls of Lake Shit. "I will say this: The only apology I really want anymore is for turning my bedroom into the inside of a cotton candy machine. You guys weren't even careful with my posters."

My mom looked up from her hands and grabbed a tissue from a pop-up box on the counter. As she wiped her eyes to clear the smudged mascara, she said, "You can thank your dad for that. I came home from the shop one day, and it was done. One of his selfish outbursts, perhaps."

I liked hearing my mom blame my dad for something, even though it was harder than expected to hear Mom talk smack about Dad. She needed to find the anger I was so lucky to discover with the help of my friends at Lakeland.

Mara bounced down the stairs in her Poms uniform.

"Good morning, O Perky One," I greeted her.

"We have a pep rally today for the football team."

"I'm sure you'll scare the pep right out of them," I said, and I tugged her ponytail as I walked into the front hall.

"Have a good day," my mom called to me when she heard the scrunch of the front door.

"You, too!" I called back.

I walked alone to school and listened to the very first Ramones album on my iPod. A righteous blast, I finished the entire album from beginning to end by the time I reached my locker.

We were assigned to finish *Catcher in the Rye* for today in English. I was ubercurious what people would say about the ending. What would they think of Holden when they found out he was in a mental hospital?

The moment class started, Mr. Groban played a CD of a lite-ish dance song I'd never heard. When it reached the chorus, the lyrics sang, "No, we're never gonna survive, unless we get a little crazy." He clicked off the song shortly after the chorus and surveyed the room smugly. "So what do you think?" he asked us. "Raise your hand if you think Holden was crazy." A few hands shot up, then a couple slow-rising hands, and lastly the too lazy to lift their elbows off the desk half-raises. Nearly all of the class raised their hands. Ouch. "Really?" Groban asked. "After all the discussions we had together, you think he's crazy?"

Steve Andrews, wearing his usual Bears jersey, blurted out, "It said right on the first page that he was going to tell us about all of this crazy stuff that happened to him and why he had to go 'there' in the first place." He held his book open to the page, as if we could read the tiny script from so far away.

I pulled out my own copy of the book and skimmed the page until I found the words he was talking about in the middle. I hadn't even noticed them when I started reading the book. "So you knew he was in a mental hospital the whole time?" I piped up. I rarely felt like an idiot in class, especially next to jersey boy, but here I was totally missing the entire point of the book while I blindly thought I was in love with the main character. I needed more info.

"So did I," said Conley Arnatz.

"Me, too."

"Well, I didn't." Thank you, random jock, for verifying what a total assbrain I was.

"I thought he might be," said Ella Santos, the girl I barely knew from my motif group.

"So we can all agree that he was in a mental hospital," Mr. Groban interjected, "but does that make him crazy? I see you nodding, but let's look back at what got him there and then make our decision."

We spent the class going over Holden's childhood, what could have made him the way he was, and things he did that may or may not have made him crazy.

But I didn't like us throwing around the word over and over again.

Crazy.

Crazy.

Crazy.

I raised my hand, but spoke before Mr. Groban called on me, interrupting a winded and pretentious diatribe from Conley. "Can we stop using the word 'crazy'? First of all, using a word a trillion times in an hour sort of takes away any meaning of the word—"

Mr. Groban lit up and tried to get all teacherly on me. "My point exactly—"

But I cut him off. "And second, just because someone's in a mental hospital doesn't mean they're crazy. *I* was in a mental hospital, and I don't think I'm particularly crazy."

Who knew there were crickets in our English classroom? Pretty soon I expected a lone tumbleweed to come rolling along the carpet.

When the silence became almost unbearable, Ella Santos announced, "I was in a hospital, too."

Well, that was unexpected.

I wasn't the only person in our class that had been in a mental hospital. And if I wasn't the only person in our class, I sure as hell wasn't the only person in our school of over two thousand students.

Mr. Groban excitedly started talking about preconceived ideas of sanity and blah blah blah. I tuned him out.

I just came out to my English class.

And I wasn't alone.

Better yet, as we left class, no one seemed to care. Maybe people whispered out of earshot, but it didn't seem like it. Ella came up to me on our way out and asked, "So where were you?"

"Lakeland. You?"

"Grover's Park," she answered.

"Cool," I said nonchalantly.

"Cool," she echoed. "See ya."

And that was it.

Everyone was so into their own shit, they didn't really care about mine. No matter how shitty. *Lake* Shitty. Get it? Oy. Coming out was exhausting. Good thing I had a physics movie to sleep through.

The rest of the day I couldn't help wondering as I walked through the halls who the others were. Could people tell I had been in a mental hospital by looking at me? My ghostly pallor was gone thanks to the walks to and from school and sitting in the stands for Tucker's soccer games, and the bruises from all of the blood taking were all but a disgusting green-and-purple memory. So could they?

Tomorrow would be exactly three weeks since the day I left Lake Shit. Three weeks in, three weeks out. I hear it takes three weeks to get over an addiction. Could my three weeks at Lakeland have gotten me over my depression? Will it come back? If so, will it be sooner or later?

I vote later.

Because sooner, I have a whole lot of normal to contend with.

NEWBIE

When Mom picked me up after school to go to Group, I started to think about whether or not I needed it anymore. Two days a week was a lot of time spent dealing with my problems, especially when I was realizing that maybe I didn't have so many of them. As much as I liked the people in my group (well, the two of them that were left anyway), I didn't need my parents' insurance paying for friends. I was doing perfectly fine in that department on my own, thank you very much.

"Mom," I started as we approached the office. "How much longer do I need to go to Group? I don't really think I need it anymore."

She took a thoughtful breath, and answered, "Will you go at least until the divorce is final?"

The car rolled up to the curb, and I watched Ali enter the building. "Mom, it's your divorce, not mine." I didn't see what that had to do with me staying in therapy.

"Anna, we're your parents. This has to be affecting you somehow."

I thought on it for a moment and knew she was right. Just because everyone else's parents were divorced and I didn't even like my parents very much when they were together doesn't mean it didn't suck that they wouldn't be. What were holidays going to be like? Who would walk me down the aisle at my wedding? Would I have a stepfamily?

"God, Mom, thanks for giving me more crap to talk about in therapy." I half laughed, and she half laughed with me. "Speaking of—your turn."

"I know. I've called two women, and I'm going to try them both out for an initial visit. If there's anything you taught me from this whole ordeal"—she waved her hands toward the Group building— "it's that not all therapists are created equal."

I taught her that. It's funny how much one person's struggles have such an impact on another's.

Which reminded me of Bart. I wondered if we'd talk more about him today. At least hear how he's doing.

Before I got out of the car, I watched a really cute guy walk through the door of my therapy building. He was tall and, dare I say, husky, with a short black Mohawk and an impossibly long chain hanging from his purple pants.

"Who's that?" Mom pried.

"No idea. Better get inside and find out." Right before I left the car, I leaned back in and said, "Love you, Mom."

"Love you, too, sweetie."

That felt surprisingly good.

Inside the circle were Miles, Ali, Peggy, Chain Boy, and a girl whose entrance I must have missed. Before I could sit down, Miles thrust a flyer at me for the Platypuses Are Mammals, Too show this weekend. "So you don't forget."

"I think I can go. My friend was actually listening to you guys in the darkroom." I smiled.

"Are you bringing her?"

"It's a guy, actually." Odd that there have been so few guys in my life, and that I'm always forced to hide or feel guilty about them. *Très* romantic.

"Your Homecoming date?" he questioned. I tried to remember that Miles had a lot of time to think, what with all those extra hours of non-sleep.

"Yep. I think you'd like him. Maybe you would. I don't know." I was quickly realizing that relationships with therapy boys are unecessarily complicated. I was ready to undercomplicate my life. I'd gently turn Miles down for Homecoming. Whoever thought I'd be saying that?

The new guy, Chris, proved my theory on therapy boys tenfold: He was not only fond of cutting himself but shared the love with his ex-girlfriend. Which I knew not only because he told us but because he had "Molly" scarred into his arm.

Tucker may have his quirks, but at least one of them was not dealing with so much shit that he couldn't possibly be there to help me with mine.

The new girl's name was Nikki. She was also weighty, although a lot bigger than I ever was. Like me, at my first day at Lakeland, she cried the entire session. Like me, she said she couldn't sit through her classes at school. Like me, she wanted to die.

I knew she wasn't me, that we had different problems, came from different families, dealt with things in different ways, but it was freakish how similar it sounded. I wanted to help her—the fatter, sadder, past sort-of version of me. So I said, "It gets better."

"I'm not gay," she defended.

"What? I meant that life can get better. I know. I went through what you're going through right now. It royally sucked, but things are getting better. I know they can for you, too."

"Spare me," she groaned.

I did sound like some bullshit self-help guru, but I recognized how my life had improved. And I never wanted to be a Nikki again. "It's not like my life is perfect, but I just, I don't know, like things again. I even kind of like me."

"I kind of like you, too," Miles interjected.

"We know, Miles. Get a grip." Ali rolled her eyes.

Miles blushed. A boy blushed for me. I wanted to point that out to Nikki, how boys never even noticed me before, and now one was actually blushing about me, but that seemed ridiculously conceited. Peggy started a discussion about self-esteem boosters, and we all went around and talked about aspects of ourselves we liked. Would I have been able to do that six weeks ago? Doubt it. But I was done with looking back so much. I wasn't even Mental Hospital Girl anymore, or at least I shared the title.

Not being alone, in misery and happiness, kind of kicks ass.

———

HAVE A NICE DAY

Everything about the next morning was so normal, I got kind of freaked out. No one said anything in English class in reference to yesterday's mental hospital extravaganza, and Groban assigned a Roald Dahl short story, "Lamb to the Slaughter," that looked promisingly unlike anything that has or will happen in my life. I mean, I don't even eat lamb.

Quizzes, movies, I even considered joining in in gym class (of which I then thought better, seeing as that would mean my reprieve was officially over and I'd have to start changing into gym clothes again). By lunchtime, I was waiting for something to happen, maybe an anvil falling on my head or a note from the front office that a relative died or a poo-laden piece of toilet paper stuck to my shoe.

But my luck continued all the way up to and through Tucker's soccer game. Maybe it was the rabbit's foot. Tucker might have to fight me to get it back.

After the game, Tracy, Tucker, Arthur, and I made plans before the guys hit the locker room. We discussed the logistics of the Platypuses show tomorrow, with Tucker driving. When it was time to part, there was a hesitant moment when Tucker and I leaned towards each other for a kiss but both thought better of it when a drop of sweat from his forehead came dangerously close to my cheek.

"Tomorrow?" He nodded.

"Tomorrow," I agreed.

I rubbed the rabbit's foot in my pocket just in case. Couldn't hurt. Unless you're the rabbit.

NO BOWL

The Whedon Bowl was in the city of Chicago proper, so me, Tucker, Arthur, and Tracy had a good forty-five-minute drive to get to know one another better. Or we would have, if the stereo weren't so loud.

We were seated in Tucker's car in pickup order, therefore Arthur rode shotgun and Tracy and I held the chauffeured positions in the backseat. By the end of the ride, my arm throbbed with Tracy's zest for Slugbug.

The Whedon Bowl is a gritty bowling alley with a small stage tucked into a corner. According to signs at the entrance, karaoke is Wednesday and Friday nights. All-ages shows were held on Saturdays at 7:30, ensuring plenty of suburban kids (such as us) access to decent music without the necessity of a fake ID. I had never actually been to the Whedon Bowl, but I tiny-lied when Tucker asked me at school. "Yeah, I haven't been there in, like, two years. I can't even remember the name of the band I saw." It felt a little too uncool to be so into music but never to the Whedon Bowl. Even uncooler when the reason I hadn't been there before was that I never felt cool enough to go. Ah, the cruel circle of coolness.

We paid fifteen dollars to get in. As soon as I paid, Tucker was all, "Oh, I was going to take care of that."

"You don't have to. If anything, I should be paying for your ticket in exchange for gas money." The tattooed guy at the door, who looked well above the legal drinking age and possibly closer to senior discount status, watched our exchange with annoyance. He jammed a stamp onto my hand that read "CoCo" and barked, "Get in there already. There's a line. He can pay for a drink."

Inside, the Whedon Bowl reminded me of the bowling alley where my family bowled when I was a kid. I almost brought myself down at the memory of my parents playing together on a bowling league but was quickly snapped back to reality when Miles bounded up to me. "Anna!" He gave me a squeeze, which caught me off guard but didn't feel inappropriate. I think we could count each other as friends, albeit ones who knew way too much about each other. "So glad you could come!"

Tucker, Tracy, and Arthur stood around me, so I introduced them, "This is Tracy, and Arthur, and Tucker." Tucker placed his left hand on my back and offered his right hand to Miles to shake. Was he being territorial or just using me for balance?

"Ah," Miles deduced, "the Homecoming date."

I nodded, and Tucker looked pleased. I couldn't read Miles's expression, since he looked both tired (as always) and vibrating with the power drink he held. He already knew I had a Homecoming date, and I think he was genuinely excited I came to the show. Hopefully, that was enough for him.

"I have to help set up. Thanks for coming, Anna. And for bringing friends. Nice to meet y'all." He slouched his way through the crowd and onto the stage, where he played around with the microphone stand.

Out of ceiling speakers, extremely loud punk cut through the crowd's chatter. Tucker had to yell to ask, "Want a drink?" I shook my head no. While Tucker and Arthur went off in search of beverages, Tracy and I stood together and people-watched. A month ago, I never would have left the house to stand in a hot, dark bowling alley packed with people I didn't know, and here I was on a maybe date, surrounded by people I didn't know to see a band with a singer I *did* know.

How does life change so fast?

Just before Tucker and Arthur returned with their drinks, Platypuses went on. Due to Miles's almost basset hound—like eye bags, I thought the music might be slow or at least emo, but it was fast, happy pop punk with hilariously clever lyrics. My favorite was, "You're as cute as a 1968 Volkswagen Beetle. Because of that, I'll never cheatle!" About halfway through the set, I noticed the room getting stiflingly hot. Was everyone standing really close to me? It felt like a wall of people a foot taller had closed in. My heart began beating harder and faster and my breathing became labored. I closed my eyes and put my hand on my chest. Not a panic attack. Not now.

A hand rested on my shoulder, and when I looked up I found Tucker. He pointed with a head tilt and mouthed, "Let's go outside." I nodded in agreement. Tucker took my hand in his, and we snaked our way through the crowd. We passed the surly bouncer, and once outside I felt my breathing open up instantly. I smiled at Tucker. "Thanks," I said, embarrassed.

"It was getting pretty hot in there, eh?" he asked. "You want to sit?" Still holding my hand, he walked me over to the curb. We sat down, and he leaned his knee against mine. Justin and I had done that, leaned our knees together in the back of a taxi. It was forbidden contact, filled with excitement and longing. This wasn't anything like that. And yet, I loved it. Someone I liked leaned his knees on mine, held my hand, and rescued me when I was falling. Maybe not everything had to be so hard.

"What did you think of the band?" Tucker asked. We both watched people come and go from a White Castle across the street.

"Pretty good, actually. I probably shouldn't sound so surprised," I admitted.

"I know what you mean. I dated this girl who was a bass player, and her band sucked. I had to go to their shows every weekend and pretend they sounded good."

Oooh. Ex-girlfriend talk. I must have made a face because Tucker asked, "Should I not bring up exes?"

313

"No. I mean, why not, right?" After I said it, I realized I had no interest in hearing about Tucker's exes. Except maybe one. "What was the deal with you and Eleanor?"

"You know, nothing. I mean, I liked her, but nothing ever happened. I think I have a weakness for strong women. Hence you, of course."

I blushed at the prospect of him having a weakness for me. "Hence me? How am I a strong woman?"

"What? You were in a mental hospital. That's badass."

I busted out laughing. "You're kidding, right?"

He shook his head no. We looked at each other for a while. I liked how I could see his eyes through his glasses, but focus on the glasses when things felt too intense. Which they were starting to. And those lips, which I had noticed one too many times before and had so far only graced my cheeks, were looking mighty tasty. Then they spoke.

"I have something for you." Tucker dug into his front jeans pocket and pulled out something silver and shiny. He held up a bracelet that appeared to be made out of . . .

"Staples?" I couldn't believe it.

"I made it. I sanded down each staple so it wouldn't poke you. Here . . ." He opened the clasp—yes, he had added a clasp—and wrapped the bracelet around my wrist. "It fits perfectly. I thought I might have made it too long because I was going by my mom's wrist size and—"

I didn't let him finish. I was so overcome by how life had changed that I couldn't let the moment go. With my newly bejeweled arm, I reached up to place my hand on his cheek and pulled him towards me. His lips were every bit as cushy as expected. Kissing him was so comforting and comfortable, I didn't want to stop. And I didn't have to. There was no one forcing us to stop. That is until the bouncer cleared his throat and coughed, "Get a room."

314

We separated and giggled, or I giggled. Tucker bumped my forehead gently with his before he pulled me up off the curb. Hand in hand, we walked back into the Whedon Bowl.

The drive home was as loud as the drive there, but I snagged the shotgun seat. I tried not to look into the backseat but made the mistake of catching Tracy and Arthur in the rearview in a compromising position. Brain bath, please.

When we pulled up to my house, Tucker began opening his door. "No, that's okay." I stopped him. "I'm sure my mom is watching. And maybe my sister." He leaned over inside the car and gave me a long, slow good-night kiss, the kind I'd watched and envied so many times on *90210*. I fumbled for the door handle and tripped my way inside my house.

My mom and Mara sat in the front room watching a movie, not the window. The second I shut the door, they pounced.

"Did you have a good time?"

"How was the band?"

"Are you guys dating?"

"Did you kiss him?"

"Did you have sex?"

"Did you use protection?"

"Oh my god!" I proclaimed. "Love you. Not pregnant. Good night."

And it was. *Such* a good night.

SUNDAY, THE DAY OF TEXT

Sunday was spent as God intended: in my pajamas watching *iCarly* reruns. You're never too old for Spencer and his rubber face.

I did a little homework, ate some food, relaxed with Rodney Yee, talked to Tracy; all in all, a good day.

While on the phone with T (we were discussing what the hell boutonnieres are and where the hell we'd get them), I received a text. The discussion was heated, so I didn't bother looking at the text, and promptly forgot about it. Around bedtime, there was that moment you have when you remember you were going to do something but you can't figure out what it was. At first, I thought it was the experiment I had wanted to try where you put toothpaste on your zits, but then I recalled that you need the white paste not the blue gel kind to make it work.

And it wasn't the zits; it was the text.

I fished my phone out of its home in my backpack, and opened the message. I anticipated it being from Tucker. Surprisingly, it was from my dad.

Anna. Hope you're well. Let's make plans for next week. Love, Dad.

I smiled that Dad felt he needed to sign his text, even though the caller ID already identified him. I also liked that he hoped I was well, and that he wanted to get together but not in an immediate, bedroom-invading manner.

I shut off my phone and nestled under my covers. Tomorrow begins Homecoming week, which means cheerleaders in the hallways wearing (even more) stupid clothes and being excruciatingly loud and energetic first thing in the morning, pep rallies and banners all over the school, as if Homecoming was actually about some football game.

I finally knew it was really all about the dance.

PEPPED OUT

The second I walked into school—nay, the second I approached the school and saw the ginormous foamy soap letters in the windows telling me to MELT HERSHEY, I knew I was in for a doozy of a week. Inside, it looked like someone had tp'd the school with orange and blue streamers, most of them already on the floor. A number of people walked around in pajamas, including a particularly well-developed senior in a negligee and high-heeled slippers with feathers perched on top. Tracy sidled up next to me and said, "I sold her that ensemble."

"I think it's one size too small," I noted. "So, what is this, dress-like-a-whore day?"

"According to the handy chart"—she pointed to a huge poster on the wall—"it's pajama day."

"My, they are clever, aren't they?"

"Don't be knockin' Spirit Week, Anna. Two chimpanzees worked very hard to come up with this stuff."

"Wouldn't it be cool," I asked as we walked to my locker, "if Spirit Week were actually an entire week where dead people roamed the hallways? Like Joey Ramone would pop out of my locker and sing to me?" I opened my locker and pretended to see him. "Joey? Joey, is that you?" I pretended to faint.

Tucker, always there when I needed a lift, helped me up off the floor. "Good morning." He kissed me, a brief good morning kiss, but a PDA nonetheless. Spirit Week indeed.

The day continued as such: screaming cheerleaders in the hall, kids in every class attempting to make a joke about falling asleep at their desks because they couldn't help it while in their pajamas, and kisses every time I saw Tucker.

In Art, we began our critiques for the natural lighting project. I volunteered to go first, something I never did, but I felt I knew I had that A already in the grade books. Mrs. Downy said my project was a triumph in spirit (I laughed when she used that word. This really *was* Spirit Week) and technical mastery. It wasn't even a big deal talking about being in the hospital. I had already come out in English, and here in Art I was surrounded by my friends. Could the day get any better?

Tracy ran up to me, excitedly out of breath after school. "You want to watch the cheerleaders beat the shit out of one another?"

"Like, metal knuckles and nunchucks?"

"The correct term is nunchucka. And, no, in powder puff football."

Powder puff was this icky, sexist thing they did every year where the cheerleaders donned barely-there outfits and played football on a wet field somewhere, ensuring that mud wrestling would ensue. Gratefully, the administration stopped pretending to overlook what was going on and last year began sponsoring the game, thus giving the cheerleaders real uniforms, a non-muddy field, and a bleacher full of parents making certain there was no drinking. Hooray?

"Why not?"

The weather had finally become autumn-cool, which meant I could wear my Have a Nice Day pink hoodie more often. I noticed people's eyes were drawn to it, and the goofiness made them smile.

Imagine that: me being the one to make other people smile.

HAUNTED BY SPIRITS

The ghostly, I mean *ghastly,* Spirit Week came to a head (which is most definitely a zit reference) on Friday with a pep rally. I had endured '80s Day, Twin Day, and Beach Day (yay! Another excuse for people to wear minimal amounts of clothing!). Today was, ahem, Spirit Day (my God—enough with the spirit already! I have teen spirit coming out of my armpits!), so lots of blue-and-orange faces and hair-sprayed heads. I almost considered dyeing my blue streak a different color just so I wouldn't look like I was participating.

The best thing about the pep rally, besides learning who made the Homecoming Court (not so much), was ditching it. Tucker, Tracy, Arthur, and I sat in the Auto Shop room and talked. Not about anything important, just movies, books, wrestling. I imagined we were in a John Hughes movie and someone was filming us waxing philosophic and looking pretty cool while doing it. A dorky thought, but it made me feel good. Over the past few weeks I had realized that feeling good wasn't about how you got there but knowing that you could.

And I didn't need a therapist to figure that one out.

DANCE DANCE

Saturday was spent preening and prepping and pooping (just because I'm new and improved doesn't mean I'm completely unpooed). Mara taught me how to walk in heels without looking like an old lady shuffler, and Mom straightened my hair to tie into a low, smooth ponytail, my blue streak tucked neatly behind my ear.

My mom had put seven dresses on hold for me at Field's, and even though I had to go down a size (thank you very much), the selection wasn't bad. I ended up with a dress concocted of various pinks draped ever-so-delicately to hide and accentuate. At least that's what my mom said. I think it was chiffon. Or silk. Whatever it was, I didn't feel ugly in it. In fact, if I were ten sizes smaller and lived at Hogwarts, one might say I resembled Hermione at the Yule Ball. If one squinted a whole hell of a lot. Tracy dropped the dress idea completely and decided to wear a tuxedo. I couldn't wait to get a picture of that.

Our Homecoming crew would be Tracy, Arthur, Tucker, and me because Eleanor and Meredith had their parents as protective chauffeurs for the evening. Probably better that way. At least for us.

For some reason, we let Arthur choose the restaurant to eat at before the dance, since none of us had a preference. Inexplicably he chose Rainforest Cafe. Not since a family trip to Disney World had I visited a Rainforest Cafe, and even then I wasn't wowed by the quality of the animatronic animals. Still, there was something hilarious about sitting there in our finery.

Around 4:30, when I was completely transformed into my Hermione-like visage, Mara opened the door (which she had waited by for a half hour) to usher in a dapper Tucker, Arthur, and Tracy. Tracy, dressed in a tux she had to rent from the boys' section, looked so cute I had to stifle a laugh. Not that I'd tell her, since the whole purpose of her wearing a tux was to look not-cute. Her right sleeve was slightly bunched due to a massive flower, some kind of beastly carnation, on her wrist. She caught me eyeing it. "Arthur refused to buy me a boutonniere."

"I let her have the tux, but I draw the line at manly flowers."

"Speaking of flowers . . ." Tucker sauntered over to me and whispered in my ear, "You look really pretty."

"Thanks." I blushed.

He presented me with a standard corsage box (who am I kidding? I have no idea what standard anything to do with dances is), but inside was a rose corsage Tucker had created made entirely out of red staples. "I thought it would last longer than a regular corsage."

My eyes widened at its beauty as he wrapped the black ribbon that was laced through the flower around my wrist. I pinned a tiny purple orchid to his jacket, and then it was time for the requisite Homecoming pictures.

It was all so surreal: a dress, a corsage, a boyfriend, Homecoming . . . Could this really be me?

Outside, I marveled at the classic red-and-white Chevy Arthur's dad had rebuilt. "He says if we hurt Candy inside or out, he will hurt *me* inside and out." Candy was the car's name.

"Scary," I noted.

"I'm not worried. He would love to have an excuse to sit in the garage and touch this car some more."

As we pulled out of the driveway, my mom still snapping away with her camera, we waved. I couldn't erase the smile from my face, and thankfully I didn't have to. The smiling didn't stop once we reached Rainforest Cafe, where they seated us directly in front of the elephants. Every time the miniaturized pachyderms trumpeted and flapped their ears, it was so loud none of us could control our laughter. Nearby kids would start screaming and crying at the ruckus. It was just like a real rain forest, except without the rain. And with way scarier animals.

We rolled into the school parking lot around 7:30, and Arthur picked a secluded spot to prevent any harm being done to Candy. Tucker ran around to my side of the car and opened the door for me, which I hadn't even realized he was doing as I fumbled with the ancient door handle. When I looked up from my buttery leather seat, I saw Tucker, hand outstretched, contacts in to highlight his hazel eyes, the sunset melting behind him, his brand-new black-and-white-checked Vans on just for the occasion. I was blown away that he was my date. I took his hand, and he lifted me out of the car. Arm in arm, we glided into the heavily decorated school gym.

Our Homecoming theme was "Dancing Under the Stars," a play on *Dancing with the Stars*. We had been joking all week that they should have ballroom dancers hanging from the ceiling, but when we saw the sparkling celestial design that transformed our smelly, torturous gym into a majestic party space, I have to say I was impressed. Way to go, peppy people.

I was grateful whoever planned this shindig chose a DJ over a band because there's nothing sadder than a song being butchered by a middle-aged woman attempting to rock out (horrific bat mitzvah flashback).

We stood on the outskirts of the dance floor and watched as people attempted to maneuver with excruciatingly tight dresses and sky-high heels. Tracy pointed out Eleanor and her date, oblivious to all around them as they slow danced to a fast-paced Britney Spears song. Meredith, in an adorable, powder blue, retro '50s-style dress, spotted us and dragged over her date.

Above the music she yelled, "This is Dutch." Hand-shaking and waving ensued, and then we continued standing still near the sea of gyrating bodies.

"Maybe we should dance," I suggested. Hesitantly, we pushed our way onto the dance floor. The Ke$ha song I didn't hate came on, and I found myself taken up by the beat. It felt both fun and ridiculous to be dancing in fancy clothes in the middle of the school gym. I looked around at everyone else doing the exact same thing, and I spied various people I knew from classes: Jenna Simpson, usually so buttoned up, had on a skimpy red dress with a neckline exposing two very pushed-up boobs; I barely recognized Steve Andrews without his sports jersey (although, was that a Bears tie under his jacket?); and there, in a pink, mermaid-style gown with a flower in her hair was Ella Santos, my mental hospital partner in crime. She caught me staring, and offered me a smile and a wave in acknowledgment. Maybe she was just saying hi because we're in the same class, but to me it felt like recognition. A celebration of "Look at how normal we are now." I had to choke back a tear.

"I'll be right back," Tucker yelled, and the rest of us continued dancing.

"This song is never-ending!" Meredith shouted.

"It's a remix!" Tracy yelled back, and then covered up her Ke$ha knowledge with, "I think!"

Just as the song ended, Tucker found us again. I was about to suggest we leave the dance floor and get a drink, when a familiar blast of guitar glued me to the linoleum.

"Aaaahhhhh!" I screamed and jumped up and down, as The Ramones' "Blitzkrieg Bop" played.

"You like it?" Tucker asked in my ear.

I grabbed his face and planted a kiss hard on his lips, then my friends and I danced and slammed into one another for the miniscule duration of the song. Even Eleanor and her date unlatched to join us.

When the song ended and we were all out of breath, we decided to step outside. The crisp air cooled off my hot cheeks, and Tucker wrapped his arms around me to keep me warm. After a minute of relaxed bliss, I turned around and took Tucker's hands. "Does anyone want to go back in?" I asked with disinterest.

Dates looked at each other, shoulders were shrugged, and Tracy proclaimed, "Not really. Anyone want to go to Dairy Dream?"

"Right on." Arthur high-fived her.

Meredith, Eleanor, and their fix-ups stayed behind, since Eleanor's mom had set up an elaborate plan where Eleanor had to take a picture at the dance every fifteen minutes and text it to her mom so she knew she wasn't doing something she shouldn't do somewhere else. Seems to me that would just make someone want to have quickie sex in the Home Ec room, but what do I know? My life hasn't become *that* complicated yet.

After an Oreo Blast Sundae and a ride in Candy that took us past cities and suburbs, farms and factories, horses and high-rises, Arthur pulled into my driveway. As I stepped out of the car, Tucker grabbed me by the waist and danced a couple awkward steps. "Dancing under the stars." He pointed at the real celestial decorations. "I've been waiting to say that all night."

"Worth the wait?" I laughed.

Tucker leaned into the car and pulled out a package wrapped in brown paper. I'd noticed it on the floor of Candy earlier, but I assumed it was something Arthur's dad left behind. Tucker guided me by the small of my back up to my front door and handed me the gift. I furrowed my brow in question, and he gently nudged, "Open it."

I carefully peeled back the tape and paper to reveal the library's hardcover copy of *The Neverending Story*. "You checked out a book for me? And wrapped it?"

"No. I took it for you. From the library. *Without* checking it out." Tucker beamed with sneaky pride.

"You stole a library book? For me?"

"Yes. Not like anyone would notice. If you look in the back of the book it hasn't been checked out in thirteen years. It's wasted sitting on those shelves. I know you'll appreciate it. You deserve to be its owner more than some metal shelves."

I turned the pages of the book, *my* book, slowly and admired the beauty of the colored ink. "It's a really amazing gift, Tucker." I looked up at him and welled with mushiness.

"I wrote something in it for you." He leaned over and found the title page, where his neat handwriting appeared. "For Anna, Who I would write into any book. Love, Tucker."

"Thanks, Tucker." I hugged the book to my chest. "That's the sweetest, most klepto thing anyone's ever done for me." A long thank-you kiss and a promise to see each other tomorrow, and we said goodbye.

No one waited up for me, and I was glad to have my own time and space to take it all in.

After I quietly got undressed, took off my makeup, and let down my hair, I snuggled into bed. Visions of paper stars danced in my head.

I couldn't sleep.

Something was on my mind that I needed to take care of. Nothing big, nothing bad, but it was there, needling me as I attempted to fall into slumber.

I crept back downstairs and turned on the decent computer. I opened my email and typed:

To: bassnomore@gemmail.com
From: gabbagabbaanna@dotmail.com
Subject: Quiet Room
Dear Justin,
Thinking of you. Hope you're well.
Love,
Anna

I hit send, and a warm feeling rushed through me. Sentiments from those who cared about you, no matter how small, were important. I remembered back to all those get well soon cards people sent me at Lake Shit.

I think they worked.

ACKNOWLEDGMENTS

Massive thanks go out to the following people in my life:

Anna Roberto for the almost two hour–phone call revision, and the million other e-mail conversations.

Jean, Rich, Ksenia, and everyone else at Feiwel and Friends for truly being my friends.

Colleen Seisser for the expert wrestling info.

The Hyuns for their help and support. I hope you like this one!

Russ Anderson and Amy Pine for inviting me to their school and providing massive *Catcher* help.

Michelle Price and her AP photo students for the photography class knowledge.

Jack Archie for not eschewing some WOW help.

Frank Portman for *Catcher* quoting advice.

Kavan Yee and Dave Cooper for science nerd quotes.

Joyce Buckley, Joe Mason, and Sandi Sprechman for Homecoming factoids.

Ali, Beth, Liz, and Tracy for being my hos and bros.

Katie for Penny's dinners, murder mysteries, and County Fair Chocolate Cake™.

Rosemary Stimola for the pep talks and keeping the Halpern-Cordells afloat.

My family for their love and support.

Matt and Romy for waking up with me in the morning, going to sleep with me at night, and fulfilling all my dreams.

And thank you to everyone who read *Get Well Soon* and wrote me loving letters. Here's hoping you all find your happy place in life.